PRAISE FOR
ANGEL OF VENGEANCE

"You will rarely see two characters as complex and compelling as these two, and you will rarely see a series as consistently well-written as this one."
—*Booklist* (starred review)

"*Angel of Vengeance* is like *Back to the Future* on steroids, with all the fears and paradoxes that come along with what we have learned from time travel. I was left in complete awe by the end of this ride, which includes a finale that provided me with a lot of revisionist history satisfaction. This may be one of Preston & Child's best novels yet—it has something for all readers to relish within these glorious pages." —Bookreporter.com

ACCLAIM FOR THESE NOVELS BY PRESTON AND CHILD

THE CABINET OF DR. LENG

"This book is a lot of fun. The writing is crisp and lightly ornate, as usual, and the story is inventive and suspenseful."
—*Booklist*

"[Pendergast] still remains the most charming, intelligent, cool, and creepy agent ever written…"
—*Suspense Magazine*

"An engaging adventure...entertaining, with a plot that twisted in unexpected ways...These are seasoned writers who know how to weave a good story and leave you wanting more."
—TheMysterySite.com

DIABLO MESA

"*Diablo Mesa* is thriller-adventure writing of the absolute highest order that takes Preston and Child back to their high-concept roots...It reads like a hybrid of the best from Wilbur Smith and Alistair MacLean, making for flat-out great reading entertainment."
—*BookTrib*

"The story has tension, mystery, murder...Down-to-earth action tackles an otherworldly mystery in this devilishly plausible yarn." —*Kirkus Reviews* (starred review)

"Excellent...The taut suspense and tight plotting that marked the authors' earliest Pendergast novels are very much in evidence. Fans of kick-ass female leads will be delighted."
—*Publishers Weekly* (starred review)

"The last third of the novel is not to be missed and is impossible to put down. Everything from Cold War espionage to Soviet agents at Roswell and, of course, our top-secret group that is behind all of this will cause enough suspense and unpredictable thrills that you will not be able to see the next move coming before Preston & Child cast a literary checkmate. *Diablo Mesa* is just what thriller junkies require, and this always reliable author duo delivers at every turn."
—Bookreporter.com

BLOODLESS

"Leave it to the imaginations of Preston and Child... Spooky and surreal [and] wonderful fun."
—*Kirkus Reviews* (starred review)

"*Bloodless* is their 20th novel featuring one of the most unique protagonists in all of thriller fiction, Agent Aloysius Pendergast, and may rank as one of the finest books they have ever penned together...*Bloodless* is a pure pleasure to read and is like candy to thriller fans—candy from which readers will drain every ounce of flavor in pure delight."
—Bookreporter.com

"Preston & Child, expertly straddling the line between reality and the paranormal, have fashioned a neo-gothic masterpiece."
—*Providence Journal*

"*Bloodless* is rife with inventive scenarios, amusing exchanges (especially between oft-impatient Coldmoon and eternally placid Pendergast) and tantalizingly spooky mysteries, topped off with a gloriously wild finale that is as action-packed as it is memorable."
—*BookPage*

CROOKED RIVER

"Preston & Child know how to craft compelling stories that are both baffling and surprising. The cast of characters feels authentic and moves the story forward in unexpected ways...The authors are masters of the procedural with a gothic flair."
—Associated Press

"[Pendergast] still remains the most charming, intelligent, cool, and creepy agent ever written...Read this. As fast as possible. Preston & Child have once again created the unimaginable, and you just can't miss it!"

—*Suspense Magazine*

"The best mystery series going today. Preston & Child display a true master's touch. This is riveting reading entertainment of the highest order."

—*Providence Journal*

"*Crooked River* is worth the price of admission, and Preston & Child find themselves with another surefire hit on their hands."

—Bookreporter.com

VERSES FOR THE DEAD

"Multifaceted and complex. Legendary. Working together, Preston and Child are masters at crafting a story that goes beyond a simple mystery or thriller...Readers unfamiliar with Pendergast will find this novel a fantastic launch point. He's a modern-day Sherlock Holmes, and the story reads like classic literature."

—Associated Press

"Doug Preston and Lincoln Child's master detective A.X.L. Pendergast is every bit the modern equivalent of Sherlock Holmes and Hercule Poirot. And his investigative skills have never been sharper than in the altogether brilliant *Verses for the Dead*...A throwback to classic crime fiction while maintaining a sharp, postmodern edge."

—*Providence Journal*

"*Verses for the Dead* is classic Preston & Child, full of complex characters, plot twists, and storylines that border on supernatural or otherworldly elements... The story is full of suspense and surprises that all converge in a jaw-dropping ending." —Bookreporter.com

THE SCORPION'S TAIL

"Expect nice twists, hairy danger, and good old-fashioned gunplay. This one's an attention grabber. Get a copy."
—*Kirkus Reviews* (starred review)

"Preston and Child have designed an intricate thriller that takes several twists and turns, but never totally diverts from the crux of the story. This is a series that demands attention." —*New York Journal of Books*

"What Preston and Child have so deftly succeeded at doing, yet again, is to combine real history with archaeological finds and forensic science to create a fascinating novel filled with the thrills of an Indiana Jones film... Buckle up because *The Scorpion's Tail* is another winner for this writing duo." —Bookreporter.com

OLD BONES

"Longtime readers of Preston and Child will love to see the beloved characters of Nora Kelly and Corrie Swanson take center stage in what is a terrific start to a new series. Their writing talent shines as this mix of history, exploration of nature, and crime will without a doubt land on the top of the bestseller lists."
—Associated Press

"*Old Bones* exceeds expectations at every juncture, a thriller extraordinaire that turns history upside down in forming the basis of a riveting and relentless tale."
—*Providence Sunday Journal*

"This outing belongs to two dedicated women whose future adventures will be happily anticipated."
—*Booklist*

"*Old Bones* has it all: chills, thrills, and a blend of history, along with archaeological expertise you can only get from a Preston & Child novel. I loved spending time with Nora Kelly and Corrie Swanson, and look forward to seeing them in future adventures. Longtime readers will be rewarded not only by this pairing but by some other surprises leading up to the conclusion of this exciting read."
—Bookreporter.com

"The two strong female protagonists [Nora Kelly and Corrie Swanson] share a dynamic reminiscent of that between Pendergast and his friend on the NYPD, Vincent D'Agosta. An intriguing series launch."
—*Publishers Weekly*

CITY OF ENDLESS NIGHT

"If you'd like to know how Arthur Conan Doyle's Sherlock Holmes tales would be reviewed today, look no further than *City of Endless Night*... A typically terrific mystery laced with the gothic overtones for which this series is known... This is mystery thriller writing of the highest order, a tale as relentlessly riveting as it is sumptuously scintillating."
—*Providence Sunday Journal*

"Preston and Child continue to write tense and compelling tales while also invoking the feel of Sherlock Holmes or other gothic stories of the late 19th century... Marvelous."
—Associated Press

"As always, the authors have crafted a story that is almost impossible to pull away from, and their prose is as elegant as fans have come to expect. Pendergast continues to be one of thrillerdom's most exciting and intriguing series leads, and the series remains among the most reliable in the genre."
—*Booklist*

THE OBSIDIAN CHAMBER

"The latest novel in Preston & Child's Pendergast series picks up from the cliff-hanger ending of *Crimson Shore* and doesn't let up. The authors keep readers guessing... The crisp writing and exemplary stories are still in abundance in this consistently exciting and never predictable series."
—Associated Press

"Rivetingly superb... great fun... thriller-writing of the highest order. A lavish, brilliantly conceived puzzle that pieces together neo-gothic plotting with splendidly rich tones."
—*Providence Journal*

CRIMSON SHORE

"It's like Christmas for lovers of suspense when the words Preston & Child once again appear on a book cover. It's a truly great Christmas when the main character of that novel is Aloysius X. L. Pendergast. For those who have read these books voraciously, it's not a surprise to learn that this latest tale is one that will keep you riveted until the very end...Preston & Child continue to make these books the absolute best there is in the suspense realm."

—*Suspense Magazine*

"Secrets and mysteries abound...the shock and twist are perfect. The unusual becomes believable and normal in the authors' capable hands."

—Associated Press

"New readers will be hooked...Die-hard fans will add this to their must-read lists."

—*Library Journal* (starred review)
LibraryReads Pick

BLUE LABYRINTH

"ONE OF THE TOP TEN BOOKS OF THE YEAR."
—*The Strand Magazine*

"Fast-moving, sophisticated, and bursting with surprises...If you're willing to surrender to Preston and Child's fiendish imaginations, you might devour the Pendergast books the way kids do Halloween candy... There's nothing else like them."

—*Washington Post*

"Preston and Child have the ability to blend contemporary forensic thrillers with a dose of Dickensian/Sherlock Holmes-era atmosphere. Add a villain to a vendetta that has spanned generations and a cast of characters that readers will find emotionally satisfying, and the end result is another bestseller for the duo."

—Associated Press

WHITE FIRE

"ONE OF THE BEST BOOKS OF THE YEAR."
—*Library Journal*

"Excellent...Small-town politics, murder, a century-old conspiracy, arson, and a detective who embodies a modern-day Holmes add up to an amazing journey...Preston and Child's best novel to date."
—Associated Press

"Sherlock Holmes fans will relish [this novel]...one of their best in this popular series...easily stands on its own with only passing references to Pendergast's complex backstory."
—*Publishers Weekly* (starred review)

TWO GRAVES

"A good thriller forces the reader to finish the book in one sitting. An exceptional thriller does that plus forces the reader to slow down to savor every word. With *Two Graves*, Preston and Child have delivered another exceptional book."
—Associated Press

"Preston and Child's high-adrenaline thriller wraps up the trilogy...with a bang...[An] intelligent suspense novel."
—*Publishers Weekly*

ANGEL OF VENGEANCE

A PENDERGAST NOVEL

DOUGLAS PRESTON & LINCOLN CHILD

GRAND CENTRAL

New York   Boston

ALSO BY DOUGLAS PRESTON AND LINCOLN CHILD

AGENT PENDERGAST NOVELS

The Cabinet of Dr. Leng • Bloodless • Crooked River • Verses for the Dead • City of Endless Night • The Obsidian Chamber • Crimson Shore • Blue Labyrinth • White Fire • Two Graves* • Cold Vengeance* • Fever Dream* • Cemetery Dance • The Wheel of Darkness • The Book of the Dead** • Dance of Death** • Brimstone** • Still Life with Crows • The Cabinet of Curiosities • Reliquary† • Relic†

*The Helen Trilogy **The Diogenes Trilogy
†*Relic* and *Reliquary* are ideally read in sequence

NORA KELLY NOVELS

Badlands • Dead Mountain • Diablo Mesa • The Scorpion's Tail • Old Bones

GIDEON CREW NOVELS

The Pharaoh Key • Beyond the Ice Limit • The Lost Island • Gideon's Corpse • Gideon's Sword

OTHER NOVELS

The Ice Limit • Thunderhead • Riptide • Mount Dragon

BY DOUGLAS PRESTON

The Lost Tomb • The Lost City of the Monkey God • The Kraken Project • Impact • The Monster of Florence (with Mario Spezi) *• Blasphemy • Tyrannosaur Canyon • The Codex • Ribbons of Time • The Royal Road • Talking to the Ground • Jennie • Cities of Gold • Dinosaurs in the Attic*

BY LINCOLN CHILD

Chrysalis • Full Wolf Moon • The Forgotten Room • The Third Gate • Terminal Freeze • Deep Storm • Death Match • Lethal Velocity (formerly *Utopia*) *• Tales of the Dark 1–3 • Dark Banquet • Dark Company*

ANGEL
OF
VENGEANCE

This book is a work of fiction. Names, characters, places, and incidents are the product of the authors' imagination or are used fictitiously. Any resemblance to actual events, locales, corporate or government entities, facilities, or persons, living or dead, is coincidental.

Copyright © 2024 by Splendide Mendax, Inc. and Lincoln Child
Excerpt from *Badlands* copyright © 2025 by Splendide Mendax, Inc. and Lincoln Child

Cover design by Flamur Tonuzi Design. Cover photo of figure © Victoria Davies / Trevillion Images; photos of alleyway and lightning by Getty Images. Cover copyright © 2025 by Hachette Book Group, Inc.

Hachette Book Group supports the right to free expression and the value of copyright. The purpose of copyright is to encourage writers and artists to produce the creative works that enrich our culture.

The scanning, uploading, and distribution of this book without permission is a theft of the authors' intellectual property. If you would like permission to use material from the book (other than for review purposes), please contact permissions@hbgusa.com. Thank you for your support of the authors' rights.

Grand Central Publishing
Hachette Book Group
1290 Avenue of the Americas, New York, NY 10104
grandcentralpublishing.com
@grandcentralpub

Originally published in hardcover and ebook in August 2024

First mass market edition: November 2025

Grand Central Publishing is a division of Hachette Book Group, Inc. The Grand Central Publishing name and logo is a registered trademark of Hachette Book Group, Inc.

The publisher is not responsible for websites (or their content) that are not owned by the publisher.

The Hachette Speakers Bureau provides a wide range of authors for speaking events. To find out more, go to hachettespeakersbureau.com or email HachetteSpeakers@hbgusa.com.

Grand Central Publishing books may be purchased in bulk for business, educational, or promotional use. For information, please contact your local bookseller or the Hachette Book Group Special Markets Department at special.markets@hbgusa.com.

Library of Congress Control Number: 2024002716

ISBNs: 9781538765715 (mass market oversize), 9781538765739 (ebook)

Printed in the United States of America

BVGM

10 9 8 7 6 5 4 3 2 1

To our friends at GCP

ANGEL
OF
VENGEANCE

Please do not discompose yourself...

Prologue

I

December 26, 1880
Wednesday

Diogenes Pendergast hurled himself into the time portal at the last minute. It ejected him into the past—into New York City of 1880—with such force that he was thrown onto the filthy cobblestones of the alleyway. With an instinctive motion, he twisted and rolled to absorb the impact, managing to cover himself with mud and horse manure in the process. Rising to his feet, he glanced back at the portal in time to catch a faint shimmer just as it winked out of existence. He briefly examined his soiled clothing with a muttered curse, but there was nothing he could do about it now. The quarry he was in pursuit of had jumped through the portal moments before...and was now gone. By no means must he be allowed to vanish into nineteenth-century New York.

Diogenes picked up the large leather valise he always carried with him—dropped in his fall—and hurried from the alleyway into a busy New York City intersection. His own era would call this place Times Square, but in these primitive times it still bore the name of the farmer's field it had once been: Longacre. He made a mental note of the cul-de-sac he'd emerged from—identified by a grimy sign as Smee's Alley—and peered around, looking for his man, taking in the horse-drawn carriages, the dusky shopfronts, and breathing in the heavy smell of coal smoke. And there he was: Gaspard Ferenc, hurrying down Broadway in the flow of foot traffic.

He took off after him at a quick walk. He had no concern Ferenc would realize he was being followed—the thick-headed fellow had no idea that Diogenes even existed, let alone that he had been spying on his doings for weeks...or had followed him through the time portal.

Why *he* had jumped back in time after Ferenc was something to ponder later. For now, he was strangely thrilled to have left his own sorry world behind.

He soon caught up to Ferenc and fell in step behind him. The man was dressed in a ridiculous motley of clothing, evidently assembled from whatever at hand might appear nineteenth century: a red plaid lumberjack shirt, black cargo pants, and Doc Martens. At least he'd tried to dress the part for this unknown errand of his; Diogenes had had no such time for preparation. The muck on his clothing was, in a perverse way, a godsend—it helped obscure the black turtleneck and trousers he'd been wearing while living secretly in the recesses of his brother's Riverside Drive mansion. Such an incongruous outfit would draw even more attention than Ferenc's.

Diogenes paused outside a restaurant, wiping his hand on a chalkboard that advertised pig trotters and smearing the chalk dust on his face. The whitening effect, he hoped, would make him look like a performer in one of the vaudeville novelty acts so popular in the theater district of the day. He then continued down Broadway after

Ferenc, as he did so taking the opportunity to relieve two affluent gentlemen of their wallets and pocket watches.

Ferenc entered a pawn shop a dozen blocks south of Longacre Square. Diogenes ducked into a nearby tailor shop and hastily purchased a shirt, Inverness cape, and hat, which he then put on. His leather valise was sufficiently worn and inconspicuous that it did not need further disguising. Buttoning the cape up to his neck and lowering the brim of his hat, he emerged again. Strolling past the pawn shop, he saw Ferenc concluding the sale of a jade figurine—stolen, by the looks of it, from the Pendergast family collection—in return for some folding money, a cape, and a cap. He left the shop and continued hurrying southward, Diogenes close behind.

What was Ferenc up to? The very mysteriousness of his errand, and the abruptness with which it had commenced, fascinated Diogenes. It was obviously premeditated, and probably involved making a great deal of money—greed, he knew, was one of Ferenc's weaknesses—but what could his plan be? Without knowing it, Ferenc could ruin everything for Diogenes, and the wisest course would be to kill the man at once. But curiosity, among other thoughts more nebulous, stayed his hand. He would let the man's little scheme play out.

It did not take long to see what he was up to. Minutes later, Ferenc crossed Twenty-Sixth Street and entered the New York Federal Bank of Commerce. After loitering a few moments at a desk reserved for filling out slips, he got in line at one of the teller stations. Diogenes got in another line. Soon Ferenc had reached the window and was being served. Almost immediately, Ferenc's intended transaction grew problematic; his teller left the iron-barred window, returned again, left once more... only to return with a functionary of greater importance. But even this gentleman could not satisfy Ferenc.

Diogenes had by now shuffled close enough to catch the conversation, and any lingering mystery veiling Ferenc's sordid little scheme quickly dissipated. The man was trying to exchange $100 in period paper for twenty-five of the rare $4 gold pieces known as "Stellas"—but the bank, unfortunately, had only two on hand, both in poor condition.

Diogenes felt a swelling of derision. So this complex and dangerous field trip into the past, where so much might be accomplished by a man of imagination and daring, was merely about filthy lucre after all. Ferenc wanted to take those rare coins back to the twenty-first century and sell them for a huge profit—but already he was making a hash of it. Diogenes's amused contempt now mingled with disappointment verging on anger. He would kill the stupid little man as soon as the opportunity presented itself.

He watched as Ferenc, enraged by the failure of his scheme, vented his ire by cursing at the woman in line behind him. A guard came forward, and the ensuing struggle revealed a cheap digital watch on Ferenc's wrist, which he'd obviously forgotten to remove. This alien object turned the minor altercation into an absurd melee, ending with the hapless Ferenc being handcuffed and dragged off in a steel-banded paddy wagon. Diogenes, watching with the rest of the crowd, overheard a policeman say the man was being transported to Bellevue Hospital. As the wagon doors closed behind him, Ferenc was loudly claiming to be from the future...and crying out Pendergast's name.

Diogenes—who, like Mithridates, had managed to steel himself against almost anything—was nevertheless deeply disturbed to hear Ferenc shouting so recklessly. He, and his babbling explanations, could expose and ruin everything.

Diogenes hailed a fly carriage and followed the paddy wagon. What a perfect idiot Ferenc was: any good numismatist could have told him the Stellas were "pattern" coins, never authorized for circulation, and not normally available at a commercial bank. As he followed the paddy wagon, Diogenes mused on the irony that a man like Ferenc—brilliant enough to help design the Mars rover, or in this case repair a machine capable of crossing parallel universes—could be tripped up in an asinine get-rich-quick scheme through the vanity of inadequate preparation. *Sic transit gloria mundi*.

2

AFTER A FIFTEEN-MINUTE RIDE down bustling, carriage-filled streets, the wagon stopped at a secure rear entrance to Bellevue—a structure whose thick stone walls resembled the Bastille more than a hospital.

The fly carrying Diogenes stopped across the street as Ferenc was being manhandled inside the hospital, metal door slamming shut behind him.

"Twenty cents, an' you please, mister," the coachman told Diogenes.

"I'd like to wait for a spell, if you don't mind," Diogenes replied, conforming his speech to *ne varietur* rhythms of the 1880s. "I may require your services further." And he handed the man a Morgan silver dollar that, an hour before, had been in the pocket of a portly gentleman on Broadway.

"All right, guv," the man said, more than happy to idle away the time with a fare willing to pay for the privilege.

Diogenes stared at the thick metal door behind which Ferenc had disappeared. This was most unfortunate. He should have killed him when he had the chance—indulging his own perverse curiosity had caused problems before.

He pondered the situation. Since Ferenc had been taken as a prisoner to Bellevue rather than the nearest station house, Diogenes knew he was bound for the insane ward. Given that, what should he do about it? He could still attempt to kill the man. That would require obtaining a disguise, putting on the false persona of an orderly or cleaner, and gaining access to the proper ward. None of these presented real problems; the most pressing issue was time.

Time... Time, indeed. He looked down at his shoes and trousers—the only articles of clothing still remaining from his own time, and which had gone unnoticed thanks to the mud and the Inverness cape. As he stared, he saw—beneath the mud—evidence of unusual charring on the cuffs of his trousers and on his work boots. He knew that Ferenc had, in effect, put that infernal machine of his on a timer of sorts—keeping the portal open long enough for him to get the coins and return. But this odd charring, along with the screaming and smoking of the machine Diogenes had observed as he followed Ferenc into the portal—

His thoughts were interrupted as a large black barouche pulled up to a different hospital entrance, one reserved for staff. The carriage door opened and a man in elegant attire stepped down. "Elegant" was perhaps an understatement: the man wore a long black double-breasted frock coat with a starched white collar, a silk ascot with a diamond pin, and a buttoned vest across which a gold watch chain traced a glittering arc. An orchid boutonniere—a purple dendrobium—was set off on his left lapel by a small fern curl.

Of intense interest to Diogenes was the pale, aquiline face, with its deep-set sapphire eyes behind small, oval-shaped glasses, and the fair hair and chiseled features that distinguished members of his own family. On his face was a look of distraction, preoccupation... or, perhaps, coldness.

Diogenes knew immediately this must be Professor Enoch Leng, famous for his novel treatment of mental alienation by operating directly on the brain. He was also known by another, even more distinguished name: Antoine Leng Pendergast, scion of the ancient New Orleans family, and the great-granduncle of Diogenes.

He watched as the consulting surgeon vanished into the walls of Bellevue.

What before had seemed a bad outcome might now become the worst possible. In short order, Diogenes felt sure, Leng would become acquainted with Gaspard Ferenc, the "madman" claiming to be from the future... and crying out for a man named Pendergast to save him.

Entering the hospital himself was now moot. Everything depended on what Leng did next. Although the cabbie protested it wasn't necessary, Diogenes flipped him another silver dollar and waited.

In less than an hour, Ferenc emerged from the employee entrance, hardly able to walk, and was assisted into the carriage by a young man in a doctor's uniform, with Leng following. Within moments, the carriage was trotting away—Diogenes giving his own driver instructions to follow at a distance.

Leng's glossy carriage wound its way southward into the poorer neighborhoods of the city, finally arriving at the Five Points, New York's most notorious slum: a maze of narrow alleys and filthy backstreets housing the most desperate and abandoned of the city's residents. The fact that a carriage such as Leng's could travel unmolested through this cesspool of vice and squalor was telling. Diogenes's coachman now earned his two dollars by drawing a conspicuous pistol, ensuring their own less elegant vehicle remained untroubled.

Leng's carriage pulled up near a Gothic Revival building on Catherine Street. An unsavory crowd was gathered before it, drawn by the gold-lettered sign over the entrance: J. C. SHOTTUM'S CABINET OF NATURAL PRODUCTIONS & CURIOSITIES. The carriage remained stationary a moment, horses stamping, while Leng stepped out, one arm curled protectively around the unresisting Ferenc. But rather than entering the Cabinet by the main entrance, they vanished immediately through a side door.

Diogenes asked his driver to move the cab to a safer spot at the end of the block and wait once again. He knew a great deal about his ancestor Enoch Leng. He knew that beneath Shottum's Cabinet—and, indeed, much of the Five Points—was a labyrinthine arrangement of tunnels and passageways, relics of an abandoned waterworks that Leng had secretly repurposed for his grisly experiments.

To follow Leng into such a place would have been far more dangerous than slipping into the hospital. But the man's carriage remained parked at the entrance. Whatever was going to happen would happen soon.

After another hour, Diogenes was rewarded for his patience. An ugly, misshapen man emerged from the side doorway, ushering a figure ahead of him over the muddy pavement and into Leng's carriage. This figure was swathed in a woolen blanket, but a pair of feminine-looking feet—pale and bare—were briefly visible before being bundled into the interior. The man barked an order, and once again the carriage set off, passing Diogenes's fly a moment later.

As Diogenes was deciding whether or not to follow the carriage, Leng himself re-emerged, moving quickly.

He dashed up the street. At first, Diogenes thought he might be chasing his carriage, as if it had accidentally left without him, and he asked his driver to follow. But no: Leng was merely headed to a nearby and less dangerous thoroughfare, Ferry Street, where cabs were waiting at a stand. Leng hailed one, got in, and headed north along the wharves.

Diogenes found it unnecessary to issue more orders to his cabbie—the man was already shaking his reins and urging the horse forward.

Leng's cab headed uptown at a good clip. The avenues broadened and straightened into a grid as they passed into the more modern part of the city. Several minutes later, Leng's cab slowed, and Diogenes realized where he was going. Remarkable, he thought, that Leng had managed to extract information from Ferenc so quickly.

"Slow down," said Diogenes in a low voice. "And be a good fellow, pull to the curb here on the left and wait."

"Good as done, guv," the cabdriver responded.

He watched as Leng stepped out of his carriage and hustled along the sidewalk, stopping to peer down a few alleyways that branched off Broadway from Longacre Square. Leng was no doubt looking for a particular alleyway—the one with the portal—and ice gripped Diogenes's heart.

Now Leng crossed Seventh Avenue—through puddles of water, his expensive clothes becoming spattered with mud and ordure—and ducked into an alley on the far side: the filthy cul-de-sac marked Smee's Alley.

"Remain here," said Diogenes, exiting and moving quickly toward the same alleyway. He slowed at the entrance and, pretending to fumble for his pocket watch to check the time, glanced toward the alley. He could see Leng looking about, sweeping the air with a gold-handled cane, this way and that, as if searching for something invisible. The portal, thank God, had not reappeared.

After several minutes, his immediate fear now allayed, Diogenes strolled past the cul-de-sac and entered a nearby grogshop, where he could sit and observe Leng's activities through a fly-specked window.

The man walked one way, then another, stopping a dozen times to look around, sometimes craning his neck up one of the bill-covered façades, other times pressing his palms against the brick walls or bending down to examine the cobbles, tapping about with his cane or poking it this way and that in the air. The afternoon lengthened; a winter dark began creeping up over the city. Finally, with evident frustration, Leng stalked from the alley and—with a curl of his index finger that reminded Diogenes of Titian's *St. John the Baptist*—summoned another cab and was quickly lost in the gloom.

Diogenes could have followed, but decided against it. The disaster he feared had happened. Ferenc, of course, was either dead or would soon be—but Leng had already gotten from him everything he needed. That meant Leng knew about Pendergast, Constance, and the time machine. He knew where the portal had appeared and had been searching for it. If he'd managed to jump through it and into the twenty-first century, that would have been disastrous...because the fate of his world, his *own* world, hung in the balance. Diogenes thanked providence the portal was gone. He strongly suspected Ferenc had red-lined the machine and left it on too long while he'd lingered in this alternate universe. Even as he'd followed Ferenc through the portal, the machine had clearly been overheating. It had likely burned out, and the portal was gone, perhaps forever.

Diogenes had been so preoccupied with the immediate danger, he hadn't stopped to consider that now he very well might be marooned here—with the others—for good.

He departed the grogshop and climbed back into the waiting cab.

"Where now, guv?"

Diogenes remained silent a moment, considering his new situation. Portal or no, there were many things he had to accomplish. First things first: he needed to set up a chessboard in his mind, ponder the placement of the pieces, and decide what the next moves should be. And to do that, he needed a base of operations. Leng knew about not only the presence of Constance Greene, but that of his own brother, Aloysius—and this knowledge made the man infinitely more dangerous.

But there was something else that Leng knew nothing about.

Diogenes cleared his throat. "My good man," he said. "Do you happen to know of any rooms to let? Preferably quiet and out of the way—perhaps a neighborhood where people can be relied upon to mind their own business?"

"I do indeed, sir," said the man. And he shook the reins again.

3

ONE MILE TO THE northeast, NYPD lieutenant commander Vincent D'Agosta was balanced precariously on a stone lintel below the first-floor window of a mansion on the corner of Fifth Avenue and Forty-Eighth Street. He began climbing the rough façade in hopes of secretly gaining entrance, but he was now having second thoughts about this plan. The uneven blocks of stone, oblong shapes in the dark, felt cold as ice. And it *was* dark—darker than he'd ever imagined Fifth Avenue could be. This was both good and bad: good because no pedestrian or passing carriage could see his lame-ass attempt at climbing; bad because he could barely see what he was doing himself.

He glanced up at the second-floor window, which was open, curtains billowing. Leng's Igor-like assistant, the sadistic bastard named Munck, had just made this same climb, opened that window, and entered the house—the precise thing Pendergast had told D'Agosta to prevent.

He started up to the next story, and reached a section where only the projecting stones and sloppy mortar offered purchase. Trying to ignore his pounding heart, he pulled himself up again, then paused to catch his breath, careful not to look down, muscles dancing and jerking from the unusual exertion.

Under no circumstances are you to reveal yourself to Constance, Pendergast had said. *If Munck appears, stop him. You may have to kill him.* Well, he hadn't stopped him: Munck, like a cat burglar, had slipped up the wall and into the house before D'Agosta—from his blind across the street—could react. Yet D'Agosta couldn't alert Constance Greene inside. That would spoil everything.

So what was he doing now? Trying to get his neck broken.

Only five feet separated him from the second-floor window—but the stone blocks here offered little opportunity for a grab-and-hoist. Still, he had to keep going—or he'd run out of muscle power and fall.

He moved to the edge of his precarious perch above the first-floor window. Nearby was a ring driven into the stone by the builders. Without giving himself time to think, he mustered strength for a hop across space, stretched out, and managed to grasp it. Hauling himself up, he got his foot on the ring, groped blindly at the sloping sill of the window ledge, and managed to get a handhold on the wooden casement. Suddenly, the mortar crumbled beneath his feet, and—with a surge of panic—he chinned up by brute force, dragging himself over the threshold and falling headfirst into the darkened room beyond. He lay on the floor, gasping for breath, heart pounding, palms and fingers and knees scraped and stinging.

A fight with Laura, his wife, had started all this. She'd walked out—and on an angry impulse, he'd gone to see Pendergast and agreed against his own better judgment to help him. And ultimately, that little fight had sent him tumbling from his comfortable twenty-first-century life into the nineteenth century, where he was now gasping on the floor in pursuit of a murdering bastard who should, by rights, have been dead for over a hundred years.

Shit on a stick, he'd better get moving. He lumbered to his feet in the dark, empty room, pulled the Colt .45 from his pocket, then tiptoed to the door and opened it silently.

Beyond lay an elegant corridor—with a man crumpled upon the floor, motionless, his blood soaking into the carpet. Munck had already murdered someone.

Closer to D'Agosta, a door opened and a cloaked figure emerged—Munck—holding a little girl by the neck. She was gagged, eyes like saucers. Munck turned, saw D'Agosta, and quickly raised a knife to her throat.

"Drop the gun now," he ordered D'Agosta in a whisper.

D'Agosta froze.

"*Now*," said Munck, pricking the girl's flesh with the tip of his knife.

D'Agosta held out his arm and let the gun swing by the trigger guard.

"On the carpet," the man said.

D'Agosta knelt to comply.

"I'm going to leave," Munck told him. "If you raise any alarm before we're out the front door, I cut her throat."

The man lowered the knife as he began backing toward the staircase. In that moment, D'Agosta realized that—despite the orders he'd been given—he had no option but to act.

He sprang up and body-slammed the son of a bitch, who in turn lashed out with the knife, slicing D'Agosta's forearm as he warded off the blow. Still gripping the girl, Munck staggered, regained his footing, then swung his knife around with the intention of sinking it in D'Agosta's back. But he was encumbered by the girl, and this allowed D'Agosta to punch upward, striking the descending forearm and slamming it against the wall, the knife flying.

Again, Munck backed toward the stairway, dragging the girl with him. Just then, the decorative drapery on one wall was flung aside, and out of a door hidden behind it appeared a woman. She rushed at Munck with a poker.

"*Meurs, bâtard!*" she cried.

Clasping the girl to him, Munck raised his left hand in an odd, martial salute, twisting his wrist as he did so. There was a clang of ringing steel—and suddenly three long, thin blades shot out from their hiding place within his sleeve, forming a spring-loaded claw beneath his fingers. The woman swung the poker, but Munck ducked and swept his arm in a wide angle, slashing her brutally across the midsection. As she fell back, Munck lunged with animal swiftness toward D'Agosta, who pivoted away, but though the bloodied claw just missed him, its metal framework impacted violently with his temple. His vision exploded in a swirl of stars as he staggered, bracing himself against the wall to avoid falling. The man raced down the stairs, hauling the girl with him. D'Agosta, head clearing, snatched his gun from the floor and lurched after them.

He could hear the house coming urgently to life. Reaching the bottom landing, he saw Munck make a beeline across the entryway and through the first of two doors leading to the street. D'Agosta raised his gun, but hesitated, unable to get a bead on the man without risking hitting the girl.

Suddenly, flying out of a darkened parlor, came a

figure—Constance—stiletto raised, terrible in the swift silence of her attack. Munck reached the outer door and grasped the handle, yanking it open, but Constance slammed it closed again with her body; D'Agosta saw a flash of steel and Munck lurched back with a cry, cut across the face. But then, collecting himself, he sprang at Constance, his nightmare device raking her knife arm and dislodging the stiletto. He yanked the door open again and leapt out with the girl into the cold December night. Constance, blood welling from her torn sleeve, grabbed her knife from the floor and took up pursuit.

D'Agosta tried to follow. But as he reached the threshold, a wave of dizziness forced him to stop... even as he saw the man—Munck—clambering into the compartment of a sleek trap that had just pulled up in front of the mansion. A gloved hand heaved Munck inside, the girl clutched close... and then the horses took off, galloping at high speed down Fifth Avenue and vanishing into the winter darkness.

He saw the pursuing Constance race down the steps and sprint to the corner... where she sank to her knees in the dirty snow, letting forth an incoherent cry of rage and pain, stretching out her bloody hands into the night, stiletto glittering in the gaslight.

The scene began to whirl around him, and D'Agosta felt himself collapse onto the entryway. Then darkness closed in and he lost the struggle to maintain consciousness.

* * *

He wasn't sure how much time passed, but it could not have been long. He found himself lying on the floor of the parlor, looking up at Constance, who stood over him, violet eyes raging.

A coachman arrived with a thud of heavy boots and

quickly took in the scene. "Your Grace, you're injured!" he cried in a coarse Irish accent.

"Murphy, attend to Féline," Constance said. "And find Joe and protect him. There may be others in the house."

More staff began arriving, frightened by the commotion. Constance was still staring at D'Agosta, her terrible look making him forget his pounding head, the dire situation...everything. He wanted to say something, explain, but he couldn't think clearly enough to speak. Instead, he struggled to a sitting position, head swimming.

A maid was attending to Constance's injured arm, wrapping it in linen cloth, but she had retained her stiletto and was now pointing it at D'Agosta with her other hand. "Before I kill you," she said in a low, trembling voice, "I want an explanation."

D'Agosta still couldn't find the words. As Constance moved closer, and he wondered with strange detachment if she was really about to cut his throat, he heard as if from very far away the clatter of a galloping horse—and then, much louder, an abrupt pounding on the door.

"Open up!" came a cry from beyond.

Constance started at the voice, then walked across the reception hall and threw open the front door. Pendergast stood there, heaving with fatigue.

"*You!*" was all she said.

Pendergast brushed past her, saw D'Agosta, then quickly came over and knelt beside him. "Did they get Binky?" he asked.

D'Agosta nodded.

As Pendergast examined D'Agosta's wound, he spoke to Constance in a cold voice. "You and I were never supposed to meet in this world," he said. "But since we have, it's best you hear all—and quickly. Leng knows about the machine. He knows who you are. He knows you've come from the future to kill him. He knows everything."

Constance stared. "Impossible."

"*Absolutely* possible. We must prepare ourselves. There's no time to lose."

"He kidnapped Binky—"

"He's been one step ahead of you—and me—at every turn. And this is just the beginning. You don't have the luxury of anger right now. Your sister is at grave risk. We must—"

He was interrupted by another knock at the door, polite and tentative.

Everyone turned toward the sound.

"It appears to be a delivery, Your Grace," said the butler, who—having recovered his composure—was now peering through the eyehole.

"Send them away!" Constance shouted.

"No," said Pendergast, drawing his weapon and standing to one side of the door. He nodded to the butler. "Open it."

A liveried messenger stood in the doorway with a handsomely wrapped gift box, tied up and garnished with white lilies. "Delivery for Her Grace, the Duchess of Ironclaw," he said.

Constance stared at the man. "What the devil is this?"

"There's a note, madam," the messenger said, eyes widening as he took in the scene.

She snatched the package from him. Holding it under one arm, she plucked away the envelope, tore it open, and extracted a card engraved with a black border. As she stared at it, her face drained of color. Then she dropped the note and tore the gold wrapping from the package, strewing the flowers about the floor and exposing a small mahogany box. She seized the lid and pulled it off. Inside, D'Agosta saw a flash of silver. Reaching in, Constance extracted a silver urn. Taking it in both hands, she held it before her face, staring at the engraved label on its belly. For a moment, all was still...and then the urn slipped through her fingers and struck the floor with a crash, its top flying off and the urn rolling across the floor, spilling a stream of gray ashes. It came to rest against D'Agosta's leg, label upward. He squinted to read it, his vision still cloudy—but the words etched into the silver were deep and clear:

> MARY GREENE
> DIED DECEMBER 26TH, 1880
> AGED 19 YEARS
> ASHES TO ASHES
> DUST TO DUST

4

December 27, 1880
Thursday

D'AGOSTA RESTED IN A wing chair, watching the rising sunlight try in vain to penetrate the shutters that wreathed the parlor in gloom.

In the hours since the assault, the house had settled into a frozen state of shock. Féline, the woman slashed by Munck upstairs, had been sutured and dressed by Pendergast and given an injection of antibiotics he'd brought from the twenty-first century. Murphy, the coachman, had taken the dead man—the children's tutor—to the basement and securely interred the body beneath a newly laid brick floor. Joe, Constance's brother, was upstairs being looked after by a maid. The rest of the servants had retreated to their rooms save for Gosnold, the butler, who insisted on remaining at his position in the parlor.

The urn and spilled ashes had been swept up and taken away. The card that had come with it, however, remained where Pendergast had placed it after reading the contents: on a side table near D'Agosta. All the rest of the night, D'Agosta had been unable to bring himself to read it. But as the light outside continued to brighten, he finally turned his head painfully toward the table, reached out, and took it up.

My dearest Constance,

I present, with condolences, the ashes of your older sister. They come with my thanks. The surgery was most successful.

Your plan was a desperate one from the start. I sensed you would double-cross me; it was just the mechanics of your betrayal that puzzled me. And then, mirabile dictu, the instrument that could lay bare the precise scheme was delivered to Bellevue... and from there into my hands.

You have the Arcanum; I have you: or rather, your younger self. Give me the formula, true and complete, and the girl will be returned to you intact. And then our business will be concluded... save for one thing. This is not your world to meddle in; it is mine. You, and those who followed you, will return to your own forthwith—or suffer the consequences.

You will signal your agreement by placing a candle inside a blue lantern and hanging it in the southeastern window of the third floor. I will then contact you with further instructions.

If I do not receive this signal within forty-eight hours, young Constance will suffer the fate of her older sister.

Until our next correspondence, I remain,

Your devoted, etc.
Dr. Enoch Leng

D'Agosta cursed under his breath and laid the note aside.

In the moments after the urn arrived, Constance had been incandescent with rage and—D'Agosta was certain—at the very brink of madness. Her feral hysteria had been the most unsettling thing he'd ever witnessed. Pendergast had said nothing, his face an expressionless mask of pale marble. He had listened to her imprecations and recriminations without response. And then he had risen, taken care of Féline, and silently supervised the cleanup of the murder scene and disposal of the body. Everyone appeared to be in unspoken agreement not to involve the authorities—which, D'Agosta knew, would only lead to disaster. And now the three of them remained silently in the parlor, sunk in a mixture of grief, guilt, and shock as a new and uncertain day crept into life outside the shuttered windows.

After her tirade, Constance had abruptly fallen silent—and remained that way. Now she disappeared upstairs. Ten minutes later she reappeared, holding a small, well-worn leather notebook.

She turned to the butler, who was still waiting in the parlor entrance. "Light a taper in a blue lantern and place it in the window of the last bedroom on the right, third floor."

"Yes, Your Grace." Gosnold turned and disappeared.

"Just a moment," said Pendergast, looking at Constance. "Is that the actual formula for life extension—the Arcanum?"

"Did you think you were the only one who had a copy? You forget: I was there while he developed it."

"So you intend to comply with Leng's instructions? You'll give him the Arcanum—and thus allow him to carry out his plan?"

"It won't matter that he has the Arcanum. Because he won't live long enough to use it—I will see to that."

Pendergast shifted in his chair. "Don't you think Leng has already anticipated this intention of yours?"

Constance stared at him. "It won't matter."

"I'm afraid it will. Leng knows everything. He anticipates everything. Whether you care to admit it or not, he is cleverer than either of us. Not only that—he now knows I'm here. He knows why we're here. He'll be prepared for whatever you do—whatever *we* do."

"He will not," said a soft voice from the darkness, "be prepared for *me*."

A match flared in a rear doorway of the parlor.

And then a figure stepped forward, lighting a salmon-colored Lorillard cigarette set into an ebony holder. The flare illuminated the pale face, the aquiline nose and high smooth forehead, the ginger-colored beard, and the two eyes—one hazel, the other a milky blue—of Diogenes Pendergast.

D'Agosta felt numb with shock. Nobody spoke. Diogenes Pendergast could not be here, he thought—not in this parallel universe, not in 1880. But here he was.

When no one spoke, Diogenes took off his coat and tossed it over the back of a chair, sat down, then carefully placed his hat on the nearby table. "I'm sorry, *Frater*. It's rude of me to intrude like this. I would have knocked, but—not wishing to disturb—it seemed best to let myself in. This is a dispiriting state of affairs," he went on, in a voice like melted butter poured over honey. "And you're correct when you say our dear ancestor will be prepared for whatever you all might do. But that's precisely what makes my presence so fortuitous."

"How did you get here?" Pendergast asked in a tight voice.

The end of the cigarette glowed red as Diogenes inhaled, and the scent of cloves began to spread across the parlor. "The garden gate was left open, so to speak. Back at Riverside Drive, where that uncouth scientist used your machine in an effort to enrich himself. Which machine, by the way, is now unfortunately no longer operational."

Not operational? This observation, despite the nonchalance with which it was delivered, sent a stab of anxiety through D'Agosta.

Diogenes paused to take a drag from the cigarette and issue a stream of smoke. "It's rather barbarous, this world without electricity," he said in the same languourous accent he'd affected since first appearing. "But at least they haven't yet discovered lung cancer."

"Why," said Constance, in a voice cold enough to freeze nitrogen, "should we ever think of associating ourselves with you again?"

"My dear Constance, let me ask you a question," Diogenes replied. "What is it I do best?"

Constance did not hesitate. "Killing."

Diogenes patted his gloved hands. "Exactly! A killer of hopes, of dreams, of love—but most especially of human beings." He stabbed out the half-smoked cigarette in a nearby ashtray—as if to punctuate this pronouncement—then drew out another and fitted it to the holder. "And now—" he turned to Pendergast— "a question for you: do you recall the last thing I said, that night I disappeared into the swamps of the Florida Keys?"

Pendergast hesitated just a moment, then quoted: "I am become death."

"Excellent. My words exactly. I'm so glad to finally be in the position of doing a favor for those I love. A singular favor." He lit another match. "I am come," he said, applying the match to the fresh cigarette, "as your Angel of Vengeance." Then the match was shaken out and he chuckled: a low and ominous sound that, though brief, seemed to linger forever before dying away, leaving the room once again in shadow and silence.

PART ONE

Darkness Drops

5

Present Day

Proctor regained consciousness slowly. His first sensation was of being horizontal, on a hard floor of concrete. His second was of pain.

He did not move. Instinct and training had taught him that when in unexpected danger of this sort, consciousness should not be betrayed until one had gathered as much situational awareness as possible.

He used the pain as a tool to take his measure. He ran his tongue gingerly around the inside of his mouth, tasting blood and dirt. A tooth was chipped, and his nose felt like it might be broken.

Without betraying any perceptible movement, he stiffened his limbs, one at a time, from elbows to fingertips and from hips to toes. He appeared to be fully functional; nothing seemed broken other than his nose and, perhaps, the zygomatic arch of one cheek.

Now, slowly, he drew in a deep breath. No pneumothorax.

Even more slowly, he unshuttered one eye, then the other. Despite being caked in blood, his eyes were fine and his vision unimpaired. The same with his hearing.

He lay without moving for another ten minutes as his senses grew fully alert and his last memories of consciousness returned. Ferenc, that bastard. He'd booby-trapped Proctor's console with some kind of anesthetic or nerve agent... while the machine was running at full power, its portal open.

He was confident Ferenc was not nearby, that the man had used the machine. The room was still—in fact, all too still, and a foul odor of burnt wiring and scorched electronics hung in the air.

Proctor readied himself. Then he rolled over at speed, balling his fists and tenting up his knees, keeping his head raised slightly off the ground to minimize the pain of his cheek and nose. Nevertheless, the agony of sudden movement was extreme. Ignoring it, he glanced around quickly. No sign of Ferenc.

Now Proctor knew he'd used the machine. Gingerly, he rose to his feet, checked his weapon, and pulled the chair from his worktable into the middle of the room and sat down.

He stared at the machine. It was a smoking ruin.

It did not matter that he'd successfully transported every piece of that machine, in its original configuration, from Savannah to this basement room of the Riverside Drive mansion. It didn't matter that he'd retrieved a scientist who could repair it—Ferenc—not only convincing him to do the work, but keeping an eye on him until Pendergast and his friend D'Agosta could go through the portal. It didn't matter, because he had failed his employer. He'd allowed that worm Ferenc to outsmart him, render him unconscious long enough to use the machine.

And because of his failure, Pendergast and the rest were stranded in a parallel universe in the year 1880.

He checked his watch. He'd been out for hours. Why

hadn't Ferenc returned? The machine remained turned up to its highest setting... and beyond. Perhaps the weasel had been delayed on the far side of the portal. Perhaps he'd died. In any case, he couldn't come back now: the machine had red-lined, overheated, and imploded. Proctor's knowledge of the device was limited to the controls on its front panels. Ferenc had been the only one to work the guts of the machine, the only one who knew enough to repair it.

Not that repair appeared to be a possibility.

Proctor sat another minute, gaze fixed on the wreckage. Then he stood and—without looking back—made his way to the door, opened it, and disappeared into the dim confines of the mansion's basement.

6

December 27, 1880

Gosnold returned to the parlor and gave a little bow. "Your Grace, the blue lantern has been placed in the window, as you requested."

D'Agosta saw Constance's hand tighten on the little leather notebook. His head now finally clear, he spoke. "So what's your game, Diogenes?" he asked.

"The stolid policeman gets right to business," said Diogenes, drawing on the cigarette and leaning his head back to blow the smoke upward. "I'll recount my activities since arriving; you'll find them interesting. I watched that hired scientist, Ferenc, as he sprang that half-baked plan of his. He knocked out Proctor and used the machine himself. I was there; I witnessed it all—and on impulse I jumped through the portal after him. That was a rash action I may still regret. I tumbled into Longacre Square and a pile of horse manure—an appropriate welcome to the nineteenth century. And that is when I made a mistake: I did not kill Ferenc on the spot. Instead, I followed him to a bank, where he tried to obtain some rare coins but botched the thing, caused a fuss, and claimed he was from the future. Naturally he was bundled off to Bellevue, where, I regret to say, Leng found him."

He took another drag on the cigarette.

"Leng took Ferenc out of Bellevue to his lair in the Five Points. One can imagine what happened there. Suffice it to say, the good doctor now knows all your secrets: the machine, the location of the portal, the real reason for your presence here—the works. His first reaction was to race up to Longacre Square and try to use the portal. Without success, I'm glad to say—can you imagine Leng, unleashed on the twenty-first century? That was Ferenc's only good deed: overtaxing and, apparently, burning out the device so Leng cannot make use of it. Of course, neither can we."

He gave a dry laugh that made D'Agosta's skin crawl. He glanced over at Constance and saw on her face a frozen mask.

"You still haven't explained why you're here," said D'Agosta. "Why help us?"

"The truth? Very well. Perhaps my use of the portal was not quite as impulsive as I've implied. When, in spying on my brother—my primary pastime these past few years—I saw the marvel of that machine, I also saw a curious opportunity. The world back there—" he flicked ash over his shoulder, as if the future lay in that direction— "is filled with nothing but grotesque memories. Here is a new world, where I am not known and have no history."

At this, D'Agosta shook his head—gingerly.

"It was only after the fact that I realized I have another purpose in this place—Leng. I wish to remove him. He murdered the sister of one I held dear—" this was said with a glance at Constance— "and kidnapped her doppelganger. On top of that, Leng is the vilest of the Pendergasts, a blot on the family escutcheon. Finally, and I am saddened to point this out, but you, Brother, have failed. Your meddling here has brought disaster and tragedy. It seems only proper I be the one to set things right."

"So what exactly is your plan?" D'Agosta asked. "He's got Binky—and any move on him will risk her death. Look what he did to Mary."

Constance suddenly stood, still clutching the leather notebook. "Gosnold, please bring Joe down here to me."

The butler left and returned a moment later with Joe. The boy had a scared look in his eyes but was fighting to keep his expression steady. D'Agosta wondered just what he'd heard and seen; he was holding so tightly to himself that it was hard to tell.

Constance knelt in front of the boy, taking his hand. "Joe," she said quietly, "I can't explain everything that's happened—because I still don't know myself. But you know enough already. Something unexpected, something very bad, has happened. Now I have to put things right. I may be back soon, or . . . I may be gone for some time."

She paused. Joe's face retained its stoical expression.

"These two men—" she gestured toward D'Agosta and Pendergast— "are reliable. You can trust them completely. Féline, too—and Mr. Murphy. These four—and no one else."

The boy remained expressionless.

"That one's name is Pendergast. The other one is D'Agosta."

The boy glanced silently from one to the other.

"Hello, Joe," said D'Agosta, unsure what else to say. "You can call me Vinnie."

The boy didn't react, his jaw merely tightening.

Constance gently grasped his arm with her bandaged hand, and for a moment some iron entered her voice. "Do you understand, Joe? Whatever Pendergast and, ah,

Vinnie ask you to do, please obey. They have your best interests at heart."

Joe nodded curtly.

"And now—" she kissed him on the top of his head—"I must leave. I know you will be strong—for your sister, and for me. Mr. Pendergast was my own guardian...once. He, along with Vinnie, will be your guardians while I'm gone."

A hesitation, then another nod.

Constance rose. "Gosnold, please get my traveling cloak and send Murphy around with the carriage." D'Agosta saw her slip the small leather notebook into her pocket.

Gosnold bowed and withdrew, and a moment later returned with a heavy cloak, which she took from him and threw around herself. A few minutes later, the carriage came around from the back, Murphy at the reins. Gosnold held open the door for her.

D'Agosta looked at Pendergast, but the man remained perfectly silent, his face like marble. Why didn't he say or do anything?

"You're not going to Leng, are you?" D'Agosta finally asked Constance.

Constance turned to him, eyes smoldering. "Naturally."

"But his instructions about the lamp... This is crazy."

"Perhaps." She exited the outer door with the swirl of her cloak, then descended the steps to the carriage. As Gosnold was shutting the door behind her, D'Agosta heard her call out to Murphy, "The Post Road..."

The door closed.

"What the hell?" D'Agosta turned to Pendergast. "We can't just let her go like this!"

Pendergast finally spoke. "I'm afraid we've got no choice. She's bringing him the Arcanum."

D'Agosta looked from Pendergast to Diogenes and back. "You're both okay with this?"

"No," said Pendergast.

"But you let her go!"

"Are you under the misapprehension she could be stopped?" Pendergast arched an eyebrow.

At this, Diogenes chuckled. "*Frater*, you and I know the nature of that woman."

"But—" D'Agosta swallowed. "After all your careful plans, after all that we've... What is she *thinking*?"

"Vincent," said Pendergast wearily, "she is not thinking. But we must let this act, however rash and impulsive, play out. We owe her that. It is bound to be unsuccessful. And when she returns—if she returns—she will be in a state none of us can imagine. What happens next will be anyone's guess." He took a deep breath. "We must prepare for the storm."

7

D'Agosta listened with disbelief. His head was pounding again, and he leaned back in his chair to ease the pain. This was insane. How were they, marooned in a strange world, going to handle Constance, save Binky, kill Leng—and then get back home again?

He turned to Diogenes. "You say the time machine was wrecked. *How* wrecked?"

"You mean, can we use it to return?" Diogenes asked him. "As I said, that fool Ferenc left its levels at maximum when he went through, timed I assume to give him sufficient opportunity to accomplish his scheme and return. The most logical explanation is that the man simply didn't return in time to ease back the power—and the machine overloaded."

"So we're stuck here?"

"Unless Proctor can repair it," said Pendergast.

"Proctor?" cried D'Agosta. "He's a chauffeur! How's he going to fix a time machine?" He felt horror settle in. Laura—he'd never see her again. The twenty-first century, the New York he loved—gone.

"My advice to you, Vincent," said Pendergast coolly, "is not to ponder such existential questions for the moment." He rose. "The first thing we must do, before something even more dire occurs, is to get the one entrusted to us safely away and far from here. Gosnold, will you take Joe upstairs while we discuss what is to be done?"

"Yes, sir."

"I can go on my own," said Joe coldly.

"In that case, pack a bag for yourself, with some warm clothes, a book, and a deck of cards. You'll be going on a journey."

Joe turned stiffly and went upstairs.

D'Agosta looked at Pendergast. "What's to stop Leng from killing Constance after he gets the Arcanum?"

"For one thing, his suspicious nature—if the formula has been tampered with, he might still need her. For another, I believe Constance has a certain amount of leverage over him."

"What leverage?"

"Constance knows a great deal about Leng—and, what's more, she knows his future."

"What I don't understand," Diogenes said, "is this: if this world is supposedly identical to our own, except that it's in the past of 1880, what is that monstrosity I saw being erected at the southern edge of Central Park? Nothing like that ever existed in the past of *our* world."

D'Agosta had seen this himself, during a carriage ride on his first trip back here with Pendergast—an ugly tower under construction, like a ten-story chimney. He'd just assumed that it, like so much else built in Manhattan, had vanished with time.

Pendergast made a dismissive gesture. "Consider it a raspberry pip under the dentures of the space-time continuum. We don't have the luxury to speculate how precisely this world mirrors our own—it's damned close. It's Joe's safety we should be discussing."

D'Agosta looked over at Pendergast as he leaned forward impatiently. Was it his imagination, or had the agent just cursed?

"Joe is in great danger," Pendergast continued. "This house is no doubt being watched, and we shall have to be clever." He turned to the butler. "Gosnold, my man, be so kind as to send a note to the closest funeral home, informing them that we have the body of Mr. Moseley in the house, and that we require a hearse and coffin be sent to pick it up. Make sure they understand that time is of the essence."

"May I remind you, Mr. Pendergast, sir, that Mr. Moseley is buried in the basement?" said Gosnold, with admirable restraint.

"And there he shall stay. Joe will be in the coffin. Here's what will happen: on the way to the mortuary, the horse will throw a shoe, which shall necessitate a trip to the nearest livery stable, at which point Joe will be removed and spirited away to a place of safety. The coffin will be delivered empty to the funeral home. Some hefty bribes will be required to make this work—to that end, please help yourself, Gosnold, to as much gold as is required from the safe."

Gosnold bowed as if this were the most ordinary request in the world. "Anything else, sir?"

"Can we rely on you to help us carry out this bit of prestidigitation with complete discretion?"

"Yes, sir."

"I see that Constance chose her household well. That's all for now; thank you."

Gosnold retreated with another bow.

Pendergast turned to D'Agosta. "You, Vincent, will be Joe's protector. After smuggling him out of the livery, you will take him to the Grand Central Depot, where you will buy passage on the New York, Providence, and Boston line. From Boston, you'll book passage on a steamer to an island far to the north, called Mount Desert. That is your ultimate destination."

D'Agosta held his hand to his head. The pounding was not going away.

"Pull yourself together, please. Joe is Leng's next logical victim, and we must immediately remove him from the field. There are reasons to choose Mount Desert Island, which I shall brief you on as soon as I've finalized the details."

"Right, okay," said D'Agosta, taking a deep breath. "Christ, I need some ibuprofen."

"There's no ibuprofen or aspirin. Laudanum is the analgesic of choice in 1880. I would not recommend it."

"Son of a bitch." D'Agosta sat up, taking a deep breath. As messed up as this situation was, Pendergast was right: he had to get his shit together.

"You'll need fresh clothes for the journey—those bloodstains would be noticed and arouse suspicion. It seems to me you are Moseley's size, more or less. You have no objection to wearing a dead man's clothes?"

"Do I have a choice?"

"His room will be on the third floor—and no doubt easy to find. Help yourself."

D'Agosta groaned and rose, steadying himself on the arm of the chair.

Pendergast turned to Diogenes. "Under normal circumstances, I would never make this gesture—but these circumstances are far from normal." He extended his hand. "Until this matter is resolved for good or ill, can we work together, Brother—without duplicity or malice?"

Diogenes rose and extended his own hand, grasping Pendergast's.

"Once Joe is safely away," said Pendergast, "we must shut off Leng's access to experimental subjects—he will want them more than ever to test the Arcanum Constance is giving him. We must stop the killing. This will have the additional benefit of frustrating him, perhaps even smoking him out."

"I have some ideas along those lines," said Diogenes, "involving the Five Points Mission." They turned away, heads together, and began to murmur.

D'Agosta made his way up the stairs, taking them slowly, one at a time. *Just get through this*, he said to himself. *Just get through it. Then worry about getting home.*

* * *

In Moseley's room, D'Agosta found a meager wardrobe of shabby clothing. The tutor's pants were too tight, so he tossed them aside: his own trousers would have to do. Thankfully, most of the blood was on his shirt. Moseley's shirts were a little snug but serviceable, as were the frock coat and greatcoat. The old-fashioned tie stumped him, so he just stuffed it in his pocket. He debated whether to take the top hat and decided it would at least keep his head warm.

Mount Desert Island—the name was not encouraging. He was going to need more clothing than this. Rummaging through more drawers turned up some gloves and socks. Pendergast would surely send up warmer clothes at the first opportunity.

Atop the dresser next to a dry sink, he saw a bottle labeled HEZEKIAH'S TINCTURE OF LAUDANUM. It was filled with a murky, reddish-brown liquid. Fucking A, he was hurting so bad, what harm could there be in it? He read the printed label on the back, which called for six to twelve drops dissolved in water. He grasped the bottle, filled up its dropper, poured himself a glass from the nearby water pitcher, and put in ten drops. Then he drank it down, shuddering at the bitter flavor.

Just then he heard a carriage arrive below. Was Constance returning already, or was it the undertaker? He quickly combed his hair with Moseley's brush, the calming medicine already spreading through his body and easing the pain in his head. *This stuff really works*, he thought. He began to stuff the bottle into his pocket, thought better of it, then returned it to the dresser and went downstairs.

It was an undertaker, but the exact opposite of what D'Agosta had imagined: a plump, rosy-cheeked fellow with a big grin, yellow teeth, and a restless manner. A coffin made of rough pine—for transport only, it seemed—was carried in the front door by four burly workmen. As they set it on the floor, Joe was brought down from upstairs by Féline, bandaged but with a look on her face almost as determined as Constance's. The boy carried a leather satchel. Pendergast detached himself to speak to the woman in rapid-fire French.

Gosnold approached the undertaker and his men with a small leather bag. Murmuring instructions, he dispensed several $20 gold pieces.

"This," said Pendergast, turning back and introducing D'Agosta to the undertaker, "is Mr. Harrison, the boy's guardian, who will be driving with you in the carriage to the funeral home. He will handle all the details of the transfer. And Mr. Harrison, allow me to introduce Mr. Porlock, the undertaker kind enough to assist us on such short notice."

"Sir," said the undertaker, bowing. "Pleased to meet you, Mr. Harrison."

"Likewise," D'Agosta said. "I'm sure." He gritted his teeth. Jesus Christ, all of this had to be some kind of karmic joke.

Féline was speaking in a low voice to Joe, leading him over to the coffin. The boy looked into it and took a step back.

How the hell were they going to get the boy into the coffin? He was staring at it, shaking his head.

"Now, young man," said Pendergast, "I realize this is not the ideal form of transportation, but it will have to do. If you please—get in."

For all his brilliance, Pendergast had no idea how to talk to a twelve-year-old boy. D'Agosta stepped forward.

"I'll handle this," he said, then knelt before the youth. "Joe, here's the situation, and I'm going to give it to you straight. Man to man. What Constance, I mean the duchess, said is true. Some awful things happened here last night. I don't know what you saw, or how much you know, but the house is being watched by some very bad people, and we've got to smuggle you out of here. You're going to have to be brave and get in that coffin. It's a disguise, a trick—nothing else. You'll be in there for about an hour, and then we'll get you out. You and I will take a train to a place where they can't find us. When things are safe again, I'll bring you home. Okay?"

The boy stared at him with a tight, hostile expression. "Who took Binky?" he asked.

So he knew that Binky had been kidnapped.

"Criminals. The same people who are watching the house. The duchess has gone to get her back. But if things—if things take too long, they'll try to take you next. That's why we have to get you out of here." He held his hand out toward the coffin. "Come on, there's no time to waste. It's you and me against the bad guys."

Joe climbed in without another hesitation. It was a large coffin, and despite its flimsy appearance the inside had been spread with cushions and blankets for the short journey. Small slits had been cut into the sides for air. As Joe made himself comfortable, Féline gave him a little bag of sweets. The boy then lay down and the lid was affixed on top. The four men hoisted it up on their shoulders and headed out the door.

Pendergast came up to D'Agosta and slipped an envelope into his hand. "You will get off in Boston, go to the Dorchester Piers, and take the Bar Harbor Coastal Packet, a steamer, north to Mount Desert Island. You will then go to the address in the envelope—complete instructions are inside."

He handed D'Agosta a traveling case of rough cloth. "There's a little more clothing in here, some sandwiches, a few necessaries, and of course money. I will send warmer clothes for you and Joe, along with instructions on how we will communicate. From now on, you're Mr. George Harrison of Sleepy Hollow, New York."

"George Harrison?"

"I picked a name you aren't likely to forget."

"Jesus."

"Good luck, my friend."

D'Agosta left the house and descended the steps as the men were sliding the coffin into the back of the hearse. He got into the passenger seat next to Mr. Porlock, the four men clambering into the back. They started off, the frost on the lampposts glittering in the morning light, the horses blowing steam from their nostrils, hooves clip-clopping on the cobblestones. D'Agosta had the strange feeling of slowly waking from a dream, waiting expectantly for the moment that these surroundings would melt away and he'd wake to find Laura in bed next to him, the sun pouring in through the curtains, the twenty-first century running on as usual outside.

8

The hearse traveled south on Fifth Avenue and was soon caught up in a scrum of carriages, horses, peddlers' carts, and all manner of conveyances elegant and shabby, mingling with the shouts of drivers, the ringing of iron wheels on cobblestones, and the cracking of whips. The smells of horse sweat and manure filled the air, along with the ever-present stink of burning coal. It occurred to D'Agosta that he was experiencing the nineteenth-century equivalent of a traffic jam.

Mr. Porlock took out a cigar case and offered one to D'Agosta. While he had given up cigars years ago and had promised Laura never to touch them again, he took one now. Why the hell not? She wasn't even in the same universe. Porlock lit up his and D'Agosta did the same, grateful for the scent of tobacco to dilute the noisome air.

When they reached Forty-Third Street, Porlock gave a histrionic cry, as instructed, and ordered his driver to pull to the side. He got out and together with the driver, made a show of examining the nearer horse's rear shoe. After a minute the undertaker's driver picked up the horse's hoof, messed around with a nail clincher, then said in a loud voice: "Mr. Porlock, we're going to have to make a quick stop at the livery stables. We're about to lose a shoe."

Porlock waved his hand with a show of impatience. "So be it."

They turned down Forty-Third Street and rode west toward Sixth Avenue, where a sign over a large brick building announced a livery stable and farrier establishment. Wooden gates, manned by two boys, opened to let them into the courtyard, closing immediately behind them.

They were met by another youth, calling loudly and gesticulating. "This way, gents, this way." Other carriages were parked in a courtyard that was covered with sand and straw, and horses were being led about by stable boys.

The boy led the hearse to a bay, where it was parked. The horses were unharnessed and taken away.

"Mr. Harrison?" said Porlock in a low voice. "Now's your chance."

D'Agosta stepped down and went around to the back of the hearse in time to see the four men opening the lid. Joe climbed out. He had the same determined expression on his face, which encouraged D'Agosta. At least he wouldn't try to run away.

The livery boy holding open the door to the bay stared open-mouthed at what he'd just witnessed—someone roughly his own age climbing out of a coffin.

"Hey, you!" said D'Agosta, stepping over to him and holding out a silver dollar. "Kid, this is to keep your mouth shut. You understand? Not a word, ever."

"Oh, yes, sir! Yes, sir!" The boy stared at the glittering coin.

"Put it away—and wipe that look off your face."

The boy stuffed the coin in his pocket and arranged his face into a serious expression.

D'Agosta turned back to the coffin and, as planned, tossed four $10 gold eagles into it—bribes to take care of those in the funeral home who would receive the empty coffin. He nodded at the four men, who quickly sealed the coffin up again. Then, taking Joe by the hand and grasping the bags in the other, he turned to the livery boy.

"Is there a back door to this place?"

"Yes, sir. But—"

"Take us there."

The boy led D'Agosta and Joe to the rear of the livery, where another wooden door was shut and barred, manned by yet another boy. D'Agosta wondered, a little idly, how many decades it would take for child labor laws to be enacted.

"Open the door for us, young fellow." He proffered the second boy a silver dollar.

The boy snatched it. "Yes, sir."

"If anyone should ask—you saw nobody."

"Right, sir. Nobody."

The open door led D'Agosta and Joe into an alleyway, dim despite the morning sun. The door shut behind them and was barred with a loud clang of wood and iron. D'Agosta looked in both directions, seeing no one but a group of young men in bowlers and flat caps, lounging on a stack of barrels, smoking cigars.

He tried to orient himself. Grand Central Depot was the precursor to Grand Central Terminal, and that should be roughly two and a half blocks east of where they were. The alleyway ran east to west, and so D'Agosta turned left, still clutching Joe's hand. They would have to pass by the toughs, who were eyeing them through clouds of cigar smoke. D'Agosta could feel the reassuring weight of the Colt .45 under his arm.

They headed down the cobbles. As they did so, the men slowly stood, hands in their pockets, and sauntered across the alleyway, blocking it.

Jesus, thought D'Agosta. It was only a random street gang—he was sure of that—and he had half a mind to just drop one or two of the bastards. But if they made a scene, it might very well attract the police—or perhaps Leng's men, who had no doubt been following their carriage.

"I don't like those men," said Joe.

"Neither do I." D'Agosta slid his hand under his arm and removed the .45.

Joe's eyes went wide. "What kind of a gun is that?" he whispered.

"A loud one."

"Hullo, guv," said a hollow-faced, rail-thin young man with pale skin, freckles, and a dented derby hat—apparently the leader. "This here's our toll booth, like. Come on, post the pony."

D'Agosta stared at the man. What the hell did that mean? Money, of course.

"What's the toll?" D'Agosta asked.

The men laughed as they spread out, some sliding long knives out of their shirts.

"As you're asking—everything, ratbag."

More knives came out... but no guns. He sure as hell wasn't going to give these scumbags the gold in his case.

D'Agosta shoved Joe behind him and showed his piece. "You know what the fuck this is?"

A silence. They seemed almost as shocked by the obscenity as by the weapon. "I guess I do, guv," the leader said.

"Then you know it can blow all your heads into little pink clouds. Want to see?"

"Boyos," the gang leader said after a moment, "let the

gentleman pass." He slid his knife back into his shirt, held his hands up to shoulder level, and said, "No harm meant, guv."

The rest of the gang followed his lead, moving aside and putting their knives away.

Was it really going to be this easy? They shuffled aside to let him pass. Would they set on him from behind once he and Joe had gone by? He rotated his gaze back as he walked on, bags tucked under one arm, gun at the ready.

At that moment, he saw—at the far end of the alleyway—a two-horse carriage come to a halt with a squeal of iron brakes. Three men jumped out, carrying iron rods. "Hey!" one yelled to the gang. "Stop that cove!"

Leng's men, thought D'Agosta. They came charging down the alleyway, still shouting. Thinking quickly, D'Agosta reached into his pocket, pulled out a gold piece, and flipped it to the gang's leader. "That's for you—if you beat the hell out of those three men."

The youth caught it and grinned. "Sure thing, guv!"

D'Agosta turned and, still gripping Joe by the hand, ran on. As they exited the far end of the alleyway, he could hear shouting and bellowing as the fight began.

* * *

Grand Central Depot rose above the surrounding city, an unfamiliar monstrosity in brick and limestone. D'Agosta bought first-class tickets on the New York, Providence, and Boston line. They boarded the train just as it was about to depart. A porter led the way to an elegant compartment, which they had to themselves.

D'Agosta took his seat with relief. His headache was starting to come back.

"So is your name George or Vinnie?" asked Joe, looking at him suspiciously.

"From now on, it's George."

The train began to chuff and groan as it pulled out of the station.

"Can I see your gun?" Joe asked.

D'Agosta thought for a moment. He had learned how to shoot from his father when he was twelve. Glancing around, he confirmed there was nobody present to see. He got up, latched the compartment, and took the gun out. He freed the cylinder and inspected it. All six chambers were still full of rounds. He shook out the bullets into his palm and flipped the cylinder back into place.

"Two rules. You never, ever point the barrel at a human being."

"Yes, sir."

"You never, ever put your finger on the trigger, or inside the trigger guard, until just before you fire."

"Yes, sir."

D'Agosta nodded, satisfied. "This is not a toy. You may hold it for a moment and then give it back. Take it by the grips, like this, and keep the barrel pointed down."

He turned the gun around and offered it to Joe. The boy took it, hefted it. "It's heavy."

"Yes, it is. It's what they call a forty-five caliber." He waited a moment. "Okay, you can give it back."

Joe did so, his face flushed with the experience of having held it, even for a moment. Funny thing about boys and guns, thought D'Agosta; something utterly primitive in the reaction. It was probably the same with bows and arrows, or spears, thousands of years ago. Joe seemed brave and resourceful, in many ways more like a small, serious adult than a kid. He must've grown up fast, living on the streets and on Blackwell's Island.

The train finally emerged from the dark tunnels beneath Park Avenue, speeding northward along the coast with a view over marshes to Long Island Sound.

"You got that pack of cards handy?" D'Agosta asked.

Joe nodded.

"Know how to play war?"

He nodded again and fished the pack out, dividing it into two piles. "That's for you," he said, pushing one pile over.

D'Agosta took the cards and they began to play. At that moment the porter came by. D'Agosta ordered a sarsaparilla for Joe.

As they played, D'Agosta's thoughts started to wander. What was it going to be like on Mount Desert Island? He'd never been to Maine in his life, never even heard of Mount Desert. The two years he had spent in Moose Jaw, Canada, as a young man on a failed attempt to write a book had cured him of cold weather and long snowy winters forever.

Mount Desert Island, Maine. End of December 1880. Sounded like hell.

9

The beautifully appointed Clarence coach, with a coat of arms on its door and a pair of black Percherons at the reins, passed the Post Road milestone at St. Nicholas Avenue and 116th Street, then turned north. It was dusk; the Hudson River was spread out to the left, glittering in its restless rush to the sea, the ramparts of the Palisades beyond. To the right was a procession of small, well-tended farms, punctuated here and there by country mansions, their broad façades facing the river.

After about a mile, at a whispered word from the occupant, the carriage pulled over at the broad entranceway to one of the mansions, larger than the others, built of dark limestone in the Beaux Arts style. The somewhat grim lines of its bulk were softened by the growing dark and the gas lanterns that illuminated both sides of the lane leading to its front doors. The iron gates yawned wide, barbed points at their tops gleaming wickedly in the failing light.

Now the carriage door opened, and Constance Greene slipped down onto the graveled shoulder. She was dressed in a long, pleated skirt and a top with tapered balloon sleeves, over which had been thrown a wrap to ward off the chill. The edge of a small bandage was just visible under her right cuff. In the shadow of the coach, her clothing looked almost plain—unless one was close enough to see the quality of the material, the fastidious tailoring and stitching, and the small chenille tassels that hung from the silk-and-velvet French wrap. She held a leather notebook in one hand, its cover scuffed and stained.

She walked up to the coachman's box, where Murphy was seated. "Remember," she told him. "On no account should you approach, no matter what you see or hear… unless I specifically call for your assistance."

"But, milady—"

"Please obey my instructions. If I require your help, I'll let you know: that I promise you." And with this, she turned and began walking toward the mansion.

As she entered the lane, the rough stones of the Post Road became smooth bricks, carefully interlaid. She walked at a measured pace, taking in the building and its surroundings. Now and then, her eyes flickered in recognition of things long forgotten; otherwise, her expression remained impassive, despite the emotions roiling within.

As she came near the wide front steps, a dozen figures materialized out of the dark topiary and neatly trimmed shrubs decorating the façade. They were dressed in clothes so similar they suggested a uniform: black trousers with suspenders and button flies; dark-gray shirts; jackets of thin leather with broad lapels; bowler hats worn cocked and low over the ears. Silently they lined up, barring her progress. They were young, moving with confidence and physical ease. Each one wore a tiny earring in the left lobe, with gemstones of differing colors.

Having grown up in the streets of the Five Points herself, she recognized this as similar to the street gangs that infested that slum: the Dead Rabbits, the Swamp Angels, and a dozen others. The primary difference was this group looked well fed and satisfied, rather than poor and desperate.

One stepped forward from the rest. The short hair, narrow stature, and delicate features told Constance she was a woman. She had eyebrows shaved to mere arrowheads, and bore on her neck the tattoo of an opium pipe. Her own tiny earring held a colorless diamond, which—along with the confident bellicosity she radiated—made it clear she held a high rank in the gang, perhaps the leader. This was unusual, and it made Constance wary.

"Search her," the woman said.

One of the young men stepped up and Constance backed away. "You do it," she told the woman.

"Not keen on a man's touch, eh?" the woman said with a leer. "Perhaps we've a wee bit in common." She approached Constance and frisked her thoroughly and professionally, finding only the Italian stiletto.

The woman took the knife and turned it over in her hands, admiring the gold workmanship. "Such a dainty little shivvy," she said mockingly. "A perfect toy for milady's soft hands." As she examined the knife, Constance noticed a long scar, purple and imperfectly healed, running across her right palm. "Can't say I've ever seen one like this before."

"That's because you've never set foot in a museum," Constance retorted.

The woman's eyes narrowed. But at that moment, the double doors of the mansion flew open and the figure of Leng appeared, framed in brilliant light.

"The Duchess of Ironclaw!" he said with feigned deference. "What a pleasant surprise—Decla, clear the way, if you please, and let Her Grace pass unmolested."

Constance stared at the tall figure in the doorway, her hatred of this murderer of her sister so overwhelming she staggered slightly before regaining her composure. If she was to get through this, she had to maintain rigid control of herself.

After an insolent moment the young woman stepped aside—without returning the knife. The others did the same and Constance mounted the broad marble steps. Leng bowed as she passed. As he closed the doors behind them, Constance could see the gang fanning out into the darkness.

Without a word Leng turned, then stepped past her, and she followed him through a long, narrow passageway, lined on both sides with suits of armor, then stopped at the entrance to the grand reception hall. She looked around, taking in the natural history collections, the fossils and butterflies, the meteorites and gemstones and stuffed animals. She felt, acutely, the assault of memory. The hall, like the mansion itself, was deeply familiar—although she had not seen it like this for many, many years.

As they entered the reception hall, she saw the misshapen figure of Munck, watching her intently from beneath the shadow of the main stairway. A hideous cut, fresh and deep, ran across his face from right forehead to left cheekbone. It had been crudely stitched and was partially covered in cotton bandages, still weeping a yellowish discharge.

"You can thank me later," Constance said as their eyes met.

Munck said nothing. But his expression changed.

Leng motioned her into the room off the right of the reception hall: the library.

She paused at the threshold. She had spent most of her recent years in this room, usually in the silent but affirming presence of Pendergast. Here was her retreat from the world, where she read, did her research and writing, or played the harpsichord. The crackling of its fireplace, the book-perfumed recesses, the baize-covered tables: everything about it had spoken to her of comfort, safety, and intellectual pleasure.

The room she stepped into now, however, was like a mirror image in chilling reverse.

She was careful to keep her expression neutral as her eyes moved across the room's contents. Here was furniture she hadn't seen in years, items Pendergast had removed upon taking possession of the mansion. The old furniture squatted in the library like malignant specters from the past: The *secrétaire à abattant* of flame mahogany, with its little cubbyholes and drawers; the hand-painted Louis XV writing desk, on which Leng kept a large leatherbound notebook; the shadowboxes fronted with Tiffany glass, containing exhibits designed to provoke madness in viewers—and Leng's most prized acquisition: three completed studies, in oil, for Jan van Eyck's *The Last Judgment*, hanging in heavy gilt frames above the shuttered windows at the far end of the room.

"Please sit down," Leng said.

Constance ignored the invitation and remained standing.

Leng seated himself behind the writing desk. "I hope my welcoming committee met with your approval."

Constance remained silent.

"Other gangs collect ears. Here, I dole out various gems to signify rank and accomplishments." He paused. "I did not expect you to beard me like this—the lion, I mean, in his own—"

Abruptly, Constance tossed the weathered notebook at him. Taken by surprise, the man fumbled it, and it fell from his hands to the floor.

Constance did not move.

Leng stared at her and then, after a moment, reached down and picked it up. He paged through it rapidly, now and then stopping to peer intently. Constance remained motionless until he at last closed the notebook and placed it on the desk.

"I went to a great deal of trouble arranging our anticipated meeting, you know," he told her. "But coming here as your own messenger, in this fashion, you've rendered all that unnecessary."

"You have the Arcanum. Now give me Binky." She spoke in a flat voice, again making a great effort not to reveal a glimpse of the overwhelming loathing she felt.

"Ah, Binky," Leng repeated in a singsong, his equilibrium already restored. "*Bing*-kee. It's very strange, you know; that Hungarian scientist Ferenc offered up so much information——toward the end, he was desperate to offer more——but he couldn't say precisely *why* you were so eager to cross universes to rescue your kin. I can only assume that Mary and Joe must have perished while still young? You, of course, survived——obviously. And you came back to change that tragic outcome?"

Constance ignored this. "I've fulfilled my end of your bargain——now you do the same."

"Ah!" Leng raised a peremptory finger, as if to silence a student giving a wrong answer. "You have brought a formula to me: on that point, we are agreed. But how am I to be sure it is *the* formula? Perhaps it has been altered slightly, compounding a painful and deadly poison into the mixture? You see——" and here he put his forearms on the desk and interlaced his fingers—— "Technically, you have *not* yet fulfilled your end of the bargain. What were my terms? 'Give me the formula, true and complete.' There's no reason for me to believe either of those corollaries have been proved. And it will take some time to confirm them."

"That is the formula, as concocted by you...over many long years still to come," Constance said. "I have no reason to lie. I want Binky—now."

"Pardon my contradicting, but you have every reason to lie. Among many other interesting things, the nosy Dr. Ferenc told me you returned to this past time, via your infernal machine, specifically to avenge yourself upon *me*."

Constance struggled to control her rage. "I won't ask again. Give her to me."

"I'm glad to hear you won't. That would be tiresome." Leng rose from behind the desk. "Now, now, Your Grace—don't look at me like that. I am not without compassion. I'd like to think you are telling the truth; that you've had a change of heart; that your mad passion to murder me has ebbed. But I can't be sure. Until I have fully tested your formula, however, here is something— shall we say?—in consideration for the trouble you've taken."

He had begun to move around the library as he spoke: slowly, as if weighed down by thought. But now his hand reached out, grasped something out of sight, and tugged it—a blind, patterned after the fashion of William Morris and blending with the wallpaper. In drawing it up, he allowed her a view out of the library and across to the east wing of the mansion. A single window was illuminated in the uppermost story of that wing, and within it was outlined Binky. When she in turn saw Constance, her eyes widened visibly, and she put up her little hands to the leaded glass, as if trying to escape.

Leng allowed the moment to linger. Nothing else was visible in the room: no furniture, no fireplace, no source of comfort. Then Leng let the blind fall—and Binky was gone.

10

As the blinds closed, and the image of her own younger self vanished, Constance felt a sensation of suffocation overwhelm her. She filled her lungs with air.

Meanwhile, Leng sauntered back to the desk. "There. Now you know not only that your young doppelganger is alive and well—but also that she is residing here...at least temporarily. I think that gesture is more than sufficient, given this formula of yours remains untested." He flung back the tails of his coat and sat down once again. "And now—it's getting late, and this stretch of the Post Road isn't safe after dark. We shall meet again, once I'm certain this Arcanum is the genuine item."

Constance stared at him, her breathing finally under control. She said, in a tone so low it might have been a whisper: "*You will regret this.*"

"I do not appreciate being threatened in my own house. As my minion Decla might say—get out."

But Constance did not get out. She gazed around the room as her heartbeat slowed. Leng had extracted much from Ferenc, but her most important secret was not in his possession. Leng did not know that Constance had once been his own experimental subject. He did not know that he perfected the Arcanum by testing it on her. He did not know she had been raised in this very house. And, most crucially of all, he was unaware she *knew his future*.

She could not wait for the time when she could reveal those secrets: when her blade was embedded in his heart.

"I see murderous thoughts on your face," Leng said. "I should point out that any effort to harm me, any attempt on my life, from you or your compatriots, will result in Binky's instant death. She is my insurance policy as I test the Arcanum. Of course, she is too young to be a guinea pig—have no fear of that."

Constance said nothing.

The doctor shook his head. "You are overstaying your welcome, Duchess. You are on foreign soil and your revetments are weak. This is *my* world, and I am well prepared to defend myself in it. Go back to whatever pestilential Pandemonium you call home."

Another important secret he did not know: the portal was closed, possibly forever.

She finally spoke, in a voice so low Leng had to lean forward to hear. "If you knew what the future holds," she said, "that would be the last thing you'd ever suggest. Because the next time you saw me, it would be with powers so formidable all your traps and your alley rats would be swept away like chaff. And you would have your own bespoke Room 101."

"Room 101?" Leng's brow knitted. "I have no idea what nonsense you speak of."

She detected, for the first time, a note of uncertainty.

"That 'nonsense' will be your doom. *Labere in gladio tuo.*" And with this, she walked toward the exit. At the doorway to the library, she turned back. "Give Augustus

Spragg, of the Natural History Museum's Ornithology Department, my condolences—I understand the poor man hasn't long to live."

Before Leng could respond, Constance walked quickly across the rotunda and through the passage lined with armor. She pushed open the front door, stepped into the chill night, and—tightening the wrap more closely around her shoulders—descended the steps.

The young woman named Decla approached. "Lord blind me, it's her ladyship!" she said. "You shouldn't frown at your betters like that—you'll be after a spanking, I reckon." She looked around. "Line up for a spanking, boys—I get first go."

Constance merely put out her hand, ignoring the ripple of mocking laughter that came from the darkness. "I'll have my weapon back now."

Decla looked at her in mock surprise. "You mean *this*?" She withdrew the handle of the stiletto from a vest pocket, so that the worked gold was visible. "It's mine now—I've taken quite a fancy to the little rib-tickler."

Constance did not reply. Her hand remained outstretched, unmoving. Slowly, Decla's eyes moved up to hers. For a minute, perhaps more, the two women took the measure of each other. Then Decla broke eye contact. With a smirk, she drew the weapon out from her vest and, palming it, slowly reached out, turned her hand over, and let it drop into the waiting fingers of Constance.

"You can borrow it for a spell," she said. "I'll take it back when I'm ready."

"In that case," Constance said, "here's a memento—until you're *ready*." She released the blade and at the same time, with a flick of her wrist, sliced open Decla's outstretched palm.

The blade was so sharp that, for a moment, there was no blood—and, likely, no pain. As the surprised Decla looked down, however, a long, narrow line of crimson began welling up.

"Now you have a matching set," Constance said.

There was a rustling sound. Within seconds, she found herself surrounded by the entire gang, weapons at the ready. They moved quickly, expertly tightening the circle. Constance's eyes remained on Decla's. For the briefest moment, she saw the woman glance over Constance's shoulder. That would be the first attack: a stab in the back.

Instantly, she pivoted to find that a hulking gang member had crept up close behind her, knife arm raised. She lunged without hesitation, her blade catching him just below the cage of his larynx. It seemed the weapon, having just tasted blood, was now hungry for more: her hand swept earthward as if directed by it, the dagger point tracing a line of death from the trachea shallowly down the sternum and then plunging into his guts below the xiphoid process before slipping out again on encountering the buckle of his belt. The man made a wheezing, gargling sound, and Constance immediately turned to the youth beside him—armed with a heavy cobbler's hammer—preparing to kill again.

There was a sudden, sharp clap from the door of the mansion. "*Enough!*" Leng cried, framed once again in the lighted doorway.

The gang hesitated—even as one of their own collapsed to the ground in ghastly slow motion.

"No more!" Leng continued sharply. "Allow her to pass."

Decla's eyes remained on Constance—a searing, feral stare. Constance glanced around at them all, frozen in various attitudes of fear and anger. Then she turned her gaze back to Leng and, raising her blade, placed her thumb and index finger against its finial; slid their tips quickly along from ricasso to point, flicking the accumulated blood from it with a quick, practiced gesture; then licked the two fingers, one after the other, while she sheathed the weapon. She spat in Leng's direction, then turned and walked into the enveloping night, back to the carriage where Murphy waited impatiently.

11

When Constance returned to the parlor of her Fifth Avenue mansion, the clocks were just striking ten. A fire was blazing on the hearth, its flickering light lending a cruel coziness to the room. Diogenes sat in a wing chair, beside a table holding snifters and a bottle of brandy, idly leafing through a book. Pendergast, meanwhile, was pacing the room, his face a mask of agitation.

Diogenes looked over at the sound of her approach. Then he glanced at his brother.

"You're back," Pendergast said, relief evident in his voice.

Constance stepped into the parlor and stood there, without removing her coat. Her fury at Leng had not subsided during the ride back—but it had settled into a cold, calculating rage.

"You gave him the Arcanum?" Pendergast asked, coming forward. "The true formula, with no alteration?"

"Yes."

"And what of Binky?"

"He would not release her. Not until he's tested it—or so he says. However, he showed her to me. Briefly."

"So she's at the mansion," Pendergast went on.

Constance nodded. "At least temporarily—those were his words."

"He wouldn't put her back in his subterranean works," Diogenes said. "The Five Points would be too obvious a move. But I've no doubt he has other places of concealment."

"Nevertheless," Pendergast said, "the Riverside Drive mansion seems a logical place to keep her for the time being. It is well fortified against invasion."

"Against invasion from those ignorant of its secrets, you mean," responded Constance.

Pendergast turned to her. "You didn't reveal anything to him? Perhaps in a moment of anger or frustration?"

Constance did not answer.

"Our knowledge of that mansion's future, and what you know of Leng's future, is our hole card."

"I'm quite aware of that," Constance said. "I betrayed nothing—because that mansion is where I plan to spend the coming days. I'll penetrate it, establish a bunker from which I can come and go unobserved... and then search for Binky—as well as probe for a soft underbelly—alone."

"What else did he say?"

"He spoke only for his own amusement. There's no point repeating any more of it."

"So you learned nothing that could be of use to us."

Constance shook her head. "One of Leng's gang members... opened himself up to me."

"And?"

"He had little to offer." She glanced from Pendergast to Diogenes, who was still seated. "And you two?"

"I, for one, have been conducting research." He tossed aside the book he'd been perusing. Constance glanced at its spine: *Puritanism and the Decline of the Reformation*.

She turned back to Pendergast. "Tell me about Joe."

"I put into motion the arrangements we discussed earlier. At this moment, Vincent and your brother should be approaching the Old Colony Railroad terminal in Boston, on their way to a 'cottage' on Mount Desert Island owned by the Rockefeller family. As you know, our family was once linked to them through shared business concerns, and when I hastily reached out to William—William Avery Jr., that is—he proved most cooperative."

"But he doesn't know you personally. Can he be trusted?"

"My dear Constance, you are correct to be on your guard. But you should know better than most that there exist certain fraternal bonds and secret societies that transcend time, money—everything except honor." And, beckoning her closer for a moment, he briefly murmured the details.

Constance, reassured, allowed Diogenes to pour her a glass of brandy. She looked from one brother to the other. It was clear that, whether or not they agreed with her plan, they knew better than to object.

After a silence, Diogenes reached for his brandy. "While you were paying your social call, Aloysius and I spoke at length—and we agreed that a critical way to start undermining Fortress Leng is to cut off his supply of victims."

"You once told me that, in order to test the new variants of his Arcanum, Leng would use a special, accelerated formulation on his human guinea pigs, in hope of success," Pendergast said to Constance.

"Correct. Followed by an autopsy."

"On those guinea pigs where his latest variant was unsuccessful?"

"Whether it was successful or not."

"*What?*" Pendergast looked even more horrified.

"Once he stumbled on the working formula, he still dosed, and dissected, half a dozen or so 'subjects'—to make sure there were no negative internal effects. Only then did he start taking it himself."

There was a brief silence before Pendergast spoke again. "I assume he'll employ this same accelerated formulation on the Arcanum, now in his possession. How long will it take him to be confident the formula works?"

Constance shrugged. "Hard to say."

"Hard to say?" Diogenes replied, lifting an eyebrow. "You don't remember?"

"I tried my best to suppress those memories," Constance said with irritation, "and I don't appreciate you scolding me for it."

"Scolding? Merely trying to help."

"That's enough," said Pendergast quietly.

"Perhaps you should remind your ward to be more grateful," said Diogenes. "I sacrificed myself by coming back here, too—remember?"

"No one asked you to," Constance said. "No one asked *either* of you," she added icily, then took in a deep, shuddering breath. "When a new version of the elixir seemed potentially successful, he allowed two weeks for observation. Sometimes a little more, never less."

"And for each new formulation—it required vivisecting the cauda equina from a victim each time, as well?"

Constance nodded.

"Then our plan should be sound," Pendergast went on. "We'll do our best to cut off his supply of victims, interfere with or destroy his laboratories of operation—at least, those we can find. You've said Binky is too young to be used as a test subject—Leng will be desperate for new victims, both as guinea pigs *and* as resources." His voice had returned to its normal level, but Constance still detected the faintest quaver of emotion. With surprise, she realized that, beyond his self-recrimination and frustration, he too was angry—angry in a way she had never seen before. Looking at his pale eyes, she could sense the same thirst for blood vengeance that filled herself.

Abruptly, those eyes locked on hers. "Constance, I'm aware you intend to operate independently. But the three of us have the same goals: save Binky—and kill Leng. We can attack the problem as individuals, but we must nevertheless agree on meeting—once, at the very least—to check on the others' progress and ensure our efforts don't unintentionally collide. And we must have a means of emergency communication."

He fell silent, and for a time everyone sat motionless. Then Constance leaned forward, picked up her snifter, drained the brandy, and then, reaching into her handbag, took out a small notebook and wrote something on it with a gold pencil. She tore out the page, folded it, and handed it to Pendergast.

He opened it, read it. "This will suffice."

Immediately, Constance rose. "In that case, good night. I need rest before I go." She paused. "Since I presume you two plan on staying, ask Gosnold to put you up somewhere on the third floor." And she turned to leave.

"Constance," she heard Diogenes say—and the uncharacteristically serious tone in his voice made her pause. "Let me caution you. You of all people must realize not to push Leng too hard or too far. If we cross his red line... Binky will die."

Constance's only response was to remain still a moment, forcing herself to let the truth of this sink in. Then she turned to go upstairs.

* * *

As the sounds of her footsteps disappeared, the brothers looked at each other. Pendergast was the first to speak.

"I'm glad you said that. I was beginning to wonder if you were really here to help us—or just goad her and stir up mischief."

"That's rich, coming from the person who's made a hash of everything—hiring that idiot Ferenc, for starters. Why didn't you just leave her here, unmolested? She was doing all right."

"She was not. She was allowing passion to govern her reason. Leng was already taking advantage of it, toying with her. She would have been doomed."

"You don't know that. Clever as we think ourselves, there are times she's surprised both of us. Besides, look at this place!" He waved his hand, indicating the room. "It's the first palace I've seen that actually has taste. And her carriage! I thought Leng's was impressive. Why, it's got the loveliest... the finest..." He stopped, at a loss for words. "I don't yet have the knowledge to articulate my admiration, but something I never expected has happened: I've developed carriage envy."

Pendergast leaned forward. "This badinage is pointless. *You* know why I returned. For the very same reason you did."

There was a moment of silence. Then Diogenes rose.

"Are you going to scare up Gosnold?" Pendergast asked him. "His rooms are just off the back kitchen."

Diogenes shook his head. "No, Brother—I'm off."

"Where?"

"That's my business. Did you think Constance the only one who values her secrets? Now, good night; I have promises to keep, and miles to go before I sleep." He paused. "I quite like the sound of that. Perhaps I'll construct a poem around those lines."

"I never took you for a plagiarist."

"One can't steal words that have yet to be written. Besides, *Frater*, plagiarism is the last thing you should fear when it comes to this new, or rather old, world of sin now open before me. I find myself looking at it with wild surmise and wondering: can so many unanticipated temptations be resisted?" He shrugged into his greatcoat, lit another salmon-colored cigarette, put on his hat. "I'll use the front door on my way out," he said as he strode into the entryway. "That will be a novelty."

"Diogenes—"

"I know. Sweet dreams to you, too." He opened the inner, then the outer door, and then—with a bow, and a slight doff of his hat—he strode off into the night.

12

Miss Editha Mallow Crean—grimacing as she picked her way among piles of ordure—crossed the area formed by Park, Baxter, and Worth Streets, the intersection that gave the area its name: the Five Points. Her own set of rooms on Mott Street, in a boardinghouse for ladies, was not many blocks away yet in another, more pleasant world. She always made her commute in haste, so as to be assailed by the vile sights and sounds of the slum as briefly as possible.

Turning west down Baxter, she fell under the looming shadow of the House of Industry. She made her way to its front door, unlocked it with a large iron key, then closed and locked it behind her, exchanging the offending odors from without for those equally disagreeable within.

She turned away from the door to see Royds, the attendant. He was in his usual place, on the far side of the reception room beyond the hinged wooden counter. There was an expression on his face that instantly alarmed her.

"He's waiting in your office, mum," Royds said.
"Who?"

But Royds did not answer. He just stood there, cringing behind the railing, looking as if he'd seen the devil himself. After a moment, Nurse Crean turned away and, opening the door in the wall to the right, stepped through it.

A short passage led past the scullery and a bookless library, terminating in the door to her private office, which was closed. She opened it, stepped in—then halted in surprise. She'd expected a distraught parent or an unwelcome messenger from the board of governors. But instead, she found herself confronted by a thin man dressed in a severe double-breasted cassock reaching to his ankles, along with a black waistcoat, starched white collar, and broad-brimmed *cappello romano*. He was standing beside her desk, rummaging through one of the drawers, and at the sound of her entry he straightened. He wore a tinted pince-nez and, at full height, was unexpectedly tall.

"What is the meaning of this intrusion?" she demanded.

He remained motionless as the echo of her question died away. Nurse Crean was not a woman to be easily rattled, and she returned his supercilious expression with a fierce one of her own. He was a clergyman of high rank, to judge by the garb. From time to time, church delegations had sent representatives to observe the daily workings of the Mission and House of Industry... and she knew how to deal with them. Her biggest concern was that, someday, she would be replaced by a graduate of the "Nightingale schools"—institutions for training nurses that in the past decade had sprouted up at Bellevue and in New Haven. Her own training may not have been formal, but it was the kind no girl could learn in a schoolroom: rather, in the Civil War, where doctors were scarce and surgeons even scarcer. She'd plied her trade at Fredericksburg and Cold Harbor, where she learned to amputate ruined limbs with a speed that made hardened veterans blanch—and later at Andersonville, after it was liberated in 1864, where nearly half the Union prisoners died of dysentery, typhus, or starvation.

But from the looks of this man's well-tailored garb and stiff expression, she doubted he had seen bloodshed. He appeared the kind of cleric who'd spent most of his life in a seminary, and she was surprised he'd braved the Five Points long enough to reach her office. But here he was—rooting through her private papers like a sow in a corncrib.

"Well?" she said.

He moved behind the desk, pushed the drawer closed, fastidiously dusted off the chair—*her* chair—then sat down in it and looked at her through his spectacles before speaking.

"Two months ago," he said, "the Elders' Council met at the yearly conclave." The man had a plummy, arrogant voice that could only come from generations of inbreeding among the British gentry. "At said conclave, the subject of the Five Points Mission and House of Industry came up. It was generally recognized that the Mission's founding objective—to house, protect, and educate orphaned girls—has been sadly neglected of late."

Miss Crean felt her corded hands tightening. This was no mere representative sent to observe. Here was someone sent to interfere.

The man went on, his voice filling the room. "As a last resort, the elders contacted my superiors in Canterbury—who in turn sent me from England to this...place." He pursed his lips. "In the spirit of Luther and Wesley, I have completed numerous reformations in Methodist schools and orphanages across England—and now I shall do that here."

"We're doing just fine, sir!" Miss Crean said. "You have no right!" This was unheard of. And with no warning whatsoever. She'd worked her fingers to the bone for those ungrateful, wretched girls—with rarely even a peep of displeasure from the Mission board or the Elders' Council.

"I have every right, Miss Crean." The cleric stood up again. "Forgive my not introducing myself. I am the Right Reverend Percy Considine. And now that I've explained the situation, I hope you'll excuse me. I have a great deal to do." He stopped. "I'll permit you five minutes to gather your things." He came around the desk, as if to afford her access to it.

"Do you mean...," she began, halting and sputtering, "does this mean I'm being *discharged*? With no recourse, no warning? I shall demand a hearing with the board!"

"On your way out, Royds will see you get two weeks' pay. We are a generous church."

The holier-than-thou smugness radiating from this man was almost as maddening as the idea he could simply waltz in here and toss her out on the street. "But you can't do this. You *can't*!"

"On the contrary—I most certainly can."

"Outrageous! I demand to see your credentials!"

With this, he reached into his vest pocket and retrieved a leather packet, which he undid and handed to her. She snatched it and went through it. It was full of official documentation from the Wesleyan Brotherhood Council—the body who oversaw the Mission and House of Industry—giving the reverend Dr. Considine full power to enact improvements and reforms as he saw fit, with no need for review or approval by the elders.

He plucked the envelope and its contents back as she was still absorbing their implications for her own future.

"This is impossible. Some devilry must be afoot." She

looked at him through narrowed eyes. "What do you know about running an orphanage and workhouse for girls?"

"A great deal. As governess in charge, you are supposed to set a standard for all the rest. Sadly, it seems you have done precisely the opposite."

He turned to the desk and picked up a small book he must have brought with him, which he raised with a sniff and held up to her.

"*The Book of Discipline*," he said. "Edition of 1858. As you know, or should know, this sets out the doctrines of our Methodist sect." He opened the book and read in a haughty manner. "*In the latter end of the year 1739, eight or ten persons came to Mr. Wesley—*" here his eyes swept briefly heavenward— "*in London, who appeared to be deeply convinced of sin, and earnestly groaning for redemption. They desired that he advise them how to flee from the wrath to come.*" He lowered the book. "I would at least have expected you, Miss Crean, to follow the Discipline and flee the wrath to come. But it seems you have done precisely the opposite. You, daughter of Crean, are no less a daughter of Satan."

Nurse Crean's rising anger and outrage topped out at this accusation. "I—I am *what?*"

"Silence! I shall number, from our own holy book, the ways you have desecrated your mission on earth." He opened the book again. "*Do no evil of any kind, such as taking the name of God in vain, or profaning the day of the Lord; or by drunkenness.* I would say to you, spawn of evil, that you have turned this godly House of Industry into a House of Drunkenness and Profanation."

She stepped forward, livid with rage, her knuckles—already clenched—turning white. "I've never touched a drop of liquor in my life! I, a spawn of evil? It is you who malign this place with such lies!"

"Still you deny your sins? I should have thought that—confronted with them—you would be glad enough to flee into ignominy and obscurity, with the money I've offered you. But perhaps I should have expected this: as my private inquiries have already shown, you continue to pile wickedness upon wickedness, crime upon unimaginable crime... including even satisfying your own bestial appetites on the virgin bodies of these poor young wretches under your care. Get thee behind me, Satan!" And, lifting the book once again, he turned to a fresh page: *"When you look them in the face, you should break forth into tears, as the prophet did when he looked upon Hazael..."*

Goaded nearly to madness by his words, Nurse Crean rushed at him, raising her hand to strike the man. To her vast surprise, Reverend Considine—displaying remarkable speed and dexterity—grabbed her left hand and wrenched it behind her back; gripped her raised right hand, forcing it down and around the letter opener atop the table; and then—his eyes fixed upon hers—maneuvered its point against her belly.

"It's impolite to interrupt a minister while he's reciting Holy Writ," he said. "Where was I? *What cause have we to bleed before the Lord, that we have so long neglected this good work!*"

With the grace of a dancer, he pivoted the two of them around so her back was to the desk. Then he pressed her against it, covering her mouth with his free hand, and plunged the letter opener deep into her peritoneal cavity. Her eyes widened white; she struggled with stifled screams.

"These letter openers are so often dull," Diogenes whispered in her ear. "Terribly sorry."

And then he thrust still deeper, turning the point upward, hooking into the abdominal aorta.

"*There were many hindrances,*" he quoted loudly, covering the muffled sounds. "*And so there always will be. But the greatest hindrance is in ourselves—and in our littleness of faith and love.*"

Then, letting her free, he leapt to one side as she collapsed onto the dusty floor, emitting a final whimper of denial as she did so, bleeding out in a crimson flood.

13

Diogenes examined his clothes. There were a few splatters of blood on his cassock, but they had missed the magenta piping and were easily rubbed into invisibility in the heavy black cloth.

"Royds!" he cried. "Great heavens! Come here!"

He glanced around rapidly, taking in the state of the office, then waited until he heard the step of Royds approaching down the hall before kneeling in front of the body.

Royds knocked.

"Come in, man, come in! Something terrible has happened!"

He came in and halted, seeing the body sprawled in a growing pool of blood, made a strange noise between a whimper and a warble, and shrank back, covering his mouth with his palm.

"God's retribution works in mysterious ways," Diogenes said. "The shock of the council's decision unhinged her. I couldn't stop her from the wicked deed."

"*She* did this—?" Royds began, backing up farther.

Diogenes stepped fastidiously away from the body to avoid soiling his shoes on the spreading blood.

"Yes," he said. "She preferred to end her own life rather than live in shame." He shook his head. "It's as I told you when I first introduced myself this morning: It would have been wiser for the General Council to give her some warning this might be coming. But they felt—especially Reverend Leeds—that were she given advance notice, her actions might be unpredictable." He paused. "And so they have proven to be." He sighed deeply. "This, alas, is precisely why I was called in. How I long to be back in Africa, delivering souls into the hands of the Lord. But it seems reforming church institutions that have strayed—a calling I never wished for—is my cross to bear."

Royds nodded shakily. Earlier, Diogenes had thoroughly impressed him with the various papers he had brought, most quite real, with the exception of one excellent forgery allegedly from the English Council, which he had presented to the head of the Council of Greater New York the day before. How convenient it was, Diogenes thought, that transatlantic communications were so primitive in the year 1880. And now the Right Reverend Considine was in full charge of the House of Industry—at least until, if ever, the New York Council confirmed his appointment with the church back in England.

"She was a right cruel taskmistress, she was—begging your pardon, sir," Royds said, looking down at the body.

"Indeed, Royds," said Diogenes.

"As hard-hearted to human suffering as any person I ever met...but as pious as you please when it came to herself. So glad to see the Mission in better hands, Reverend."

Diogenes was faintly repelled by this Uriah Heep already ingratiating himself with his new master—with the previous one still warm on the floor. "Her sadistic proclivities were known beyond these walls... And so were her vices—although 'vices' is too mild a term for her depraved peccadilloes."

"'Depraved,' you say?" Royds's shocked and frightened eyes took on a sheen of lurid curiosity.

"Some of the darkest, most vile acts a human could commit, even in this den of iniquity." Diogenes spread his hands to include the entire Five Points. "The most distinct category of vice will have its own foul subclasses. So it was with Miss Crean, too. She was cruel, she was heartless; both labels are apt. But to her everlasting damnation, the evil lusts she hid beneath that hypocritical veil would make the most hardened sailor blanch."

"It would?" Royds said. Then: "I always knowed it."

"I can trust you, Royds. And I know you're a man of character. Which is why I'm going to give you greater authority here than you enjoyed before, raising your salary to match—you've suffered under the lash long enough. But I also know of your sound moral qualities... which is why, if I mention to you just a few of the acts Miss Crean perpetrated on the helpless young women of this institution, you will be horrified—and understand why her replacement had to be undertaken in so swift a manner. You must be strong, Royds—with your new position comes new responsibility."

"Yes, Reverend, sir," said Royds.

Going back behind the desk and sitting down, Diogenes crooked a finger at Royds. The attendant came over eagerly—making a wide detour around the bloody form on the floor—and bent his head forward as Diogenes briefly whispered in his ear. Two or three horrors perpetrated by Crean upon the girls in her charge, hinted at without clarity, were sufficient to whet, but perhaps not fully satisfy, Royds's unhealthy imagination.

"Your first responsibility, Royds, is to fetch a heavy blanket to wrap this body in for disposal. We mustn't allow the church to be sullied by scandal."

Royds returned, and Diogenes helped roll up the nurse's body and place it in a handcart. He then gave Royds a generous advance on his new position, with extra funds, and sent him off with instructions on how to dispose of the corpse. Diogenes watched through the window as Royds disappeared down the street with the remains, heading for a certain private cartage he had identified not long after his arrival, known for handling unusual disposal problems.

Now was the time, Diogenes thought, to assert his role. He rang the bell for the head girl.

She arrived and halted in confusion, then gave a hasty curtsy.

"I am the master now," said Considine. "Miss Crean has left."

"Yes, sir."

"Get two other girls with mops and buckets and clean this mess up," he said, with a wave of his hand. "Scrub it down to the boards; leave no trace."

"Yes, sir." She stared at the bloodstain, eyes wide, but no questions asked. The brutal Miss Crean had cowed them well, thought Diogenes.

"And then, when you're done," he added, "gather the girls in the chapel. I should like to introduce myself as the new director of the Mission and House of Industry."

14

Through the half-open door of his office, Warburton Seely, chief inspector of buildings for the City of New-York, eyed the man who had just stepped into his outer chamber. He was dressed in the latest style: an expensive herringbone tweed sack suit with a wingtip collar and four-in-hand tie, low brogues with spatterdashes, a green vest, and a heavy gold watch chain, the ensemble completed with a formal top hat and Malacca cane. He would have been the very picture of a prosperous banker or financier, save for the fact it appeared he'd bought the clothes that very morning.

Then there were his peculiar features. The man had a hideous scar across his pale face. He was unshaven; his hair was long and greasy, fingernails cracked and dirty. Seely could hear the man's voice as he engaged in conversation with the clerk—a high-pitched, whiny voice with a western drawl so pronounced it was almost a foreign language. He had arrived without an appointment, and it was a wonder he'd managed to get past the municipal police who guarded the inner sanctum of city hall.

"I'm a-here to see Mr. Seely," the man was saying.

"The name is Pendergast. Aloysius X." He spoke his name as pompously as an English lord, the effect ruined by the ridiculous twang.

"Do you have an appointment?"

"No, I do not. But I 'spect he'll want to see *me*."

"Mr. Seely does not receive visitors without an appointment," said the clerk, voice laced with contempt. "Now, if you'd care to leave your card—"

"I'm newly arrived from Leadville, Colorado, and they tell me this here Mr. Seely is the man to see if you have—" he coughed with a ludicrous attempt of delicacy— "money to invest in real estate."

"I'm terribly sorry, sir, but an appointment is necessary. I'll have an officer see you out."

Leadville, Seely thought. Wasn't that where the gigantic silver strike had been made last year?

He rose from his desk and leaned out the half-open door. "Mr. Charles? I think I can find a moment for the gentleman now."

"Yes, sir."

"Thankee," said the man, shuffling into the office, hat in hand, the ruddy scar across his pale face like a streak of blood on marble. After a hesitation, Seely held out his hand. "Good day, Mr. . . . ?"

"Pendergast."

"Of course. May I offer you a cigar?" As he proffered the box, he closed the door to the outer office.

"Most obliging of you, sir," said the visitor, taking up a cigar. Seely selected another, lit the man's cigar, then his own. He gestured to a seat in front of his large desk. "Please sit down."

The man did so. Seely, settling back into his own chair, could smell the newness of his clothes.

"Now, I understand that you're from Colorado. May I ask what business you're in?"

"Well, sir, I was in the mining business. Silver."

Seely nodded.

"Yes*sir*. God has been good to me, very good to me, when it come to silver. You heard of the Belle Gulch Mine? Twenty-four million troy ounces, not to mention lead, zinc, and bismuth. Well, that there Belle Gulch was my claim."

"How fortunate for you, Mr., ah..." What was that damned name again?

"Pendergast. Now, Mr. Seely, I'm not one to milk a prized cow dry: I cashed out my claims when the opportunity was ripe, and now I'm here to invest the proceeds. City's growing. Property is the future. They told me you're the man to see."

"Ah, of course. Of course." Seely wasn't sure exactly where this was headed, but he had a tingling sense there was going to be money in it for him—maybe lots of it. This bumpkin and his wealth would be quickly separated in New York, and Seely figured there was no reason he shouldn't be present for the division.

He let his instinct guide the conversation. "As I am the chief building inspector of the city, I don't actually have real estate for sale... Was there some other way I could be of help?"

"That's exactly right, Mr. Chief Inspector—you can most certainly help a feller out. Since arriving, I've spent my time, well... doing prospecting of a different sort." He seemed to find this privately amusing. "There's a brewery up by Longacre Square. Called Hockelmann's Brewery. Main entrance on Forty-First Street, back gate down Smee's Alley. You know it?"

Seely did not.

"Good strong ale. Prosperous enterprise, too. The brewery has bought up the block and is emptying out the tenements for development. That Longacre Square is going to be some valuable property, sir, as the city grows—I'm from Leadville, like I said, and I've watched a dozen towns spring up in the territories. I saw which ones boomed, which went bust...and why. New York here may be a mite bigger, but business is business, as sure as men are men. And I've learned to sniff out an opportunity like a stallion sniffs out a mare."

Seely nodded, his hands folded, waiting.

"Well, that's the property I want. Them empty tenements."

"And you've tried to purchase it?"

"No, sir. I'm too smart for that. I inquired around first. The devil who owns it won't sell. He's turned down many offers. Can't see past his flourishing beer business enough to realize there are other things like to flourish more. Thing is—" and he leaned closer— "I was talking to this friend of mine, lives over the Stonewall Inn, and he told me I had one shot at getting them buildings. One shot, and one only—and that was to get the property condemned." He leaned back again. "I understand you're the man who can do that."

"Who might have told you such a thing?" Seely felt a slight twinge of alarm at the thought his name was being bandied about in this way. It was true, he'd condemned two, maybe three, buildings—that were unfit to live in, of course—for certain considerations. But he had his reputation to consider. On the other hand, twenty-four million ounces of silver, at a dollar an ounce...Thoughts of reputation fell away as he realized this Pendergast must be as rich as Croesus—and a lot wilier in business matters than his rube-like appearance implied. Looking closer, Seely saw that the man's silvery eyes were positively glittering with greed and cunning.

"A friend," was his only response. He drew a line on his cheek with his thumb and followed it with an exaggerated wink.

"I see," said Seely. He thought for a moment about how this might be done in such a way that, if it ever came out, there'd be deniability. As he was ruminating, the man, Pendergast, spoke up again, his voice falling to a hush.

"Mr. Seely, I got it all worked out. You loan me one of them badges, make me into an inspector. I take it up to Hockelmann. He don't know me from Adam, and I scare him with it. Soften him up. I won't actually condemn nothing, because then it'd be on record. I'll just do an inspection, find a passel of things wrong, and make a lot of noise. Ain't no harm in that, is there?"

Seely was careful not to let his expression betray his thoughts. It actually seemed like a sound plan—and it had deniability baked in.

"And while I'm here," Pendergast said, "I'd like to take a squint at the construction plats of them tenements. I believe they're filed with your office?"

Seely tented his fingers. There was a reason this man had grown so rich—and it wasn't just stumbling on a silver lode. As he waited for the offer, he told himself not to judge strangers too rashly in the future.

"You do this for me, Mr. Seely—just loan me the badge for a couple of days and give me some papers. You know, the kind with fancy stamps and seals on them."

Seely again waited.

"You do that for me, friend, and I'll see you right."

Seely raised his eyebrows, indicating his interest.

"Five hundred dollars now, five hundred when I return the badge."

A thousand dollars—this was at least five times what Seely had been expecting. Stunned, he managed to control himself, even fashion a little frown on his face, and allowed his silence to drag on.

"One thousand dollars now," Pendergast said.

More silence.

"Damn it, man!" Pendergast urged.

"Fifteen hundred. All up front."

"Twelve hundred."

"Thirteen hundred."

Pendergast scowled. "All right. Give me whatever I need to put a scare into that damned brewmeister, and I'll give you the money. But I'm going to need the badge for at least a week, maybe more."

It was as easy to enlist a false inspector as it was a real one—even easier—and Seely had all the necessary accoutrements at hand. He went to his closet, unlocked it, took out a badge and a portfolio of embossed leather. He brought them over to his desk, filled out several lines here and there, then showed them to Pendergast. "I've put an alias on the paperwork—Mr. Alphonse Billington. I'll have my clerk bring up the plats for you to look at—not, however, to take with you. I'll give you the credentials when you bring me the funds."

The man reached into his suit, extracted a slim packet of $100 banknotes, peeled off thirteen, and placed them on the desk. Seely felt his heart accelerate, even as he noted with dismay there were still quite a few left—he could have done even better. But thirteen hundred was a gigantic backhander, and the risk was negligible. If Hockelmann ever followed up with a complaint, Seely would simply deny all knowledge of the miner and his scheme; "Alphonse Billington" would be just a man with a stolen badge and forged papers.

"Mr. Pendergast, may I give you some advice?" he said on impulse.

"Yes, sir."

"Don't arrive dressed like that. No building inspector would wear such an outfit. You will need much more conservative attire: frock coat, vest buttoned high but open below, string tie, and above all, workingman's brogues without spatterdashes. And a derby hat—that top hat's too formal."

The plats arrived and Pendergast spread them out, glanced them over rapidly, then stepped away. "That is all. I thankee, sir," he said with a bow, taking up the badge and portfolio. "I will return these in a week's time."

"No. Don't return them. Burn everything made of paper, and make sure the badge gets lodged at the bottom of the East River." He paused. "But within a week, mind—after that, I'll have the badge number removed from active service."

Seely rose, opened the door for the prospector, and saw him into the outer office, where he murmured to his clerk. Nodding, Mr. Charles saw the visitor out.

Seely then retired once again to his inner office and eased the door shut. He placed his hand on the pocket of his suit coat, feeling the crinkle of the banknotes nested within. Thirteen hundred dollars—three months' salary. Not a bad morning's work.

15

THE "COTTAGE" ROSE ABOVE the spruce trees like a gigantic, shingled castle, its eaves shagged with icicles, the windows shuttered and mysterious. The distant Atlantic stretched out beyond and below the mansion, a gray heaving surface smoking in the bitterly cold air. D'Agosta, holding Joe's hand—the only warm thing anywhere—could hear the distant sound of surf crashing on the rocks. The steamship ride from Boston had been brutal—he was sick as a dog on the rough winter seas—then followed by a ride in an actual horse-drawn sleigh with jingling bells, which might have been interesting if he hadn't just about frozen his junk. Not until he'd spent these last several days in this strange universe did it occur to him just how many twenty-first-century conveniences he took for granted. On top of that, the train ride had given him way too much time to mull over the idea that he was trapped in this world; that he'd never see his wife, Laura, again, have another beer with his work buddy Coldmoon...or even drive a car.

At first, D'Agosta had felt the silent Joe to be a

millstone around his neck—one he resented being saddled with. How was he going to keep this kid occupied? Would there be a school on the island? There was so much Pendergast hadn't told him. But he and Joe had both enjoyed playing cards—the kid was a determined and clever player. While clearly anxious, he was a tough kid, not prone to showing emotion, and for that at least D'Agosta was grateful. Nothing, in fact, seemed to faze him. On the contrary, it was D'Agosta who was put out by the whole assignment. And then, on the steamship to Bar Harbor, Joe had refused to leave his side even as he fled to the windswept, frozen deck to puke his guts out. And when they were back inside the cabin, Joe had fetched him, without being prompted, a pot of hot tea. The kid didn't talk much—except when asking directions at the station and elsewhere. D'Agosta himself had tried to keep silent, thinking his manner of speech might cause suspicion. At heart, Joe was a steady, reliable kid, and might surprisingly enough even become a comfort to D'Agosta, overwhelmed by this absurd situation and the horrible thought he might never get home again.

Initially, he'd wondered if Joe might bolt at the first opportunity. Pendergast had briefed him on the boy's background and disposition. Only recently sprung from prison, Joe had just gone through a terrible spasm of violence that had torn his family apart and left him alone with a strange man to boot. But it seemed, somehow, the boy was smart enough to sense D'Agosta was an ally and friend, someone he could depend on and even look up to.

His presence had stirred up memories of D'Agosta's son from his first marriage. At twelve, Vinnie Jr. had also been reserved and stubborn—a tall, serious boy. He had kept his stalwart nature even at eighteen, as he was dying of acute myeloid leukemia. D'Agosta knew Joe must have suffered a lot in Blackwell's prison and as a homeless kid on the streets, but he faced it just as Vinnie had faced his illness—with stoic bravery and silence.

"That's big," said Joe matter-of-factly, staring up at the mansion.

It was gigantic. D'Agosta wasn't sure he had ever seen a bigger house. "Yeah, sure is," he said, trying to put some cheer in his voice.

"I thought it was a cottage."

"Apparently, that's what the very rich call their summer homes—no matter how large they are."

"Right this way, sir," said the sleigh driver, as he came around and directed them toward the porte cochere. "Right this way."

"I'll bet there's a ghost," said Joe.

D'Agosta was startled; he'd been thinking the same thing as he stared up at the dark bulk, with its steep roofs, square towers, gables, and eyebrow dormers. The place looked forbidding, if not downright menacing. "I'll bet it just looks scarier than it is," he said. "Anyway, it'll be nice and warm inside."

The driver hustled up to the door and, fumbling with his gloves, removed a key and inserted it into the lock. The door swung back to reveal an entryway opening into a vast salon, the windows showing a few cracks of light through the shutters. Far from being warm, the mansion felt even colder inside than without. All the furniture and paintings were draped in white sheets, the carpets rolled up, the tables covered. Even the chandeliers hanging from the ceiling were tied up in sheets, floating overhead like great shapeless apparitions.

"The heated part of the house is through here," said the driver, bustling across the salon to a passageway. After several windings through chill corridors, they came to a stout door, which the man opened. Out poured the yellow light of kerosene lanterns and a welcome flow of warmth. They entered a cozy set of rooms: small and plain, apparently the kitchen and scullery of the servants' quarters. Perhaps this would feel more familiar to Joe, less alien. In any case, it was warm, gloriously warm, the heat radiating from an iron stove at the end of the room, on which a pot of coffee exuded a welcome scent.

Two people, a man and a woman, sat on either side of the stove. The woman was knitting while the man nursed a cup of coffee. She set down her work and rose to greet them. They made a funny pair, D'Agosta thought—both in their fifties, the woman big and bosomy and cheerful, with a red face and curly orange hair, and the man thin as a rail, stooped and dour, with droopy mustaches. He did not rise. He didn't even look up.

"Mr. and Mrs. Cookson," the driver said. "Caretakers."

Mrs. Cookson enveloped D'Agosta's hand in hers with a beaming smile. "Mr. Harrison, welcome to Norumbega," she said.

Norumbega? D'Agosta felt a momentary confusion.

"That's Mr. Rockefeller's name for the house," Mrs. Cookson said. "It was a mythical land of gold and pearls that the early English explorers looked for around these parts but never found—of course."

"I see. Thanks for the explanation."

"And who is the young master?" Mrs. Cookson turned toward Joe and bent down to take his hand.

"Joe," the youth said gravely.

"Very nice to meet you, Joe. How old are you?"

"Twelve."

"That's a fine age."

Joe, in his typical silent fashion, merely nodded.

"Will you stay for a cup of coffee?" she asked the carriage driver.

"I'd best be off afore sunset," he replied. Then he wrapped his scarf back around his neck and disappeared out into the main house, closing the door behind him with a gust of frigid air.

"Coffee?" Mrs. Cookson asked D'Agosta.

"Don't mind if I do."

"And for you, young man? Hot chocolate?"

Joe nodded.

"Have a seat." She fetched D'Agosta a mug of coffee. "I'm so glad you've come. Mr. Rockefeller is concerned about security, and at our age we're just not able to keep up as we should. The house is full of valuable things, of course. I know your presence will be such a reassurance to Mr. Rockefeller—you being an ex-policeman and all."

D'Agosta wondered who might rob a house in the dead of winter on a remote island in Maine. Even more to the point, he wondered how Pendergast had gotten an in with the Rockefellers on such short notice, let alone arranged for him to be hired on as extra security for the premises. But it was useless to speculate: he'd long ago given up trying to figure out Pendergast's inscrutable methods or trace his wide-ranging connections. The important thing was the place, being at the ends of the earth, seemed safe from Leng and his henchmen.

"I was sorry to hear of the loss of your wife," went on Mrs. Cookson, apparently in a talkative mood—and no wonder, with a husband as taciturn as hers. "I hope you'll find the peace and quiet up here to your liking."

Loss of his wife. D'Agosta, aka George Harrison, was playing the part of a grieving widower with a child—that was part of the hasty biographical sketch Pendergast had provided as he bundled them off. But the phrase hit home: if he couldn't find a way to return, Laura truly would be lost to him.

Mr. Cookson got up from his seat, fetched two sticks of wood from a pile beyond the warm kitchen, inserted them into the stove, and sat down again. Mrs. Cookson refilled his mug as if by habit.

"As you can imagine," Mrs. Cookson said, "the island's quiet during the winter. There's a small year-round community of lobstermen, a two-room schoolhouse for Joe and the other children, a one-horse fire station, and a church. Of course it all changes in the summertime, with all the wealthy folk arriving, dances and theatricals, lawn parties and boating and the Lord knows what else. What church do you attend, Mr. Harrison?"

D'Agosta couldn't remember Pendergast's instructions on this point, or even if there had been some, and he stammered: "We're, uh, we're Catholic."

This statement caused even Mr. Cookson to look up briefly.

"Oh dear," the woman said. "*Roman* Catholic? We've not got a church of that persuasion on the island."

D'Agosta hesitated. He really didn't go to church anymore, to be honest, but he sensed that Mrs. Cookson would not be happy to hear that. "I'm sure God won't mind if we attend your church while we're here."

"Very good. I think we're going to get along well." She eyed the two newcomers for a moment. "Mr. Harrison, I was warned you and Joe might not come prepared for a Maine winter. I can already see that to be the case. Mr. Rockefeller instructed me to make sure you are both properly dressed, and he offered some of his secondhand family clothing. I shall have Mr. Cookson bring some down from the attic." She cocked her head. "You're a trifle stout, but I'm a good seamstress and we'll be able to accommodate."

"Thank you. I'm not used to this kind of cold."

"That will change soon enough." She smiled, looking like an oracle. "Now—Mr. Harrison, Joe—let me show you to your rooms."

D'Agosta started to follow her, then paused at the staircase, turned back to Joe, and leaned down conspiratorially. "If there *is* some old ghost, we'll give him what for—what do you say?" And he mimed a gun with his thumb and index finger.

Joe's eyes lit up in a way D'Agosta hadn't seen before. "We will, by jingo!" he whispered back almost fiercely. "He'll get such a thrashing he'll just have to go haunt somewhere else."

And the two shook on it.

16

Pendergast sauntered down to the seaport, where a huge board fence had been erected around a construction site on the East River. The fence was painted green and had been up long enough to be plastered with many layers of playbills and announcements. Slots had been cut in the boards so that passersby could view the activity beyond, and there were quite a few availing themselves of the opportunity.

Pendergast made use of one of these slots. Peering through it, he saw a massive site crawling with hundreds of workers. There were great piles of cut stone, steel, cranes, steam shovels, huge metal caissons. A monstrous cut had been made into the bedrock of Manhattan Island along the river's margin, mostly filled with concrete, stone, and steel. A half-built tower of granite and limestone rose up from the river itself, and a second could be seen in the distance, near the far shore.

The Brooklyn Bridge was nearing completion.

After observing the activity for some minutes, Pendergast strode alongside the fence until he came to a gate manned by a guardhouse. He offered his inspector's badge and papers and was allowed to enter. He walked down to a large staging area near the tower just in time to hear the noon whistle blow.

Not long afterward, men began to emerge from the top of the gigantic caisson at the base of the tower, their faces and work clothes black with muck. These were the sandhogs, the men who removed mud and rock from beneath the riverbed, replacing it with massive granite blocks as they sank the foundations of the bridge into the bedrock below.

Pendergast positioned himself strategically, inspecting the filthy, exhausted men as they filed past on their way to clock out. The sandhogs were the toughest construction workers in the city, and many had died—and more would still—before the bridge was completed.

The men paid no attention to him, but he paid keen attention to them. As they lined up at the exit, Pendergast strolled down the line and tapped the shoulders of ten men in particular, including one of the foremen, motioning them to step out, while at the same time opening his coat to display his badge. They did so, looking apprehensively at the badge, while the foreman eyed Pendergast suspiciously.

"What's this all about, sir?"

"Inspection," said Pendergast. "Perfectly routine. Not to worry—nobody has done anything wrong."

The foreman nodded dubiously. Pendergast turned to the men, who eyed him, unsmiling, exhausted—wanting nothing more than to go home.

"Gentlemen," said Pendergast with a smile, "I understand you are earning two dollars a day down in the caissons. And you, sir," he said, turning to the foreman, "make three."

They shuffled nervously.

Pendergast lowered his voice. "My name is Alphonse Billington, and I'm here to offer you an overnight job. One night only. The pay is ten dollars each."

At this, a gleam of interest shone in the men's faces.

"Go home, gentlemen, clean up, change, get some rest—and then meet me in Smee's Alley off Longacre Square at nine o'clock sharp. As a gesture of my sincerity, I'm offering a signing bonus of one dollar, right now." He put his hand into his pocket and went down the line, slipping a coin into each filthy hand, along with a freshly printed card.

As the men turned to leave, he stayed the foreman with a hand to the elbow. "I'll just need a moment more with you, sir. Mr. Otto Bloom, is it not?"

The foreman looked surprised and suspicious all over again. "How did you know my name?" he asked in a thick German accent.

"Your reputation precedes you, Mr. Bloom. Now, I'm placing you in charge of this group of men—which means you'll receive double wages." Pendergast pulled a piece of paper from his pocket. "Here is a list of supplies I will need you to bring to Smee's Alley an hour before the other men arrive. That means you might need to be quick with your purchases. Hire a wagon for transport, and spare no expense."

Bloom took the list and stared at it. "Explosives, sir?"

"A trifling amount. I understand that as foreman you have the requisite license."

"I don't want to be involved in any funny business."

"It is all perfectly legal, I can assure you, if a bit unorthodox." Pendergast dipped into his pocket and took out an envelope. "Here are the funds you'll require. And your full remuneration of twenty dollars—in advance. I shall be offering bonuses upon successful completion of the job."

The man hesitated, then took the envelope.

"I'm an honest man, Mr. Bloom, and I believe you to be one as well," said Pendergast in a pleasant voice. "Should you prove otherwise, it would be most unfortunate—for you, I mean."

"Yes, sir." Bloom touched his forehead with the envelope, then slid it into his jacket pocket. "Eight o'clock, Longacre Square."

17

On occasion, Dr. Enoch Leng enjoyed taking the reins of his four-in-hand barouche himself, feeling the power of the fine horses under his own hands. This evening, he headed across Chatham Square and angled down Chatham Street at a fast trot, Munck sitting beside him. Not far past the square, he was obliged to stop, due to a commotion in front of Fatty Walsh's Saloon. This was often the case in the slums of the Five Points. Leng watched with interest as a superannuated whore was chased from the saloon by a group of drunken ruffians shouting catcalls and abuse. A crowd of gawkers had also gathered, temporarily blocking Leng's progress as they watched the pursuit of the prostitute who, weeping, tried to escape her harassers. Such displays of human cruelty only further confirmed his deepening sense of Weltschmerz.

Soon the commotion had passed southward into the Fourth Ward, and Leng was able to proceed, turning right onto Baxter and then left onto Park Street. Midway down the block rose the forbidding, four-story brick façade of the House of Industry. He pulled the carriage up to the arched portal and turned the reins over to Munck, then alighted, clapped on his top hat, and pulled the visitor-announcement chain on the door. A moment later, the door opened half a dozen inches and the rubbery face of Royds appeared in the gap, creased with anxiety. Leng expected the man to open it the moment he was recognized, but instead Royds began to stammer.

"Dr. Leng, good to see you, Professor, very good indeed, sir..." His voice seized up.

"Is something the matter, Royds?" Leng asked.

"Well, Dr. Leng, sir, there's been a terrible tragedy..." Again he seemed to freeze, at a loss for words.

"What sort of tragedy? Are you going to admit me, man, or just stand there gaping?"

Leng heard a voice sound out from the darkness beyond. "Who is that?"

"Ah, sir, it's the Mission doctor, sir—"

"Open the door so I can see him."

Royds eased open the door, and the light from outside revealed an extraordinary figure—a thin man, imperious, clothed in clerical severity, with reddish hair and a short beard, staring down at Leng with glittering eyes: one green, the other milky blue.

"Who are you, sir?" the man demanded.

Stepping farther into the entrance hall, Leng lost none of his composure despite this odd turn of events, arranging his face into an agreeable expression and removing his top hat. "Dr. Enoch Leng, at your service. May I enter?"

"Please do, Doctor. I am the Right Reverend Percy Considine. Come to my office and we shall discuss your business, whatever it may be."

At this, the reverend turned on his heel with a swirl of

his black cassock and retreated into the darkness, Leng following. Royds, he noted, scurried away as soon as he could.

The reverend led him out of the entrance hall, down the east corridor, and into Miss Crean's office, where he seated himself behind her desk with a flourish and held out his hand to indicate where Leng was to sit.

"Now, Dr. Leng, you may not know this," the man said, "but tragedy has visited the House of Industry."

Leng kept his features arranged in as pleasant an expression as possible. "I had not heard."

"The details are strictly confidential—for the present. Suffice it to say, Miss Crean passed away quite suddenly, and I am her replacement, appointed by the Methodist Judicial Council. You can imagine, Dr. Leng, that I am still getting acquainted with the particular affairs of this mission. I regret to say I'm not familiar with you or your business here." He clasped his large hands. "So tell me, Doctor: what can I do for you?"

"Thank you, Reverend Considine," said Leng. "I am very sorry to hear of Miss Crean's passing, and I offer you my condolences."

"No such condolences are necessary. As it happens, I was here to replace her."

Leng was taken aback. "Indeed? May I inquire as to what happened?"

"You may not. It is church business, and as such must remain private."

"I see. Well then, allow me to congratulate you on your assuming the duties of director." Leng paused. "I am a doctor of, if I may say, excellent repute, who offers his therapeutic services pro bono to the unfortunate girls of the Mission. I am credentialed at Bellevue Hospital and am an adjunct at Columbia, with advanced medical degrees from Heidelberg and Oxford, specializing in mental alienation and psychosurgery. I would be most happy to present you with my credentials."

"That won't be necessary, Doctor. I naturally accept your word."

"Thank you. In my private clinic, I sometimes offer treatment to a very few patients from the Mission and House of Industry. In addition to Bellevue, of course."

"And you are here today, sir, on what purpose?"

"My hope today is—as has been my practice of some time now, as indicated—to tour the wards, examine any new arrivals, and if necessary transfer to my clinic any worthy Christian girl in urgent need of medical attention. As you know, many of the impoverished inmates rescued from the streets bring with them mental and physical diseases in need of management—especially epidemic diseases that can spread quickly."

Considine frowned. "Do you have a contract with the Mission?"

"No, Reverend. It was all handled informally, since no payments or obligations were involved—and since, to put it plainly, the Mission has little money to spend on medical care. This has been a way for me, as a devout Methodist of the Wesleyan Church, to offer such talents as God has given me. To live my life, as the Discipline instructs us, 'to continue to evidence the desire for salvation.' "

"And you believe that removing these lost, sinful souls from the House of Industry, where they are put to hard work in service of the Lord, and in hopes of redemption from their wicked ways, will somehow bring them to salvation?"

"Naturally. By healing their bodies *and* their minds, I can help them on their journey toward becoming good Christian ladies. And, if I may say so, I have seen the effects of such healing—through my observation of the results." He smiled piously, carefully hiding his growing disdain of this cleric.

"You mean to say, sir, that by overindulging them, by offering them luxury, by providing them soft beds and medicines and fine food, that somehow you are preparing them for redemption?"

"I would not go so far as to call their hospital quarters luxurious, or their food fine. But as the body is the temple of the soul, then: yes, Reverend, I do believe I am doing God's work."

"Sir, I take exception! Rather, what we must do is give them 'a desire to flee from the wrath to come, and to be saved from their sins,' as is stated in the same *Book of Discipline* you have just quoted. Doctor, cosseting these wicked women only leads them farther down the path to perdition. Why, the only charitable, Christian thing I can perceive Nurse Crean to have done in her tenure is to move the Mission offices here—to the House of Industry—where we can keep a closer eye on their labor!" Considine's voice was rising in volume. "Doctor, I have only been here a day, but it took me far less time than that to observe these women are used to wallowing in depravity and sin—Sabbath-breaking, gaiety of apparel, profanation, brawling and quarreling, and worst of all—worst of all—the *accursed thing*... You know that of which I speak!"

Leng remained quite still, gazing into the reverend Considine's face. Clearly, he had suffered some injury to the dead, milky eye; he wondered what it might have been, and whether it was the source of the man's fanatical nature.

The reverend was now in full throat. "As the Discipline instructs us: *Look round and see how many of them are still in apparent Danger! And how can you walk, and talk, and be merry with such People? Methinks you should set on them with the most vehement Exhortations!*"

He rose from his chair. "Now, Dr. Leng, prithee get thee hence! I doubt not that your intentions are honorable, but I fear your practice is sadly misguided. Ponder my words and, above all, read and study the Discipline. Because verily, verily, I say unto you: no longer shall this mission be a place from which depraved souls shall be permitted to wantonly fly to sanctuaries for mollycoddling of the body—while their minds remain fettered by filth and wickedness!"

Leng understood that no argument he could muster would move this sanctimonious creature, especially now that he was roused into self-righteous fury. There was nothing for it but to rise stiffly and offer his hand. "You have explained your position, Reverend. I wish you good day."

Considine stood across the desk, cassock and vestments wrapped around him like a shroud, his face pale and beaded with sweat. He looked down at the hand and, seeming to recollect himself, took it in his own, clammy and wet, and gave it a limp squeeze. "*Dominus vobiscum*, Doctor."

18

Leng exited the House of Industry, his face cool and placid, but he was raging within. He pulled a handkerchief from his pocket and wiped the reverend's loathsome exudations from his hand. Stepping out into Park Street, he saw his carriage parked at the corner of Pearl, where a small group of guttersnipes were fawning over it. Munck, seeing Leng emerge, immediately shook the reins, and the carriage moved forward.

What a damnable thing to happen, Leng thought, just when he was in greater need than ever of experimental subjects on which to test the Arcanum. He could, of course, take the matter up with the Mission elders or the council—but that would take too much time. It would be preferable to simply kill the insufferable ecclesiastic. But before he arranged for this mental cataleptic to meet a tragic end, it would be prudent to learn precisely what had happened to Miss Crean and where precisely Considine had come from. Removing the cleric prematurely might possibly lead to an even more objectionable result. At some time in the very near future, he would need to have a conversation with the unctuous Royds.

He climbed in the cab. "You drive," he said curtly to Munck.

"Yes, Doctor."

The coach pulled away from the curb, Leng deep in thought. The more he considered this, the more disastrous the development appeared. There were at present no young females at Bellevue of the right age and health to be suitable—he had run through all of them. On top of that, he could not afford to appear too eager for more, especially since Dr. Cawley, the medical director, was showing annoyance at Leng's having spirited Ferenc off so quickly. It was within the bounds of his Bellevue credentials to do so, of course, but the patient had been sufficiently intriguing that the hospital was eager to examine him themselves. Indeed, they were asking when they could expect Ferenc back.

As Munck headed northward on the Bowery, Leng eased his mind by considering the most appropriate way in which the Right Reverend could meet a dreadful end. After a few minutes, his attention shifted to the view outside his window. They were just passing a crowd in front of the Bowery Theater.

As he gazed, an idea came to him. "Take a left on Canal, then another on Mott," he said.

"Yes, sir."

The carriage made the requested turns, which brought it back into the slums of the Sixth Ward and then once again toward the Five Points. As they moved south on Mott, a town house, more elegant than its neighbors, rose up ahead. Several young dandies loitered about in front: Bridget McCarty's brothel. His eye swept the group, and he decided taking a victim here would be unnecessarily dangerous— he should seek someone who would not be missed.

"Munck, turn right on Bayard, please. When you reach Centre Street, slow down."

They came out on Centre Street. In the middle of the block was a low limestone structure that—with its squat columns and narrow windows—had an ironic resemblance to an Egyptian temple. This was the ancient, infamous prison known as the Tombs.

Munck, seemingly anticipating his master's thoughts, expertly slowed the horses down to a walk, while Leng peered at the street through a gap in the carriage curtains. A woman had just come out of the Tombs: one whose thinness, rags, and filth could not entirely hide her youth. It appeared she had just been released. She looked dazed, squinting into the hazy lamplight, struggling to wrap a threadbare shawl around her shoulders.

"Stop."

The carriage came to a halt along the curb, beyond the woman. As she drew alongside, Leng opened the carriage door and swept off his hat. "Miss? May I have a word?"

"I'm not in that business no more," said the woman, quickening her step.

Leng sprang out of the carriage and paced her. "No, no, miss, you misunderstand. Allow me to introduce myself—Dr. Enoch Leng of the Five Points Mission. My business is saving souls, and I've found the surest way to do that is by *feeding* souls. Now, I have some grapes and sweetmeats in the carriage—if you'd care to step inside?"

The woman stopped and looked at him, her face grimy and drawn, a few locks of blond hair straying out from under a bonnet. "I know what you're after—sir. You don't fool me."

Leng paused. "Well, perhaps you do know what I want. But I'm a good clean gentleman, miss, and I've a fine place where you can take a hot bath, have a good dinner, and be given a fresh change of clothes. And where, I might add, you'll be treated with respect."

She gazed into his face with an expression of resignation mingled with exhaustion. She resumed walking.

"Where are you going to spend the night, dear girl?" Leng added as she moved away. "It's bound to be a cold one. And it appears you've been cold a long time. Prison is no place for a fragile creature like yourself."

She hesitated, slowing her pace.

"A fine saddle of beef and potatoes drowned in butter await."

She halted. Munck had eased the carriage forward to where Leng was now standing, and as she looked back, he held its door open invitingly. A long moment passed. And then, with something like self-disgust, she turned and climbed inside.

"What is your name, dear?" Leng asked.

"Daisy."

Leng reached for a small lacquered carrying case affixed to the inside of the carriage, opened it, and withdrew a small porcelain box, within which were nestled candied apricots. "Would you care for one?"

The girl hesitated, then reached out and took one, cramming it into her mouth.

"Have another."

She took another.

"Take them all, my dear Daisy. Sit back, relax, and enjoy the journey to my home."

19

Loitering in the shadows of Longacre Square, Pendergast saw the loaded wagon approaching, drawn by a pair of stout Clydesdales driven by Bloom. He waved to the foreman and had him pull up to the curb near the entrance to Smee's Alley.

"All in order?" he asked in a low voice.

"Yes, sir."

"Let's have a look at those explosives."

Bloom got out, went around to the back, and pulled aside the canvas flap. He lit a small lantern and Pendergast quickly surveyed the interior. Everything looked to be in good order: wooden planks and braces for scaffolding; a neat stack of bricks; some bags of dry cement, sand, and aggregate; tools, nails, and spikes. To one side, cushioned between sacks of lime, was a small wooden box. Bloom slid it out and opened the lid, revealing four sticks of dynamite with fuses and a clock apparatus. Pendergast took one, hefted it, took another, and then slid each into interior pockets of his frock coat, along with the clock.

"Now, Mr. Bloom, kindly wait with the wagon. I am going into Hockelmann's Brewery to pay the owner a visit."

Pendergast strolled along Seventh Avenue, then turned into Smee's Alley, where he paused. The shimmering portal was still nowhere to be seen: just dirt, horse manure, and peeling playbills on the brick walls. The cul-de-sac had a single entrance into the tenements on the right side. At the end stood a wooden gate that, Pendergast knew, was the back entrance to the brewery's courtyard. Even at this hour the brewery was going strong, coining money for the owner, Heinrich Hockelmann, who in turn was busily buying up and emptying the surrounding tenements in preparation for expansion.

Pendergast walked to the end of the cul-de-sac and noted the padlock on the wooden gate. He grasped the lock in his hand and, using a metal pick, gave it a twist. The lock fell open. He let himself into the courtyard beyond, where two burly men were rolling barrels of beer up a ramp into the back of a wagon. A strong smell of fermenting barley and hops drifted in the air.

The two saw him and halted their work. "Who might you be?" one yelled out.

Pendergast opened his frock coat to display his badge. "Building inspector, here to see Mr. Hockelmann."

"A moment, sir." The workman murmured a word to his companion before heading into the brewery itself. Without waiting, Pendergast followed the man inside.

The brewery was a remarkable example of nineteenth-century industry: huge oaken fermenting barrels, twenty feet tall, lined one wall, with a welter of copper pipes going every which way. At the far end, a great iron cauldron of boiling mash sat on a fire, fed by a group of men shoveling coal, the flames casting a reddish glow across the dim space.

After a moment, the burly man returned with a short, fat fellow hustling along behind him on stumpy legs, with a white beard, flushed face, and red button nose, looking very much like an alcoholic Santa Claus.

"What's going on here?" the man demanded, coming up to Pendergast. "A building inspector? At this time of night?" His voice was thick with beer. He stared at Pendergast's badge. "What's your name? I want to see your bona fides."

"Alphonse Billington, at your service." Pendergast removed the portfolio from his case.

Hockelmann opened it, looked over the credentials within, grunted, and handed it back. "So what might you want here? Everything's in order!"

Pendergast let an uncomfortable silence build. "The brewery may be in order," he intoned at last, "but your tenements are certainly not."

"What d'ye mean? Those tenements are mostly empty."

"I am aware of that. I'm here to inspect them." Pendergast brushed past and, working from his memory of the plats in the building inspector's office, walked briskly through the huge space and down a corridor, the brewmaster skipping and hopping to keep up. He stopped at a heavy door in the east wall of the building and, apparently just brushing his hand over the lock, opened it.

"Hold on here—I'm telling you, sir, that building beyond is empty."

Pendergast stepped into a passway through two adjacent walls and found himself on the ground floor of a tenement building: a dark, foul passage illuminated by a single gaslight that led past a row of stinking garbage containers and leftover construction materials. He knew Hockelmann had been mercilessly evicting the immigrant tenants, intent on using the buildings for his growing business.

He charged along, turned a corner, and halted at an alcove containing a stack of old lumber. "This, Mr. Hockelmann, is a serious fire hazard."

"But there are no tenants in this building—"

"A fire endangers the *entire* city." Pendergast was in motion again. He paused at a brick wall, stopped, took out a tiny ball-peen hammer, and tapped the wall with it. He tapped again, putting his ear close to the masonry. *Tap tap tap.*

"Oh, dear," he murmured.

Tap tap tap.

"Gracious me."

Hockelmann waited, face red.

He straightened. "This is a bearing wall, is it not, my good man?"

An exasperated sigh. "It's the outer wall of the building, yes."

"Just as I thought. Substandard. Unstable. Shoddy construction. It could collapse at any moment."

"Wh—?" Hockelmann began to splutter. "This is preposterous!"

They continued on, Pendergast pausing now and then to tap on the walls, his frown deepening. At one point, two rats broke away from a heap of construction trash.

"Vermin," Pendergast observed. "Uncontained trash. Dangerous storage of paint and oils, leading to possible spontaneous combustion. Extraordinary to think that people live in this environment."

"But I keep telling you, the building is unoccupied—!"

"Violations are violations, whether there are presently tenants or not."

It was almost comical how Hockelmann huffed in his attempts to keep up with Pendergast, while simultaneously trying to vent his surprise and indignation.

"What is behind this door?" Pendergast suddenly

cried in a suspicious voice, turning a knob and finding it locked.

"An empty apartment," said Hockelmann. "Like all the others."

The door suddenly opened as Pendergast pushed against it, and he fell into the darkened space beyond, the door slamming behind him: a bit of business so well executed that a vaudevillian actor would have admired it. Hockelmann tried to follow, but the door had somehow locked itself.

"Let me out!" came Pendergast's muffled voice. He banged on the door. "This is intolerable!" He rattled the knob and, a moment later, flung the door open, looking alarmed and disheveled. "This door is dangerous and requires immediate attention!"

He slammed it behind him and, tugging his jacket straight, continued on. In a matter of minutes he had made a complete circuit of the ground-floor hallways of the tenement building that fronted Forty-Second Street, and they were back at the door they had initially passed through. Pendergast stepped once again into the brewery, Hockelmann at his heels.

"These are immigrant tenements that I acquired *as is*," Hockelmann said, gasping for breath. "You know perfectly well, sir, no tenement landlord ever follows building regulations!"

"*Never* follows building regulations? I don't see how that could hold up in court, sir."

"Court?" Hockelmann's eyes briefly went glassy as he considered a potential chain of future events.

"The city is up to its neck in lax and irresponsible landlords. Do you think I'm out here, at this time of night, conducting inspections for my health?"

With a mighty effort, Hockelmann held his temper in check. "No, sir, I don't."

"Or that I enjoy performing them with the owners at my heels, complaining and insulting me from start to finish?"

Hockelmann said nothing.

"Recall that I have examined only one of the tenement buildings that overlook Smee's Alley—the other, fronting Forty-First Street, has yet to be examined. Need we conduct this same exercise *again*?"

Hockelmann took a deep breath, shook his head. "What—what is your recommendation?"

"That you see to it these grossly negligent violations are attended to—and posthaste."

"I shall do so immediately, Mr. Billington."

"In that case, having given you this warning—I shall take my leave." And with a supercilious little bow, he turned away, walked out of the brewery into the courtyard, and approached the gate leading to Smee's Alley—but not before hearing the words "Bloody *scoundrel!*" shouted in a voice so loud that it echoed even over the noise of horseshoes and the shoveling of coal.

20

Daisy woke up and for a moment was in a panic, uncertain where she was. She sat bolt upright as her memory came flooding back. The doctor had taken her to his grand mansion, given her a bath, fresh clothes, and a dinner of beef and potatoes, just as promised. There had been no demand for sexual favors as she'd expected—the man had not so much as put a hand on her. Instead, weary beyond all measure, it seemed she'd been allowed to fall asleep right there at the dinner table—only to wake up in this unfamiliar place.

She looked around. The room was spare, with a narrow but comfortable bed, a chair, and a bedside table with some books. The walls were of windowless stone. A riveted iron door stood at the far end, with a grated window, into which was set a small panel, also shut. A single taper burned on a table by her bedside. It was warm and dry—not at all like the Tombs—yet it had the feeling of a prison chamber.

Daisy tried to shake off the feeling of sleepiness. She felt grateful the man had not pressed himself upon her, but it also made her wonder: what was he after, if not that? She rose from the bed and went to the iron door; the handle was, as she expected, locked.

She went back to the bed and sat down. For the first time in months she was neither cold nor hungry. The clothes he'd given her were of good quality, a cotton dress and woolen shawl, along with clean, warm undergarments, stockings, and slippers.

She idly picked up one of the books on the bedside table and squinted at the title. *The Light Princess*, by George MacDonald. With a shock, she recognized it as a book her father had read to her as a child, about a princess who had no weight and floated everywhere. The unexpected sight of the book was like a knife twisting in her heart, and back flooded all the memories that, for five years now, she'd tried to suppress: her father, killed in the factory; her mother, dead of consumption; her little sister, dead of hunger—and herself now part of the lost sisterhood, forced like so many other penniless women to walk the streets in order to stay alive. She didn't know what this man—this doctor—wanted, but he hadn't tried to interfere with her; he'd promised to treat her with respect, and in fact he had, calling her "dear" and making sure she was warm and well fed.

She opened the book with a trembling hand.

Once upon a time, so long ago that I have quite forgotten the date, there lived a king and queen who had no children.

Reading was difficult and slow—it had been so long since she'd had anything of interest to read—and she found herself sounding the words out aloud as she went along. As she did so, more recollections came back—of her mother, teaching her to read. She felt so old and worthless now, so vile, even though she was only eighteen. If her father hadn't been drawn into the machinery, they'd still be living in their three rooms down on Peck's Slip at the bottom of Ferry, with the steamers coming and going and blowing their whistles, and maybe her with a seamstress job on Pearl Street and a young suitor bringing flowers—

She put the book down. What time was it? She got up from the bed again and went to the door. She knocked politely.

Nothing.

She knocked again, louder this time. "Hello? Dr. Leng?"

Again, nothing.

"Hello?"

She felt a twinge of alarm. What did he want? Despite his nice talk and the fancy meal and clean clothes, he seemed a strange, cold man, and thinking of him made her shiver.

Then she heard footsteps outside the door. She held her breath.

There was a grating of metal on metal, and the panel in the window grate slid open. The light beyond was dim, but she could see the doctor's wet lips glisten as he spoke.

"Please do not discompose yourself," he crooned. "All this will be over shortly. Forgive me for not playing the host at the present moment, but I have some pressing business to take care of. I assure you that, in the near future, I will be able to give you the benefit of my undivided attention."

"But, Doctor, sir—?" Daisy began, then stopped when she noticed the little panel had already shut with a rusty scraping sound.

21

Pendergast waited with Bloom on the seat of the large wagon, parked on Broadway across Longacre Square from Smee's Alley. A winter wind blew across the empty intersection, bringing with it the smell of coal smoke and horse manure. The gas lanterns cast pools of yellow light at regular intervals in the sea of darkness.

Held out in Pendergast's hand was a gold pocket watch, which both men examined closely. At one minute to nine precisely, Bloom nodded at Pendergast. A moment later a muffled explosion came from across the street, followed by the sound of collapsing brickwork. A great cloud of dust issued from the mouth of Smee's Alley.

Pendergast turned to his companion. "Mr. Bloom, if you are as good at construction as you are at demolition, I shall be the first to cross the Brooklyn Bridge upon its completion."

"Thank you, sir."

"Now, would you be so kind as to block the alleyway?"

Bloom urged the horses across the square and stopped

directly before the alley, the horse prancing nervously as dust from the explosion billowed around them. The air, full of pulverized brick, slowly cleared—revealing that a portion of an empty tenement's outer wall had collapsed into the alley, bricks strewn about.

On cue, the nine sandhogs converged on the scene, as if drawn by the noise.

"Gentlemen!" Pendergast called out. "You've come just in time. There's been an accident—a wall of this tenement has collapsed, as you can see. Shoddy construction, naturally—unfortunate, but hardly uncommon. I want this alleyway permanently blocked off. In the wagon you will find all the tools and materials needed to erect scaffolding, shore up the walls, and begin repairs. We have no time to lose! Mr. Bloom, please see to it that the work is done correctly."

"Yes, sir," Bloom said, hopping off the wagon and crying out orders to the men. The sandhogs immediately began unloading. Pendergast also alighted to watch the process, drawing his greatcoat around his narrow frame.

Within ten minutes there came the sound of horns and engines, and then a firewagon arrived: pulled by four stout horses, uniformed men hanging off the sides. They came to a halt and leapt off, bell clanging.

"Over here, fellows!" Pendergast cried, approaching and waving his badge. "Alphonse Billington, at your service. I commend you on responding so promptly. I happened to be passing, and it was my great luck to enlist the workers that you see here to put things temporarily aright. Nothing to worry about—the collapse of a wall of an alley tenement. I have inspected, and there's no fire or further danger of instability, thank the Lord."

"All the same, we'd like to take a look, sir," said the fire chief.

"I'd be relieved if you would." Pendergast led the man

around the wagon and halfway down the alley, where a five-by-ten-foot hole could be seen in the tenement wall, the bricks spilling into the street. The sandhogs were already bracing the ragged opening with timbers and jacks.

The chief peered inside the hole for a few moments, then nodded. "Very good, sir."

From the corner of his eye, Pendergast saw Hockelmann burst from the wooden gate at the end of the cul-de-sac and come charging up on stumpy legs, evidently drunk on his own wares.

"What's this?" he cried. Then he spotted Pendergast. "Damn your eyes, man, you're behind all this devilment!" he huffed as he approached.

"You're drunk, for one thing, and talking rubbish for a second." Pendergast took a step back and viewed him disdainfully. "Did I not tell you the wall was shoddy and prone to collapse?"

"That is all part of your japery somehow, you—you—mountebank!"

"Mountebank, is it?" Pendergast assumed an offended expression. "Perhaps we should inspect more tenements of yours, Mr. Hockelmann, now that we have an excellent team here to look for fire violations... as well as the other signs of neglect by an irresponsible landlord." He glanced at the fire chief, who stepped up beside him.

This pulled Hockelmann up short. "*More* inspections? Haven't you done enough?"

"Enough? I should say not! Here we have proof of dangerous, substandard construction. In fact, given your unwarranted resistance and insulting behavior, we should inspect *all* these buildings!"

Hockelmann swallowed, looked from Pendergast to the fire chief and back again, and then rearranged his facial features with considerable effort. "My sincere apologies, sir. I didn't mean to cast aspersions—"

Pendergast raised a hand to stop this flow of words. "I possess a tough hide, sir; I've had more than my share of landlords climb out of their beds to insult my person. Perhaps we needn't inspect them all...at *this* time of night. But due to the dangerous conditions in the alley, we're going to have to temporarily padlock this gate to prevent any ingress or egress. You shall be obliged to make do with your main entrance on Forty-First Street."

Hockelmann, face once again growing dark with fury, retreated back down the alley, slamming the wooden gate behind him.

Pendergast turned to the fire chief. "Thank you for the swift response," Pendergast told him, shaking the man's hand firmly. "I shall be sure to take special note of your efficiency in my report."

"Much appreciated, sir." The fire chief climbed back aboard his conveyance, then yelled to his men, and—with greatly diminished clamor—the wagon began making its way down Seventh Avenue.

22

Just after one am, a skiff detached itself from the thicket of wharves and moorings that jutted into the Hudson around the terminus of the Christopher Street ferry. Although the West Side of Manhattan wouldn't truly bristle with piers and transatlantic liners for another forty years, there was nevertheless some river traffic even at this late hour; but the skiff blended into it easily, calling no attention to itself.

Constance Greene sat aft, rowing upriver on the incoming tide, to the faint creak of oarlocks and the splashes of oars. She wore a man's outfit, that of a supercargo, cap set low over her short-cropped hair. A large bundle in the bow, covered with an oilcloth, served as more than just counterweight: beneath the canvas lay clothing, food, tools, and weapons.

The skiff's shallow draft allowed it to skim across the water's surface, while the planking, hand-notched and pegged, rendered its frame sturdy enough to weather a heavy sea without foundering.

Constance rowed easily, keeping her gaze on the glow

that lit up the southern tip of Manhattan. As the glow faded, she piloted the skiff in a little closer to land.

It was a cold, cloudless night, and under the stars the natural features of Manhattan stood out to her practiced eye. Continuing with even strokes, she passed "Mount Tom," the outcropping where Edgar Allan Poe had once enjoyed taking in the view. Farther north, the island's bedrock began forcing its way upward into bluffs, leaving only the West Side Line of the New York Central at sea level—along with the ruins of shanties abandoned a decade earlier, during the land condemnation that would prepare the ground for Riverside Park.

The tiers of graded land forming the park were soon visible between patches of bare trees, and here Constance briefly shipped oars and drifted with the tide, looking carefully at the landscape to make sure of her bearings. The park's outlines, still under construction, ended around 125th Street. Her own destination was a mere dozen blocks farther on.

She looked over her shoulder, using the dim cliffs of Washington Heights for triangulation. Then she took up oars again and brought the skiff still nearer to shore. There she continued with easy strokes, examining the twisted trees along the shoreline with care.

Once, she thought she'd found what she was looking for—but when she angled the skiff in toward land, it grounded on a muddy bank thick with undergrowth, and she quickly used an oar to push back into the river again.

A second attempt, minutes later, was more successful. She knew it before she reached it: the brace of bare plane trees, standing athwart a tangle of scrub, dead weeds, and hanging ivy. More cautiously this time, she approached the spot, expertly bringing the skiff about and letting its bow pierce the prickly curtain of winter undergrowth.

It was thicker than she remembered, however, and for a moment she was surrounded by a mass of vegetation and branches. But then the skiff broke through the mantle of undergrowth, which swung back into place with a dry rustle, sealing the gap and giving no indication it had been disturbed.

Constance shipped oars once again and let the skiff glide freely. Her nocturnal vision was acute, but under this vegetative canopy it was so dark her senses of smell and hearing became equally important. No sound but a faint lapping; no smell but that of briny, icy water and dead foliage.

Reaching forward, she retrieved a dark lantern from beneath the oilcloth and lit it, turning up the wick just enough to faintly illuminate her surroundings. This was the place: the slight opening in the rock just ahead, a familiar outcropping shaped like a moonshine jug both confirmed this was the natural water cave the pirate king who once owned this land had used to access his lair from below ground level. As her skiff entered the stony tunnel, her lantern illuminated centuries-old patterns of smoke on the granite ceiling.

More quickly now, she took hold of the oars and maneuvered the boat around the bend in the grotto. The skiff bumped against the worn rocks at the far end, and she stepped out, knelt to test the ancient bronze ring driven into the nearby bedrock, then tied the painter to it. Reassured by the silence, she straightened up and took a deep breath, shining the lantern around and refamiliarizing herself with the space.

She knew that Leng had purchased the mansion above this cave five years before. At this early point, he had not yet discovered the hidden cellar entrance to the extensive and dangerous sub-basements below, infected with damp and encrusted with niter. And it would be several more years before he discovered this secret water-level access that they ultimately led to. The last person to use this passage to the river had been the one to discover it in the first place: the pirate himself, an Englishman named Nathaniel Bell. "Bloody Bell" had established this stronghold not long after the English acquired New Amsterdam from the Dutch, and he operated as a privateer with a wink and a nod from the new English rulers, who were happy to see him prey on the annual Spanish treasure fleet. After he'd left on what turned out to be his final, fatal sea voyage, no treasure was discovered. Bloody Bell had buried it somewhere—speculation pointed to most likely the Maritimes, probably on Oak Island off the coast of Nova Scotia.

Constance held her lantern close to the walls, moving her fingers lightly over the stones that made up the far end of the grotto, occasionally applying pressure. At last she stopped before a rock face that was smoother than those around it but showed no signs of a doorway. Unsheathing her stiletto, she used the edge of its blade to lightly probe along the rock face, encountering mud and niter. On the fourth try, the blade sank deep. Carefully, she exerted downward pressure—and the blade began tracing a vertical incision without obstacle.

Constance removed the knife. Now that she'd located it, the task of unsealing the hidden door could wait temporarily. She turned back to the skiff, pulled aside the oilcloth, and—quietly, but with haste—unloaded the contents from the bow and arranged them along the damp stones nearby.

23

A COLD DAWN WAS JUST breaking over Longacre Square as the sandhogs finished their work. Pendergast looked it over with no little satisfaction. These men were the best of the best at such tasks; they had done all he asked and more. Smee's Alley was now completely secure. The mouth of the alley was thoroughly blocked off, the tenements surrounding it offering no access; the hole in the wall caused by the dynamite was boarded over, and the brewery gate at the far end of the alley had been reinforced and padlocked. Just inside the alley's Seventh Avenue entrance, a sturdy, two-story guard station had been built into the temporary joists, beams, and supports, ready to watch over this small—but critical—alleyway.

Pendergast understood only too well that, if the portal were ever to be opened again, it was vital to control the surrounding space and—even more vital—to prevent Leng from using it. If *he* ever passed through the portal and gained control of the machine from the twenty-first century of Pendergast's home universe...the results would be unthinkable.

"Mr. Bloom," he said, turning to the foreman. "Please assemble your men."

Bloom quickly lined up the nine members of his crew. They stood straight in their motley work clothes and heavy boots, faces smudged with concrete dust and dirt.

Pendergast eyed them and, after a few words of fulsome praise, reached into his pocket and took out a fistful of $10 gold eagles. He walked down the line, dropping one into each outstretched hand. The expressions on the faces of the men at the sight of the gold were remarkable indeed.

"You," said Pendergast, tapping one man on the chest. "What is your name?"

"Patrick McGonigle, sir."

"Do you have any squeamishness regarding fisticuffs or acts of violence?"

"Squeam? I don't have the clap or the coughing sickness, if that's what you mean. As for violence, I can handle myself with fists or me shillelagh."

"Very good. Step over there."

Pendergast paused at another man. "And your name?"

"Tony Bellagamba, sir."

"I can see where you got that moniker. Step over there."

He placed his hands behind his back and turned, strolling once again along the line of ragged men, who were all trying to stand as straight as possible.

"And you?"

"Emil Krauss."

"Where did you get that scar on your cheek?"

"In a duel, sir."

"A duel! How marvelous. With what type of weapon?"

"A Korbschläger, sir. Back in Prussia."

"And what happened to your opponent?"

"I spared his life, sir."

"Why?"

"Humiliation is worse than death."

"Excellent, most excellent. Please join the others."

One final turn along the line. "And you, my good fellow?" He paused before a giant of a man.

"Francis Smith, sir."

"What did you do before starting work on the Brooklyn Bridge?"

"I was in the iron mines, sir. In the Adirondacks."

"Can you read and write?"

"No, sir."

"Step over there, if you please."

Pendergast questioned one other—a man of rather mysterious pedigree but obvious lethality named Perigord—then nodded with satisfaction. "Please join the others. The rest of you, thank you for your good work. You may go."

After the others had left, just Bloom and five of his band remained. Pendergast waited until they were alone, then turned to address the group.

"You men now work for me. The pay is six dollars a day. The hours will be irregular, and you will be on call at a moment's notice, any time of the day or night. You may well have to take up temporary residence within these buildings, but I will see to it you're made comfortable. Any objections?"

No, there were no objections—just vigorous nodding and muffled expressions of satisfaction.

"Mr. Smith, you will stay here and occupy the guardhouse for the initial watch. Mr. Perigord, please patrol the surrounding tenements—and keep an eye on that brewery and its owner. It is of the utmost importance that no one enters the alley or surrounding buildings, now empty. Consider this our territory, not to be intruded upon. If either of you sees anything odd occur in the alley, such as strange lights or colors, you will stay where you are, remain calm, and get a message to me. The rest of you I'll expect at this address at five PM this evening." He handed out cards to each of them. "And now, Mr. Bloom, let us take a few minutes to finalize, to our satisfaction, the duties and responsibilities of your most excellent brigade."

24

The sprawling bulk of the Drury Hippodrome—the largest entertainment and theater complex in New York City—occupied an entire block of Fourteenth Street. By eight PM on a Saturday night, it resembled an anthill of activity. Within, the various entertainments, from concert saloons to circus performers to geek shows, were in full swing, and the pavement outside was busy with patrons coming and going.

Due to the variety of spectacles and the need to collect separate tickets for each, the building had been subdivided into many venues. Short alleyways led into the enormous beflagged bulk of the complex from various streets, serving as admission for the public as well as backstage entrances for performers, stagehands, and vendors. The Hippodrome was a miniature city so labyrinthine that no one, it was said, fully knew its byways, corridors, tunnels, and catwalks.

In the midst of the chaos, between a dressing area and a repair shop for theater sets, was a room kept locked at all times. Its heavy door held no sign, and it was ignored by passing workers as just another storage or maintenance area. This room, with its thick walls and lack of windows, belonged to Leng: one of the more unusual of many bolt-holes he used for his hydra-headed enterprises. While it might seem incongruent to situate a retreat in one of the busiest places in all New York City, it was precisely such busyness that rendered it anonymous. This was where he gathered his "crew."

Decla stood beside the door, with a bandaged hand, restlessly tossing a bowie knife into the air, catching it by the tip, and flipping it into the air again. Looking at her, Leng almost smiled. Despite their differences in class, education, and age, she was his favorite, the one he relied on for pragmatic, streetwise advice. They first met when she'd tried to pick his pocket on the Bowery, eighteen months before. He'd turned at speed and seized her hand, preparing to sever her carotid artery with a scalpel, then push her away to bleed out while he blended into the crowd. But something had stopped him: something in her eyes that showed—instead of fear—calculation, even resignation.

And so an unusual partnership had begun. She was the leader of the Milk Drinkers—a gang whose very name was a contemptuous challenge to the Plug Uglies, the Slaughterhousers, the Roach Guards, and the other gangs who ruled New York's nastiest slums. The Milk Drinkers were a small, tightly knit gang, feared for both their secrecy and their lethality. Unlike others, the Milk Drinkers had no turf to hold and battle over; they came and went where they pleased. Leng had taken Decla not exactly under his wing—she would never stand for that—but into an alliance of sorts, one that he financed himself. In return, she'd agreed to let him thin the gang's ranks of deadwood until it was as lean, mobile, and dangerous as humanly possible. The Milk Drinkers were his bodyguards, his night agents, his messengers of death—and in return he allowed them not only sanctuary and unlimited funds, but the freedom to work independently, maintaining their position atop the gang hierarchy and performing tasks of their own hatched up by Decla's clever, feral mind.

Right now, she was unhappy—the confrontation with Constance Greene had put her out. Leng knew she would never be satisfied until she'd finished it. Decla viewed female gangs with particular hatred, and over time she had arranged for the murder or neutralization of every member of the Sow Maidens, who had dressed like stevedores and filed their teeth to points. Watching her, Leng felt it only proper to give her satisfaction with the fake duchess... when the time was right.

He looked around the room. Some two dozen figures were in attendance, slouching in chairs or lounging on packing crates, motionless, waiting. There were just a few more to come—blending with the throngs of visitors and attracting no attention as they made their way to the room through the myriad routes that, in an emergency, also served as multiple exits.

While they all looked tough, he could read their faces like a book. They feared him; they respected him; they called him "Doctor." Of course, they knew nothing of what he was really about. He kept his true, overarching work—the harvesting of cauda equina, the elixir he was seeking, his grand project—a secret known only by Munck. Instead, he had given them the vague impression he was a sophisticated gangland boss like no other, dealing in the most dangerous, remunerative black-market operations and illegal activities—and that he functioned behind the scenes sub rosa, as their guardian angel... or perhaps *demon* would be the more appropriate term.

A series of low raps sounded a brief tattoo on the

door. Decla cracked it open, then allowed the last two outstanding members—Sloopy and Wolfteat—to enter. As they took seats, Decla locked the door and Leng rose to address the assembly.

"My dear friends," he said, gazing around. "Welcome."

Nods, murmurs.

"I regret to say I have a little problem. It involves Smee's Alley, off Longacre Square. Do any of you know it?"

No one did—it was too far uptown.

"This man I've spoken to you about, Pendergast, has blocked it off. I want access."

Nobody asked him why. They knew only too well that to show curiosity about his private matters was not a salubrious practice.

"Search for a secret way in—underground; through a skylight; as a member of the crew presently guarding it. I don't need to tell you how; just let me know when it's done."

He paced for a few seconds. The gang was well aware of his need for young women, his "jammiest bits of jam"—and the speed with which he went through them—even if the particular nature of that need remained his secret. He let them assume the usual.

And this led to the next topic on the agenda. "A new cleric has been installed at the Mission," he said. "He's forbidding me access to the inmates. No longer am I able to take select girls for necessary medical treatment at my clinic."

At this, several smirks were traded among the assembly.

"I can gather no useful information from that mooncalf at the Mission, Royds, on either the details of Miss Crean's death or background on the cleric himself. The man so precisely hinders me that, initially, I wondered if it might be some sort of plot—but his papers are in order and, in short, it's clear the man must be genuine and not a fraud."

"Let us take care of the cleric for you, Doctor," came a voice. "The river's always thirsty for more bodies." A low chuckle arose.

Leng nodded slowly. "Precisely my thinking. Decla, please give this job some thought and let me know your recommendations."

At this the pout left her face, to be replaced by a slow smile. Plotting murder was one of her favorite pastimes. "Scrape here will have him grinning in the muck of the East River in no time."

Leng nodded again. "Very well. Just let me know when it's done. And take nothing for granted with this one—be on the lookout for unexpected outcomes."

"Why not do this mutton-shunter Pendergast at the same time?" another voice asked, to murmurs of agreement. "Get him out of the way along with the cleric."

"I'm afraid he's too wily for that. Trying to get the drop on him would only reduce the size of your crew. Rather, I think a breadcrumb gambit might be of better success." He paused, thinking. "Yes...a double-breadcrumb gambit, perhaps."

Even as he spoke, the idea was formulating in his head. A man as clever as Pendergast might, in fact, be too clever by half—that would prove his downfall.

Leng glanced at his watch; twenty minutes had passed since he'd first arrived, and he preferred to keep these gatherings short. "Just one more item of business. Humblecut, you have something to report?"

There was a brief stirring in the rear of the room, gray against black. Then a taciturn-looking man, who'd been leaning back in his chair, eased himself forward. He was older than the rest, midforties perhaps, and instead of the gray shirts, suspenders, and bowler hats, he wore a long, double-breasted trench coat of fine black leather. His eyes were hidden beneath the brim of a homburg, but he had a waxed handlebar mustache that he smoothed faintly with the tips of his fingers before he spoke.

"Thank you, Doctor. The boy, Joe, was spirited out of the house using a hearse and coffin as a ruse," he said in a quiet, almost melodic voice. "It was meant to hold the body of his tutor. Instead, the boy was placed in the coffin and switched out when the hearse stopped briefly to mend a horseshoe—a contrivance, of course. From there, he and his policeman escort made their way to the train station. We didn't cotton on to it until the last minute, and we were hindered in following."

"Go on," said Leng.

"We ultimately learned they had purchased tickets to Boston."

"I see." Leng thought a moment. That portal from the future, through which these adversaries had come—if he could only determine when it would reappear, access it...the results would be almost incalculable. Constance Greene had used its mere existence to threaten him: *If you knew what the future holds... The next time you saw me, it would be with powers so formidable all your traps and your alley rats would be swept away like chaff.*

My God, he thought. The great project that he'd always assumed would take decades, even a century, to complete could perhaps be accomplished in a matter of months, even less. What he needed was more information about the portal *itself*; information that only those who had used it would know. And he needed knowledge of the future century from which Ferenc and the rest had come. Once again, he bitterly regretted pushing Ferenc over the edge. That left only three.

"We can kill that meddlesome cleric, but Pendergast and the policeman—I want them alive for now." He paused. "That is all. Thank you, my friends. Mind how you go. And remember—*keep it dry*."

He lifted an index finger to his lips. The group began shuffling to their feet, preparing to leave the Hippodrome by their various routes.

Leng waited until his detective, Humblecut, approached. Then he motioned the man aside and—while Decla stood guard at the exit—began giving him further instructions in a low, urgent whisper.

25

Pendergast stood in Catherine Street, gazing past the oyster cellars and cheap lodging houses toward an imposing brick building with granite cornices that dominated the corner: Shottum's Cabinet of Curiosities. A cold winter mist drifted along the street, tinged a reddish orange from the gas lamps of the establishments lining both sides. The air smelled of old fish and urine, and he could hear the distant sound of drunken singing, the clatter of hooves, and the whistle of a steamship on the East River.

Dressed as a late-night grogshop patron in a shabby greatcoat and dirty spats, Pendergast made his way down the lane, weaving slightly. It was nearly three o'clock, there were few people in the street, and no one paid him any attention. Nearing the corner, he lurched into an alleyway that ran behind Shottum's, bending over as if to vomit. When a quick glance around indicated he was alone and unobserved, he straightened and leapt up a wrought iron fence at the end of the alley, quickly hoisting himself over and down onto the other side.

There was a service door here into Shottum's Cabinet, padlocked—but the padlock seemed to prove no greater obstacle than an unlocked door. He slipped inside, easing the door shut behind him.

All the gaslights inside were off and it was pitch black. New odors assaulted his senses—formaldehyde and mothballs, overlaid with the faint odor of suppuration. Pendergast removed the stub of a candle from his pocket and lit it, casting a feeble glow. He was in one of the exhibition halls. Bizarre and, supposedly, authentic displays loomed out of the shadows, which he viewed with detached amusement: a rearing "man-eating" grizzly bear with a fake arm clenched in its jaws; a mummified orangutan; the skeleton of a French countess executed during the French revolution, appropriately missing its skull. Crossing the hall, he passed through an archway marked *Gallery of Unnatural Monstrosities* and into a narrow corridor sporting such additional grotesqueries as a dog with a cat's head and a hideous brown mass identified as the liver of a woolly mammoth, found frozen in a Siberian glacier. At last the corridor bisected at the display of a second-rank western outlaw, hanged by the neck until dead.

The passage to the left ended in a curtained alcove. Pendergast drew these back to expose a wooden wall. He pressed a small knothole and the rear of the cul-de-sac opened inward. A closet with a padlocked metal door lay beyond. Once again, this padlock seemed to melt open in his hands. The metal door led to a small landing, with a staircase both ascending and descending into blackness. Downstairs, he knew, was the basement coal tunnel. The staircase upward led to Leng's first laboratory.

Before Leng had begun acquiring victims from Bellevue and the House of Industry, he had used this cul-de-sac in the Cabinet as a snatching point for victims. He would lie in wait, like a trapdoor spider, and seize an appropriate victim, smothering her with a chloroform-soaked rag and dragging her behind the wall. He sought out young women, poor, alone, often prostitutes—those who could disappear and never be missed. Shottum's Cabinet was in fact frequented by many such women, as it was one of the few popular amusements available in the Five Points, and—at a cost of only a few pennies—a momentary respite from their hardscrabble lives.

Pendergast had learned there were currently no patients at Bellevue Hospital that met Leng's particular needs. That meant Leng, having also had his flow of victims at the Mission and House of Industry shut off by Diogenes, might turn back to this scheme for acquiring victims—and he was determined to shut it off, as well.

Candle wavering, he ascended the staircase to the floor above. Leng had abandoned this laboratory when one of his dying victims had been discovered up there by the landlord, Shottum himself. What Leng had done with the man after killing him, Pendergast was unsure; this was another purpose of his visit.

He came to the third-floor landing, picked the lock and opened the door, and paused to survey the large, partitioned space beyond. Its vaulted roof lay under the eaves of the building, and one side contained several black soapstone tables, displaying the remains of partially stripped and abandoned chemistry apparatus and other scientific detritus. There was a strange smell here, not unlike a cured ham that had, perhaps, been left in the sun too long. The smell came from behind a heavy oilcloth curtain at the far end of the room.

Pendergast made his way past the tables to this partition and drew it aside.

There, on a marble gurney, lay two long wooden

crates, each containing a human corpse. As Pendergast held the candle out to provide illumination, he saw the cadavers had been packed in coarse salt and what looked like natron as a preservative. Even though the features were distorted by shriveling and curing, one of these corpses could only be Shottum. The other probably belonged to Tinbury McFadden, a curator at the Natural History Museum to whom—Pendergast knew from old letters and journals—Shottum had conveyed his suspicions about Leng. No doubt the unfortunate gentlemen had been a little too curious about Leng's doings on his rented third floor of the Cabinet. The salt was obviously how Leng had kept the bodies from possible discovery until—in Pendergast's own timeline—Leng had ultimately burned Shottum's Cabinet to the ground, leaving no trace. They were now of course in an alternate timeline, and anything could happen. Pendergast had contemplated burning Shottum's himself but discarded that notion as being too risky to innocent lives in the crowded slum.

He had been in the Cabinet before—first as a construct of his own intellect, and later in person—and this would be his final visit. He was now satisfied as to the fate of Shottum, but he had further business down below, in the coal cellar, where Leng's vivisected victims had been walled up in empty alcoves.

Leaving the laboratory, Pendergast padlocked the door and descended as far as the basement. At the bottom of the stairs, he paused to listen. He knew Munck was probably nearby, but he could hear no sound beyond the dripping of water. A coal tunnel ran away to the left, and to the right, another tunnel led deep into Leng's underground complex.

Pendergast stepped into the coal tunnel, the candle's glow feeble but sufficient for his sharp eyes. A number of alcoves had already been sealed up; extra bricks and mortar were stacked nearby, along with trowels and a wheelbarrow, ready for Munck to entomb future victims of Leng's search for his elixir.

After the preparations for the structural collapse in Smee's Alley, Pendergast had asked Bloom to purchase several more crates of dynamite and store them on the premises, against the need for possible future use. From his greatcoat, Pendergast removed three wrapped sticks of dynamite, attached to a ten-minute fuse—prepared separately for him by Bloom. Now, examining the structural pillars and arches, Pendergast identified the point of greatest weakness. He placed the dynamite against its base and uncoiled the long, waterproof fuse, stringing it along the stone floor for several dozen feet. Then, crouching, he lit the end with his candle.

With a hiss, it caught and began to burn. Straightening, Pendergast moved rapidly out of the coal tunnel and up the stairs to the landing, entered the Cabinet proper, exited the alcove, walked past the gruesome exhibits, then went out the side door and back into the alleyway. It was still deserted. He relocked the door and climbed over the wrought iron fence, dropping down into Catherine Street. It was now close to four, and the street was just as he left it. Back in the guise of a grogshop drunk, he made his way down the street. A lady of the night, standing in a doorway with her dress raised to display one ankle, called out to him as he staggered past. He politely declined her companionship.

At the corner, he paused. Moments later, a deep, hollow boom sounded, followed by a brief vibration beneath his feet. A cat, startled, shot out of a corner; a dog barked somewhere; the drunken singing paused. But it took only a few minutes for the street to grow silent once again.

26

Edwin Humblecut stood in the dark fastness of Boston's Old Colony Terminal, a location fragrant with the odors of tobacco juice, stale urine, and rotting fish. He'd taken the same train that the policeman and Joe Greene had ridden just a few days before. There was a good chance most, if not all, of the same employees were at work today, as well.

Humblecut had been untethered from Leng's other operatives and left to accomplish this task on his own—which was the way he liked it. The Milk Drinkers were excellent at striking fear into adversaries and following through on threats, but Humblecut did not enjoy time spent in their company. Leng kept him on retainer for jobs that were more sophisticated, refined—and secret.

He glanced up and down the platforms, once more going over what he knew. He did not know the name of the policeman, though that hardly mattered—no doubt both he and the boy would be traveling under pseudonyms, most likely as father and son. Munck, however, had been able to provide a decent enough description of him. Leng had told him to assume the man "would appear to be somewhat unfamiliar with this time and place"—precisely what that meant Humblecut wasn't sure, but it led him to believe the boy would be the one who'd do most of the talking and other necessary business. And it had been the boy, in fact, who'd purchased the tickets to Boston.

The manner in which they'd left the mansion—the trick with the coffin—was clever, but it also had the whiff of having been planned in a rush. This was understandable, of course...but it was also useful to Humblecut. This nemesis of Leng's, Pendergast—who was probably involved in the planning—had been given very little time to work between Munck's kidnapping of the girl and the policeman slipping Joe out of the house, no doubt to keep him away from Leng. This rush would work in Humblecut's favor, because the getaway plans would have been necessarily simple and straightforward. A place, somehow, had been hastily arranged for them to hole up in; any elaborations to or additional precautions for the plan would follow later.

From what he had learned and observed, Humblecut now moved on to speculation. The two might have gotten off at one of the numerous stops; if he found no further trail in Boston, he would backtrack. But instinct told him that the same urgency employed to get Joe out of New York would also send them as far as possible—perhaps even beyond Boston—without making a return too onerous.

The policeman was a stranger, and the boy—while street smart—was young and would have no practice throwing a hunter off the scent. Humblecut had little problem putting himself into either of their shoes and then running through the various actions they might have taken from this terminal.

Straightening his homburg and smoothing down the polished black leather of his long overcoat, he ambled over to the ticket booths, adjusting his hold on his valise so it appeared more like a gift than a traveling case. None of the ticket agents on duty, however, remembered selling tickets to or speaking with anyone that fit Joe's description.

This did not trouble Humblecut. In fact, even though a single inquiry such as this could not cover every ticket agent who worked at the terminal, it fit the mental picture he was putting together. On the run as they were... however they proceeded from this train station, it would almost certainly be by a different kind of conveyance. That jibed with plans being made in haste.

He looked around slowly, taking in the long wooden benches, the newsstands, the row of ticket booths, the food concessions. Mentally, he put himself in Joe's position: young, excited by what was probably his first long train ride, but scared at the thought he might be followed... Where would he go next?

Now Humblecut made his way over to the large, ornate gentlemen's comfort rooms, where shaves, haircuts, facials, nail polishing, shoeshines, emergency tailoring, and numerous other services were available beyond the mere satisfying of the urges of nature. Many and varied attendants were on duty there, and Humblecut was rewarded, after half a dozen unsuccessful queries, with a barber who recalled a stout-looking man fitting D'Agosta's description who had come in to use the facilities the day before yesterday; his son had asked the barber for directions to the New Commonwealth Dock.

Humblecut thanked the man and returned to the main waiting room, sitting down on one of the long benches to think.

New Commonwealth Dock was in South Boston, not

far from Dorchester Heights. The city was a major port; if one no longer wished to travel by train, Boston held many opportunities for traveling by water instead.

Local ferries used the closer wharves on Atlantic Avenue; New Commonwealth Dock was the departure point for more distant realms.

Humblecut was too taciturn to smile, even to himself, but he allowed a small glow of satisfaction to briefly warm his vitals.

Another person might have gone scuttling off immediately. But Humblecut knew there was no rush. It was too late in the day for any ferries—to Cuttyhunk, Martha's Vineyard, or elsewhere—to set off. Joe and his minder would have spent a night in one of a handful of ramshackle inns near the South Boston docks, probably on Congress Avenue, which Humblecut knew well enough. That gave him plenty of time to visit these establishments, make casual inquiries, and determine the next—and perhaps ultimate—destination.

He put down the traveling valise beside him. The hunt itself was his second-favorite part of this kind of job. Originally, he'd been a member of the New York City Metropolitan Police, but they had always been more interested in fighting rival law enforcement agencies like the Municipals than in catching criminals. After a few years he left to join the Pinkerton Detective Agency, rising quickly in those early days, working directly with Allan Pinkerton and becoming part of Abraham Lincoln's personal security detail from 1862 through 1864. But the same personal characteristics that made him so good at investigation— Pinkerton himself called them "unhealthy"—had another, darker side that prompted him to leave the agency and become a journeyman. And it was not long after that he found Leng. Or perhaps Leng had found him; Humblecut, for all his perspicacity, had never been quite sure.

Now he rose from the bench, picked up his valise, and made for the nearest exit. One thing he was sure of: Leng did not harbor any priggish reservations about his methods. Nor did he get in the way of what, for Humblecut, was the best part of jobs such as this: leeway to proceed as he saw fit—once the quarry was caught.

It might, perhaps, have been useful if he'd maintained a contact or two at Pinkerton's—the detective agency was busy assembling the largest collection of what were termed "mug" shots in the country. But Blackwell's Island would never have bothered to take a picture of young Joe. Besides, Humblecut had very subtly gained two descriptions of the boy—one from the ticket agent, another from the barber—and in their own way, they were better than a photograph.

He left the station and headed for South Boston, his step now slightly brisker.

27

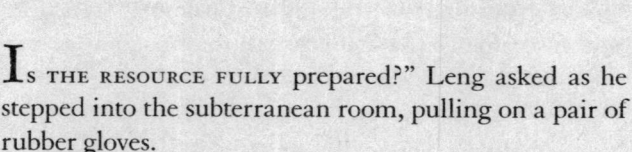

"Is the resource fully prepared?" Leng asked as he stepped into the subterranean room, pulling on a pair of rubber gloves.

"Yes, Doctor," said Munck, turning toward him. The short, powerfully built man was breathing heavily from exertion, and a bead of sweat trickled down his forehead, stopping at the fresh scar that served as a reminder of Constance Greene's fury.

"Excellent." Leng directed his gaze around the operating chamber to ensure all was prepared. Obtaining this resource off the street, where such an action could easily be witnessed, was dangerous, and he wanted to make sure the extraction process went like clockwork. Until that sanctimonious cleric was dealt with, he would have to undergo an excess of risk to obtain resources. But he was confident the Right Reverend Considine would soon be hastened to his reward in the next world and he could return to obtaining resources from the Mission: a far safer and easier method.

He finished his survey, satisfied everything was in

order. That spectral companion to the duchess, Pendergast, had breached his tunnels, no doubt in fury after finding the corpse of Ferenc. What a lovely surprise that must have been; Leng was sorry he hadn't been there to see the man's face. But though the fellow's explosives now prevented his gathering future resources from the site, the pale detective did not know of this hidden operating theater of his, located in a walled-off section of the old Stuyvesant aqueduct underneath Shottum's Cabinet. He could not help but be struck by the contrast of the weeping brick archways of the aqueduct with the gleaming metal walls that sealed this most modern and advanced of operating rooms situated within it. It gave him comfort to view the trays covered with glittering steel instruments that Munck had sharpened to perfection, the latest oak surgical table covered with oilcloth, the brilliant electrical light and reflector that ran from his own custom-made voltaic pile.

The extraction of the cauda equina had to be as precise and antiseptic as possible.

The cauda equina—"horse's tail" in Latin—was the bundle of nerves that diverged at the base of the spine into hundreds of gossamer-like strands. This miraculous biological structure was the very foundation of his Arcanum. Its extraction was only possible if postoperative recovery was not an issue. But the processing of the cauda equina into the Arcanum—the elixir of life extension for which he searched—required a chemical process of great complexity and precision, procedures and titrations that had so far eluded him. Perhaps that book the duchess had given him, seemingly written in his own future hand, had the answers. Perhaps not.

An additional problem was the resource itself. As he gazed down at the surgical table, he felt a twinge of dissatisfaction. This one was on the lean side, malnourished, pale. He would prefer to have had the time to fatten it up, but he was in a hurry. A tremendous hurry. It would have to do.

The resource—he'd already forgotten her name—was lying facedown on the oilcloth atop the surgical table. One of innumerable sad cases: abandoned, desperate—more proof (as if it were needed) of the worthlessness and suffering of the human species. She was covered with a crisp white sheet, hands and feet securely strapped, a thick wad of chloroform-doused cotton over her mouth and nose, held in place by gauze wound around her head. Leng knew that in Munck he had an assistant who took pleasure in preparing the resources—he himself found the inevitable struggling, screams, and pleas a tiresome prologue.

He gave a sharp nod, and Munck drew back the sheet, exposing the naked body.

A faint moan sounded. The chloroform was a minor sedative only, but it was all he could risk using. He had learned it was important to keep the resource conscious as long as possible, in order to harvest the nerves in an active state.

Now he approached the table, taking a last glance at the instrument tray to make sure all was in readiness. Munck stepped back, clutching the white sheet between his hands, eyes shining. Picking up a surgical scalpel, Leng expertly palpated the lower back with his fingers and thumb, locating each vertebra and mentally identifying them: T12, L1, L2. Then, with a single, decisive swipe, he severed the longissimus thoracis and other "true" muscles of the lower back. There was more noise now, but Leng did not notice: he was engrossed in his work and pleased with the start he'd made. Only a true surgeon would appreciate the skill it took to transect all four layers of deep back muscle with one stroke.

Using retractors, he exposed the laminae of the vertebrae, the curved sections of bone that made up the rear of the protective spinal ring. A medical chisel was sufficient to chip these away, along with the vertebral arches. After plucking away bits of interspinous ligaments with a forceps, he picked up a finer-bladed scalpel and opened the dura, clamped it away on both sides with retractors, and—scalpel in one hand, forceps in the other—probed the meninges of the spinal cord, looking for the precise place to cut.

...And there it was. He nodded to Munck, who presented a glass jar, partially filled with sterile water tinctured with a mild preservative. With the resource now motionless Leng made the final cuts, exposing his prize, freeing it from the peripheral nerves, and extracting it carefully with the forceps.

The anatomical perfection of the structure, its delicacy and intricacy, never ceased to impress him. How amazing were the works of God!

He submerged it with infinite care in the beaker, and Munck sealed the top and placed it in a small portable icebox kept for that purpose. Leng stepped back, then pulled off his mask and gloves while Munck turned his efforts to packing the open wound with gauze and covering the resource—now spent—with the sheet.

How amazing indeed, he thought again, were the works of God. But it seemed the Supreme Being cared too much for his creation—Leng could think of no other reason why such a destructive creature as man would be permitted to remain on earth. But that, in essence, was the foundation of his life's work.

What a kind and merciful God did not have the heart to do, Leng would do for Him.

28

Otto Bloom unrolled the soiled plat on the dining room table of the Park Avenue dwelling and pinned down the corners with lead weights. Three of his sandhogs looked on, dressed in work clothes and exceedingly ill at ease in the opulent surroundings. Bloom himself felt intimidated by the extreme wealth, as well as the way Alphonse Billington threw around huge sums of money for all kinds of crazy things.

"Well," he said, glancing up at his new employer, who was examining the plat with glittering eyes, "this is quite some plan of yours. I have to warn you: there will be rats."

"They are practically Manhattan's mascot."

"I'm talking about a *lot* of rats. When we unseal the reservoir of the old Collect Pond here, and its water floods the underground tunnels, the rats are going to flee in the only direction left to them—up."

"How interesting," said Billington.

Bloom shook his head. He wondered again what he'd gotten himself into, tangled up with this strange, pale man and his peculiar tasks. But the pay was high, and the work was preferable to the brutal and dangerous caissons of the Brooklyn Bridge, where dozens of his comrades had died. He was keenly aware that Billington had not told him all, or even most, of what he was doing, nor had he explained the spiritual gobbledygook that motivated his brother, whom Billington had mentioned but Bloom had yet to meet. Yet despite all the secrecy and unfathomable dealings, Bloom's instincts told him that Billington was a person of goodwill and integrity—and had ways to ensure the work they did, lawful or not, would appear to be so.

"Are you confident, Mr. Billington, that there's no one down in those old tunnels? Once the water comes, they won't be able to escape. I don't want to be responsible for . . . you know, drowning anyone."

"Bloom, the truth is there is probably one person, perhaps two, down there. But you can trust me when I tell you they are guilty of heinous crimes against humanity. A side effect of this operation is, in fact, to rid the world of their presence."

Bloom nodded. He *did* trust the man—although he didn't know exactly why. His men seemed to, as well.

Billington rubbed his hands together. "Now, Bloom, please tell me the plan you've devised."

Bloom smoothed down the plat with his calloused palms. "Just to warn you, sir: it was difficult to get this plat, and I'm not sure it's entirely accurate. The Collect Pond was drained and filled in about sixty years ago, but much of the water remains trapped in these reservoir canals, kept filled by underground springs. To stop the water from spreading, these holding canals were sealed off from the rest of the old aqueduct complex, which is now free of water. That's what we're going to flood—these tunnels, here and here. There may be—in fact, there certainly *are*—other tunnels and abandoned spaces down there, not recorded on the plat, that may also be flooded."

"I hope to flood them all. But is there any danger the water might rise above ground level?"

"No. The water won't rise farther than its natural level, which is well below the street and most of the current basements in the area."

"Where will you put your charges?"

"The way I've worked it out, my men will enter at these access points. Three charges will be set: here, here, and here, each timed to detonate more or less simultaneously. Once these connections have been blown, the water will issue from these transverse aqueducts, meet in the middle, then spread out to flood the rest of the old reservoir tunnels."

"Excellent. And how long do you estimate this will take?"

"Not long at all. Ten minutes, perhaps." He glanced at the three men, who were eyeing the plat with furrowed brows. "These are reliable men, and they've been thoroughly briefed."

The men shuffled awkwardly at the praise. Billington straightened up and turned to them. "You're clear on what to do?"

"Yes, sir," they said.

"You will all be handsomely rewarded."

"Thank you, sir."

"It goes without saying," Billington went on, "that everything we do here, as at Smee's Alley, is totally confidential. The consequences of idle chatter, barroom bragging, and so forth would be severe, if not fatal."

None of Bloom's men were under any illusion that this work was ordinary, or even legal, and they all nodded their understanding.

Billington withdrew a gold watch, glanced at it, then turned to Bloom. "Midnight is approaching. Mr. Bloom, I wait upon your leisure."

29

H. P. Munck removed his soiled steel-toed boots, leaving them outside the iron door of the room, and tiptoed inside in bare feet. The plush Persian carpet tickled his toes—horned with calluses—in a most luxurious way. Holding up his kerosene lantern, he paused to take in the opulence. It still smelled slightly foul—the recent corpse of that man, Ferenc—but he was not one to find such a natural stench off-putting. Quite the contrary.

He took several more steps into the room. The bed, piled with rich coverings and overtopped with a satin puff, had not been made since he'd removed the corpse, but it nevertheless looked inviting, the clammy air of the room merely adding to the coziness. Taking a small taper from his pocket, he lit it from the lantern, then applied the flame to the many candles that had been placed about the room, filling it with a warm, flickering light.

Ahhhh, thought Munck. This was delightful. He was tired—very tired. Master had kept him especially busy of late, and Munck hadn't had any time to himself in weeks. Until this morning.

The candles having been lit, he approached the bed and crawled in feetfirst, and then drew the covers up to his chin. As he lay, feeling the cold sheets warm up, he thought about how perfect this moment of privacy promised to be. The smells, the knowledge of what had taken place here—all that was missing was... Wait! Just as he was turning his head on the pillows and closing his eyes, he made out a few droplets of dried blood. They must have oozed from Ferenc's ear after his death but still been fresh when his body was laid here: a present for the Pale One.

For a *Hämophile* such as Munck, this was now truly perfection. As he grew nice and toasty, he reached into his pocket and withdrew a silver flask, raising it to his lips to take a long pull on the contents—raw, unfiltered vodka from his native village of Elkhotovo, rare and expensive, available only in the small Russian ghetto of Hamilton Heights, a mile or so east of the master's mansion.

As the liquid burned its way down his throat, old memories came back—the days of his youth, before Russia's almost total extermination of his native Circassian lands—and the depravity and carnage he'd witnessed. But it was not the violence and bloodshed of Tsarist Russia that he dwelt on, but rather scenes of depravity and carnage he'd committed on his own, hidden for the most part by the greater genocide going on all around him. Another sip of the harsh liquid, and the memories grew still more vivid. Eyes closed, he murmured words in a strange tongue as he nuzzled against the bloody pillow.

Abruptly, his mind snapped back to the present. He'd heard a noise: a distant *crump!* followed by two more in rapid succession. *Crump, crump!* With each, a faint shudder had passed through the stone walls.

What was that?

He listened intently, but no more sounds came to his

ears. It had been distant—and as the silence stretched on, he decided it was nothing to be concerned about. He once again drew up the covers and closed his eyes, his mind returning to a particularly arousing incident in which he had taken a long—but again, his stream of bloody reveries was interrupted. This time, it had been by a faint breeze stirring his greasy hair.

A breeze, down here? He didn't recollect ever noticing one before. How was that possible?

And then another sound reached him, very different this time: like the whispering of a distant storm, mingled with a strange chorus of squeaking and squealing. It was drawing closer—and growing rapidly in intensity.

Munck sat bolt upright. He recognized the squeaking. It was rats: many, many rats. He had no idea what the whispering was, except it was rising fast—and coming his way.

He got out of bed, went to the half-open iron door of the room, and stuck out his head. The wind in the tunnel was, incredibly, not only strong, but increasing, carrying with it the commotion of the rats. And underneath that horrible chorus of squealing, that other sound was growing louder: not so much a whisper as it was like the continuous reverberation of surf.

He stepped partway outside, holding his lantern up to cast light farther along the tunnel, and saw an astonishing sight: hundreds—thousands—of tiny glowing eyes jittering and bobbing toward him. It was a multitude, an army, of rats—running his way in frenzied panic.

Just as they reached him, he jumped back into the room to avoid being overwhelmed. But none of them had any interest in swarming his chamber. Instead, they just streamed past as he watched, their coarsely bristled tails glistening pink, their bodies mangy, filling the corridor with their squeal and stink.

Munck had a most vivid imagination, but even he could not begin to guess what was happening, or why. He stood, dumbfounded, until the stampede had finally passed, leaving only a few crippled or sick animals in their wake. He'd been so dumbstruck at the sight of the leaping, crawling rodents that at first he didn't notice that the wind had continued to rise and, along with it, that other sound—growing in volume until it was a deafening roar, loud as an approaching train.

Suddenly, Munck understood: water. Not just water: a subterranean flood. He quickly pivoted away from the sound, intending to flee down the corridor in the same direction as the rats, but he was too late. With a roar, a wall of black water came barreling down the tunnel, moving like a living thing, the force of it knocking him back into the room and pushing the iron door shut. Munck scrambled to his feet in a panic: the door, he knew, was designed to lock itself from the outside.

He was trapped.

The door shook from the force of the water, torrents of foul viscous liquid squirting from under the sill and pouring out of a feeding slot in the door, the pressure of its gush quickly covering the floor.

"*No!*" Munck cried as he tried to slide the feeding slot shut, but the pressure of the water made it impossible. More gushes were surging in from beneath the door.

Water was now filling the room with astonishing rapidity, icy cold and horribly greasy, swirling around his ankles and surging upward, first to his calves, then his thighs. He cried and pounded on the iron door, but he knew no one could hear him—let alone save him. Even if he could open the door himself, he would be drowned in the rush of water beyond. The water swirled about, and as it rose it formed a violent whirlpool that circled the room and began snuffing out the candles. This flood couldn't keep up, the water couldn't keep rising...and yet it did. Munck placed the lantern as high over his head as he could, atop a bureau, then climbed into the bed that smelled of death and pulled the covers up above his head, wrapping himself in a resignation of abject terror. Even though he shut his eyes tightly, he felt the water top the level of the mattress and flood into the sheets, churning around and invading his cocoon; he felt it rise and rise, flooding him until he was choking and spitting. Then it rose above his head and he found himself floating, his mind collapsing in confusion as the clothes and blankets dragged him down from the roiling surface. When his head slipped beneath it and he could no longer take in air, he held his breath until he could hold it no more—then, in an automatic and unstoppable physical reaction, breathed in the frigid black liquid, and that was the end.

30

COMFORTABLE WITHIN THE RECESSES of his coach, curtains partially drawn, Murphy at the reins, Pendergast waited. They stood on the corner of Little Water Street and Anthony Street, as deep into the heart of the Five Points as Murphy would go, the horses wearing heavy blinders and their bits tight under the reins. Around the coach were decrepit tenements, with strings of laundry hanging over the street, itself piled with uncollected garbage and coal ash, prowled by emaciated cats and furtive, abandoned children. His gold watch was in his hand. Even though half past nine on a Monday morning was normally a relatively tranquil time in the slum, Pendergast's carriage might nevertheless have been overwhelmed by curious residents, save for the underground explosions that had occurred as they pulled up, exactly three minutes before.

"*Jesus!*" Murphy abruptly yelled. And then a moment later, as if finishing an equation, he added: "*Mary and Joseph!*"

Pendergast drew back the curtain and peered outside.

He had seen many incredible sights in his life, wondrous and terrible, ghastly and awe inspiring—but he had never seen anything quite like a cityscape becoming suddenly engulfed in rats. They poured out of every drain, every cellar hole, every ditch and manhole and crack and hollow: a streaming horde of wild, insane, gibbering rats, all tumbling over each other, biting and thrashing, accompanied by a deafening chorus of squealing and squeaking. Pendergast had never seen so many rats; he'd had no idea so many rats could exist in one place. They poured through the streets and alleyways, tributaries into rivers into deltas and then, at last, into a living ocean of brown and pink, frantically seeking escape or cover, streaming past and underneath the carriage, some trying to climb its wheels or scrabble up its slick, varnished sides. The entire floor of the city seemed to shudder and rock.

Despite their expert training, the horses began to prance and stamp in fear. Murphy wielded his whip, expertly flicking off one rat after another as they tried to climb aboard. "*Sir!*" he cried, a note of panic in his voice. "Sir, we better be moving on!"

"Stay just a bit longer, please. It will be over soon, I promise."

As the rats slowly began to thin out, a growing hiss could be heard over their shrieks—the sound of pressurized air being forced from the same holes, vents, and openings the rats had come, blowing out bits of trash and effluence with it. And then came an unfamiliar noise, but one Pendergast presumed was the hollow sound of water swilling in caves, coming from everywhere and nowhere at once.

The few people in the street had fled in terror at the invasion. Now, with a rhythmic sloshing, the sounds gradually died away until, ten minutes later, all had grown still once more. A most unusual silence fell on Little Water Street, now empty of both rats and people, the winter mists settling down again as if nothing had happened—only a sticky layer of short, matted, brownish-black hairs, clinging knee-high to every surface, to show where the flood of rats had passed.

"Thank you for indulging me, Murphy," said Pendergast, with a rap of his cane on the carriage roof. "You may drive on."

31

Pieter De Jong scraped marmalade over his toast with the same slow, methodical deliberation he employed in all things. The toast was just to his liking: baked on the hearth that morning, a faint burst of steam rising with a crackle of crust as the cook first sliced it; the marmalade was made by his maiden aunt and shipped to him from Delft. Every bite reminded him of his childhood.

Although it was winter, the sun was out—and not all work on the farm could wait for spring. He heard the bleating of sheep in the ten-acre bottomland, and the calls of William, his factotum, to the sheepdog as he kept them from straying. Just a few years ago, New York City had carved its latest borough, the Bronx, out of the western edge of Westchester, which included his farm. This did not trouble him; the area remained rural, and his thirty acres—surrounded as they were by other dairy farms—would not be encroached upon. The road had been somewhat improved, and that had been a godsend: it allowed him to transport his prize cheeses across

Hell Gate and south, to the eagerly waiting grocers and restaurateurs of Manhattan.

"Some more toast, Master De Jong?" asked Clara, the housekeeper.

"No, thank you, Clara. Please tell the cook she hasn't lost her touch with the bread."

"I'll do that, sir." Clara curtsied and left the breakfast room.

With a contented sigh, De Jong returned his attention to the *New York Star*, perusing it from front to back, occasionally grunting in approval or displeasure as one article or another caught his eye. He didn't get out to the farm often enough, and he enjoyed the relaxed, pastoral air. But at last he took out his pocket watch and peered at it. Ten o'clock: time to get busy with chores.

Enoch Leng had created several identities with meticulous care, of which Pieter De Jong was one. Some, like the good doctor Leng himself, required frequent curation, while others—such as this pastoral Dutch farmer in Whitlock Dell, West Farms, New York—needed only infrequent effort. Each of his identities was of unimpeachable pedigree and could stand a thorough background check. He was equally careful in choosing his staff. In this regard, the insane ward at Bellevue had proved a veritable cornucopia of potential talent. William, for example, out tending the flock—he'd been locked up for expressing a strong desire to eat his older brother. After several examinations and interviews, Leng decided this request was not as outrageous as it seemed on the surface; the brother, a vile person, had abused William abominably as a child. Leng intuited that William would be forever grateful if given the opportunity to achieve his heart's desire. This Leng was able to arrange without much difficulty. After the repast was complete, Leng took on the appreciative—and quite handy—William as farm help. Clara, on the other hand, had the occasional need to burn down a building. As long as she was given a day off once or twice a year to do so, and assisted in locating a suitable target, she was the best of housekeepers. Several others had required the use of a surgical device of Leng's own design, which resembled an icepick; this device was inserted into the brain through the lower edge of the orbital socket and then given a very specific up-and-down wiping motion. The operation worked wonders, turning the most refractory patients docile and obedient—and, under Leng's grooming, fanatically loyal, with none of the normal ethical constraints that might encumber ordinary servants.

Leng passed through the rooms of the large old farmhouse, exited through a side door, then crossed snow-encrusted stubble to a wedge-shaped structure with two metal doors rearing out of the ground: the cheese cellar. He removed the padlock with a key, pocketed it, and pulled one of the heavy doors wide with a grunt. Stone steps led down into darkness. A kerosene lamp hung on a peg nearby and, lighting it, he began to descend.

The cellar was deep—thirty steps into the earth. One reason his cheeses were in such demand at the city's finest restaurants was the hay, wildflowers, and pasture grasses unique to the soil of his farm; another was the cellar itself. Carved deep into the pink feldspar of the land's substratum, it afforded the ideal, constant temperature and humidity for his cheeses to deepen in flavor and complexity as they aged.

Reaching the bottom landing, he moved down a long corridor whose stone walls curved into a groined archway overhead. As he passed, he glanced over the rows of cheese stacked on both sides, sitting on wooden shelves and marble trestles, observing the progress of their aging. A number were now ready for sale: his finest crumbly sharp cheddars, aged up to three years; a nutty Gruyère that he found needed fifteen months to bring out its natural firmness; and the pride of the De Jong cellars—grana Padano, an Italian cheese no one else in America knew the secret of—voluptuous yet fine-grained, with a faintly sweet flavor.

Reaching the end of the storage area, he descended a few more steps to another, heavier door, which he unlocked. In the room beyond, he turned up the lamps until what was obviously a laboratory became visible.

On one table sat a tray of test tubes in a centrifuge ring full of liquid. This marvelous device had been invented less than a decade earlier for separating milk from cream. Leng had found a more important use for it. He picked up one of the test tubes and held it to his eye, examining it for both color and viscosity.

Perfect. He knew from prior research this light saffron color was the hallmark of a properly prepared elixir, but he had never before achieved such clarity and uniformity. Perhaps Constance had given him the true Arcanum after all. Time would tell.

He reached into a drawer, pulled out a syringe of metal and glass, and filled it from the tube. Then he returned the tube to its rack, dimmed the lights of the laboratory, and—keeping the syringe behind his back—unlocked and entered a door at the rear of the lab.

Beyond was a small, spartan room, with a bed, a desk, a clothes hanger, and an armchair. None of these, nor the single print on the wall, helped alleviate the cell-like claustrophobia. The room was lit by a single lamp, set high on one wall. There was a chamber pot under the bed, and a tray of plates covered with half-eaten food on the desk.

A girl in her late teens lay on the bed, dozing fitfully. Rousing herself at the sound of his entry, she sat up.

"Dr. Leng!" she said.

"Hello, my dear," Leng answered, in a gentle voice, as he approached.

"I'm so frightened. You said you'd explain everything—ouch, what's this?"

He smoothly injected the fluid into her plump arm.

"Just some vitamins." He glanced disapprovingly at the half-eaten food. "You really need to eat more—it's important to keep up your strength. Clara will bring you some fresh oranges."

"How can I eat while stuck in this cell, Doctor?"

Leng sat down on the bed and took her hand in his. "I did explain everything, you know... Perhaps you don't remember. Quite understandable. There was an outbreak of smallpox, and I had to move you from the hospital before we were all quarantined." He paused. "It's a severe outbreak, a true pestilence; had we stayed, I fear it would have done you mischief."

"But what about my brother, my—"

"Everyone is fine. You just have to be patient," Dr. Leng said, patting her hand, then releasing it and rising again. "I'll have Clara bring you fresh sheets and bathwater with the oranges—you'll feel better afterward. And you won't have to wait much longer down here—I understand the pestilence is beginning to subside."

Leng moved quickly toward the door and grasped the handle. "Just a week, perhaps a little more. I promise."

She looked at him. "Promise?"

"Yes, Mary. I promise."

PART TWO

Things Fall Apart

32

They arrived at the garish brownstone on the outskirts of the Tenderloin district at different intervals between midnight and one. First came the dandy, an obviously wealthy English fop whose mincing gait and exaggerated Oxbridge accent were reminiscent of so many callow younger sons of the peerage sent on "grand tours" to get them out of the way. Next came the traveling purveyor of dry goods, recently arrived in New York for an annual company meeting, whose very attempts at being inconspicuous in this high-priced house of turpitude were made all the more risible by his hayseed accent and awkward manners. He passed through the gaudy parlor, gaped in astonishment at the ladies lounging about on sofas and ottomans, dropped his hat in an attempt to doff it, then—after getting his bearings—ascended the stairs.

Last came the nightingale: the expensive lady of easy virtue, whose well-appointed charms could be had by the hour. The English dandy had paid the proprietress for the use of a large set of rooms on the third floor, and nothing about these two additional arrivals excited the faintest of curiosity in the parlor. Other groups of various sizes and compositions had already come in that evening, bent on celebrating the New Year, and more would be arriving soon enough.

* * *

Closing the door to the third-floor suite, Pendergast took off his ill-fitting hat and shrugged out of the shabby salesman's overcoat. Diogenes was already seated in a gaudy Louis XV armchair, one that clashed appallingly with the rest of the furniture, a mishmash of faux pieces from other French periods. His back was to the door, but he glanced up briefly into a framed mirror, saw Pendergast, then returned his attention to a notebook balanced on one knee.

Pendergast looked around: at the huge four-poster bed with fringed canopy; the painted dressers and wardrobes; the various basins of fine china, already filled with water for *post-laborem* washing.

"Aren't you going to get out of that ridiculous costume?" he asked his brother.

"This 'ridiculous costume,' as you call it, is my armor. It protects me from those who might seek out the Right Reverend Considine for assassination. It is also the uniform of the other life I now lead here: a certain Lord Cedric. I rather enjoy that life and the extracurricular opportunities it offers."

At Diogenes's mention of his other life, a pained expression crossed Pendergast's face. "Speaking of Considine, how has Leng reacted? Does he suspect?"

"Not at all. Leng is so annoyed at being deprived of his victims that I suspect he will soon make an attempt on my life. I've grown adept at inflicting on him the finer points of Methodism, and in his rage he suspects nothing."

"I'm glad to hear that." Pendergast's eye fell on the notebook Diogenes had just opened. The page consisted of a list of names, of which he could make out only the first few:

Martha Jane Cannary
Clarissa H. Barton
Anna Mary Robertson

"What's this?" Pendergast asked, as Diogenes finished drawing a line through the first name. "Martha Jane Cannary?"

"Better known as Calamity Jane," said Diogenes, flashing a grin.

"And Clarissa Barton, no doubt better known in our day as Clara... Precisely what depraved extracurricular opportunities are you availing yourself of?"

"That, *Frater*, is none of your affair," Diogenes replied, closing the book at the same moment that Constance opened the door.

The brothers, as one, looked over at her while she silently entered. Her disguise was so effective in its promise of loose sensuality, its disturbing mix of elegance and poor taste, that for a moment neither could say a word.

She took off her hat and hair netting and came over, glancing each of them up and down as if to assure herself neither had suffered serious harm in her absence. From the ease with which she moved, it was equally clear the injuries sustained from her altercation with Munck had healed.

"Let's proceed with this meeting, shall we?" she said. "The winter wind off the Hudson is positively Siberian tonight."

Pendergast frowned. "Very well. As agreed, this is the one meeting we dare allow ourselves before we complete our tasks and get in position. And since we last met, you've calculated the date by which we must be ready. Correct?"

Constance nodded.

"Then let us go over our individual progress and finalize our strategies. Leaving room for the unexpected—if we can."

"Unexpected developments are Leng's stock in trade," said Diogenes. He slipped the notebook into a pocket of his waistcoat. "Have you arranged for my access to the alleyway?"

"Yes."

"This fellow Bloom knows all that he needs to know—but no more?"

"He does," Pendergast said, taking a seat himself, "and I'd suggest you pay him a visit, make his acquaintance, and see what he's done." He turned to Constance. "You're sure that Binky is no longer in the Riverside Drive mansion?"

Constance tugged her white gloves tighter and spread her fingers, like a cat unsheathing its claws. "She is not."

"Do you have any further suggestions to add?"

"Not particularly. She has left Riverside Drive, so I *suggest* you get on with your mission, Aloysius—find her."

Pendergast's normally unreadable face creased with irritation. "That is my intention," he said almost coldly. "Let us get down to particulars, shall we?"

Constance seated herself on a chaise lounge. It was clear Pendergast's mood had darkened since her arrival. Diogenes looked from one to the other. Then he bent forward, elbows upon his knees, and they began a murmured conversation.

33

Constance estimated that the conference between the three of them could not have lasted over twenty minutes. When all the necessary points had been covered, Diogenes rose.

"I believe we've talked enough," he said. "I've completed the lion's share of *my* assignment already—cutting off Leng's supply of victims from the workhouse. But just to be sure: Constance, you said that—given Leng's methods—we have until January ninth to get all the chess pieces in place?"

She nodded. "Within a day or so, yes. After that, Leng will have made ironclad arrangements for my siblings that... effectively, will render everything we've done, or tried to do, useless."

Diogenes thought a moment. "This deadline—unfortunate word, under the circumstances—doesn't leave us much time. However, since there are no other options, I'll proceed with arranging an emergency signal, in the manner we've just agreed on—with the hope that all goes well for you both in the interim. Yes?"

Constance nodded, and after a moment Pendergast did as well. It was clear to her they all believed that—however necessary—this assignment for Diogenes remained an exercise in wishful thinking.

"Just so the two of you know," Constance said in a low voice. "Even if we fail, and the deadline comes and goes—there is one thing that I *will be certain* to accomplish."

"And what is that?" Pendergast asked, a note of alarm in his voice. "Why spring this melodrama upon us now—once we've already gone over our plans?"

Constance did not reply.

"I am allergic to melodrama," Diogenes said. "And Horace was right when he said: *Indignor quandoque bonus dormitat Homerus*. Let me deal with this accursed signal, so I can return my full attention to debauchery once again. Can you not hear it, crying out from the haunts of iniquity and demanding my attention? Such a delicious world this is! So for now, *adieu*." He walked over to the coatrack, donned his cape with a flourish, gave a low bow, and left the suite.

Pendergast remained silent for a long moment. Then he glanced over at Constance. She could see an unusual flush of anger in his pale face. "Constance, I find your attitude to be, frankly, not only willful, but ungrateful."

"'Ungrateful'?" she repeated acerbically as she stood up. "That would be ungenerous of me indeed, given how poorly I was making out *before* you arrived here... neither invited nor expected." She held up a fist before his face—aware that her limbs were trembling with repressed emotion—and began raising her fingers, one after another. "What had I accomplished? Oh, yes. *First*: I had established an identity as a European duchess, with the pedigree, household, and wealth necessary to maintain it. *Second*: I had rescued both Joe and Binky and brought them safely under my wing. *Third*: I had contacted Leng directly, put him off balance, and made my demands clear. Had you not blundered into my carefully laid plans, the four of us would already be far away from here: a family once again, sailing for lands where he'd never follow. Never—because as soon as I had made Mary safe, I would have killed him."

Pendergast stood as well, listening in icy silence. Then he placed his hand over hers, folding her fingers back down into her palm. "*Fourth*," he said, "instead of this fantasy you fondly imagine, a more accurate picture would be this: all of you dead by now, tortured at the hands of Leng—or, worse, awaiting the bite of his scalpel into your lower back."

"That's ridiculous."

"You blame me for blundering in and confounding your plans. That's clear enough. But what I 'blundered' into—at that ball where you literally danced with the devil; and later, when you flirted with him at lunch— was the spectacle of a woman unknowingly headed for the slaughterhouse door."

Constance was taken aback. This was Aloysius as she had never heard him before—brusque, lacking the courtesy with which he habitually treated her. From the meeting just concluded, she'd already sensed he was acting with uncharacteristic recklessness—destroying Shottum's basement, flooding the subterranean tunnels of the Five Points. She realized this impulsiveness stemmed from anger, even fury.

And yet she felt her own anger rise at this presumption— Aloysius, daring to be angry? He had disregarded her express intentions, entered her world, and spoiled her plans. His irritation was as hypocritical as the swordsman who, upon decapitating Marie Antoinette, grew annoyed when her blood stained his shoes. And it was the last straw.

Snatching away the hand he'd just forced closed, she slapped him. His face went pale, with just a blush where her hand had struck him, and his eyes glittered dangerously.

"It was all going perfectly until you came. I had Leng precisely where I wanted him."

"You had him as a doomed rabbit has a fox when caught in its jaws. Leng, where *you* wanted him? Quite the reverse. He was simply enjoying the spectacle, toying with you, as you foolishly exulted in your so-called success."

"Spectacle?" she raged. "This was *my* home, *my* world—" Her throat grew tight with emotion, and for a moment she could not speak. "Make all the excuses you want, but your meddling is what ruined everything... and killed Mary."

He stood his ground. "This is not your home," he said. "It is not your time. It's not even your universe. This delusional image you paint of your 'family,' sailing happily off to lands unknown... it never would have happened. The decades you spent in his house have left you blind to how consummately clever Leng is, and—"

"This *is* my home—as much as I can ever have one! You think my home is back on Riverside Drive, with you? I had to escape. You were cold. And what's worse—indifferent."

"Cold? Indifferent? I've been good to you in every way."

"Is being good to me sharing only a sliver of your life—denying me the part of you I most wanted?"

"I always treated you with the utmost respect and decency."

"Decency?" She was almost crying. "If only you'd showed me a little less of your damned *decency*."

"What would you have me do?"

"Be human. Give in to impulse. Be *indecent* for a change, and not such a weak-kneed prude!"

She could see from his expression this had struck home, and she was glad. Before he could respond, she went on. "And then the heartlessness you showed by following me to this place, even as I was trying to put the misery and loneliness behind me. Didn't the note I left make it clear? Did you even *read* it?"

She raised her hand to strike him again, but this time he caught her wrist. The ferocity of her intended strike unbalanced her, and she tipped forward against his chest. When she tried to pull back her arm he continued to hold it in a grip of iron.

"Let me go!"

He said nothing, pulling her closer to him, his face inches from hers. She felt the sudden warmth of his breath; she could see his pupils dilate in the ice-chip eyes, see the mark of her slap blossoming on the alabaster of his cheek.

"I read it a thousand times," he said, his voice low and urgent. "I know it better than you do yourself."

"Prove it."

"*I see my own lonely, loveless future,*" he said, voice lower still. "*If I can't have you on my own terms, I can't have—*"

But he was abruptly silenced as Constance pulled him still closer, joining her mouth with his. There was the briefest of intervals—brief, yet strangely limitless in its counterpoise of anger and hunger—and then they came together in a passionate embrace.

34

Diogenes Pendergast walked along Central Park South, slowly swinging a billy club by its leather strap and whistling "She Was Poor but She Was Honest," a tune that seemed to be on everyone's lips that season. He had temporarily exchanged his foppish dress for the uniform of the Metropolitan Police—a disguise that both made him forgettable and ensured he could do almost anything without arousing curiosity.

Not that there would be any witnesses: it was two in the morning, and he had only the gas lamps for company.

Ahead and to the right rose a dark outline that, he thought with distaste, resembled the "Big Ciggy"—the grotesque Skidmore, Owings & Merrill sculpture that, a century in the future, would dominate a section of the Richmond, Virginia, skyline. The half-completed structure thrust up into the sky like a square straw, devoid of decoration. Tiny slots punctuated its flanks, following an invisible spiral, like the arrow slits of Caernarfon Castle. These, Diogenes assumed, were for wind bracing. The full moon threw a spectral illumination over its bulk, and he could see that its surface was covered in brick for perhaps two-thirds of its height: above that rose a wooden skeleton and steel frame. This was the work of Daniel Burnham, architect and developer, and it was awaiting the final delivery of bricks and precut steel.

He moved closer. Peering into one of the lower slits, he could make out a plumb bob, a sort of pendulum made from a string with a piece of chalk fixed to its base and touching a slate board—a rude implement for measuring the sway of the tower in the wind.

Unfinished, its top partially exposed to the elements, it was easy to see why the eccentric-looking thing was already being called "Burnham's Folly." It had none of the finishing touches that would make it the observation tower scheduled to open in three months. But Burnham's intentions were still bigger: in Chicago, bids were currently being taken for the commission to design the Montauk Building. That, Diogenes knew, was where Burnham's true interest lay: in constructing the tallest building in America—at fourteen stories, taller than either the Equitable Building or the Tribune Building, both erected in Manhattan over the last ten years. And in the future universe of Diogenes, Burnham *had* succeeded in building the Montauk—one of the most spectacular high-rises built up to that time, even though it enjoyed only a short life, being demolished around 1900. *This* ugly tower was the one thing that, to him, seemed an anomaly of this place—a construct that never existed in the Central Park of his own world. It was a vulgar and intrusive excrescence.

Stepping smartly up to the barricade erected around the structure, he undid the padlock with a policeman's skeleton key and slipped inside. The base of the tower was surrounded by construction site detritus: piles of dirt, sawhorses, cut bricks, and pieces of steel. One foundation section was still exposed, and Diogenes noted the massive footings.

He made his way through the clutter and reached the entrance to the tower itself, which he unlocked with the same method. No workmen would be on site, day or night, until the rest of the building materials arrived. No guards were on hand, either, if for no other reason than there was nothing worth stealing.

After closing the door behind him, Diogenes lit a dark lantern. In one corner, surrounded by worktables, stood a small steel room, fashioned out of sheet metal, carefully welded. This functioned as a vault in which tools and other things of value were normally kept. Its door was set in place with a combination lock.

Diogenes approached the lock and twisted the dial right, then left, then right until the tumblers fell into place. The interior of the vault contained an array of equipment and four small, stout wooden boxes, covered with a drop cloth. Aloysius had been as good as his word: his man, Bloom, had contrived to have the fraternity of New York construction workers drop off the boxes earlier in the evening. Setting the lantern on a peg, he stepped in, pulled away the tarp, and—grabbing a nearby claw hammer—pried off their tops. He examined the neatly stacked red tubes of black powder with their coils of fuses, caps, and plaster inside.

He spent the next half hour gingerly carrying the sticks of explosives up the wooden steps and affixing them at various well-hidden spots. He made his way upward until, at last, he placed the final load directly beneath the wooden ceiling.

He paused to catch his breath, sitting on one of the steps and unbuttoning the top of his policeman's overcoat. The moonlight, which had not deserted him during the last half hour, shone not only through the tall narrow windows, but also faintly through the cracks in a rectangular shape in the heavily braced ceiling. This, he realized, was the opening to the unfinished viewing parapet. Placing his palms against it, he dislodged it, then hoisted himself up onto the surface.

On the roof, there were not yet railings or posts of any kind: each side of the wooden square dropped off into darkness. Diogenes approached the south edge. He did not suffer from vertigo, but he nevertheless braced himself against the wind gusts that came and went at this height, which he estimated to be one hundred and seventy-five feet above ground.

As he raised his glance from the supporting platform and looked out over the city, he forgot all about the wind. There, below him, was the heart of Manhattan. Directly under his feet, where Central Park met a line of new apartment buildings and hotels, was the "Grand Circle" that, in ten more years, would host a statue of Christopher Columbus. Beyond it, Broadway ran crookedly south, breaking the otherwise neat grid of streets until it encountered the maze of alleys and lanes south of Houston. Despite the late hour, and the emptiness of the streets, faint sounds rose up to greet him: the nicker of a horse, a shout of laughter. The city was breathing, but it was a peaceful breathing... nothing like the garish cacophony of twenty-first-century New York. He could see countless twinkling lights, gas lamps illuminating the streets and margins of lower Manhattan with tiny jets of fire—but there were more, many more, that he could see only indirectly, shining within windows and from alleyways, and these gave the city a mysterious lambent glow, only increasing for Diogenes the sensation that he was staring down upon a living thing.

This was his new home—his domain. This was the place upon which he would make his mark. For all its technology, all its advances, the twenty-first century was sterile, insipid, and pitiless. It had been exceptionally cruel to him—and he to it. It was a flabby world, ruled by detumescent Babbitts, where ease had replaced vigor; a world *nihilo ac malem*.

He took a step back as this sudden, unexpected transport of emotion threatened to carry him over the edge. He stood still a moment, letting the strong wave of feeling pass and his breathing return to normal.

Now that everything was in place, he had only to attach fuses to each charge as he descended, each one of a length he'd already calculated. Not for the first time, he wondered why he was going for such overkill: the load beneath the roof was perfectly sufficient. But no: removing this excrescence in its entirety would be his opening gift—his housewarming present, so to speak—to 1881.

He slipped down into the tower, pulled the ceiling cover back into place, and picking up the dark lantern, descended the stairs one last time, uncoiling and attaching the fuses, ensuring that all his handiwork had been properly secreted away, before returning once again to the city.

His city.

35

ONCE AGAIN, THE DINGHY passed through the rustling weeds along the banks of the Hudson and into the hidden passageway, Constance silently dipping the oars. The lantern hung in the bow cast a dim light down the stone passageway as the boat eased forward, until finally the landing came into view. She steadied the boat against the stone quay, tied the painter to the bronze ring, and unloaded an oilskin duffel of fresh supplies. She stepped out herself and, slinging the bag over her shoulders, opened the hidden doorway and crept along the tunnel beyond, until she had passed under the Boston Post Road and entered the sub-basement of the Riverside Drive mansion.

Constance made her way to the blind she had chosen as a hiding place and set down her duffel. As she sank onto the crude cot, covered with a mattress of straw and canvas ticking, she had to force herself not to close her eyes. She hadn't had a moment to think, or muse, since the night before.

She contemplated the small stone chamber that,

almost two centuries earlier, had been the treasure room of the privateer king whose stronghold had been replaced, years earlier, by Leng's mansion. The chamber, and most of the surrounding passages, had been carved out of the natural bedrock. The half dozen gold ducats and scattering of crude gemstones remaining in the cracks and corners led her to assume the pirate had vacated his lair in a hurry.

She'd intended to return here the night before, under cover of darkness, directly after the meeting with Diogenes and Aloysius. But she had been significantly delayed, and dawn was breaking by the time she exited the house in the Tenderloin district. Nevertheless, she'd put the day to good use. First, she'd stopped at a purveyor of gently used women's clothing—well made, simple, but out of fashion—and used a dressing room there to change into a new outfit, leaving her brothel-style dress behind. She'd walked a mile along back alleyways before hailing a cab, which she directed to her town house on Fifth Avenue. She entered to the amazement of Féline, Gosnold, and the servants. This unexpected arrival, she hoped, would further confuse Leng and his spies regarding her comings and goings.

Once she had settled the household's nerves with a combination of half-truths and lies, she retired with Féline to her private study. The young Frenchwoman was recovering well from her injuries, but she, like the others, was distressed by the current state of the house. Constance had no time to waste in commiseration; there were vital affairs to settle and little time to do it.

She explained her plans to Féline. The private secretary was aghast and pleaded with Constance to change her mind. Ultimately, however, she was forced to concede the logic behind her mistress's intentions. Constance then sent her out to summon the lawyer with whom she had already done business. He arrived; Constance explained what she wanted, then overrode his protestations at the legal irregularity with the help of an extra-large fee. She waited while he drew up the paperwork, then reviewed and signed it, with Féline as witness. Lastly, she took Féline aside for a few final words, and they embraced.

By this time, it was dark. Constance donned black, close-fitting clothes, took up a small traveling satchel, and slipped out a basement window into the dim alleyway behind the house as quietly and invisibly as a cat.

She had made a show of her arrival, but she intended for her departure to remain unseen. Flitting westward from alley to alley, she ultimately gained the Hudson River and the shoreline weeds where she had hidden her dinghy. She rowed up the river, once again with the tide, to the pirate's secret entrance.

Now, in the silent stone chamber, she gazed meditatively at the tallow candle whose guttering light illuminated her washbasin, the unopened satchel, a whetstone, and a dog-eared copy of the poems of Catullus. It was odd: when she'd returned to the past of her childhood, she had expected to be confronted by long-forgotten memories. What she had not anticipated were the specific things that would trigger them. This cheap candle, for instance—its gray-black smoke, coiling toward a small vent in the ceiling, just now resurrected a ghostly image of her mother, sprinkling salt on a candle precisely like this one in order to extend its burn time. It was the most ephemeral of memories, thin as gossamer and just as fragile.

Constance shook it away. Now was not the time to indulge in reminiscence. She rose up and, lighting a taper from the dying flame, moved out of the chamber into a clammy stone tunnel.

Leng had owned the mansion for only five years, but

he was already filling the basement with a collection of weapons, torture devices, anatomical relics, poisons, chemical compounds, and other items of interest to his criminally curious mind and dark ambitions. She was in possession of a vital fact: in her world, at least, Leng would not discover the secret entrance to these caverns below the mansion's basement complex for another thirty years. Constance, however, already knew them well. On her first arrival underneath the mansion, she had searched the basement and sub-basement with methodical precision, comparing this with her own memory of how it looked in her own present day, and within thirty-six hours she had learned, or refreshed her recollection, of all its secrets. Leng was already busy in the basement, setting up his collections and labs, and she had to be exceedingly careful to leave no trace whatsoever in those spaces. But she could spy on him through certain peepholes and masonry cracks, from the spaces between and inside the walls that honeycombed the rambling structure.

Her first effort had been to find Binky, but it quickly became clear (and was no surprise) that she was no longer in the house. Tracing where she had been taken was now Aloysius's task. Constance was ready to move on to the next stage of her own plan: the one thing, she'd told the two brothers, that she would achieve—no matter what.

Quickly and stealthily, she made her way past false walls and up secret staircases through the basement and to the main floor, then up a narrow flight of disused back stairs and through a doorway whose outlines were hidden in the wallpaper. She tiptoed between beams, joists, and small piles of nogging, until she came to the inside wall of Leng's library. There was a tiny hole five feet above the ground, hidden by a minuscule flap of loose plaster in the deepest shadows. She lifted the flap and looked through... to see the man himself, enjoying a glass of postprandial port.

She allowed herself only a split-second glimpse; she knew the doctor was not someone to take even the slightest chances with. But it was enough. That hateful image would carry her through the days of work that lay ahead.

"*Te post me, satanas,*" she whispered as she secured the tiny flap. Then she turned and slipped away, back down into the darkness, ready to prepare a beverage of her own.

36

Cedric Deddington-Bute, Fifth Baron Jayeaux, lay sprawled across the stylized reproduction of an Egyptian sarcophagus, circa 800 BC, carved out of lignum vitae. From the eiderdown bolsters cushioning his limbs, he gazed with satisfaction around his salon.

The real Cedric Deddington-Bute, newly arrived from Southampton, was now decomposing peacefully in the muck of the East River, and Diogenes had smoothly appropriated the man's identity and worldly goods. To honor his memory, Diogenes had created this opulent nest with an extravagance that would have been impossible in the twenty-first century. The salon itself was decorated in the Etruscan style; the bath, Egyptian; the dining room, Roman Empire; and the bedroom, a mélange from the fevered minds of Huysmans and Baudelaire. Years ago, Diogenes had learned that money—when spent extravagantly—could spin straw into gold. At present, he had an enormous amount of money: with his knowledge of future market movements, he'd acquired an immense fortune on the New

York Stock Exchange with astonishing speed and was now deploying it to his own gratification. It had been easy to do in this Gilded Age, when labor laws, OSHA, building codes, UNESCO conventions, and the Lacey Act remained far in the future.

The Etruscans had been famous for their skilled goldsmiths, who could coax gold to granulation and work it into intricate filigree. Nearly every inch of Diogenes's salon—from the caryatids sculpted to look like living pillars, to the very jointure of the furniture—was covered in such Etruscan gilt. The drapes of the third-floor room were thrown wide, and the winter light that flooded in gave the natural sheen of every surface a brilliance. Thirty-Fourth Street lay outside the five-story town house he'd purchased, and he'd paid a great sum to have it immediately secured with iron bars, special locks, and soundproofing. There were other retrofittings he planned to make himself... when time permitted.

With a sigh of leisurely enjoyment, he looked over at the dish set beside his couch and the various fruits that lay upon it, glistening with tiny droplets of water. He quoted dreamily to no one in particular:

The silent man in mocha brown
Sprawls at the window-sill and gapes;
The waiter brings in oranges
Bananas figs and hothouse grapes

"Livia," he said in a somewhat louder voice, "would you be an angel and peel me a grape?"

For a moment, all was still. Then one of the caryatids lowered her hands from their mock position in support of the ceiling, stepped down off her plinth, and walked toward him. Unlike the room's other ornaments, she was flesh and blood; dressed from the waist down in billowy white silk, but also covered from face to navel to toes in fine baker's sugar, of a golden color.

"Of course, my lord," she said, approaching him with a sly smile.

She took a seat on the couch beside him, lifted a paring knife from the plate, and began expertly preparing a grape. Diogenes watched, appreciating her artless poise, the lissome manner in which she moved. It was a gift that only nature could confer: dancers might practice for decades and never achieve it.

Diogenes liked Livia very much indeed. She reminded him of another woman with a similar name he had been very close to: Flavia. The women were also similar in their self-assurance, their lusts, and their willingness to experiment. But while Flavia had been obsessed by the art of causing pain, Livia—who had been born into a family of destitute academics—was much more interested in things intellectual. As such, she and Diogenes were twin adventurers in the realms of the mind and senses. Flavia, alas, had died a few years back in the Florida Keys, assisted into the next world by Constance Greene, among others. So many of those in his brother Aloysius's orbit seemed to suffer a premature demise.

Livia delicately placed first one grape on his tongue, then another. And then—eager to draw off the sugar from her limbs by slow strokes of his tongue—he smiled and beckoned her to lie beside him.

Soon, the sweet taste was flooding his senses even as his mind continued to roam. He reminded himself: Flavia was not dead; she hadn't yet been born. Neither had he, for that matter. How strange it was, this parallel universe. Diogenes, agent and abettor of chaos, found himself fascinated by it. With his entropic turn of mind, he couldn't accept that such a precise duplicate of his world should exist. As he'd moved through this mirrored New York of the nineteenth century, he'd been alert for discrepancies. What if Thomas Edison championed AC current, rather than DC? Or John Keats had avoided tuberculosis and gone on to write another dozen famous odes? Yet wherever he looked, he'd detected no departure from history, however minute—aside from the changes he and his compatriots from the twenty-first century had wrought in their arrival.

And that bloody tower. There was no such tower in his New York, and he had never heard of such a one previously existing. This lone discrepancy from his own timeline vexed him.

Meanwhile, the tip of his tongue had traced a line up Livia's left arm and was now moving in semicircles toward her breast, taking away arcs of golden sugar with each stroke. But as the Egyptian Revival clock struck the hour, he realized he had dallied too long—the workhouse required his presence.

"Livia, my pulchritudinous poppet," he said, lifting a fingertip to trace one of her eyebrows, then drifting it along the center part of her brunette hair, "would you mind terribly if we pause for just a while?"

"Of course not," she said. "As long as you promise to finish."

"I swear to make it a climactic event of the first order."

"Should I regild—?" She paused, looking down at the streaks on her smooth flesh where the gold was now gone.

"Oh, please don't bother. I have some additional adornments in mind for tonight."

"How delicious!" Livia knew better than to spoil things by asking what these might be. "I'll order up some caviar and read *Justine* while I wait."

Of course she meant the novel by the Marquis de Sade, rather than the other, yet unwritten, one by Lawrence

Durrell. He kissed her, whispered something in her ear that made her gasp, then rose and left the salon.

In his private dressing chamber, which nobody—including Livia and his manservant—ever entered, he changed clothes and washed, transforming himself into the Right Reverend Considine, the stiff-necked, narrow-minded bane of Leng's existence. He left the dressing chamber through a hidden panel and passed down a narrow, blind staircase that ended at a door beneath the level of the street.

Beyond was a narrow, low-ceilinged passageway that had once been intended as a crypt for a church, demolished fifty years before. A new, larger church had been built in its place, and its entrance—at the end of this passageway—was as carefully hidden as the one within his own town house. He had no idea which prior owner built the secret staircase to his dressing room, or why; he only knew it had sat unused and forgotten for half a century.

Reaching the far end, he slipped into an unused basement room of the rebuilt church, closed a hidden door behind him, then threaded a circuitous path up into the active area of the building. Although he saw nobody, he had already devised a backstory for his clerical presence in the church at any time of the day or night.

Diogenes went out the front door of the church onto Thirtieth Street and walked in the direction of Broadway, where he planned to hail a cab to the Five Points. According to Royds, Leng was still attempting to gain access to the Mission and the House of Industry. Diogenes was determined to deal definitively with Leng—the only man capable of seriously threatening his own existence in this strange old snow globe of New York.

He soon became aware he'd been observed leaving the church and was now being tailed. It was one of

Leng's Milk Drinker gang, of course. No avoiding that: he realized he cut a conspicuous figure in the getup of Considine.

Diogenes caught a glimpse of the tail as he passed a mirror in a barbershop window. A gangly, unkempt fellow—he felt offended the man hadn't done him the courtesy of a decent disguise, remaining clad in the unofficial Milk Drinkers uniform. Diogenes slowed a little, smiling as he saw the thug quicken his own walk. Now it became clear: the man wasn't just following him, but planned to kill him.

How delicious.

Bringing himself into acute awareness of everything going on around him—on the street, the sidewalk, the buildings above—Diogenes waited for the right opportunity. Two coaches were clip-clopping down the cobbled street, and here, in midblock, the pedestrians had thinned out.

He dipped three fingers into the hem of his cassock, withdrew them, and then suddenly turned to face the man, a beatific smile on his face, hands cupped together before him as if preparing to administer the Eucharist.

"Would you care to confess your sins, my son?" he asked.

The man's grimy face screwed up in confusion—just long enough for Diogenes to sink the short-handled icepick he'd palmed into the man's solar plexus, the movement hidden by his billowing cassock. As the would-be assailant wheezed in surprise and pain, Diogenes leaned in familiarly, patting the man's shoulder with one hand while the other—as with Miss Crean—probed the point for the sweet spot.

The man's eyes widened as Diogenes found the artery and pierced it, neatly stepped back, and then with a sharp nudge tripped the man up, over, and into the street—even as he feigned a gesture to arrest his fall—directly in front of the wheels of the closest cab. The horse neighed; the driver pulled on the reins with a curse; but nevertheless a satisfying thump-*thump* informed Diogenes it hadn't stopped in time.

But he was already looking toward the second coach. As the driver slowed instinctively, Diogenes grabbed the door and hoisted himself up and in.

"What in thunder?" the cabbie cried, looking back into the compartment and spying the white dog collar around his customer's neck. "Begging Your Grace's pardon, I mean."

"I believe he was drunk, poor soul. I tried to arrest his fall, but failed—alas. We can only hope the next life is easier for him than this one was, my friend."

"Aye, true enough."

Diogenes, glancing out the window, saw the first cabbie was now down on the street and kneeling by the thug lying motionless between the wheels. The icepick guaranteed there would be little external blood. And there was not even the remotest chance Leng, thorough and clever as he was, would note the similarity in wounds between this fellow and the former director of the workhouse—for the simple reason that Ms. Crean's corpse no longer existed, save at the atomic or subatomic level.

"Well, my man, time waits for no one," he said gravely. "Canal Street, please."

With a whistle of the whip cracking the air, they lurched immediately into a trot.

37

"Would you care for some more damson-plum jam, Mr. Cassaway?"

"No thank you, Mrs. Plaice. If the holidays weren't so close behind us, I'd think you were fattening me up as a Christmas turkey."

"What sauce!" Mrs. Plaice tittered as she picked up the tea-things and made her way out of the parlor and into the kitchen.

Humblecut watched her disappear. Mrs. Plaice was, indeed, a most excellent cook, but he was strict about his diet.

Mount Desert Island—where his slow, methodical inquiries had ultimately led him—was a curious place indeed. It was quite large—dwarfing Martha's Vineyard far to the south. And it had recently undergone a transformation. For years, the island had been the haunt of "rusticators"—artists of the Hudson River school searching for remote, rugged landscapes to put on canvas. But over the last decade, these would-be Thoreauvians had been displaced by the wealthiest of the wealthy, eager to build large summer "cottages" far from the city. Various Carnegies, Astors, and Rockefellers arrived on the island by yacht and steamship for summers full of lawn parties, yachting, and croquet. This was good news for provisioners, carpenters, masons, and house staff...but bad news for the cheap boardinghouses patronized by the artists and naturalists. How lucky then for Scots-bred Emmaline Plaice, who ran just such a modest establishment, that Mr. Cassaway—middle-aged, handsome, lean and sinewy, with impeccable manners—had arrived, looking for a place precisely like hers, where he could research his history of the postrevolutionary New England coast. Better still, he seemed to find the tranquility of the winter season inspirational and appreciated being her only boarder. In fact, once he'd chosen her best room—overlooking the main street of Northeast Harbor—and secured it by paying a month in advance, she'd taken the small ROOMS TO LET sign out of the front window.

In his brief stay on the island, Humblecut had already taken long walks along its rocky coastline and meandering carriage rides through the sleepy winter towns, braving the godawful freezing temperatures, to ensure he became a familiar figure to the locals. He was also spending time at the library and chatting with self-professed island historians in the local coffee shop, displaying his bona fides, along with establishing that he was there for private research and minded his own business. This last quality masked the fact he was skilled at coaxing rumors and gossip out of others without their realizing it. That morning, he'd learned from a lobsterman that a man had taken up residence in the Rockefeller estate as a security guard, bringing his young son with him. Another encounter with a housepainter informed him that a boy of twelve years old had begun attending the

Seal Harbor school—noteworthy because the painter's son had teased the boy on account of his peculiar accent, to unfortunate results.

"I think I'll go out for a stroll, Mrs. P.," he told the landlady as she bustled back in. "Work up an appetite for supper."

"What—after tea?" She frowned in concern. "It gets dark so early, these days."

"I won't go far—just up the Foster Farm Road."

"Will you, and all? There's nothing to see out that way but them dirty great mansions. Not much history thereabouts—some of them are but half-built."

"What we find contemporary, future generations will call history."

The woman frowned as if trying to parse this statement. "Future generations aren't about to walk out that door and catch their death of cold."

He smiled. "Have you, by chance, ever heard of historiography?"

"Can't say that I have." Mrs. Plaice opened the closet door. "Here, take my late husband's scarf. White cashmere—it's ever so soft."

"I'd prefer that other one, if you don't mind."

"What...the black? But that's a lady's scarf...that's mine!"

"In that case, I shall be sure to tuck it especially close to my heart."

"*Such* a saucebox!" She tittered—then paused. "What was that word again?"

"Historiography. The study of how written history changes with time. I suppose you could call it the history of history. In any case, someday *my* history book will be studied in such a way...if I'm lucky."

"The history of history. I never. It's like...like walking backward on a moving train. What's the point?"

"That's a question even historians can't answer."

At this, she burst into laughter. "You always give me something to think about, you do! Now remember: supper's at half past six. We're having roast hogget."

"In that case, I'll come back with an extra-sharp appetite." Wrapping the scarf tightly around his neck and tucking it into his coat, he opened the front door and—black upon black—strode out into the failing light.

38

THE ODD FIGURE WOBBLED down West 137th Street, a man with long black hair, a swollen nose with burst veins, a shabby frock coat and filthy gaiters, and a partially crushed stovepipe hat perched on his head as the final touch. He trailed a distinct smell of whisky behind him. He approached the corner of Riverside Drive, passing by the somber Beaux Arts mansion that dominated the block, turned the corner, and continued north, humming tunelessly. Veering diagonally across the drive, he jauntily staggered down into newly built Riverside Park, converted from a railyard only a few years before and still not finished. Here, he spied two other malingerers sitting on a stack of granite blocks not far from the tracks of the Hudson Railway.

"A good evening to you, fellow bindlestiffs!" he cried, pulling out a quart bottle and waving it like a white flag before taking a good pull. The two tramps, who had been guardedly watching his approach, softened their expressions.

"Come join us, friend," said one.

The tramp seated himself and offered the two others his bottle. "Old Overholt," he cried. "Not as aged as one might like—perhaps Young Overholt would be a more appropriate name. Ha ha ha! But never mind: fine stuff, fine stuff!"

One took it, swigged, and passed it on. The newly arrived tramp stuck out his hand, fingers protruding from dirty fingerless gloves. "Stovepipe's my moniker."

The two tramps introduced themselves as Galloon and Howitzer.

"Help yourselves to more refreshment," said Stovepipe, courteously refusing to accept the bottle reluctantly passed back to him. This considerably cheered the tramps, who took several more enthusiastic pulls each.

"Thank you, friend," said one, wiping his mouth. "That's some good coffin varnish."

Stovepipe issued a cracked laugh and gave the man a slap on the back. "Yes*sir*!"

The bottle went around again, the two tramps indulging themselves even more liberally than before.

"Haven't seen you in these parts," said Galloon.

"Just arrived," Stovepipe said. "Looking for work."

"What kind of work?"

"As little as possible."

This got a round of laughs, and the newcomer continued. "Stableman, when I have to be. Just got here from old Boston. I'm a little light on the spondulix at the moment, and I heard the city's a-growing, lots of jobs."

Galloon spat. "Not for us."

Stovepipe waved his hand. "With all the rich people around here? Take that mansion up there. They must have at least a coach and four."

Galloon shook his head, taking another pull. "Skinflints."

"You seen what kind of coach they drive? Asking for professional reasons, you understand."

"Oh, a big old varnished thing, four-in-hand, like you said. Comes and goes at all times of the night and day."

"Anything else?"

"A wagon, pulled by a Belgian."

"A four-in-hand and a Belgian? My word. Where do they keep the horses?"

"In the mews right around back of the house."

"Now that's some useful information!" Stovepipe scratched thoughtfully at his stubbly chin. "What kind of wagon did you say?"

"A farm wagon, just a horse and cart. I saw it not but a few days back, headed out around midnight."

"A few days back? You mean, Monday?"

The tramp frowned. "Not sure I recollect." He shrugged. "Monday sounds right. Then again, it might have been Sunday."

"Which way did it go?"

"North."

"Who was driving it?"

"He was all mufflered up on account of the cold, black scarf and greatcoat, but I think it was the master of the house himself—he's a right tall feller." He hesitated. "Why so interested? You some kind of second-story man?"

"Good gracious, no! My interest, sir, is for the very simple reason that they couldn't find a better drayman than yours truly! Why would the master be driving some old farm wagon if he had a decent wagoner? Now, if he had a man like *me*—"

"I wouldn't knock on that door if my life depended on it—and that's a bottom fact."

"What do you mean?"

"Thems are some rum coves lounging around that place, comings and goings at night—all sorts of doings. It's a strange house with queer folk, and you'd do better to toughen your knuckles on doors farther up."

"Well, you've scoured the place, and I haven't... but crikey, it's the biggest mansion on the whole stretch! More horses, more money. And with a separate stables, a man can likely get a fair amount of shut-eye in without being overly troubled."

Galloon shook his head.

"What was it carrying?"

"A load of hay, I believe."

"Out of the city? For dunnage?"

Galloon shrugged. "It was dark, and they was moving fast. If I were you I'd pack away that curiosity—it's like to get you into deep tar."

"I thankee for the advice, Mr. Galloon, sir, and I leave you with the bottle as a parting gift. Now, good night. I had better freshen up my wind afore I go a-knocking on doors."

The tramp rose and headed north along Riverside Drive, eyes scanning the ground. In short order, his vigilance was rewarded with two items—crumpled pieces of damp hay and a single round pellet, which he recognized as the dung of a sheep.

39

THE FLICKERING LIGHT FROM Constance's candle gleamed and winked among the hundreds of glass jars, bottles, beakers, and phials that crowded the shelves in the chemical storeroom housed in the basement of 891 Riverside Drive. She moved silently on stockinged feet, holding the candle to the labels in each row of vessels in turn, on which an impeccable hand had written the name of the item or substance within—a venomous insect, snake, or other noxious creature; a swollen poison gland dissected from a toad; a deadly plant, mineral, liquid, powder, crystalline, or colloid.

This was the heart of Leng's collections—poisons, toxins, banes, and venoms. He had only begun to stock this most valuable and dangerous storeroom; over the years, Constance knew, it would grow to embrace virtually every lethal substance known to exist, as he searched for the ultimate poison capable of driving the human race to extinction. It had been an unpleasant experience for Constance—delving into her memory, back to the time when she was a young girl living in this same mansion, acting as Leng's assistant in various chemical and toxicological experiments—but necessary, if she were to reacquaint herself with its layout.

She was looking for a certain toxin Leng had been fascinated with, found in the death cap mushroom, *Amanita phalloides*. The toxins of that infamous species of mushroom were thermostable: they could be cooked yet remain deadly. In addition, the mushroom had a pleasant taste resembling beef broth, allowing food to be heavily laced with it yet take on no bitter or unusual flavor. But what primarily attracted Leng was the fact that the mushroom's deadly effects took days to appear—much too late to purge the stomach with an emetic. By the time you felt sick enough to realize something was seriously wrong, you were already a dead person. You could ingest a fatal dose and remain unaware of it for as long as two weeks—until your liver began inexorably to fail. For this reason, the death cap had been used as a poison for thousands of years, playing a role in the demise of, among others, the Roman emperor Claudius, Pope Clement VII, and the Austrian emperor Charles VI.

Once the poison finally manifested, it made itself felt in a most unpleasant manner indeed. An antidote was not developed until some time into the twenty-first century. Prior to that, nothing could save the victim except immediate liver transplantation.

In the nineteenth century, there was no cure at all.

She recalled that, during the 1890s, Leng had labored in this laboratory for weeks: preparing a desiccated and powdered form of the death cap, trying to isolate and identify its poison. He had discovered it contained not one, but seven toxins, each biochemically distinct and with different effects. The empress of these toxins, alpha-amanitin, was the deadliest and also had the advantage of taking the longest to manifest itself. The ingestion of as little as ten milligrams was fatal.

Constance had helped Leng isolate the toxin, and she had searched her memory for the exact process. She wanted to make sure to prepare an absolutely fatal dose, and that meant concentrating the poison through biochemical extraction. Although it would be a decade before he turned his attention to studying its properties, even as early as 1881 she knew Leng had kept a cache of powdered *Amanita phalloides* somewhere in his storeroom.

At last, the candle flame flickered over the label she was searching for:

> AMANITA PHALLOIDES
> DEATH CAP
> DESICCATED

She could not simply take the jar of white powder—Leng frequently haunted the laboratory, and she planned on leaving nothing to chance, not even the remote possibility he might spy that the level of powder had dropped in a single jar. Removing a small bottle, a piece of paper, an empty phial, and a packet from the pockets of her dress, she placed them on a shelf. Rolling the paper into a funnel, she gently shook out two tablespoons of the amanita powder into the phial; then, transferring the funnel to Leng's jar, she took the packet—containing confectioners' sugar—and restored the powder to its former level, stoppering the jar and shaking it to disperse the sugar.

As she slipped the items back into her pockets and returned the jar to its place, she heard a faint noise. Instantly, she extinguished the candle and stopped its smoke with a pinch of her fingers to the wick. Another

sound—a door, scraping a sill with a creak of hinges—
and then a gleam of light appeared. It was Leng. The
man, so regular in his eating habits, otherwise kept the
most unpredictable hours. And it could only be him: no
one else, not his gang or his servants or even the hated
Munck, was allowed in the basement laboratory and
storerooms. None of them, Constance believed, even
knew of their existence. She had—over time—become
the only person Leng allowed to assist him.

She shook away further recollections.

As the light moved into the chamber, Constance
shrank back behind a row of shelves and pressed herself against the damp stone wall. The light continued to
move down the central aisle, slowly and silently. From
the dark of her hiding place she could see the patrician
face of Leng, pale and hollow in the light of his lantern,
his eyes glistening behind violet-tinted glasses. He was
hatless, and his light blond hair, brushed back, gleamed
with Macassar oil. At the sight of him, a hatred rose
within her so violent that she feared he might detect the
angry beat of her heart. But he passed by like a specter,
intent on some late-night business of his own. Soon he
had left the room and gone into the next—full of weapons, for the most part still boxed from shipping—and
she took the opportunity to creep out of her hiding place
and move deeper into the basement, away from Leng.

To isolate alpha-amanitin from the powder would be
her next step. It would involve another trip to the laboratory, the borrowing of certain reagents along with a
titration burette, analytical balance, mixing beakers, and
tubes. It would have to be done tonight, and the equipment returned before morning—once again, to its precise position in the lab.

40

Pendergast turned onto 139th street and headed east to Tenth Avenue, where Murphy was waiting with the carriage, along with a riding horse, saddled and bridled, tied up on a lead rope behind. He stepped into the coach, drew the curtains, then swiftly changed out of his disguise, shedding the crushed stovepipe hat and shabby greatcoat for a cloth cap and scarf, leather trimmed breeches and high boots, a musette bag, and a woolen riding coat of fine quality.

"He's a good gelding, this one," said Murphy, offering him the reins as he stepped out, completely transformed. "Name's Napoleon."

The chestnut beast eyed Pendergast, his ears perked. Pendergast stroked his neck, let the animal smell him a moment, and then took the reins, slipped his boot into the stirrup, and mounted.

"Take care, sir," said Murphy.

"I will, Murphy, and thank you. He seems a fine horse."

The two parted, and Pendergast started northward

up Tenth Avenue, bent on his last and most important objective—finding Binky. He'd decided to layer his disguise: a farmer, supposedly returning to his farm from a day in the city, who in reality was an insufficiently disguised Pinkerton agent in pursuit of a fugitive.

By ten that evening, with the moon struggling to rise through icy vapor, Pendergast arrived at Kings Bridge, where the Boston Post Road crossed Spuyten Duyvil Creek, the body of water at the very northern tip of Manhattan Island separating it from the Bronx. Kings Bridge was the oldest bridge connecting Manhattan with the mainland, and as he approached he saw a faint light in the wooden tollhouse at its near end.

Pendergast halted, dismounted, and tied his horse at the hitching post. The toll master opened a small window and leaned out. "Greetings, traveler," he said, in a tired voice.

As he approached, Pendergast took in the cozy hut, warm from a woodstove, with a coffeepot and a pan of corn bread. "Greetings to you," said Pendergast.

"Ten cents, if you please."

Pendergast removed a silver dollar and laid it on the sill. "My good man, permit me a question: early this week, did you happen to be on duty at about two or three o'clock in the morning?"

"I did indeed," the man said, rousing himself at the question and by the sight of the silver coin. "What's it to you?"

Pendergast assumed an arrogant tone. "I'm a farmer, returning from a day in the city, and I'm wondering if my brother came through here around that time, Monday or perhaps Sunday night. He's an uncommonly tall fellow, thin, pale, face and neck wrapped up in a dark scarf, driving a cart loaded with hay hitched to a Belgian draft horse."

"Your brother, you say?"

"Yes."

There was a pause, and Pendergast ostentatiously laid a second Morgan dollar on top of the first.

The toll master eyed him up and down. "What's it all about?"

"I'm afraid that's none of your business," came the officious reply, pitched in a tone designed to arouse suspicion.

"It is my business if you're looking for information." The toll master paused. "And if I may say so, sir: if you're a farmer, then I'm President Hayes."

At this, Pendergast paused a beat. Then he broke into a slow, cold smile. "I can see you're not one to be easily fooled."

"I am not," the man said, a touch of pride in his voice.

Pendergast lowered his voice. "Well, then, I'll be straight with you. Confidentially, of course."

"That's more like it."

"I'm in pursuit of a fugitive from justice."

The toll master nodded, eager to hear more.

"Let's just say I'm a private detective from an outfit that isn't exactly unknown—if you get my meaning."

"The Pinkertons?"

"I didn't say that!" Pendergast leaned forward and lowered his voice still further. "The man I just described is a murderer and kidnapper. The fiend was last seen spiriting a young girl out of the city, trussed up in a hay wagon."

The man's eyes widened. "No!"

"I fear greatly that it's a fact. Now: did you see the man I described pass by?"

"Sir, I did in fact see the man you're describing. It was after midnight, in the wee hours of Monday morning. Not only that, but at the time I thought I heard a sound from the hay. It seemed the mewling of a cat... but I suppose it could just as well have been the muffled crying of a child."

"Is that so! I commend your abilities of observation. Did you exchange any words with him? Any clue, say, as to where he might be going?"

"He was completely silent. He drew up to the window, paid his dime, and then shook the reins and was gone over the bridge in a flash."

"He was moving fast, then?"

"Yes."

"No idea which road he took on the far side, where the toll road branches?"

"No, sir."

"Had you ever seen him before, coming and going?"

"I can't say—his face was entirely muffled up, as you noted, and it was a dark night—like tonight."

"Had you seen the horse before?"

"Can't say that, either. There are a lot of Belgians come through this way, pulling loads. That's a popular breed. The wagon looked like any old market wagon. Stank like sheep shite, I recall."

"You've been quite helpful." He gestured at the two dollars. "You've earned them."

"I'm not one to take money for doing good. I hope you catch the man, sir. I did feel he had an evil air about him."

Pendergast retrieved the coins, replacing them with a dime. "You are an honest man and a fine citizen to boot. Now: if anyone should inquire about me or this encounter, what might your response be?"

"That I've no idea what they're talking about and never saw the gentleman in question."

"Excellent. Thank you, toll master." Pendergast unhitched Napoleon from the post. And then, with a single, agile movement, he leapt into the saddle and pressed the flanks of the horse with his heels; in an instant they were galloping across the bridge and into the deep gloom of night.

41

Around four pm, Pendergast halted at the second major fork in the Boston Post Road and looked about. It was an even lonelier spot than the first. Here, the Post Road continued northeastward, while another road went off to the left heading due north, in the direction of White Plains. It was rutted and strewn with dead weeds crushed into the frozen mud by wagon wheels.

After he'd passed Kings Bridge the night before, the road had entered a hilly region of farms and small villages, and after half a mile he'd come to the first main fork. The left-hand fork followed the route of the railroad, past the grand estates perched on the bluffs over the Hudson, meandering through such villages as Dobbs Ferry, Tarrytown, and Pocantico Hills. The right-hand fork was the continuation of the Boston Post Road.

At this point, Pendergast had been presented with his first decision. He stopped the horse and took a deep breath of the cold night air. The crossroads was cold and silent. He was on a high point of ground, and from it he surveyed the countryside. It was remarkable how dark the world had been before the advent of electric lights; how starry the night sky, and silent the landscape. He could see to his left a faint illumination of the Hudson Line, and a sprinkle of dim lights he assumed must be the village of Spuyten Duyvil. To the right, the Post Road continued on through Williamsbridge and Pelham, then northeastward along the shores of Long Island Sound and its many seaside villages.

It seemed likely Leng was taking Binky to a working farm, not a nouveau riche mansion set on manicured grounds, where a dirty farm wagon would attract attention and a flock of sheep would not be welcome. But he'd reminded himself that nothing about Leng could be taken for granted—and he'd spent much of the morning and early afternoon examining the least likely routes before returning... and choosing the right-hand fork.

Another few miles had brought him to the second major fork—and another decision. As he sat on Napoleon, looking up the long, desolate lane that again veered off from the Post Road, with mist rising from its halffrozen ground, he felt a strong sense of desuetude. He knew from a recent study of local maps that this road led to the scattered dairy farms and smallholdings of the Van Cortlandt region, initially settled by Dutch farmers in the seventeenth century and still relatively remote. He closed his eyes, calmed his mind, and considered the matter. Within moments, he felt certain no more time was needed investigating probable red herrings—this was the road Leng had taken. The man was going to a place he knew well and had long used. This northern road led into an area that was quiet and isolated, far from the gossipy small towns on Long Island Sound as well as from the conspicuous mansions along the Hudson. Somewhere along this road there would be a prosperous, working farm owned by Leng, no doubt in another guise—one with livestock and, in particular, sheep.

Sheep. That seemed odd. He had learned, firsthand, that the wagon that had spirited away Binky stank of sheep. But the wool trade was no longer practiced in the Hudson River valley, and mutton, being a poor man's meat, was not a profitable trade. Why sheep? There were many dairy farms in the Van Cortlandt valley—but they were stocked with cows. And as he tried to penetrate the *Umwelt* of Leng, he suddenly understood: this farm to which the haycart had been headed was not about mutton or wool: it was about cheese.

He opened his eyes and breathed deeply of the cold winter air and then exhaled, staring as his breath took on shape and form as dark once again began to fall. The air smelled of ice. He gave Napoleon a nudge and sent him down the road less traveled.

* * *

As Pendergast rode along, he became aware that this might be the most difficult part of his pursuit: finding the right farm in this vast winter nightscape. But he also felt certain there would be evidence of one kind or another to guide his way.

A mile down the road, he halted his horse and dismounted. He lit a small lantern, then crouched to examine the frozen surface of the road. He noted the ground had become rutted during the freeze-thaw cycle of winter; the relative warmth of the day softened the muddy surface of the road, which would then freeze again at night. The previous Sunday, however, there had been an overcast sky; in the city it had not gone below freezing, and he surmised that had been the case out here as well. Leng's cart would have left tracks. Unfortunately, he could see that too many wagons and carriages had passed in the intervening time, erasing any useful information.

Pendergast remounted Napoleon, loosened the reins

to let the horse have his head, and closed his eyes once again. As the horse continued at a rocking pace, Pendergast used a series of mental exercises to clear his mind of stray thoughts, letting it become like a crystal pool of water. Gradually, the image of Binky in the hay wagon formed in his head, like a reflection on the water. The girl lay with her feet shackled, hands bound before her, a gag around her mouth. Blindfolded, as well: Leng would take no chances with a resourceful, energetic guttersnipe who'd learned the arts of survival in the worst slum of New York City. In the reflected image of his mind, it seemed to Pendergast that she was also tied or otherwise bound to the wagon itself, in order to prevent her from wriggling up and over the sideboards.

But as he observed the scene, he grew convinced that Leng, careful as he was, had made a mistake. Binky's hands were bound in front... but her fingers were free.

Now Pendergast opened his eyes and halted the horse. He dismounted, relit the lantern, and—leading the animal by the reins—walked slowly along the road, head down, lantern held low to illuminate the ground. The road dipped and rose, and the night deepened as he continued on.

He had gone a quarter of a mile when he found what he was looking for: a piece of damp straw folded into a loose, crude knot.

Remounting Napoleon, he continued on. The tranquil crystal pool vanished from his mind, leaving two images behind. One was of Binky, cleverly tying pieces of straw together with her nimble fingers and dropping them over the side to serve as a sort of breadcrumb trail. But that image dissolved into another, very different, one: Leng, seated at the reins, a handful of straw in his lap—now and then tossing out precisely the same thing.

42

THE NEXT FIFTEEN MINUTES, Constance felt sure, would be the most important—and dangerous—of her time in Leng's mansion.

With infinite care, she had learned the rhythms of the house. Leng's outstanding characteristic, she had noted, was a strict adherence to dining routine. When he was in, usually three or four nights a week, he had dinner punctually, alone, and ate a limited menu. At eight o'clock promptly he was served *le premier plat*, usually smoked buffalo tongue, a pâté of snipe in jelly, or jugged hare. This was followed, invariably, by terrapin soup at eight fifteen. Then at eight forty-five came *le plat principal*, usually beef or lobster, with a glass of claret or white burgundy, which occupied the doctor for half an hour, until he was served pastries and coffee.

Because Leng was fussy to the point of metathesiophobia when it came to food punctuality, the preparation of dinner was always a fraught affair. The doctor would let it be known, before leaving in the morning, whether he'd be in for dinner, and the necessary arrangements would begin around noon, with marketing and the assembling of ingredients. The cook, with his sous chef and two assistants, would begin work at around five. The kitchen and pantry were on the first floor, their rear wall partially below ground due to the slope of the land, while Leng's private dining room was almost directly above it, on the second floor. A dumbwaiter served both to bring up the various dishes—then served by the butler—and to send down dirty plates. The preparations reached a crescendo around quarter to eight and slacked off at eight thirty, when Leng briefly left the dining room to sharpen his appetite for the main course with a pipe of tobacco. The dinner reached its zenith between eight forty-five and ten. That was when Leng retired to his private salon and the last plates were sent down to the scullery maid.

This unchanging *concerto de cuisine*, so very surgical in its demanding nature, was a boon to Constance, especially given Leng's otherwise unpredictable schedule. From her hidden chambers in the sub-basement—two floors below the kitchen, three floors below the dining room—she choreographed her plan of action. She had timed and rehearsed her plan and tried a dry run to ensure it could work. Now it was time for the main event.

Dressed in her black catsuit, she ascended from her hidden quarters to the basement, and from there to the first floor at five minutes after eight, taking up position behind a panel in the passage between the kitchen and the scullery. She had contrived to keep her hands and arms free by employing a crossbody strap, slung over her neck like a leather scarf and containing a pouch on either side. One held the poison she had managed to extract and concentrate with infinite care, along with a small glass beaker of hydrofluoric acid that she intended to fling at any attacker, should she be discovered. The other pouch contained a "top break" Enfield Mk I service revolver with a full complement of .476 cartridges. This was not for defensive purposes—it was to be used on herself as a last resort.

As the minutes stretched on, she remained still as death. Then, from her vantage point behind the panel, she silently withdrew her pocket watch: eight thirty precisely. And, just as precisely, the dumbwaiter descended with a whir; the scullery maid opened its door, removed the dirty plates, and trotted off down the corridor. A moment later, the sous chef returned with the dinner plates, arranged them in the dumbwaiter, and sent them up. The butler waiting above, Constance knew, was ready to deliver the main course to the table—and then discreetly withdraw.

This was Constance's window of opportunity. She waited one hundred seconds exactly, then slipped across the corridor, freed the mechanism holding the dumbwaiter at the floor above, and manually wheeled it downward. Then she opened it. As expected, it was empty: the dinner had been taken to the table.

She clambered into the cramped space and closed the door behind her. Then she opened the trap in the roof and used the rope-and-pulley mechanism to lift herself up the fifteen feet from the main floor to the dining room. The dumbwaiter was of too primitive a design to have an interlock, so she bolted it in place manually, then paused to listen. The dining room beyond was silent. Once again, she checked her pocket watch: 8:35.

A faint smell of tobacco permeated the interior of the dumbwaiter.

Now Constance opened the door on the back side. Leng's dining room came into view. The dinner was set, china and sterling glittering, butler gone, and the food in place, waiting for Leng's return in a minute or two—or even less.

Constance quickly stepped out of the dumbwaiter and up to Leng's chair, glancing over the meal: *filet de bœuf et sa sauce Bordelaise*.

That would do nicely.

Keeping alert for the sound of footsteps in the hallway outside, she plucked a wad of cotton wool from the pouch and unwrapped it, revealing a tiny ampoule with a cork stopper. Without hesitation, she opened it and poured the clear liquid contents into the gravy boat holding the rich sauce. She mixed the sauce briefly with an index finger. Unconsciously, she raised the finger to her tongue—then stopped herself with a mordant smile at this almost fatal mistake. Instead, she dipped it into a large finger bowl and rinsed it off, the copper container masking any faint brownish hue that resulted. After a final glance around, she climbed back into the dumbwaiter, lowered it to the first floor, and put the ceiling trap back into place. Once again she looked at her pocket watch: 8:41.

The corridor outside was silent. Constance opened the dumbwaiter, crawled out, closed its door, raised it back to its proper level, and returned to her hidden observation post on the far side of the hallway.

Leng returned to the dining room, and she could hear the faint sounds of his meal for the next half hour. Finally, the dirty plates were loaded on the dumbwaiter and sent down. Looking out from her peephole, Constance saw that the filet had been wholly consumed—and that the gravy boat with the Bordelaise was at least half-empty.

"The condemned man ate a hearty supper," she murmured to herself as she ducked out of the nook, then through the door leading down to the basement—and beneath.

43

GEORGE HARRISON—WHO, DESPITE HIS name, had no musical gifts whatsoever—closed the servants' entrance to the Rockefeller "cottage," helped Joe remove his coat, and then took off his own. He hung them on pegs while Joe ran ahead into the kitchen. Every day, Mrs. Cookson had raisin porridge waiting on the stove for Joe when he got home from school. This morning, however, they'd made the journey to the schoolhouse only to learn that one of the teachers was ill, and that class would not resume until tomorrow—Saturday. Which meant, Mrs. Cookson said, that Joe would get his porridge early...once he'd completed his studies.

Joe was fitting in well at the two-room schoolhouse. On the first day, his accent had attracted the attention of an older bully, but after Joe had used his fists to place the fellow into a recumbent position, the other students quickly came to respect him. The teacher had initially planned on a remedial syllabus for the boy but, on discovering his reading and writing skills were unexpectedly strong, found a place for him in the upper schoolroom.

It was, D'Agosta supposed, one of the benefits of a tiny school, where such labels as *fifth* or *sixth grade* had little meaning. He was pleased by the way Joe, even though still keeping much to himself, had begun to make progress in his studies and was getting along with his classmates. The only thing the least unusual was the six-day school week: because fathers needed extra hands to help work during the season, there were sixteen weeks off during summer instead of the usual twelve.

D'Agosta moved through the warm kitchen and proceeded on to the back parlor, where a fire was burning and a copy of the Portland newspaper, a week old, was waiting. He picked it up and began leafing through it. He found these 1880s papers pretty thin: six or eight columns of print set off by ornamented headlines. The most interesting stories were buried inside, lurid descriptions of criminal goings-on, reports of strange marvels from "the uttermost corners of the Orient," or the like. The stories on the front page were more or less incomprehensible to someone who had no background in the politics or controversies of the day.

He put the paper aside and sighed. Life on the island, he had to admit, was dull. He dutifully made uneventful, daily rounds of the common rooms of the freezing mansion. Mrs. Cookson was friendly and eager to minister to their needs, but her conversation was limited and her worldview cramped. He missed his wife, Laura, terribly and felt broken up that they had parted in anger. She had to be freaked out by his sudden disappearance.

Mr. Cookson turned out to be a surprise. He had initially remained taciturn and indisposed to small talk, but that changed when D'Agosta offered to help paint the ten small bedrooms in the servants' wing. The man made a feeble attempt to rebuff the offer, but it was clear he was no fan of standing on ladders and slopping paint on ceilings. As they worked together, D'Agosta began to like the wizened, mustachioed man, who only spoke when he had something worthwhile to say, and often with a wit so dry it took a moment to realize that it was wit at all.

The island seemed safe enough. Strangers were rare and immediately noted. A few artists and writers arrived from time to time to spend a week or two in the offseason, wandering around the shores and cliffs. D'Agosta himself had decided the less time he spent out of the mansion, the better: he'd been accepted as one of Mr. Rockefeller's "people" and was happy to leave it at that. His outside excursions mostly consisted of walking Joe to and from school, and he used the opportunity to look for anything out of place. Nothing raised his suspicions. And Joe, thank God, knew how to keep his mouth shut.

Now the boy himself stepped into the back parlor to join D'Agosta. One hand gripped the leather strap that bound his schoolbooks together, the other his prized possession: a metal dip pen. This pen, though it was used like the others in school and even looked rather common, was in fact very special.

Two packages had arrived from Pendergast since they reached the island: both addressed from Mr. Rockefeller to Mrs. Cookson, but holding inside smaller packages with George Harrison's name on them. The first contained necessaries, including money and instructions he had burnt after reading. The second package contained a present for Joe. Pendergast, who knew Joe had been developing an interest in astronomy before being rushed out of the Fifth Avenue mansion, had given him a dip pen with a metal shaft. D'Agosta, reading from Pendergast's note, explained to Joe that the pen was exceedingly rare, having been machined from a piece of the Bendegó meteorite, which had impacted in Brazil almost a hundred years before. In the package Pendergast had also included a pamphlet on meteors and meteorites, along with some photographs. It turned out to be the perfect gift. Joe treasured it above all things and kept its origin as secret as if his life depended on it. D'Agosta smiled as he watched the boy unfasten the strap around his schoolbooks. No doubt half the fun of the gift was being the only one to know just how valuable the ordinary-looking item was.

A thump sounded from downstairs. Immediately, Joe's eyes met D'Agosta's. A minute later, the basement door opened and Mr. Cookson could be heard emerging, preparing to do the morning chores, speaking briefly to his wife before shuffling away again. D'Agosta could see Joe's shoulders sag, his eyes wandering. The boy was easily bored—and no wonder, being stuck on a frozen island.

The combination clock–barometer–temperature gauge on the mantel told him it was nine thirty—an entire day ahead, unexpectedly without school.

"You know what?" D'Agosta asked. "I think it's high time we went looking for that old ghost. You can do your studying afterward. What do you say?"

Joe's eyes lit up.

D'Agosta leaned forward conspiratorially. "We'll just have a quick look... for now. If we find anything suspicious, we'll make preparations and investigate more thoroughly tomorrow. But we'd better put on our winter coats—those closed parts of the house are as cold as Siberia."

"*Jiminy!*" Joe half slid, half jumped out of his chair, then followed D'Agosta into the back kitchen to collect their coats and a kerosene lantern.

* * *

Almost an hour later, a freezing D'Agosta sat on the top step of the attic staircase, wrapping his scarf more tightly around his neck. He hadn't considered just what an ordeal a "quick look" through a mansion entailed. While he'd regularly made a circuit of the primary rooms of the house as part of his cover, he'd never penetrated its recesses. He was shocked at the sheer number of storerooms, larders, closets, and shut-up bedrooms the mansion contained, all of which Joe had insisted on exploring. They were now both covered in dust and cobwebs.

When he'd made the suggestion, it had seemed like a way to make good on his promise to entertain Joe, and in the process give the structure a really thorough going-over. And now, he estimated that, in the last sixty minutes, he had walked up and down at least two dozen flights of stairs. They had ended up here in the freezing, sprawling attic, filled with dust and mothballs and rat traps, many already accommodating frozen rats not yet disposed of. Brick chimneys stood here and there like sentinels, rising through the gloom to pierce the gables overhead.

So far their explorations had not revealed any sign of ghosts, and no rattle of chains had greeted their passing. Joe, however, was having a marvelous time. D'Agosta was exhausted.

"Well, if there were any ghosts," he said, "we scared 'em off for sure. Time to call it a morning."

"What about back there?" Joe asked, still eager, pointing to the darkest ends of the attic, where the eaves sloped down into a series of crawl spaces.

"No ghosts in there," D'Agosta said.

"How do you know?"

"Too cold."

"Ghosts can't feel cold," Joe said authoritatively.

D'Agosta shrugged. "*I'm* cold."

Joe accepted this explanation. "What about the carriage house?"

"We'll look there tomorrow," D'Agosta replied. "Come on: careful with these stairs—they're steep." And, rising, he led the way down to the third floor. Joe followed, closing first the attic door, then the door at the bottom of the stairs.

* * *

For several minutes, silence returned to the attic. Then, with a brief, almost indetectable scraping noise, a packing crate shifted in the darkness beneath a far gable. A shape emerged. Edwin Humblecut rose and moved to the front of the crate, on which he took a seat, wiping dust from his heavy clothes and setting his homburg beside him. And then—idly fingering his handlebar mustache—he settled down to wait.

44

The sun had already risen in the eastern sky an hour before Pendergast peered down from the top of a hill, surveying the landscape with a pair of binoculars. After spending the night in a meadow some distance away, where he'd made sure Napoleon was fed and watered, he'd left the horse tied up in a copse, well hidden, while he made his way up the hill at dawn, creeping the last few yards. Mists had risen from the fells and dales of the surrounding farms.

The trail of knotted straw—sparse to begin with—seemed to have vanished. Whatever its origin, it seemed likely Leng's wagon had turned off the road and headed to one of three farms Pendergast could see in the valley. All were isolated, the farmhouses and outbuildings buried in hollows or surrounded by trees, the encircling fields spreading out broadly across the land, separated by hedgerows and windbreaks. This was dairy country, and he saw small herds of dairy cows, released from the barns, make their way to grazing areas that, despite the season, were clear of snow and offered some meager sustenance. He remained in his blind—motionless, watching—until at the farthest farm he saw what he was looking for: a flock of sheep meandering up a hill, driven by a shepherd with a dog.

The sheep's milk, he felt sure, was for making cheese. If the farthest farm specialized not in dairy per se, but in cheese making, such an establishment would have cellars or natural caves of the kind necessary for aging cheese— and useful for other, more nefarious purposes.

He crept down from the summit of the hill and back to Napoleon. Stroking the horse, he praised him and murmured a soft goodbye in his ear. Then he unbridled and unsaddled the horse, hung the bridle on a tree branch, propped the saddle on a rock, and turned the horse loose. He knew such a beautiful animal would soon find a good home, and the lucky traveler who happened upon the abandoned saddle and bridle would be grateful indeed.

He ventured back to the road, where he could just make out the gables of the target farm's main house peeking above the protected dell in which it lay. A stream ran past the rambling old structure, deep in shadow, and it was along these wooded banks that Pendergast decided he would make his approach.

He cast a final glance back at Napoleon, who was standing next to the road, ears perked, watching him quizzically. Another murmured goodbye, and then the horse turned and trotted away, tossing his head with newfound freedom, breathing out clouds of condensation as the sun broke over the horizon.

Crossing the road, Pendergast vaulted a split-rail fence, then traversed a field, moving rapidly and keeping to low areas of ground. He had fixed the terrain in his mind during his long vantage from the top of the hill; he had seen no movement except in the immediate vicinity of the barn, and it was a simple matter to work his way to the small stream burbling along a pebbled course edged by ice, overhung on both sides with bare trees.

He moved downstream, following the meandering course of the rivulet and staying under cover. He calculated it was about eight-tenths of a mile to the farmhouse—a distance he could cover in less than fifteen minutes. Keeping rigid track of both time and distance allowed him to follow his progress across the landscape as clearly as if he were viewing his location on a modern GPS. As the sun rose over the bare tops of the trees, the stream brightened and he began moving more cautiously, keeping to areas of heavier vegetation. The farmhouse was now one final turn of the stream away, and as he came around, creeping through the bushes, he could see it clearly across a broad expanse of matted grass. The farm was showing robust signs of life: smoke streaming from the house's chimneys, a strange-looking man carrying wood inside, another rolling open the door of the adjacent barn—but the shepherd was away with his sheep and, once he'd satisfied himself as to the rest, Pendergast could plan his final approach.

He heard a stealthy sound behind him in the nearby bushes, then another, farther and to his left. He did not turn, did not even move, but merely tensed ever so slightly. The sounds approached from two sides. Still, he did not react... until he felt the icy steel of a muzzle press itself into the back of his neck, while a second individual with scabby lips and a boil on his face emerged from the thicket to his left, rifle leveled.

"Mr. Prendergrast," came the voice from behind him. "Raise your arms nice and slow, like."

"That's *Pendergast*," he said coolly as he complied. "Please do get the name right, at least."

45

Pendergast waited while the man with the boil searched him.

"Got a knife here," the man said.

"Keep searching. Master De Jong says this one's slippery."

They found a second knife in his boot. Further searching turned up nothing beyond what he carried in his musette bag, which they also took away.

"Keep your hands on your head where's I can see 'em," Boil said.

Pendergast complied.

"Now move."

He was shoved forward. The man with the boil walked behind him while the second man fell farther back, covering him from twenty feet with his revolver. As they came out into the field surrounding the farmhouse, Pendergast could now see the second individual who had captured him—a small, bow-legged fireplug of a man with a massive neck, bullet-shaped head, and giant handlebar mustaches. Several other farmhands had now come out of the house, also armed, including one who was clearly in charge.

"Mr. William," said the man with the boil, "we caught him sneaking up on the house, just like you said we would."

"Good work, Berty. Put him in the cheese cellar. I'll get word to Master De Jong that we found his man."

Mr. William put his fingers to his lips and gave two strident whistles. A moment later, Pendergast saw still more armed people rising from places of concealment along the edges of the property. It seemed not only that Leng had prepared a welcoming party for him—he'd prepared several. He wondered just how long they'd all remained hidden, laying their trap and giving him a false sense of confidence—it had to have been twelve or eighteen hours, at least. Remarkable.

As these people began approaching, Pendergast was shoved again from behind. The sun rose farther in the sky, casting a bright, cold light over the frozen landscape. He allowed himself to be led past the house and barn to a wedge-shaped structure emerging from the ground, dug into the side of a hill and fronted by two metal doors. The man named Berty undid the padlock holding the doors closed, and another man pulled them open, one at a time, with loud creaking sounds. Stone steps descended into a cellar to a long passage with an arched ceiling, the air pungent with the smell of cheese and mold. As they walked along, Pendergast could see rows upon rows of cheeses curing on wooden shelves and marble slabs. At the far end, a low archway led to another set of descending steps and, in turn, to a second locked door. This opened into a small laboratory, which appeared to be mainly for processing and testing the cultures needed to make cheese, along with some other, more unusual items of equipment. In the back was yet another door.

"I'll open the door," said Berty. "You, stand back and cover in case there's trouble."

Berty spoke to his fellow worker in a clipped, hostile manner. That, along with his obvious flat affect, led Pendergast to believe the man probably suffered from an antisocial personality disorder. It would make sense, of course, for Leng to employ sociopaths to tend his farm—not only would they be completely reliable if handled correctly, but they would have no moral compass or feelings of sympathy for Leng's victims.

Now the door was unlocked and opened. Pendergast saw, by the light of a kerosene lantern within, a small stone chamber containing two prisoners. One was a girl of about nine, who sprang out of an armchair in surprise as the door swung open. It was Binky, whom he immediately recognized—having seen her from a distance more than once during his initial surveillance of Constance's Fifth Avenue mansion. The other prisoner sat on a bed—a girl of eighteen or nineteen. Pendergast had never seen her before, but based on her resemblance to Constance, he instantly realized who she was.

Mary. Alive. So she had not been murdered by Leng after all. This was something Pendergast had speculated about but never been certain of—until now.

"Get in there," said Berty, nudging him with the rifle.

Pendergast stepped inside as Mary rose in apprehension. The door slammed and there was the sound of padlocking on the other side.

The two girls looked at each other. "Who are you?" asked Mary.

"My name is Pendergast. I'm a close friend of...the person Binky knows as Auntie. The duchess."

"Where is Auntie?" Binky blurted, like Mary keeping back a little guardedly from this stranger.

"She sent me here. It was my task to find Binky—and save her."

"But you haven't saved her," Mary said, matter-of-factly. "You've just joined us—in this cell."

Pendergast gazed at Mary. He could almost see the face of Constance staring back. But whereas Constance's eyes always seemed to radiate defiance, Mary's hazel eyes looked sad and resigned.

46

Decla slouched in the shadows of the brownstones lining Twentieth Street just east of Park, keeping an eye on the plain-looking brownstone that stood, windows shuttered against the cold, halfway down the block. It seemed a perfect residence for a clergyman, a dour, ugly structure, shuttered to the street, in a plummy neighborhood miles from the stink of the Mission. Biscuit had sworn this was the reverend's home, and he was the best tail man she had. Twice, Reverend Considine had, for some unfathomable reason, given him the slip... No, that couldn't be right; Biscuit must have just been off his game. On the third attempt, he'd followed Considine straight to this residence—and stayed long enough to see the clergyman taking off his outerwear and getting comfortable in a room full of books before the shutters were once again closed to the outside.

She'd arrived early, and she still had a few minutes to wait. Digging into a pocket of her jacket, she pulled out a small, thin chapbook whose cover she had deliberately defaced to be illegible. Angling it toward the light of the nearest gas lamp, she turned the pages, then began to read:

When the world is burning,
Fire inside, yet turning,
While fierce flames uprushing
Over the landscape, crushing

She scoffed, then took out the nub of a pencil, licked the lead, and spat onto the pavement. She crossed out a few words and added others, altering the opening lines of the poem—and in so doing, improving the doggerel significantly.

Seeing movement in the distance, she looked up to see the thin figure of Longshank approaching from the evening gloom. She shoved the book back into her pocket and tucked the pencil stub away.

Decla had spent ten of her first sixteen years alone on the streets of lower Manhattan, begging for food and tagging behind gangs for protection, learning by necessity the cruel street arts of survival. She'd been helped in this by a fearlessness, which the sight of blood encouraged rather than repelled. But then a missionary—at least that was what he'd called himself—had come across her while preaching salvation on a street corner and taken her under his wing. Naturally, she'd been suspicious, but he had been patient and kind and, above all, erudite, and in time she had let her guard down and learned not only to read, but to appreciate the long-dead poets: Andrew Marvell, Robert Herrick, John Keats. But over time, the man's lessons began to come at the cost of intimacy: first hinted at, then taken. Decla was so attached to this person she saw as her mentor that at first she hadn't resisted. But then, as his attentions became more frequent, her repulsion and innate violent nature had risen up against this betrayal. Leaving the bloody remains of the man and his life behind, she returned to the streets of the Five Points, fueled by a fatalistic cruelty that allowed her to rise quickly through the ranks of her chosen gang, which in time caught the attention of Enoch Leng. They had become associates of sorts, enriching each other in many ways. While she did not trust him, she respected his cleverness and the way his cruelty was unvarnished by hypocrisy. He also showed a welcome lack of interest in her private life... And, knowing he was a man of many secrets, she returned the favor.

Seeing Biscuit materialize at the corner of Park, she stepped out of the shadows and began moving down the dark street toward the town house. The three met in a small carriageway that ran alongside the residence. Tom Handy arrived next. Last came Woodstock, who more than compensated for his club foot with an uncanny ability for throwing knives.

"You're sure it's the reverend, now?" she whispered to Biscuit, gesturing toward the house.

He nodded in his usual phlegmatic fashion.

"Get to it, then. And keep your peckers up—remember what happened to Scrape." With four of her lieutenants on hand, she'd decided to let them do the actual job, while she kept lookout. Four against one—that smart-arsed preacher wouldn't stand a chance; and besides, it would be good practice.

Tom Handy, the picklock, disappeared around the front of the building. Five minutes later, he returned. "No go."

"What do you mean, 'no go'?"

"Can't be done. Like no lock I've ever tried."

Decla cursed under her breath. "And the windows?"

"Barred."

"Fine bunch of night men you lot are."

"This one ain't," said Woodstock, pointing at a

window partway down the façade. Decla crept up and examined it. There were, in fact, no bars—just wooden shutters, closed tight.

"Think you can handle this?" she asked Tom, sarcastically indicating the window frame.

The young man grinned. He pulled out a rag, a cobbler's hammer, a tiny jar of lard, and some strange-looking tools he'd made for himself, and arrayed everything silently along the ledge. Within five minutes he'd cracked the glass, undone the lock strike, unfastened and pushed aside the interior shutters, then greased up the jamb liner and raised the lower sash halfway.

Decla waited a minute, then peered into the room. It was unlit, but from beyond she could hear a woman's laugh, then the murmur of voices. Enough light came into the dark room to illuminate Considine's black cassock and distinctive broad-brimmed hat, hanging on hooks by a fireplace.

She stepped back from the window. "Is this good enough, then, or should I rap on the door and have his nibs ask you lot in for tea?"

Nods in the darkness. She'd roused their spirits, given them something to prove.

"Right, then. Sounds like he's got a filly with him." What a surprise—hypocritical cleric bastard. "Do him proper—fast, clean, and quiet. I'll watch the street and whistle up a signal if I see anything."

She watched as, one after another, the four slipped quietly through the window and into the town house. Then she moved back to where the alley met Twentieth Street, pulled out her knife, and waited.

* * *

Woodstock was last inside, but he was used to being last—the other lads didn't give him extra consideration, but they also knew better than to make any jokes about his being a gimp.

By practice and silent agreement, the four waited in the darkness to make sure their entrance had roused no curiosity and to let their eyes, and their limbs, prepare. They knew what Decla expected of them. Even if they wouldn't admit it, they were all afraid of her—except perhaps for Longshank, and that was only because he was too stupid.

The voices continued as before. The door of the dark room was partway open, and beyond lay a plain hallway. The voices came from down the hallway, to the right—what Woodstock assumed was a bedroom.

Biscuit, leader in Decla's absence, looked at each of them in turn to make sure they were ready. Everyone had their blades out; Woodstock had two of his heaviest throwing knives ready, with another in reserve. Quietly, they made their way across the room, through the door, and then—slowly, in single file—out into the hall. Woodstock hadn't known what to expect, exactly, but the hallway looked as barren as a prison. There was a strange odor in the air: smoke, but sweet smelling.

Out here, the voices were much clearer: they were coming from a room at the end of the hall, from which also came light that, it seemed to Woodstock, must be the result of many candles. He listened to the exchange going on beyond the door.

"Why, Reverend, I don't think I should." A giggle, half-awkward, half-coquettish. "I mean, given what we've said, what we've *done*—"

"And what we have still to do, Anna. Remember, please call me Percy."

"It seems sinful to do so. But then everything feels so sinful—I mean, we only met three days ago, and—"

"And that makes me the luckiest man on earth.

Imagine, if I hadn't been there by the train station, and you hadn't been on your way back to your father's flax mill in Greenwich, we might never have met."

"And I would still be a good girl."

"No, Anna, no—you would have been, pardon my saying so, an *ignorant* girl, unaware of all the sensations that God in His goodness confers on us...if we only open ourselves to them."

The four had been creeping toward the door during this exchange, and now they formed a half circle around it: Biscuit, Longshank, Tom, and Woodstock. Through the partially opened door, Woodstock could glimpse only a portion of what was indeed a bedroom, spare and severe, but with a massive church candelabra of brass, with its candles throwing off a mellow, flickering light.

"Is that from one of your sermons?" Another nervous giggle.

"No—although there's no reason it couldn't be. God works in mysterious ways, as He is doing here with the two of us—and with your art."

Biscuit looked at them each in turn, making sure they were ready. He held up three fingers, then lowered one of them, silently counting down.

"What do you mean?" came the female voice.

"I'm showing you how to express yourself in a new medium—oil paints instead of yarn. As for me, I have an excellent exemplar in John Donne. He was dean of St. Paul's Cathedral in London, and a most excellent cleric. But he also wrote several elegies that would make the saints in that cathedral's whispering gallery blush despite their marble skins. One in particular, 'Going to Bed,' is particularly apropos: 'To teach thee, I am naked first; why then / What needst thou have more covering than a man?'"

But this quotation was punctuated by the splitting

of wood as Biscuit kicked open the door and the four of them poured into the room. The sight that greeted them, however, gave even the unflappable Biscuit pause. A woman of about twenty sat before a painter's easel, one hand holding a brush up to the canvas, the other holding a palette. She was entirely naked, hair down, a chemise gathered carelessly at her ankles. A somewhat older man—apparently the model, and most certainly the reverend Considine—reclined on a nearby settee, naked as well. Although the man was thin, his body looked surprisingly strong, its chiseled musculature brought into high relief by the candlelight.

Woodstock took all this in during the fragment of a second when everything remained still. And then, instantly, all was sound and motion. The woman screamed, dropping the palette; the man leapt off the settee with remarkable speed, threw the silken coverlet on which he'd lain over Biscuit, then plunged a knife that appeared out of nowhere into the coverlet—once, twice—and yanked the coverlet off again as Biscuit sank toward the floor, blood spurting from his neck. Throwing the easel in the path of the onrushing intruders, the naked man seemed to vanish into the walls. The remaining three halted, frantically casting about, frozen in shock, while Biscuit writhed on the floor. The naked woman fled down a far hall. And then, suddenly, Considine appeared again, now in a billowing silk robe, darting out from, apparently, a hidden entrance. Instinctively, Woodstock whirled and threw a knife; the man dodged it, then yanked the knife from the wall and, with an odd spinning motion that looked almost like ballet, cut Tom's throat from ear to ear. Woodstock skipped backward, raising the other knife and aiming for a second throw, but with a bound Considine covered the distance, grabbing Woodstock's wrist with one hand and twisting it with the other, breaking the bone. "Mind if I borrow this?" he whispered as he wrenched away the knife, flipped it round, then thrust it into Woodstock's eye with the soft *pop* of a rupturing grape.

Woodstock staggered back with a hideous scream and fell upon the hard floor just in time to hear Longshank's own gurgling screams begin to rise. In agonizing pain, Woodstock coiled himself into a fetal position, both hands cupping the blade that protruded from his eye, joining in with the other screams, hoping this was just a bad dream and, given all the noise, he would soon wake up.

47

D'AGOSTA COULD SMELL MRS. Cookson's heavenly dinner rolls baking in the oven—but he could not find the housekeeper herself. It was his habit to let her know each time he went out to pick up Joe at school, despite the event being as regular as the tides on nearby Godwit's Beach. He never bothered looking for Mr. Cookson—that scarecrow could be anywhere about the house or the outbuildings. And so he left the mansion through the servants' main-floor passage as usual, locking the door, ducking his head against the bitter wind, and making for the Seal Harbor schoolhouse a mile and a half away.

When he arrived, he was surprised and alarmed to learn Joe was not there. He had dropped Joe off in the morning as usual, and the teachers confirmed he had been in school until the final bell—but now he was nowhere in the vicinity of the red-painted structure.

D'Agosta paused outside the schoolhouse door to look around. The last thing he wanted was to cause a fuss and draw attention. Scanning the winter landscape revealed nothing. He had not met Joe along the way. Had he gone off with some newfound friends—sledding, perhaps? Or was this some small rebellion of independence? Earlier, Joe had complained about D'Agosta walking him to school, saying it was making him look bad to the other kids.

Or could something worse have happened?

D'Agosta hurried back toward the cottage to see if Joe had turned up, setting off up the frozen lane at a faster pace than he'd come down it. But when he entered through the servants' entrance, there was no sign of Joe—and the kitchen was full of smoke and the smell of burnt bread.

An icy foreboding gripped his heart.

"Mrs. Cookson!" he called as he walked through the back quarters of the mansion. "Joe? *Joe!*"

Only echoes returned.

He ran up to Joe's room; it was as he'd left it when they'd set off for school that morning. The Cooksons' rooms were also empty. He went back outside, scanning the horizon, now in a full-blown panic. He quickly checked the barn and carriage house—nothing there either. They had all simply disappeared.

Was it possible Leng had tracked them here? His policeman's training reasserted itself—anything was possible. He next searched the mansion from attic to basement—maybe Joe was ghost hunting again—but the building was empty. He looked outside for fresh tracks in the snow—nothing.

Returning to the first floor, panting for breath, he considered what to do next. God *damn* this nineteenth century and its lack of communication. There was no way to contact Pendergast, or anyone else for that matter, beyond the slow and truncated telegraph system.

He was turning, ready to head for the back exit again, when he saw something outside the large windows of the parlor. A man, at the reins of an old wagon, its top covered and tied down with canvas, was approaching the mansion up the private lane.

In all the time he'd spent on the island, D'Agosta had never seen a stranger drive up to the cottage. Mrs. Cookson did the marketing herself, and Mr. Cookson took care of the milking and the limited livestock on the property. But nevertheless this alien wagon was coming closer by the minute, the driver holding the reins and sitting back in his seat as casually as if he were going to Sunday-morning service, wearing a well-brushed homburg and covered in a long, tailored trench coat of black leather. He must have caught sight of D'Agosta staring at him out of the window, because now he raised a hand in greeting, then gestured he was going to take the horse around to the servants' entrance. Without bothering to wave back, D'Agosta left the parlor, checked that the front doors were bolted, took out his revolver, and went back into the heated section of the mansion.

This couldn't be a coincidence... could it?

When he reached the servants' entrance, he found the man had already tied his horse to a post and was approaching the door, a small oilcloth bundle draped over one shoulder. Their eyes met through the glass, and he once again raised a hand in greeting. D'Agosta unbolted the door, then stepped back several steps, bringing up his weapon and pointing it at the man. If the man noticed, it didn't seem to faze him, because he opened the door and came in, stamping his feet against the cold, then doffing his hat.

"You're Harrison, I presume?" he said in an accentless American voice as he replaced the hat on his head.

D'Agosta was careful not to register any surprise. "Who are you?"

"My name is Humblecut."

"What do you want?"

"To speak with you for a bit."

D'Agosta kept his face expressionless. He was just about to order the man to turn around and prepare to be searched when Humblecut spoke again.

"It would probably save us a lot of time if I simply told you that we have Joe. Also the housekeepers. If you cooperate, it would be better for them—and for you." As his hand came down from arranging his homburg, it had a derringer in it. "And you could start by handing me your revolver."

D'Agosta stared at the small weapon, astonished and dismayed at the way the man had gotten the drop on him. Here, in this strange place, on this distant island, his twenty-first-century cop instincts were of little use.

"Come now, let's not waste time." Humblecut twitched his gun hand slightly. "I'm not going to hurt either you or Joe—unless you force my hand. That's not why I'm here."

"You seem to forget I have a gun pointed at you," D'Agosta replied.

"If you kill me, it would be the same as killing Joe. And I will get a shot into you, besides." Keeping the derringer pointed, the man reached into his pocket and pulled out Joe's deck of cards. He tossed them at D'Agosta's feet. "If you care at all about Joe, put down your revolver... Mr. Harrison."

D'Agosta hesitated, then placed his revolver on a nearby bench.

"A wise decision. Now, be kind enough to put your hands against that wall while I check you for other weapons. I hope you won't mind my lack of trust—a necessity in this business, I'm afraid."

The man frisked D'Agosta quickly and expertly, then pocketed his revolver. "Now," he said, motioning again with the derringer, "shall we have our little talk?"

Keeping a safe distance to the rear, Humblecut

instructed D'Agosta to walk through the scullery and the kitchen and into the rear parlor. Motioning D'Agosta to take a seat in the far corner, the man quickly locked the pocket door leading into the dining room passage, then took a seat of his own near the entrance to the kitchen. The confidence with which he did all this told D'Agosta the man was already acquainted with the interior of the house.

The man took off his homburg and laid it and his bundle on the floor, then opened the top buttons of his overcoat and pulled out a pencil and a leather notebook.

"Shall we begin?" he asked.

D'Agosta took a deep breath. The man had been sent by Leng; that much was clear. What did he want from D'Agosta? Maybe he could smoke the man out.

"I have a better idea," he said. "Why don't you kiss my ass?"

This was followed by a disapproving silence. "I can understand you're annoyed by your own failings," Humblecut said. "Nevertheless, we can still proceed like gentlemen."

"Tell you what: I'll loosen my pants, stand up, and turn around. That will make it easier for you to kiss my lily-white Italian moneymaker."

Another silence. "Very well," Humblecut said. "If you won't act courteously, you don't deserve courtesy in return. You *will* answer my questions... one way or the other." He paused, looking D'Agosta up and down, as if considering. "Perhaps an audience will help." And with this he reached over to the oilcloth bundle, loosened it, and—with a motion that, for D'Agosta, was ghastly in its similarity to a bocce player aiming for a pallino in Flushing Meadows Park—rolled the severed head of Mrs. Cookson out into the middle of the room. D'Agosta watched as it tumbled over and over, staring eyes glinting sunlight with each rotation, trailing a thin line of fluid, until—with a final bobble—coming to rest a few feet in front of him.

48

"MOTHER*FUCK!*" D'AGOSTA SAID, RECOILING.

Humblecut smiled, amused by his reaction. Then, keeping the derringer pointed, he rose, stepped forward, picked up the head by its hair, and planted it upright in such a way that the saucer eyes stared fixedly at D'Agosta.

"Perhaps now we can steer our conversation back onto a more civilized course," Humblecut said. He readied pencil and notebook. "Shall we begin?"

But D'Agosta was still staring at the decapitated head of Mrs. Cookson. "*Jesus*," he gasped.

Then he forced his gaze back to Humblecut. The man took out a pocket watch and glanced at it. "Time is passing. Are you ready to answer my questions? Or shall I go fetch Mr. Cookson and add him to our audience?"

D'Agosta stared at him, trying to recover himself. "You son of a bitch!"

"You're taxing my patience. You will answer my questions, with none of your own, or perhaps the next head you'll see will be Joe's—which, for now, remains where it belongs."

He was a madman, and D'Agosta believed him. "Don't hurt Joe, for God's sake. Please. I'll answer your questions."

Humblecut smiled broadly. "Bear in mind, I know the answers to some of them already, so if I find you are lying, Joe will die. Now—" he consulted his notebook— "who won the World's Championship Series in the year 2000?" He looked up inquiringly.

D'Agosta struggled to focus. What the hell was this about? "World's Championship... You mean, baseball? The World Series?"

"Yes. Who was the winner?"

It was hard to think, with the dead eyes staring unblinkingly up at him. D'Agosta took a breath, then another. "The Yanks."

Humblecut consulted his notebook again. "You mean, the Yankees?"

"Right. The New York Yankees."

Humblecut raised his pencil and made a check mark, apparently satisfied. "What is the greatest invention of the twentieth century?"

Again D'Agosta was overwhelmed with confusion mingled with horror. Why was Humblecut asking these questions, instead of demanding to know where Pendergast was hiding out, or what their plans were—or something? "I don't know. The computer, maybe?"

"Which is?"

"A device," D'Agosta stammered. "A machine. Everyone has one. Electronic brains that can do incredible things."

"For example?"

"Beat any human at chess. Store huge amounts of information. Do difficult mathematical calculations. You can reach anyone in the world, instantly—and see their faces as you talk to them. You use them for banking, making friends that seem like real people..." He raised his hands. "Everything."

This was followed by much note-taking and more probing questions, one leading to the next. D'Agosta had to explain what the telephone was, radio, television, the internet, cars, airplanes, spaceships, men on the moon.

Humblecut wrote it all down. Then he changed the subject. "What was the worst event of the twentieth century?"

"Christ... 9/11, maybe. No, that was... The Holocaust. World War Two. The bomb. Jesus, I don't know where to begin."

"Let us go through each one, then."

Falteringly, D'Agosta explained the Holocaust, World Wars I and II, the atomic bomb, the terrorist attacks of September 11, 2001. As he spoke, Humblecut occasionally interrupted with shorter, more pointed questions, still writing everything down. What were the principles behind the bomb? How powerful was it? Who had them? Were there other genocides besides the Holocaust? The questions now probed the darkest, most horrific corners of the twentieth century, an area that Humblecut seemed to relish.

"Now," the man said at last. "What were the greatest medical advances of the twentieth century?"

D'Agosta racked his brain. These questions were so off the wall. "Um, let's see... penicillin... the heart transplant... DNA... cloning... CRISPR..."

Humblecut held up a hand. "Enough. Let me have an explanation of those items."

D'Agosta struggled to explain as Humblecut probed into each medical discovery. What was a vaccine? How did it work? What were antibiotics? Did they cure smallpox? Were there still diseases in the twenty-first century? How long did people live?

Yes, there were still famines and epidemics. There were no cities on the moon. The question of life after death had not been answered. Nobody had proved or disproved God's existence. You could go anywhere in the world in twenty-four hours. Robots were exploring Mars. D'Agosta, nearly certain he was in the hands of a madman, answered each question as truthfully as possible.

An hour passed, then another, before the questions finally ceased. "Thank you," Humblecut said—and his tone had regained the fake friendliness he'd shown initially. "I believe you've answered my questions truthfully." He put down his pencil and notebook. "Under the circumstances, I think we can reunite you with Joe now."

Hearing this, D'Agosta silently thanked whatever god was orchestrating this nightmare. But when Humblecut stood up to put away his gun, a blackjack suddenly replaced it in his hand; and when he stroked D'Agosta's skull with it, the thankfulness was cut off prematurely.

49

Enoch Leng had his medical office and consulting practice in an ornate suite of rooms in Manhattan's fashionable Murray Hill neighborhood, on Twenty-Eighth Street just off Madison Avenue—New York's equivalent of Harley Street, housing the city's best Gilded Age physicians. He practiced no surgery for private clients—confining his surgical experiments to the mental patients at Bellevue and his personal victims. He maintained a lucrative practice instead by treating wealthy women of a certain age who suffered from a host of fashionable nervous ailments—neurasthenia, the vapors, hysteria, and assorted female maladies. He had recently acquired a device, patented by Dr. Granville, that was remarkable in its ability to restore the nervous vigor of women.

In truth, however, Dr. Leng was wealthy and had little need for the fees he charged these blushing matrons; rather, it was necessary for him to have a professional face for the public at large. And so once a week his practice was open, with a secretary, a nurse, and a medical assistant. The other six days, when the elegant rooms were empty, Leng employed them for other projects.

At present, he was seated in his private office: a large space paneled in mahogany, boasting rippled glass display cases, bookshelves full of medical treatises, diplomas and awards framed on the walls, and two tall windows overlooking Madison Avenue. Several members of his private security staff were in the outer offices, and Decla herself was in his office, sitting moodily across from Leng.

Leng knew what was preying on her mind. Decla needed violence like a shark needed motion. There *had* been some violence of late—but it had concluded in a manner unsatisfactory to both of them.

A knock sounded on the door.

"Enter," said Leng.

A member of the Milk Drinkers—dressed in the garb of a newsboy, one of the messengers known as "runners"—stepped in. He nodded to Decla and came forward, leaning over the desk, to murmur in Leng's ear. Then he produced a thick envelope, which he placed on the desk blotter.

"Thank you, you may go." Leng sat back, waving vaguely in the direction of the door. He waited until the runner had left, then turned to Decla.

"This reverend Considine is a damned enigma," he said. "First, he does Scrape a fatal mischief. That was a surprise—Scrape was normally good at that kind of work."

"One of my best," Decla said.

"And now, even more surprising, this whoreson making short work of your squad. Please give me the details, as you witnessed them."

"I was keeping watch outside. Four on one—seemed a good chance to sharpen their skills, like."

Leng knew this failure had left Decla in a dangerous mood. "Quite understandable. I should have done the same."

"There were two side windows next the alleyway. The first was barred, but the farther was only shutters over glass—Tom got that open and they all slipped in, like Bob's your uncle. It was dark, but before they closed the shutters, I noticed a little light from the back of the house, and the laugh of a woman."

Leng raised his eyebrows.

"It wasn't loud. A minute later, I heard shouts, then screams. At first, I thought that meant all was going aright. But, quick as you like, I realized the voices—some yelling, some begging—as our own boys'. I thought I was hearing things. Then I wondered if we'd walked into a trap somehow—maybe the preacher had hired some other gang for protection. I almost slipped inside myself to take a butcher's... but I remembered what you said about unexpected outcomes, and I kept my position as lookout—for a time."

"Undoubtedly the right thing to do." Leng knew what most upset her was the loss of three Milk Drinkers and the half blinding of another—on her lookout.

"It didn't take long. Five minutes, and the cleric opened the back door. Then, after taking a gander, he carried out Biscuit, Tom Handy, and Longshank—one at a time, over his shoulder—and dumped them into a cart near the stables."

"A cart?"

"The kind you use for night soil."

Leng shook his head.

"Just a few minutes later, now it was the front door what opened, and out pitched our Woodstock. He hit the pavement and rolled into the gutter. Had one of his own blades sticking out of his eye. I thought it might be a trap, so I whistled up a crew as fast as I could; then we brought a dray cart up and hustled him away."

"You left the other bodies?"

"Had to save Woodstock—and then later, the bodies had disappeared."

Leng grunted. He had patched the youth up himself. He'd be all right, in time... but his knife-throwing days were over.

He thought a minute. Woodstock had whined and gabbled out fragments of what had taken place within, but he'd wanted to hear Decla's own story, as well. "So the first of the side windows was barred."

She nodded.

"But the second one—farther back—was merely a normal window, covered with wooden shutters?"

"Yes."

"Odd. It does sound like a trap. The fellow claims to have been a missionary in Africa. Perhaps that proved rather more perilous training than I assumed."

"All I know is, for a preacher, he's damned handy with a knife."

"Fancy him for a member of your gang?" Leng asked, trying to cheer her. "He'd be handing out salutary tracts with one hand while administering *coups de grâce* with the other."

Despite the light tone, he was troubled. There was something extraordinary about the man. Leng did not doubt he was a cleric sent to do work in the Five Points; he was just too authentic and eccentric to be an impostor. Nevertheless, there was an intangible air about him, something ineffable and dangerous. He would require an entirely unconventional approach—but Leng, with rather a lot on his own plate at present, could not take up the task himself.

He glanced privately at Decla, who was now staring

off into space, eyebrows narrowed, running her fingertips over the fresh scar on her palm. His *chargée d'affaires* was like a Thoroughbred: extraordinarily talented, but requiring careful handling.

"What if I gave him to *you*?" he asked. "As a special gift, so to speak? Now that you know what you're up against."

Decla raised her eyes to his, a hungry smile slowly replacing her abstracted look. "I'd have a free hand?" she asked.

"Just as you please. But hold off a week or two—and take your time formulating a plan. That cleric isn't going anywhere."

She was, he noticed, still idly stroking the scar. "I'd be happy to give you the woman who gave you that, as well."

The fingertips froze, and something flickered in her eyes. "The duchess?"

"Yes. She's highly skilled, but I think she could, if goaded, become rash or even impetuous. It would be lovely if you could arrange to have a mano a mano someplace where I could be a spectator. Just be careful: I should be particularly unhappy if I ended up having to replace you, as well as the others." He stretched, adjusted his cuffs. "On a related matter: not only was that Pendergast fellow caught yesterday at a property I own up north, but now—" he paused to pat the envelope on the blotter— "given this message that just arrived from Humblecut, we have all of these pestilent nuisances in chains."

"Except the girl," Decla said in a low voice.

"Except the girl." Leng mused in silence for a moment, then reached for the envelope, slicing it open with a scalpel. He drew out a sheet of paper nearly three feet long, folded at least six times and covered with thin ribbons of text pasted into paragraphs.

"Good heavens!" he said, scrolling through it. "It must have taken the telegraph operator hours to convey this." He put the document on his desk, smoothing it out carefully.

"I'll be off, then," Decla said, rising silkily to her feet, energized by the thought of stalking Considine.

"Mind how you go," Leng told her. But his voice was low and distracted; his attention was now fixed on the telegram, which he had already begun to decipher.

50

THE ROUGH BURLAP SACK had been over D'Agosta's head for so long that when it was finally removed, his eyes were already adjusted to darkness and he had no problem getting his bearings in the moonlight. He looked about, his head still pounding. He was on a commercial wharf, arms bound behind at the wrists, mouth gagged. It appeared to be early evening, but at this time of the year the place was deserted: a stone building that fronted the quayside was empty and dark, and the only noise was the chugging of a vessel. It appeared to be a fishing trawler, with an upthrust bow covered in netting and a small cabin from which rose a smokestack.

He looked around. There was the wagon that had carried him and Joe from the mansion to the dock. Humblecut pulled Joe out from beneath the wagon covering and stood him on his feet next to D'Agosta. He, too, was bound and hooded. He watched Humblecut pull the hood free, exposing Joe's face, red and defiant, his mouth also gagged. They exchanged a look. D'Agosta tried to communicate with his eyes that everything was going to be okay—even if he felt precisely the opposite. They were clearly about to sail from Mount Desert Island, bound for God knew where.

How much time had passed since he'd been clobbered, D'Agosta wasn't sure; Humblecut had locked him alone in a basement storage room with stone walls and an iron door, no windows, and only rows of preserved peaches for company. He guessed that a night and a day had passed, and that it was now the following evening. After finishing his questions, Humblecut hadn't said another word to him—not when he locked him in the storeroom, not when he put the sack over his head and bundled him into the wagon, and not now.

The crew of the boat seemed limited to two: a mate, who was currently unloading half a dozen oilcloth bundles from the wagon and carrying them on board, and the captain: a man with a deeply seamed and scarred visage.

"Put these two in the hold," Humblecut told the captain as he boarded the boat.

"Aye, aye, Mr. Cassaway," the man said.

The captain came up, grabbed him and Joe by an arm each, then escorted them roughly along the dock and up the gangplank onto the vessel. As he ushered them toward the bow, D'Agosta caught sight of the mate again. He was in the stern and, having placed the oilcloth bundles in some heavy netting, was now drawing the netting close around and wrapping it with an iron chain. A rough hand between his shoulders pushed him down the hatchway and onto a rank pile of fishnets. A moment later, Joe was shoved down next to him and the hatch banged to, shutting out the moonlight. There were enough open seams in the wall to let in light from the aft cabin. He'd never seen the youth look worried, and he did not look worried now—only angry and defiant. Remarkable how resilient he was.

D'Agosta heard the light rap of mooring lines hitting the deck; then the engine took on a throatier roar. The boat started to vibrate as it pulled away from the dock. As it moved out into the open water, it began to roll in the swell. At a certain point the engine throttled down, and the boat slowed. There was the murmur of voices, the sound of chains being dragged aft across the deck, followed by a loud splash. It seemed that Mr. and Mrs. Cookson, separated on land, were now to be united in death on the seabed. The callous brutality of it enraged D'Agosta.

It was bitterly cold and dim in the hold. Joe wriggled up against him to stay warm, resting his head on his shoulder. D'Agosta was glad of the human contact; it helped him focus his mind. He turned his thoughts to what might happen next. He wondered if he and Joe were going to shortly join the Cooksons in their journey over the transom. It seemed unlikely: if that were the case, they'd already be dead and gone. Leng was keeping them alive for some reason, probably as bargaining chips. They were securely tied up, and even if they could get loose, they were on a boat in the winter Atlantic with no possibility of getting off... unless he could seize control of the vessel, which seemed an impossibility without weapons. Or, if they could get untied, they might wait until docking to fight or make a break for it.

He wriggled his wrists. Humblecut knew how to tie a knot, that was for sure. The rope that bound his hands and encircled his waist was stout hemp, tight and inflexible. There was probably nothing in the hold that could be used to free them, but D'Agosta knew it was better to keep busy—not only for Joe's sanity, but for his own. He nudged Joe, not sure how to explain that he was going to search the hold. He pointed his chin around, then got up on his knees and began to crawl about, looking around as best he could in the faint light for anything that might help. Joe immediately caught on and—nodding his understanding to D'Agosta—began a search of his own.

51

Edwin Humblecut eased himself into an armchair by the fire, feeling the warmth of the glowing coals. It was quite a handsome library, revealing enormous wealth, quietly displayed.

"Brandy?" asked Leng, standing at a side table with crystal decanters and glasses.

"No, thank you, Doctor. I am a teetotalist."

"Of course. I, however, shall have a tot to warm myself on this cold evening."

Leng poured a brandy and settled into the seat opposite. It was a chill winter night, and Humblecut was grateful for the warmth of the fire after his stay on Mount Desert.

It had been a gratifying trip on several levels. He had particularly enjoyed his time with that pair of island rubes—what were their names? Cookson. And he treasured the moment when he revealed to the policeman what he'd done—the look of perfect horror on his face. The sojourn itself, however—especially his attic vigil—had left him chilled to the bone. But the twenty-four-hour sea voyage back to Manhattan was now complete; he had handed off Harrison and the boy to Leng's lackeys...and all that remained was to collect his reward.

As Leng settled into the seat, Humblecut observed him with keen but covert interest. Humblecut had the uncanny ability to peer into other people's minds and see their thought processes. But Leng was absolutely opaque. His thinking was hidden and his goals shrouded in mystery. That intrigued Humblecut. This last assignment had been truly inexplicable: questioning a copper who, apparently, had come from the future. Humblecut was a man who believed in rationality and science, and the concept of traveling through time was too much to swallow. Ordinarily he would have discounted it as madness. But what convinced him of its veracity was that Harrison, the policeman, was clearly an ordinary sort of person, without any particular imaginative gifts—and yet he'd painted a picture of the future that was original, unexpected, utterly grotesque...yet entirely believable. If George Harrison was a fantasist, he showed no other signs of madness or even abnormal thinking. It seemed impossible for him to invent, on the fly, all that he had said.

Thus, Humblecut was inclined to believe it was true—that he was indeed a man who had traveled from the future. And what a future he'd depicted! The remarkable inventions, the even more remarkable violence...Humblecut wished he could live long enough to see it.

He knew better than to ask Leng what it was all about—but nevertheless, he had mentally filed away every detail. There had to be value in it; exactly what to exploit, and how, could wait. Humblecut was not only a careful man—he was a patient one.

He'd brought the police officer and the boy back to the mansion, where Leng's people had taken over and imprisoned them somewhere in the house. And now it was time for Humblecut to be paid a liberal fee—which he felt he richly deserved, after that long perambulation through a frozen hell.

He waited for Leng to initiate the conversation. But Leng seemed content to sit by the fire in silence, sipping his drink.

"I am wondering," Leng finally began, in a low voice, "what your thoughts are on this most recent assignment?"

"I don't think about my assignments, sir," Humblecut replied. "I accomplish them. And then I move on."

"But surely," said Leng, "you must have wondered where that fellow Harrison came from? Why I had you ask him all those questions? Above all, you must have wondered how he could possibly know the answers. Not the slightest glimmer of curiosity about that?"

Humblecut felt the conversation moving into hazardous territory. "Dr. Leng, I pride myself on a lack of inquisitiveness when it comes to the dealings of my clients. I've never allowed the kind of curiosity another man might find natural to interfere with business. What you intend to do, or not do, with the man—or the telegram—is none of my affair."

"A very commendable attitude. I hadn't pegged you as an incurious man. Had I been in your shoes, I would have had many questions about how such a man could possibly exist, and whether his information could be put to some use. I would have retained notes, at the least."

"I never take notes," said Humblecut. "I possess an eidetic memory."

"Ah! An eidetic memory."

"Very useful in my line of work," Humblecut said, allowing himself an uncharacteristic measure of pride.

Perhaps such an asset could up his bargaining price in future assignments.

"I imagine so," Leng said, rising. "Cigar?"

He picked up a box of cigars from the mantel, opened it, and held it out to him. Humblecut selected a cigar—a Don José perla—and used the proffered cutter to notch the end. Leng lit it for him with a large, chased silver lighter. Then he took one for himself, and trimmed and lit it.

Humblecut puffed on his cigar—it was, as he anticipated, excellent.

"Eidetic memory, most useful," said Leng. "Now, is there anything else you'd like to tell me before we settle our accounts?"

"I'll just leave you with a word of advice: that man may be an ordinary, unimaginative copper, but he's cleverer than he looks. He almost managed to escape the boat on our way down from Maine. And keep an eye on the boy—he's a resourceful little squib." He took a moment to draw smoke into his mouth and expel it in a little stream.

"Thank you, I shall do so. Now, I believe I owe you a tidy sum."

Humblecut inclined his head.

"Twenty thousand dollars is what we agreed."

He inclined his head again.

Leng pulled a tapestry cord next to the chair. One of his white-gloved lackeys came in, conferred with Leng, and left. A moment later he returned with a leather satchel, which he handed to Humblecut. He took it by the handle, opened it, and saw it was filled with neatly banded bricks of notes. He quickly riffled through them, pulling out a random few to ensure they were genuine—more from habit than anything else; Leng was not the kind of client to pull a low stunt such as that. He closed the satchel and placed it next to his chair. "Much obliged, Dr. Leng."

"It's a funny thing, Humblecut," said Leng. "I just can't get over the fact you aren't more curious. Surely you've been wondering what it's all about...and how you might profit from it."

"I've already answered that question," Humblecut said sharply. "I do not seek profit from my clients' business." Now was the time to get out—he didn't like the direction in which Leng continued to steer the conversation, and it occurred to him that revealing his eidetic abilities to this man might not have been wise. "And now, Dr. Leng, I thank you for your trust in me. I hope to do business with you again." He laid his half-smoked cigar down on the ashtray and rose.

"Not quite yet."

On his feet, Humblecut felt a sudden spell of dizziness, and a strange weakness in his knees that forced him to steady himself against the arm of the chair. He instantly realized he'd somehow been poisoned. The dimness was coming on fast, his mind filling with confusion. He took a step toward Leng, stumbled, and then lunged, in an effort to strangle his client with the last of his fading strength. But despite the will of a lion, he was overwhelmed with weakness and merely collapsed on the floor in front of the dying fire. Staring up at Leng, all he could manage was a gurgle of fury. He had badly misjudged the man.

Leng rose and stood over him, calmly puffing his cigar. Humblecut stared up at him, burning with an internal paroxysm of rage, but—now entirely incapacitated—with no ability to act on it. Worse, he was finding it increasingly difficult to breathe. It must have been the cigar—or something dusted on the money.

"While I appreciate your help," Leng said, "I know

you were already scheming to turn the knowledge you gained to your profit. That cannot be permitted. A man from the future is an inestimable commodity. And, yes: that is indeed what Harrison is. Extraordinary, don't you think? The value of his knowledge of what is to come is priceless, and I know exactly how to use it. You, on the other hand, would only ruin everything in an effort to capitalize on the information."

Now all Humblecut could think of was getting more air into his lungs, trying to keep his chest expanding, his breathing going. But the paralysis had now reached his core, and no matter how hard his mind screamed at his lungs to expand, they refused. His eyes danced with points of light, and then fog, and then finally night.

* * *

Leng pulled the tapestry cord again, and the white-gloved lackey returned, a second on his heels. He wordlessly gestured at the body and the satchel, and both were quickly removed.

A few minutes later Decla entered. Leng had asked her to wait until Humblecut left—if she was surprised at the way he'd done so, she did not show it.

"Have a seat," Leng said.

Decla sat. She looked displeased—Leng knew the trappings of wealth made her uneasy: they were to be looted, rather than make oneself comfortable in. Her eyes darted to the fire and back to him.

"Drink?"

She shook her head.

"My dear, I find myself increasingly concerned about a mutual acquaintance of ours."

"The churchman?" This piqued her interest.

"No—although, as we've discussed, you can have his head in a day or two. Now: I've accomplished my goal of capturing and imprisoning our main adversaries—all except one. Three more are due to arrive soon—that interfering fellow Pendergast, along with the sisters, Mary and, ah, Binky. There's just one loose thread—the other person we spoke of at our last meeting. Despite everything I've done, despite all the nets I've dragged across the city, I can't find her. I'm sure you know of whom I speak."

"The *duchess*," Decla said in a low, hateful tone.

"Exactly. The Duchess of Ironclaw. Whose real name is Constance—Constance Greene. A meddlesome creature, here to interfere with my—*our*—plans."

Decla nodded with increased interest.

"As you know, I only purchased this abode a few years ago and have yet to find time to explore every last corner. Be that as it may, over the past few days I've had the sense—only a feeling, mind you—that there's a foreign presence here; a hostile revenant, if you will. I've no solid evidence; it's mere intuition...but I believe that presence is our mutual friend."

Decla remained silent, listening.

"I don't know the details—neither did the source of my information—but it seems that, for at least a few years, she once lived in this house. And my sense, my intuition, wonders if in fact she might be hiding here, in this house, right under my nose. It's just the sort of thing she'd do. If that's the case, it's possible she knows passageways and rooms I have not yet discovered. Your assignment is to take your squadron and search this house, top to bottom. You will be permitted to enter even those areas previously off-limits, such as the cellars. In fact, you should probably concentrate your search there." He held up a ring, from which dangled an iron key. "Here is the master key to the house: you may go anywhere, search any place. My only exhortation to you is not to touch anything in my storerooms, laboratory, surgery, or collections. I say this out of concern for your own safety—there are poisons that will kill by mere touch, weapons that will discharge at the slightest jostle, gases that will suffocate. Do you understand?" He removed the key from the ring and tossed it to her. "Go find Constance. I'm not interested in her capture, if you understand my meaning. You may have your way with her—as you may also, in the near future, with the reverend. That will be your reward: but I find this business of the Greene girl rather more pressing than even Considine. Please see to it at once."

Decla's only response was the wicked gleam that appeared in her eyes, and a smile she could not fully restrain. She nodded, stood, and left the room.

52

Constance peered at the coin in her hand: a gold doubloon struck during the Spanish empire, bearing a date of 1699. She had found it wedged in a crack of her temporary quarters and appropriated it as a sort of good luck piece. She turned it over in her palm. Its cool heaviness was soothing to the touch—but it did little to ease the agitation she felt.

She assumed—hoped—that Aloysius had found Binky, allowed himself to be captured by Leng's men, and was now headed back to the mansion—as they had planned in their meeting at the Tenderloin bordello. She'd successfully poisoned Leng—a private plan of her own she had told neither Aloysius nor Diogenes about, for obvious reasons. The man was doomed: it gave her immense satisfaction to know that no matter what he did, no matter what happened to her, he would be dying in agony within four to six days. But poisoning him had started a clock ticking, and it meant both she and Pendergast had a limited period to complete their combined assignments: free her siblings and get them to safety before

Leng's initial symptoms kicked in. These symptoms could manifest themselves as early as tomorrow, January 9. As soon as the poison began to work on Leng and he realized what was happening, he would kill them all. But he'd *already killed Mary*—which, almost subconsciously, had narrowed her own goal to one overriding thing: destroying Leng. Hence the irreversible poison. Aloysius and the others—they must have known when they came through the portal that the chances of survival were slim. Now, with the machine broken, all their fates were even less certain.

She stared at the coin. Her feeling of unease was not going away. She'd lived in this house—or at least its simulacrum—for a hundred years, and she trusted her instincts. She decided a reconnoiter would be in order, to see if conditions had changed.

Grasping a lantern, she rose from the cell and moved out into the corridor leading to the secret staircase that connected this sub-basement lair to the basement proper. She cautiously ascended the stairs and paused at the exit, peering through a pinhole to ensure nobody was there before she opened the door.

She froze. There *was* someone. She could see a dim lantern moving down the far end of a basement corridor. Soon, two more appeared behind it.

She watched as they approached. Slowly, the face of the leader became visible. It was Decla. She and the others were clearly searching for something: examining the walls, tapping on them, occasionally holding up lighted matches to test the flow of air.

Constance shrank back. The secret door into the sub-basement was well hidden—and securely locked—but would it stand up to such close examination? Despite the thickness of the walls, she could hear the tapping move closer, and closer, until it reached the hidden door. There the tapping hesitated briefly. Then it started again, now going up and down, then sideways. Clearly, they had noted a change of tone.

This was followed a few minutes later by a low scraping: a knife being used to examine the spot for cracks or unnatural edges. Then a sudden, excited murmur of voices, and the tapping immediately accelerated.

They had found the door to the sub-basement caverns.

More scraping and chiseling as they uncovered the hidden seams. They weren't going to be able to open it right away—the inside of the door was shielded in solid iron plate—but it would be only a matter of time before they broke through and uncovered the sub-basement—and her lair.

She waited, ear pressed to the iron of the door. More chiseling, hammering, chatter—and then all went silent.

They had gone off to fetch heavier tools.

She had to act immediately. When they got the door open, they would eventually find her hiding place, and everything she'd stored within it. This left her with a choice: she could flee the mansion via the watery tunnel, leaving everything behind—or she could flee into the house itself, hoping to remain hidden in its secret passageways and hollow walls long enough to accomplish her objectives.

In reality, this was no choice at all. To follow through on her end of the plan required her presence—here. To run away was to fail herself and the others, and to perish... sooner rather than later.

Extracting a heavy key from her pocket, she unlocked the door and cracked it open, easing her lantern into the now empty hallway. They would be coming back momentarily—she had to move fast.

After shutting the door and locking it again from the other side—given the scrapings and chisel marks, there was no longer any point in trying to disguise it—she crept along the basement corridor. With her lantern partially shuttered, she moved in the direction opposite Decla's path of return. It would take the gang an hour, perhaps longer, to break through the door and explore the sub-basement, which should give her time to locate a new bolt-hole from which to operate in the time that remained. Of course, the water entrance—the intended escape route—was almost certain to be discovered. They would have to leave the mansion through the main floor—a dangerous complication.

She moved along the maze of corridors into an abandoned and unstable area of the basement, far from Leng's labs and collections. A small cave-in marked the opening. She made her way over the rubble and continued along in silence, looking for a place to hide. There were rows of ancient storerooms, some with rotting casks that once held amontillado; stacks of old bricks; hardened sacks of cement; shovels and trowels and other rusting tools.

She heard a distant sound and froze, quickly shuttering her lantern. Listening intently, she identified it as a girl weeping.

In utter darkness, she stole toward the sounds, occasionally touching the basement walls for orientation, her progress aided by her preternatural night vision. Slowly, the sounds grew more prominent, and the darkness diminished—she was approaching a section of the vast, never-mapped basement that was reachable from another passage. Someone had been imprisoned down here—and recently. And as the weeping grew nearer, she realized it was Binky. This meant Pendergast *had* completed his part of the compact; he had located Binky, been captured by Leng, and already been brought back to the house. But as she turned a corner, and the weeping grew louder, she could hear another voice murmuring words of comfort.

In a moment of profound astonishment, followed instantly by joy, Constance recognized the other voice. It was her sister, Mary. *Alive.* She was whispering words of comfort to Binky. And then another voice chimed in—Joe.

The shock of this discovery, with the simultaneous rush of gladness and fear she felt, was so powerful that she had to steady herself against a nearby wall. Mary wasn't dead after all. *Mary was alive.*

But now all her siblings were prisoners.

It had been a cruel deception of Leng's—and she had to temporarily put aside her emotions to think the consequences through. If Binky and Mary were here, Pendergast had succeeded. And if Joe was here, too, then Leng had discovered D'Agosta's hideaway. D'Agosta, if still alive, would probably be imprisoned with Pendergast in another section of the mansion.

She forced herself to pause a moment, to refrain from acting on instinct. Her natural impulse was to rush to them, free them, take them to safety. But without more intelligence of the other developments that must also have occurred, that plan would surely fail—especially now, with the basement crawling with Decla's gang, which meant Leng was on high alert.

Even as she pondered this, she heard other voices coming down the hallway—loud, male—and then saw a dim light, shining from around the corner of the path opposite to the one she'd taken. More of Leng's confederates. She shrank back into a nearby storeroom, flattening herself against the inside wall.

She heard the men bang on the metal bars of the cell door. One shouted Mary's name. There was a defiant yell from Joe and what sounded like a tussle; Binky sobbed loudly and Mary began to scream.

"Don't take me!" she heard Mary cry. "Oh God, don't take me *there!*"

Another angry shout from Joe, followed by the sound of a blow, and then the clang of the iron door. Mary's voice, still crying out, began to fade as she was manhandled down the hall and away.

A new shock flooded over Constance. Mary was alive... She had not factored that into her plans when she vengefully poisoned Leng. But more immediately, she knew from the echoing sounds exactly where Mary was going: Leng's new operating theater, built in this very basement.

If Leng had not killed Mary for her cauda equina, then what had he done? There was one obvious answer: he'd been using her as one of his guinea pigs, testing an accelerated version of the Arcanum on her. And since she herself had given him the proper formula, it would no doubt work—Mary would be showing no signs of aging.

And Constance recalled something else. When Leng's guinea pigs began to present like Mary—indicating a successful formula had been reached—Leng had the first of them dissected, looking for internal malfunctions caused by the elixir but not obvious externally.

This meant that Leng was preparing—right now— to autopsy her sister, Mary... alive.

53

Vincent D'Agosta sat on a straw bale in the corner of the room, watching Pendergast examine the walls, door, floor, and ceiling—something he'd been doing for the past hour. D'Agosta had been locked in this cell the night before, but Pendergast had only arrived today. It seemed that—although Pendergast had been caught earlier than D'Agosta—Leng had taken his sweet time arranging transport for him and the others from his farm down to the mansion... no doubt realizing how cautious he'd have to be in doing so. Upon his arrival, Pendergast had closely questioned D'Agosta about his conversation with Humblecut, taking extreme interest in both the questions and the answers.

"We're fucked six ways to Sunday," said D'Agosta wearily. "There's no way out of this iron box."

"Your curses are as amusing as they are logistically and anatomically impossible," Pendergast replied. He broke off his investigation and began pacing the room. His outfit—tight riding breeches and shirt, cloak, and high leather boots—made him look like some highwayman of old.

"You don't seem all that worried."

"I assure you, my dear Vincent, I would be extremely worried—were I merely pondering our predicament. But worry is a debilitating emotion, and so I suppress it in lieu of other things." He paused, staring down at D'Agosta's shoes. "Pity your footwear has been ruined."

"Who cares?" D'Agosta said. The overwhelming emotion he felt was one of failure—failure to protect Joe and keep him safe, failure to detect Humblecut's presence on the island, failure to escape from the boat. That last had been an interminable voyage, the two of them stuffed in the freezing, foul-smelling, almost lightless bilge. At least Joe hadn't been affected by the seasickness that plagued D'Agosta. They had almost escaped when Joe managed to loosen some rivets in a bulkhead, but their efforts were discovered by that bastard Humblecut. As soon as they docked, a carriage with guards took them to Leng's mansion; there, Joe had been led off elsewhere, and he, D'Agosta, had been locked in this cell under the eaves of the building. Earlier that day, Pendergast had been thrust in as well. A single candle illuminated the grim, windowless room, its floor covered in straw, a tiny, barred slot in the door presumably for meals—although they had been given only water. The four walls, ceiling, and floor were all riveted iron. Not even Pendergast, it seemed, could find a way out.

When Pendergast spoke, it was as if he'd read D'Agosta's thoughts. "If you're blaming yourself for getting caught, please don't. That was part of our plan all along."

"Our plan? What are you talking about?"

"Constance, Diogenes, and mine. You see, under the circumstances it was virtually impossible to hide you somewhere you would not be found, while still being able to reach you. No: the trick was to delay Leng's finding you until his plans and schemes began to focus more and more on the future—and the portal we used to get here. That is why the first thing I did after you left the city was seal off all access to the portal. Whatever Ferenc told him, Leng does not know for certain whether or not we have control over it. I was confident he wouldn't kill either Joe or Binky, because he could use them for leverage. My assignment was to find Binky—which I did—and then arrange to be captured. I felt certain Leng would return all of us here, under this roof... and as you see, he has done exactly that—including, as it turns out, Mary."

D'Agosta looked up at him in surprise. "Mary?"

"Yes. Those ashes in the urn were just a cruel deception."

"Christ." D'Agosta shook his head. "So now that your plans have succeeded and we're all under one roof, what next?"

"Now we are tortured in an attempt to force us to give up the secret—not that there's any to give—of accessing the portal."

D'Agosta grimaced. "In other words, we have him just where he wants us."

"You're forgetting that three of us put this plan together, not just me. One person's job includes watching our alley, just in case... Well, I need not spell it out. More to the point is the third person's assignment, which, now that we are all here, is to get Binky and Joe free."

"You mean, Constance?"

"She knows the house better than anyone—including me and Leng. And she is extremely capable and stealthy, as you know. Although certain variables I did not consider have been introduced to the equation."

"Such as Mary?"

"That—and precisely how clever and intuitive Leng

is. I fear he may have guessed, or will guess shortly, that he has an uninvited guest."

D'Agosta could imagine this all too well. "How nice for Binky. How nice for Joe. What about us?"

"Constance has a devilishly difficult task merely freeing her siblings."

"I see. So it's up to us to free ourselves."

"Speaking of that—may I see your left shoe?"

"What?"

"Indulge me."

D'Agosta, still struggling to absorb what he'd just heard, and in any case no longer surprised at any of Pendergast's enigmatic demands, took off his shoe and handed it over. Pendergast turned it around in his hands, examining it. He then flipped it over and, with a jerk, removed the heel, exposing a pattern of small tacks. Another series of yanks peeled back the sole. He managed to pull out one of the tacks, which he examined with a frown.

"This won't do," he said.

He reseated the tack, pressed the sole back on, and reattached the heel. He stared at the shoe a bit longer. Then he unlaced it, extracting the lace and testing its strength with a few jerks.

"Better," he murmured, weaving it inside his waistband. He handed D'Agosta back his ruined shoe. "Try not to draw attention to its condition."

"Planning on strangling someone?"

"I fear the lace is too short for that purpose."

"What's it for, then?"

"Better you should not know. I'll gladly replace the shoes with another pair when we get back."

"*If* we get back," D'Agosta said, putting the shoe back on.

"I feel, Vincent, that I owe you a rather profound apology for dragging you here."

D'Agosta waved his hand. "Why, exactly, is Leng keeping us alive—even just for the time being? I mean, he could kill us and be rid of the problem permanently."

"Because we're invaluable to him. As I said, he doesn't know the time machine might be ruined for good. He anticipates needing our help."

"Why does he care so much about the machine?"

"Think of the questions he asked you. His goal has moved beyond the Arcanum, although that is still of intense interest. Extending his life is only a proximate goal. His ultimate ambition is to—"

D'Agosta heard the sound of a heavy tread in the corridor. They immediately fell silent.

"We're going to open the door," said a loud voice. "Stand in the back of the cell. We're well armed. Don't be stupid."

Pendergast and D'Agosta moved back against the far wall. The door swung open and two men stepped in with rifles, taking positions on either side of the door, while a third came in bearing wrist and ankle cuffs, linked by iron chains. He tossed them across the room, where they landed with a clang at Pendergast's feet.

"Put those on."

D'Agosta watched as Pendergast did as ordered, latching each cuff.

"Turn around and lie facedown on the floor."

Pendergast complied. One of the guards now walked over and tested each cuff, pulling on it to make sure it was latched. They patted him down, finding nothing.

"Stand up."

Pendergast rose awkwardly, chains clanking. "May I ask where I'm going, all dressed up like this?"

"To the boss."

"Will there be tea and cakes?"

"Shut your mouth, numpty."

D'Agosta watched as Pendergast was ushered, unresisting, out the door, which was slammed shut and locked behind him. He sat down on the hay bale, putting his head in his hands, wondering if there was even the slightest chance that he'd ever see Laura again.

54

The guards began escorting Pendergast down from the attic room. He shuffled along clumsily, hindered by the chains binding his legs and arms.

"Hurry up," one guard said, poking him in the back with his rifle.

"My dear fellow, I would like to see you move nimbly while shackled like an ape," Pendergast responded, slowing even further.

One of the guards snickered and imitated his upper-crust New Orleans drawl—*"My dear fellow"*—before giving him another push. "You can move faster than that."

Pendergast, who knew the mansion well, guessed he was being taken to the library, where no doubt Leng would join him. The house was laid out almost exactly as it would be in his day—but the fixtures, decoration, and wallpaper were, of course, very different. The most striking change was the lack of electricity: the house was lit with glowing gas mantles in frosted glass globes, which cast a mellower light than the electric bulbs of the future.

The shortest route from the attic to the library would involve descending three floors, and along the way it would go past a small, windowless room on the third level that served as a music chamber, where musicians could practice or tune up without bothering people on the lower floors. As they passed by the door to that room, Pendergast abruptly veered into it, opening it with his shackled hands and then pivoting to slam the door shut and wedge it in place with his foot.

There was a moment of consternation as the guards pounded on the door, at last forcing it open. They rushed in, shouting and waving their weapons and surrounding him—Pendergast had barely had time to reach the far side of the darkened room—one smacking him across the face.

"What the hell do you think you're doing?" the lead guard asked, seizing Pendergast by the shackled hands and dragging him back out into the hall, shutting the door behind him.

"You can't fault a man for trying to escape," Pendergast said meekly.

This brought a round of laughter. "Some escape!"

"*My dear fellow*," another mimicked again.

More laughter. He was manhandled down the rest of the stairs, through the drawing room and salon, then past the archway leading to the library.

"Bind him," the lead guard said.

They hauled Pendergast over to a freshly installed iron post inside the library, locking his feet to its base and his hands to loops welded higher up. Then the two stepped back, rifles trained on him.

"Tell the boss he's here," said the lead guard, who had been supervising.

One of the guards left while the other took up a position by the door. A moment later, the first guard returned with Leng.

Now Pendergast looked on as Leng sauntered into the room and took a seat in a wing chair. He adjusted himself, took out a cigar, trimmed and lit it, then settled back, turning intently toward Pendergast. The guards backed off, rifles leveled.

"I'm sorry," Leng said. "I'd offer you a seat—but you're a slippery devil, and I can't feel easy unless you're chained to that post. Now, we are going to have a rather important conversation. Are you ready?"

* * *

While Leng was speaking, Pendergast noticed in his peripheral vision the flash of a single violet eye. It was shrouded in darkness, peering out for a brief moment from a tiny hole formed in the library's intricate wallpaper. Then it vanished—and where it had been, only wallpaper remained.

55

Enoch Leng set down his cigar and removed a notebook from his pocket, into which Humblecut's long telegram, cut into leaves, had been bound. He opened it and began perusing it, turning pages covered with his own extensive notations in a tiny, perfect hand.

"Well, well, Aloysius," he said. Then he added: "May I call you Aloysius? You may call me Enoch. That is the name I prefer now. We are, after all, blood relatives." He smiled at Pendergast. "But I'm not quite clear *how* we're related. My father was Hezekiah Pendergast... who must have been, let's see, your great-great-grandfather?"

Pendergast said nothing.

Leng took a long moment to examine Pendergast. It was the first time he'd really had a chance to examine the man at leisure, and he was somewhat unsettled by the resemblance to himself, and by the keen intelligence evident in those silver eyes; the lean physique; the patrician visage. He was indeed a Pendergast, through and through. All the more reason to take the most extreme care.

"Since I have no children," Leng continued, "and have no intention of fathering any, you must be descended from one of my brothers. Comstock? Maurice? Or...Boethius?" He leaned forward, gazing into those silvery eyes, but could not interpret the expression. "I would guess Boethius. He's the only one who has married so far. Atia is the name of his wife, and they just had a strange little child named Cornelia. Atia must be your great-grandmother. Which makes you my great-grandnephew. And I, your great-granduncle." He smiled. "So glad that's settled."

Pendergast remained silent.

"Amazing how the Pendergast likeness follows the generations."

Sitting back, he took a long, slow puff on his cigar, laid it down in the ashtray, and crossed his legs. "Now, Aloysius, are you in the frame of mind for this important—indeed, for you, decisive—conversation? How it goes will determine whether you and your associates live or die. If you plan on remaining silent, I shall have you taken back to your cell immediately, so no more of my time will be wasted—and you will all be disposed of accordingly."

"I do not object to a conversation," said Pendergast coolly.

"A wise decision. Have you guessed my plans?"

"You wish to extinct the human race."

At this, Leng gave a little laugh. "Wrong. The word isn't 'extinct.' The word is '*cleanse*.'"

"What do you mean by that?"

"The idea is to eliminate the vast bulk of humanity, leaving behind a small group to continue the species in a superior way. Purified. Decontaminated. Perfected."

"And you, naturally, are to be part of this small group."

"Naturally. Do you think my plan is evil?"

"Is the mass murder of innocents evil?"

Leng smiled broadly. "Human beings—innocents? I think not." He licked his finger, turned another page in the notebook. "Let us review the century to come, the twentieth, and what will happen. It featured two so-called world wars, correct?"

"Yes."

"In the first, forty million people died. In the second, eighty million. Correct?"

"Approximately."

"Among the dead were six million Jews, murdered in a coldly systematic and scientific way by Germany under a man named Hitler, in an attempt to eradicate an entire people. Men, women, children, helpless old people, babies—everyone. And it went beyond Jews: Romani, homosexuals, the retarded... Anyone considered genetically or intellectually inferior was liquidated. Correct?"

"Unfortunately, yes."

"The second war was ended by the use of a new weapon called an atomic bomb, which killed two hundred thousand people in just two explosions. After that, an even more devastating weapon called the hydrogen bomb was developed, which in your current day a dozen or so countries possess. Correct?"

"Where are you going with this inquisition?"

"You know perfectly well where I'm going. Also in that century of yours, there was a man named Stalin, who killed nine million of his countrymen. Another named Pol Pot, who killed a third of the entire population of his country, and a man named Mao, who killed forty to eighty million in China—through mass starvation, prison camps, and executions. A truly staggering figure. Again, correct me if I'm wrong."

"You are not wrong."

"Let us return to the case of Germany. I am

particularly interested in this, because I spent many good years there studying medicine. It is a country I know well—and when I learned from your associate about Germany's conduct in the mid-twentieth century, I could scarcely comprehend it. Germany today—I mean, in 1881—is the most advanced country on earth. It produced Bach and Beethoven, Goethe and Gauss. It fathered some of the greatest advancements in medicine, science, and mathematics the world has ever seen. And yet this country, at the very apex of so-called civilization, made this man, Hitler—and through him, perpetrated the most profound evil in all recorded history."

"Yes."

"Staggering. And appalling. But I've learned a lot more about the twentieth century, and quite frankly this summary has barely scratched the surface." He paused. "Which leads me to an overwhelming question."

"Which is?"

"You know very well what it is. How can you believe the human race is worth preserving?"

He waited, and after a slight but meaningful hesitation, Pendergast said, in a low voice: "I concede that, as a species, we are anything but exemplary. I assume that's why we blame the serpent in the garden for all our faults. But we have also produced good things, beautiful things—even magnificent things."

Leng looked at him, then flipped another page in his notebook. "I also understand from your colleague that the sole thing humans of the twenty-first century are united in doing—humans who otherwise are more divided than ever before, having learned nothing in the intervening century—is destroying the earth. All eight billion of you. Polluting the oceans, heating the planet, burning the rainforests, exhausting the mineral wealth. Your own scientists are now calling your age the Sixth Extinction."

He stared at Pendergast, the man's pale face now tinged by a slight flush. He might be breaking through. "You admit these things occurred and are occurring—do you not?"

"I admit it."

"You admit the technological advances of the twentieth century pale in comparison to your descent into barbarism?"

"There is nothing exceptional about the evils of the twentieth century."

"You can't be serious."

"As a species, we have always been bloodthirsty. The twentieth century merely gave us the technology to conduct killing on a mass scale."

Leng clapped his hands. "You are only reinforcing my argument: this godlike technology will eventually lead the species to self-destruction. Do you agree?"

A hesitation. "It seems likely."

"Then, if we are to destroy ourselves: shouldn't it be done in a logical, controlled way, with the idea of starting afresh?"

"You're speaking of the massacre of billions of people."

"Irredeemable people."

"There are many bad people. There are also good and even great people."

"But most are brutal, stupid, and selfish."

"I might point out that you, while not stupid, are one of the brutal and selfish ones."

"I beg to disagree. What I'm doing is nothing less than providing a path to salvation for our species. I've always had a low opinion of humankind—but when I learned of the evils of the twentieth century, I could scarcely believe it. Good God! Now I'm certain our species—if unchecked—will not see the twenty-second century. So: instead of destroying ourselves completely, or leaving behind naked savages fighting rats and cockroaches for sustenance, I would rather see a carefully conducted cleansing that will *preserve* the species, which, when combined with a longer life expectancy, will yield marvelous benefits. My methods are lethal—yes. But they are necessary. I am an agent of good."

"Good?"

"My dear nephew, how can you possibly support the status quo—the continuation of this madness? Especially given the fact that we have a chance to wipe the slate clean, start afresh."

"We?"

"You, me..." Leng halted.

"Is this an invitation?" Pendergast asked.

"Of course. But not one issued lightly. You have proven yourself a most superior man. You are just the kind we need to rise from the ashes, phoenixlike."

Pendergast said nothing.

Leng added, in a significant tone: "The invitation is extended to Constance Greene, if she will lay aside her vengeful mission. The children will come, too—Joe and Binky; that is, young Constance. They are highly intelligent. Even Mary, whom I am on the verge of vivisecting to ensure the Arcanum does its work without damage to the internal organs—I'll spare her, as well."

"A family affair. I see."

"I'll even throw in your friend D'Agosta as a sweetener, although he is hardly suitable material for our new world. Together, Nephew, we can create a just society, a logical society, one rooted in respect, stability, and obedience to rational principles of good order."

"And how will you accomplish this?"

"Through use of your portal. Our small band will travel to your century. Science in your time is superhuman in its power. From what I understand, a biologically engineered pestilence—like the Black Plague, but far more virulent—combined with a special vaccine for our select few will do the trick. As I've said, humanity is going to destroy itself regardless. I have no doubt bad actors in your century are already working on doomsday weapons."

"No doubt."

"But we," Leng said triumphantly, "will beat them to it!" He paused, finding his heart rate elevated. He took a deep breath and looked at Pendergast, trying again to see into his mind. He thought, not for the first time, that he spied glimmers of curiosity, if not actual interest.

"Just so we're clear: your 'wiping the slate clean' means, at its core, ridding the world of ninety-nine percent or more of its inhabitants—and beginning again with a handpicked few. Not unlike Dr. Strangelove."

"I'm unfamiliar with this doctor you speak of, so I imagine his brilliant work lies in the future. But that's beside the point. Will you join me?"

A long silence ensued. "It is worth considering," Pendergast finally said, slowly and deliberately.

"My dear nephew, the time has come for you to make a decision. I will not wait. What is it to be? Will you join my endeavor: yes or no?"

A long silence. And then: "Yes."

56

Sitting on a fly-blown couch in an otherwise barren second-floor room, Otto Bloom had just finished rolling a cigarette and was about to light it when he heard a commotion among the sandhogs milling about on the floor below.

"Look—it's his nibs!"

"So it is. And he's got his muffin with him, looks like."

"Between the two of them, I don't know which one's the more barmy."

Dropping the cigarette, Bloom jumped to his feet and raced downstairs to the small group clustered about the sole entrance that remained open to Forty-Second, sniggering and chortling.

"Shut your pieholes!" he said, pulling the men bodily back from the doorway, leaving only the two guards in place. "Back to your posts!"

As the bricklayers, carpenters, and other construction workers scattered into the dim fastness of the empty tenement, Bloom stepped out onto the street to watch the glittering cab pull up. There was a brief pause, then the door opened and a resplendently dressed man descended, pausing on the lowest step to glance right and then left through his monocle, grimacing as if the street were made of cowshit and he were searching for the spot most thinly daubed. At last he condescended to tread the pavement, where he paused to snatch a silk handkerchief from a vest pocket and polish the handle of his snakewood walking stick. Giving the enameled surface a final stroke, he tossed the kerchief into the gutter, shot his cuffs to a precise amount of Mechlin lace, then turned to assist his companion out of the carriage. This was a young woman—young and, Bloom had to admit, very beautiful—whose shoulders were wrapped in sable and whose sweeping silk gown exposed—given the cold January air—an unhealthy amount of décolletage. The dandified gent gave her his arm and then guided her to a cart where a woman was selling apples to select one for his companion and another for himself. Reaching into a pocket of his satin waistcoat, he extracted a coin and tossed it to the vendor, a glint of gold flashing end over end. He looked up at the building before him, his gaze moving languorously east to west across the heavily scaffolded façade. He patted his companion's hand with satisfaction and proceeded toward the guards framing the doorway, their expressions carefully stolid. As he did so, Bloom moved back a few steps into the maze of carpentry, preparing himself for another meeting with Lord Cedric.

When Mr. Billington had employed Bloom and his gang to contrive a small collapse in Smee's Alley, then fill the alley and its surrounding buildings with enough obstacles—in the form of structural girders and buttresses—to keep out a small army, Bloom hadn't asked many questions. The pale-looking man had paid handsomely indeed. It was only once the site was fully secured that he was let in on the secret. And it was bizarre indeed.

Billington said his family had an estate in Surrey, where he had an older brother—Cedric, Lord Jayeaux, fifth baron in his line. Thanks to the English system of primogeniture, Lord Cedric got all the money, and Billington's allowance was dictated by his brother's whims.

One of these whims, Billington explained, was Lord Cedric's study of the occult. His Lordship was a member of various mystical orders and secret societies devoted to alchemy, divination, necromancy, and other occult sciences. Billington described to him Cedric's interest in mummy "unwrapping parties" and "spirit boards" and his devotion to the charismatic Helena Blavatsky, a Russian spiritualist who had arrived in New York a few years earlier and founded the Theosophical Society.

Bloom's recollections were interrupted by the high, nasal tones of Lord Cedric, searching for him.

"Stab me if I've ever seen such a beastly mess in all my life! *Bloom!*"

Summoning patience, Bloom stepped out into the corridor.

"Odd's fish, where is that layabout? Bloom, I say! Come out of your hole and face me!"

Turning a corner, Bloom reached the spot where Lord Cedric currently stood, spreading his costume out to full glory, like a peacock fanning his feathers.

"There you are!" cried Lord Cedric. "Bloom, have you been introduced to this, my trembling hyacinth of the Dartmoor bogs, my hothouse Brixton orchid—the Lady Livia?"

"We've met," Bloom said, putting a hand to his cap. Lord Cedric had, in fact, brought the woman here only once before, to the great entertainment of the sandhogs.

He fell in behind Lord Cedric, who was now continuing on through the dust and intervening joists, making for a shaft of light that marked the interior entrance to Smee's Alley.

Years earlier, Billington had told Bloom, his brother Cedric and Madame Blavatsky had joined forces to establish the precise point on earth where unearthly forces could manifest themselves to worldly beings. Billington had referred to this mysterious spot as the "nexus of ectoplasmic energy" or some such thing. The baron and Madame Blavatsky had determined it was located somewhere in New York City—but then they'd had a falling-out. Not long afterward, Lord Cedric had narrowed down the location of the nexus—the middle of Smee's Alley. Blavatsky and her henchmen had learned about the discovery and were moving in to take it over.

When Bloom heard this and realized all their work in the alleyway was merely to indulge the ridiculous whims of a batty English lord, he'd come close to quitting. He had, however, noticed a variety of shady characters loitering here and there, evidently acolytes of Blavatsky. Billington had warned him they were serious people—and would not hesitate to murder anyone who might stand in their way of gaining access to the nexus.

Bloom, of course, didn't tell his men anything about the occult tommyrot. Lord Cedric was paying them lavish amounts of money to keep the alley and its surrounding buildings secured, in addition to providing unlimited food and small beer. With three hots and a cot, and the spondulix literally pouring in, the men were happy to shore up the works and keep watch without asking questions. In fact for them, the occasional visits by Lord Cedric were moments of comic relief. Not so for Bloom, who had to keep his men in line while at the same time humoring the dandified Brit.

The three of them stepped into the empty alley, and Bloom watched as the baron took a moment to peer around with his monocle, satisfying himself that everything was in good order. Bloom had to admit that the man—once he'd allowed his monocle to drop—had a keen, observant eye—at least one eye, the green one. The other was a deadish white-blue, perhaps blind.

There was a rustling from one of the few open windows looking over the alley, and then a rough voice sounded, scornfully feigning a cough. "Kaf-kaf-kaf... ponce!! Kaf-kaf!"

Lord Cedric looked up indignantly. "Who said that?"

Silence from above.

"Insolent puppy! Show yourself!"

Another rustling, then the grimy, indistinct visage of a workman peered out a second-floor window, grinning. Immediately, Livia took aim and let fly her half-eaten apple, the overhand heater—despite the dim light—hitting the man's face squarely above one eye with a spray of pulp and juice. The figure disappeared from view with a stream of invective.

"Why, Livia!" Lord Cedric turned toward her, delighted. "How reassuring to see you haven't lost your slum pitching arm."

Livia—who, it seemed, didn't appreciate being reminded of her pedigree—sulkily turned her back on them and began to stroll toward the guardhouse sealing off Smee's Alley.

"Don't mind 'em, milord," Bloom said, making a mental notation of the heckler's name in order to dock his wages. "Just blowing off steam, you know—making a little harmless fun of their betters at the end of the day."

"Blowing off steam, you say? Well, you can tell him for me—in the words of Mozart—*Leck mir den Arsch fein recht schön sauber.*" The baron looked around once again. "All quiet? All remains as it was? No sign of the nexus coming to life?"

"No, milord. And my two brothers arrived just yesterday from Virginia. They've been working the mines there. Brought three of their sons with them, too: big, strapping boys they are—to keep out them spies."

"Stab me, that's capital! Bolstering the ranks is a bully idea, especially—"

"Cedric?" Livia's voice came floating over, interrupting the conversation.

"Yes, my dove?" the baron said without looking over.

"Whatever on earth is that?"

Bloom watched as the other man spun around. Halfway down the alley—hovering directly in front of a set of old dancing-hall posters plastered to the brickwork—strange sparks were appearing in the air, hovering a moment like fireflies, and then disintegrating in odd rainbow curlicues.

Bloom was struck dumb. He had never seen anything like it. Good God, could the hocus-pocus actually be *true*? Even more remarkable was the transformation of the baron's face, the silly expression vanishing into one of surprise, then concentration. "Bloom," the man said in an entirely new voice, "have someone get that woman into a carriage and send her home. Not in my own conveyance—that is to stay. Hurry, now."

As Bloom led the protesting woman away, he could see Lord Cedric approaching the sparkling lights. By the time Bloom returned, the baron was standing—warily—in front of the multicolored flashes, which now were vibrating the very air of the alley. As he watched, the vibration turned to a shimmer, then began to take on an ovoid shape. Bloom stared, mesmerized and astounded.

"Bloom," Lord Cedric said, turning to him.

But Bloom found himself unable to move.

"*Bloom!*" came the low, urgent voice. "We must hurry and cover this thing up. Let us drop the cloths now—as discussed. And, for God's sake, keep everyone away."

Spell broken, Bloom—who had more than once been instructed on what to do in this situation, however unlikely—began issuing orders to his men. In quick succession, they tugged a series of guide ropes that loosed heavy black tarps—each suspended from scaffolding above, five feet on either side of the shimmering thing—and let gravity roll them to the ground. The baron meantime scrambled up a ladder and, running along a catwalk, kicked free another tarp, mounted horizontally, that unrolled along a frame, covering the open space above the thing. Descending the ladder again, he helped Bloom fix the tarp panels in place with hooks. In minutes they had, in effect, produced a twelve-foot cube, the thick black material of which enclosed and obscured from all eyes the brilliant light of the thing within.

"You remember what to do next?" Lord Cedric asked him.

They were currently standing inside of the enclosure, and Bloom, having fixed the last tarp into place, was again staring, mesmerized, at the...*thing*.

"Yes, sir. Triple the guard."

"Exactly. Your best men. And for the love of Christ, keep everyone away. You understand? It won't be long now. Twelve, maybe twenty-four hours, and either Billington or I will see that you and all your men get a thousand dollars each. Now, *hop it!*"

"A *thousand*—?" Seeing the look in Lord Cedric's eye, Bloom nodded. The baron, for his part suddenly a different man, ducked out of the canvas cube and began running—actually running, having lost all his mincing affectations—for the alley exit, then disappeared.

PART THREE

Mere Anarchy

57

Constance stole through the basement corridors, avoiding the occasional roaming gang member, heading for Leng's suite of laboratories. She had been shocked and dismayed to see Aloysius chained to a metal post in the library, but she believed—as they had agreed at the bordello—that if their plans managed to reach this point, they each had clear and specific tasks to accomplish. The task she'd been assigned—and demanded—was to rescue her siblings.

She had to move with infinite care. The lack of electricity was her friend—the basement had no gaslights, and the kerosene lanterns carried by the searchers were dim and hardly penetrated the murk. She, for her part, was able to move without light—an ability gained after a hundred years spent in these same corridors. But the discovery of the sub-basement grottos, and the focus on them that immediately followed... these were things she had not planned on.

As she neared the laboratory entrance, she could hear the muffled cries of a protesting Mary. As much as it filled her with relief, it also—cruelly—filled her with desperation.

She remembered all too well that Leng had vivisected the first half dozen successful guinea pigs—just to be certain—before he began injecting it himself. This was likely one reason he'd kept her alive this long; the other was his need for a decent laboratory to perform the procedure...and which was where Mary had just, almost certainly, been taken.

She crept up to a corner and peered around. Ten yards ahead lay the entrance to Leng's suite of labs. One of the Milk Drinkers stood guard at the doorway. Even as she waited, considering what to do, she heard Mary's cries drop in tone and volume and become softer, more confused. It was safe to assume she'd just been injected with a sedative, rendering her pliable and helpless.

It was also safe to assume she was being prepped for surgery.

Grasping her stiletto, Constance picked up a pebble and tossed it against a far wall, where it made a faint rattling noise. Then she ducked back around the corner.

"Who's there?" came the guard's voice. Another guard then appeared in the doorway of the lab. Leng was taking no chances.

"Oi, what you moaning about?"

"I heard something out there."

A clank sounded as they unshouldered their rifles and began moving forward. They raised the wicks of their lanterns for more flame, and the dull light beyond became brighter.

Two of them. Constance, with her keen hearing, could tell they were moving in parallel along either side of the corridor. That meant one would come around the corner directly in front of her, while the other remained on the opposite side.

She crouched, tensing. She could hear the nearest guard approach the corner, then pause. What would follow was obvious—he'd wheel around the corner, weapon aimed at waist level—but she was ready. He made his move and she leapt up, knocking the rifle barrel away so quickly he couldn't get off a shot, while spinning him around and sticking the stiletto deep enough into his throat to render him incapable of speech. She held him in front of her as a shield while turning toward the opposite guard, who'd heard the scuffle and trained his weapon on her but was unable to get a clear shot.

"Drop the weapon or I'll skewer your confederate," Constance said matter-of-factly.

The man rushed her.

She sliced through the guard's throat, then heaved the body at the approaching man, who ducked aside to dodge it. This was an equally obvious move—Constance, anticipating it, came at him from the side, slashing him deep across the neck as he fired, missing her.

She stepped aside as he sprawled across his partner, the two men gurgling a dying chorus.

Now Constance snatched up a rifle and sprinted down the hall through the laboratory door, past rows of jars and equipment, into the operating theater. She looked around, gun at the ready. Mary was on the operating table, two assistants apparently in the middle of draping for surgery. A third assistant had been laying out surgical instruments and phials on a tray. All three, having heard the shot, were standing rigidly, faces turned toward her, frozen in surprise.

It seemed that, in addition to improving and migrating his laboratory from the one now underwater in the Five Points sewers, Leng had also upgraded his surgical staff from merely the untrained but enthusiastic Munck.

Their confusion lasted just long enough for her to take down two with rapid shots while still on the move. But the third grabbed a scalpel and, to her surprise, threw it at her. She was forced to dodge it as she swung the rifle around. Her next shot went wide and the man was on top of her, strong as an ox. He grabbed the scalpel from the floor and raised it, but she blocked his arm. She lunged upward and sank her teeth into the man's nose, twisting her head viciously. The man reared back with a roar, his grip loosening enough for her to twist the scalpel out of his hand and cut his throat with it, the spray of blood temporarily blinding her.

She rolled his body off her own, rose to her feet, and went quickly to Mary, laid out on the operating table. She was dressed in a white surgical gown, only partially conscious.

"Mary," she whispered. "*Mary.*" She gave her a gentle slap across the face.

Her eyes did not come into focus.

"Get up." Constance slipped her arms under Mary's and helped her off the table.

"What's...going on?" Mary slurred, knees buckling as she sank to the floor.

Constance tried to pull her to her feet, but Mary was heavily drugged. Still, there wasn't an instant to spare; Leng might appear at any moment.

She hurriedly sorted through the contents of the medical tray, looking for adrenaline or some nineteenth-century equivalent. She found a bottle labeled COCAINE HYDROCHLORIDE 7% AQUEOUS SOLUTION.

Cocaine? It was a stimulant, and she was out of options. She inserted a needle into the bottle, sucked up a small amount, then stuck it in Mary's arm.

The response was dramatic. Mary's eyes fluttered open, then she looked around in a panic. "Who are you?"

"A friend. I'm here to get you out." Constance wiped the guard's blood off her face with a nearby roll of gauze. "Come with me."

They exited the lab the way they had come. Constance grasped the hand of Mary, who staggered along behind her, confused but compliant, slowly regaining her senses. At the tunnel intersection, Constance paused and yanked a revolver from the belt of one of the dead guards. Now she led Mary in the opposite direction: a turn, another turn, then—up ahead—a third. The cell holding Binky and Joe was just beyond it. She could hear, somewhere down the halls, the sound of shouts and running feet.

She took a breath, then swiveled around the corner. Just a foot away, a guard was standing in alarm, rifle raised, back turned to her. She jammed the gun into his kidneys and pulled the trigger. Grabbing him as he fell, she plucked the keys from his belt, ran up to the cell door, and opened it. The two children rushed to her and Mary, Binky crying out loudly.

"Quiet!" Constance said sharply. "No time. Follow me."

The only way out still available was now up, rather than down: to the main floor, and then out...one way or another.

Heading away from the sounds of footsteps, she made for a back corridor that led to the basement wine cellar; a stairway to the kitchen, she knew, was nearby. She pulled the confused Mary along by the hand, Joe and Binky careful to keep up.

It quickly grew so dark that, with no lantern, they were unable to see. Constance paused, then whispered to the two youngest: "Keep hold of my dress."

She held Mary's hand as they continued down the black corridor. Agitated voices echoed through the basement; people were approaching. Constance felt along the damp wall, found a niche, and pulled the rest in with her. A light grew brighter as a patrol approached. Constance slipped the revolver out of her waistband and eased the hammer back, finger on the trigger. The men appeared, walking fast, one holding a lantern, arm outstretched in front of him. They passed hurriedly, not seeing the little group shrinking back into the niche. Constance turned the muzzle to follow them.

Ten seconds later, she eased back the trigger, led the way out of the niche, and continued on. Soon, a musky scent of old oaken barrels told her they were passing the wine cellar. She touched the wall from time to time as they moved—and then her fingers contacted the doorframe of the staircase leading up to the kitchen.

"This way," she whispered.

They mounted the stairs awkwardly, children clinging, Mary being led by the hand. As they moved, the image of Aloysius, chained to the iron post, returned to Constance. It was true, the three of them had had solo tasks to perform, without aid from the others—but at this late hour, the thought of leaving him alone with Enoch Leng, poisoned or not, was troublesome indeed.

At the top of the narrow stair, she cracked open the door, then emerged into a back kitchen. It was dim, but there now was enough ambient light for everyone to make out their surroundings.

"You can let go," she whispered. "We're almost there."

The children released their hold. Constance cast around, and her gaze stopped at a ground-level window above a long marble counter. She picked up a heavy copper saucepan, wrapped a dishcloth around it, and swung it into the glass, shattering the window, then used the saucepan to break away the sharp edges around the frame. She grabbed Binky, hoisted her up and out; Joe scrambled out on his own and Mary followed.

"Run to the road along the river," Constance told Joe, pointing toward the front of the mansion. "Stay near the bushes. Féline is waiting at the Post Road with Murphy and the carriage."

"Aren't you coming?" Joe asked.

She hesitated a moment. "No. I've got unfinished business inside."

58

Leng stared into his descendant's glittering eyes. The face remained slightly flushed, and Leng noted a trace of moisture on his brow. This man was a formidable opponent and had to be handled with excessive caution. He quashed a momentary impulse to unshackle the man and allow him to sit by the fire to enjoy a glass of brandy and a cigar with him. No, not yet. He had to be sure the man's conversion was genuine.

He took a moment to relight his cigar. After a few satisfying puffs, he stood up, went to the cabinet, and poured himself another brandy. He came back and reseated himself, swirled the brandy in the glass, and took a long, lingering sip. Then he set it down, picked up the cigar again, and puffed it back into life. Blowing out a long stream of smoke, he said: "I am pleased to hear your declaration. How did you come to believe?"

"My opinion of myself stands, or falls, on logic. And I find your logic unassailable."

"It *is* unassailable."

Pendergast bowed his head in assent.

"You would no doubt like to be released from those chains."

"I was hoping. And a brandy would be most welcome on a cold night."

"It pains me to say—not quite yet. Might you, however, be interested in hearing my plans more specifically?"

"I am indeed. Perhaps I can even make some suggestions, given my familiarity with the next century."

"I'd appreciate that. The group I propose to assemble will use the machine to go to your time, as I said. We will establish ourselves on a very large piece of land, well fortified, preferably in the American West. We will stockpile food, weapons, and all the necessities of life."

"I would advise against certain aspects of that plan."

Leng arched his eyebrows. "Such as?"

"Many bizarre religious cults have sprung up in the twentieth century. They often favor the American West, for all the reasons you might imagine. These cults are usually armed and unwilling to submit to the rule of law—as a result, there have been massacres, large-scale suicides, and shoot-outs with law enforcement. In my time, the authorities are on the lookout for precisely the kind of well-fortified camp you propose."

"I see. What would you suggest?"

"That the true purpose of your group, at first, be carefully concealed under the cloak of benevolence. An institute or foundation, devoted to human improvement—what we sometimes call a think tank—would be ideal. Or perhaps even a health resort, a therapeutic retreat for the wealthy. We would need to accumulate vast sums of money in order to accomplish this and cover our tracks—but that would be the least of our problems. Years must pass if we are to do this right...but you strike me as a patient man."

"I am. And I greatly appreciate the caveats you

mention. To continue, then: we will create our, ah, benevolent institute, with your warnings in mind."

"It must be kept under the radar."

"Excuse me?"

"I mean to say, quiet."

"Precisely. There, we will assemble the scientific expertise and equipment necessary to develop a fatal and virulent plague germ, as well as the vaccine against it, and unleash it on the world. Of course, not everyone will succumb—that I understand would be impossible—but the remnant population will be starving, and savage, and no doubt soon kill themselves off anyway."

"I'd assume so."

"We will be safe in our enclave, which at this point will assume its true nature. Everything will be orderly. The rules will be strict but fair. There will be no violence, no disobedience to authority. All crime will be dealt with through banishment."

"What political system will you establish? A democracy?"

"Absolutely not. Democracy is misrule by the stupid, greedy, and corrupt. No, it will be an enlightened oligarchy, or rather a geniocracy, which I'd call the Convocation of Twelve. Twelve wise men and women, who will confer on the important questions of state and move forward with consensus."

"And how will these twelve sages be chosen?"

"Those individuals most active in civic duty, displaying leadership qualities, and also scoring in the ninety-ninth percentile on a rigorous suite of intelligence quotient tests and measurements. Hence my labeling it a geniocracy—the rule of the excellent."

"So far what you propose sounds logical. It also evades the shortcomings of those political systems that have emerged since 1880," Pendergast added with something like approval. "And your economic system?"

"Capitalism, but with the convocation owning and controlling the means of production. As the outside world returns to wilderness and the savage remnants of humans die off, we will expand our borders, laws, and civilization, until we have reoccupied the planet under an intelligent, rational, and compassionate world government." He paused, then smiled broadly. "What do you think, Nephew?"

"A geniocracy, a convocation... I can see you've given much thought to this. I, too, have long wondered why we don't require politicians to pass an intelligence test. It seems that stupidity is almost a requirement to run for office."

"Indeed." Leng gave Pendergast a long, searching look. Then he went on. "And with the added gift of the Arcanum, we'll live much longer lives. Think of the scientific breakthroughs we could achieve, the music, the mathematics, the art, if we could live eight hundred years instead of eighty. Of course, new births will need to be greatly restricted, but the world will be a better place, in my view, without mewling children underfoot."

"The word 'utopia' comes to mind, Uncle."

"It is indeed most apt." Leng hesitated for a long moment. "I'm truly sorry you won't be among us."

"You're rescinding your invitation?"

"I am. You lied about joining me. I only just realized it."

"I did not lie."

Leng chuckled. "Of course you did. You are an opaque and devious fellow, but I am more a student of human prevarication than even yourself. Although I'll admit, Aloysius, you had me convinced you were sincere—briefly. But I heard your lie in the single word you just spoke now: 'Uncle.' You couldn't help yourself: there was the tiniest note of irony, or perhaps distaste. Which, in turn, tells me you have *not* been convinced. What have you to say to that?"

Pendergast stared back at him, denying nothing.

"I could see I was making inroads. When you stated

that my solution is the only workable one, and when you offered suggestions for improvement, I believe you were speaking the truth. Perhaps all you need is a bit of time to reflect, because my logic *is* unassailable. And my methods, while I freely admit them to be cruel, are equally necessary. You are a cruel man, too. I know what you did to my man Munck—drowning him like a rat in a cage."

Pendergast remained silent.

"But allowing you the luxury of considering my offer at your leisure would be a waste of my time—not to mention a needless risk. So now the demand is simple: you have one hour to give me access to the portal, or you and all of your friends will die—and most horribly. I am that rarest of souls, *Nephew*, who can treat the same person either magnanimously or with extreme vindictiveness. Your refusal—which would be a pigheaded and obstinate act, given what you've heard and been unable to refute—would cause me extreme vexation. So—if I suddenly find myself with a period of leisure I'd hoped to spend instead by employing your portal—I would be pleased to turn my mind toward a temporary project: watching you and your merry band die in the most excruciating ways imaginable. And, believe me, I don't lack for imagination—even if I did, Decla could no doubt embroider the details. The breaking wheel; molten gold, General Crassus's cocktail of choice; scaphism; the blood eagle; and, of course, combing and flaying. You'd be the audience for them all, of course—and I can promise that when, at last, you die yourself, you will be wearing the skin of your friend, the constable."

He let this image hang in the air for a moment. Then he gestured toward the guards. "Take him back." He stood up and bowed good-humoredly to Pendergast. "I have an important operation awaiting me downstairs; as it happens, the preparations will take roughly the same amount of time you have to make up your mind."

59

Diogenes moved through the fretted shade of the alleyway, pushing workmen and guards aside as he ran, until he burst out onto Forty-Second Street. Tossing his monocle to the ground, he spotted his carriage and waved. His driver, Cato, seeing him, briskly moved the carriage forward.

Diogenes leapt onto the running board and signaled directions. Cato nodded and cracked his whip, and the cab shot out into the bustling traffic. Diogenes swung himself inside, closed the door, and sat back, removing the lace-edged gloves and other frippery encumbering his clothing as Cato navigated the broad avenue.

His coach, despite being tastefully appointed within and without, might have been looked at derisively by much of the beau monde: small, driven by a single horse, and in general resembling a hansom cab. In fact, it *was* an English hansom cab, chosen by Diogenes because its low-slung profile and center of gravity allowed it to take corners at speed. With a single horse at the reins, it could cut in and out of traffic when necessary, easily overtaking larger and more ponderous vehicles.

At that very moment, in fact, Cato was demonstrating the cab's agility by turning north on Broadway at— Diogenes estimated—nearly fifteen miles an hour.

He had already added luxurious touches to the cab while replacing needless weight with lighter, stronger materials. He had ordered the springs and wheels altered according to certain laws of mechanics and gravity that, in 1881, remained undiscovered. Even more important had been his choice of driver. He'd visited the Belmont Stakes at Jerome Park, but decided Thoroughbred jockeys were not what he was looking for. Instead, he'd found his man at Coney Island Racetrack in Brighton Beach: a harness racer who had won a large number of trotting competitions. It turned out Cato was ready to trade in his "sulky" for a professional cab, especially for the money Diogenes was willing to pay.

It was precisely this moment for which Diogenes had hired Cato.

The cab was jostled as another, larger carriage tried to pull away from the curb and elbow into the throng; Cato, with the instinctive training of a harness jockey, made a quick double feint that sent the driver of the other vehicle into a terrified halt, horses neighing and rearing as their reins became entangled.

Some distance ahead, in the fading light of approaching evening, Diogenes could see their destination: the Grand Circle where Broadway met the southwest corner of Central Park.

Not only, Diogenes mused, was Cato the best possible cabman, but childhood meningitis had rendered him deaf and mute. This proved no difficulty to Diogenes, who was fluent enough in American Sign Language; if anything, it was a benefit. Cato was a man with a remarkably even keel: nothing he had witnessed while in the employ of Diogenes seemed to have excited his deadpan nature.

Cato had one other advantage: his superb knowledge of horses allowed him to control the kind of animal whose speed and stamina were usually found on the track, not the boulevard. Cato himself had found the horse for Diogenes: Bad Influence, an American standardbred of tremendous strength who, it seemed, relished being free of the racecourse. Pulling ahead of the surrounding carriages, they caromed around ninety degrees of the Grand Circle, then cut nimbly across traffic and made a U-turn, slowing and pulling to the curb directly in front of the unfinished observation tower.

Diogenes pulled out his pocket watch: ten minutes to five. Grabbing a box of matches from one of the inlaid drawers of the cab's interior, he opened the door and jumped nimbly to the street. *Cato*, he explained in ASL, *create a brief diversion*. Then he darted into the park while, from behind, he could hear Bad Influence already beginning to whinny and rear.

No one was looking his way as he slipped into the construction zone and then the tower itself. He fumbled for a lantern, lit it, placed it on the floor, then looked around to ensure nothing had changed since his last visit. All was as before; no further work had been done.

He went to the far side of the dark space, pushed aside some crates and scaffolding, and then—more gently—rolled back a large tarp and placed it in a corner. Beneath was a double strand of jute, wound very tightly with fine gunpowder dust and then dipped in tar: the main, arterial fuse.

He had set four charges in the tower, the primary at the top and three secondaries at intervals below it. He'd also altered the safety casing of the fuse so it would burn at five seconds per foot instead of the usual thirty. If he'd calculated properly, once he lit this main fuse, it would make its way up the stairs, lighting the three secondary fuses in turn as it reached them. The higher up the load of dynamite, the shorter he'd made the secondary fuses—this way, the primary charge beneath the roof would go off first, followed in succession by those below it.

Diogenes had found amusement in explosives from an early age: placing squibs on the underside of a trash can lid; in a bed of roses; in a dog's chew toy. Rather extreme measures had been taken to snuff out this childish pastime, and it had been years since Diogenes had toyed with, or even thought about, gunpowder. But now, watching the thick fuse take on a life of its own under his match—and the flame begin crawling its way up the stairway, leaving nothing but a wisp of smoke in its wake—he felt once again a boyish quickening of the heart.

The angry cigarette end of flame vanished up the curve of the stairwell, and Diogenes took his leave. He blew out the lantern and passed through the construction debris to the curb. The lamplighters were moving along the streets, heralding night's advance. His cab was now parked on the far side of the circle, Cato holding Bad Influence calmly by the bridle.

Looking out for traffic, he made his way across Central Park South, and then west to the far side of Broadway. Diogenes was about to warn the ex-jockey to cover his ears, then remembered it wasn't necessary. And so instead he gestured for Cato to keep the horse calm. They both put reassuring hands on the animal's neck, and Diogenes turned toward the tower to make sure he didn't miss the show.

60

"WHAT THE *DEVIL*?" ENOCH Leng roared, staring at the dead bodies of the two guards splayed in a puddle of blood across the basement corridor outside his surgery. He rushed into the surgery suite itself and saw a sight that curdled his vision: three dead assistants sprawled across the floor—and surrounding an empty operating table.

"Cheese and crust," murmured Decla, coming up behind him with a posse of Milk Drinkers.

Leng knew instantly what had happened: Constance. She *had* been in the house, spying, plotting. That bloody bitch had stolen his patient—and no doubt she'd also freed, or was freeing, the other children. He had underestimated her. He felt an intense, destabilizing fury... but quickly recovered himself.

Where was she now? Had she fled with the children? Did she know Pendergast and his policeman friend were locked in a distant wing?

He turned to Decla and the gang. "Seal up the house. Now. I want that woman."

"So do I," said Decla.

"By God, you shall have her." He paused. "In fact, it's possible I can save you some work in searching."

* * *

Constance pulled back from the broken window after watching Mary, Joe, and Binky disappear into the shrubbery, apparently unseen. She slipped into the main kitchen, then paused in the dim light, listening. She could hear voices, running footsteps, a door slamming—the house was now on full alert. Aloysius was being kept on an upper floor—almost certainly in an attic room under the eaves that on an early reconnaissance she'd seen being converted into an iron room with bars. But the upper floors were a very dangerous place to roam. Above the first floor, there were few hollow walls or secret passageways—and that meant sneaking around in unfrequented halls and rooms, hoping to avoid discovery.

Slinging the rifle over her shoulder, keeping the stiletto in hand and the revolver tucked in the waistband of her dress, she went to the kitchen door and listened. The activity, though extensive, sounded for the most part distant. She eased open the door, slipped through, and closed it. Beyond, a broad archway led across a main hall to the salon, and she could see the gas there was turned on brightly. As she waited, an armed figure passed by—one of the Milk Drinkers. That was no way to go.

She returned to the kitchen, pondering how to get to the higher floors. The stairs to the servants' quarters, next to the pantry, were a possibility. She flitted across the kitchen and through the pantry to a closed door that led to the back stairway. She pressed her ear to the panel and listened. Silence. She turned the knob and opened the door. The narrow, unpainted, claustrophobic stairway was dark. Shutting the door, she crept up, one hand on the beadboard wall. The wooden stairs creaked and groaned with every footfall. She paused to listen after one particularly loud creak. This part of the mansion still seemed quiet, with most of the activity taking place in the front of the house and, no doubt, in the basement and even deeper.

The stairs came to a landing with two doors, right and left, both closed. One went to the cook's bedroom and sitting room, the other to the scullery maid's chamber. The latter was a dead end. The cook's rooms, on the other hand, led to a door that opened onto a rarely used second-floor hallway. From there, the hallway led to a large room and, beyond, a staircase to the third and fourth floors—and it was on the fourth floor, under the eaves, that the iron room had been built.

She could see a faint light under the doorsill of the cook's bedroom. Again, she pressed her ear to the door. Was the cook in there? It was impossible to tell. He might have retreated to his room to get away from all the excitement—or he and his assistants might have been enlisted in the search. There was only one way forward, and it was through those rooms. Constance flung open the door, stiletto in hand, and rushed in.

The room was empty, the gas turned low.

With a sigh of relief, she moved through the bedchamber and sitting room, to the door leading into the side hall. Beyond, she could hear running and intermittent shouts, growing fainter even as she listened. She used this moment of relative calm to map out in her mind the route to the iron room. She would have to traverse the hall and large room beyond in order to reach the staircase to the fourth floor.

Making sure all remained quiet, she opened the door from the cook's chambers and darted down the hall. The light remained dim. The door at the end of the hall led into a private entertainment room, which in her own present day was used as a gym by Proctor. Back in 1881...she tried to remember...it had been a billiards room, with a leather seating area and cocktail tables for smoking and drinking. The windows were usually drawn with heavy drapes. Beyond the room was the service stairway leading up to the third floor and then to the attic areas.

No sound could be heard in the space beyond, and the sill was dark. It was empty, the gas off: not surprising, since no one would be playing snooker at a time like this. She opened the door and stepped into the darkness beyond. There was no light at all. But nevertheless, she was aware of shapes, moving quickly—

A gaslight flared up, illuminating a half dozen Milk Drinkers, including Decla. They had been lying in wait and were heavily armed, all guns pointed at her. She shrank back toward the door, pulling the revolver as she did so, but a shot rang out and a blow to her left shoulder spun her around, the gun flying out of her hand. As she struggled to lower the rifle, she was rushed, seized, and thrown to the ground.

Struggling and twisting, she tried to escape, but four brawny men pinioned her, and all she could do was writhe. The shot had merely nicked the upper part of her left arm; the wound didn't seem serious, but one of the men, seeing a bloodstain, ground his knee into it anyway.

Decla sauntered over, hands in her pockets, and stood over Constance.

"I'll slit you open like a Christmas goose," Constance said, struggling.

"What a wildcat you are," Decla replied. She bent over Constance and methodically searched her clothing, extracting the stiletto, a second knife, matches, a tiny pair of opera glasses, a phial of white powder, and a one-shot ladies' derringer with a pearl handle.

"Heading off to a fancy-dress ball, are we?" Decla said, inspecting the derringer and putting it in her pocket. "Such pretty little toys." She held up the white phial. "Don't tell me you smoke the Shangri-la tobacco, too?" She turned to one of her gang. "Go tell the doctor we caught her just where he suspected."

The man left, and Decla turned back to Constance, this time playing with the stiletto. "You're all mine now, love," she said, rotating the glittering, razor-sharp blade. "This is the beauty you cut my hand with, isn't it?"

"Too bad I didn't cut your throat."

"Oh, it hasn't seen its end of throat cutting, I'd wager," said Decla.

Constance struggled but was firmly pinned down. "Is this your idea of a fair fight? Let me up—then I can kill you one at a time."

With a tight smile, Decla merely bent more closely over Constance, the stiletto point gleaming in the gaslight. "Such shiny thick hair you have," she said. "In my trade, I can always use another wig—or a merkin, for that matter."

Carefully placing the edge of the blade at the line of Constance's scalp, she let the tip slowly sink in.

61

PENDERGAST SHUFFLED ALONG, CHAINED hand and foot, as the three guards escorted him back to his cell. Their ascent had been briefly interrupted by a surge of noise and activity erupting from below, but when it grew fainter, the guards resumed forcing him up the stairs heading back to the iron room.

"You're an arse-dragging cove, aren't you?" one of the guards said, giving Pendergast a shove with his rifle. "Here, get a wiggle on."

Pendergast stumbled and fell to his knees, then laboriously got to his feet.

"For Jayzus sake—"

They were now opposite the door to the third-floor room Pendergast had barged into on his way down. Just at that moment, the cuffs fell almost magically from Pendergast's hands, and with that he whirled around, snatching a revolver from one guard and, continuing his pivot, shooting him and the man beside him, ending up facing the third man, barrel planted in his ear. Taken utterly by surprise, the guard froze.

"Live or die?" Pendergast asked quietly.

The man swallowed, his Adam's apple bobbing. "Live."

"Drop the gun."

The man did so.

"Unlock these leg irons."

With shaking hands, the guard knelt and did as instructed. Pendergast kicked off the irons, picked up a candle and matches from a nearby table, then rummaged through the pockets of the two dead guards until he found a penknife. Keeping an eye on the remaining guard, he used the knife to split the candle lengthwise, then—carving away excess wax—he extracted the wick. He slid the wick under the doorsill of the room he'd entered earlier, wedging it in place with the penknife. Then he lit the end of the wick, which would act as a fuse to the chamber, now full of explosive gas: a result of the torchlight stopcocks he'd managed to twist open in the moments after he broke into the room on the way to see Leng. He watched long enough to ensure it was burning steadily, the wick inching down toward the doorsill. He hoped they could escape the mansion before the improvised bomb went off—it all depended on how quickly, or slowly, that candlewick fuse burned.

Then he rose, keeping the gun trained on the guard. "Walk ahead of me. Unlock the door to our room."

62

Diogenes did not have long to wait. Within fifteen seconds, he saw a small flash of intense light at the top of the tower, which was instantly engulfed in a fast-expanding gray cloud. He opened his mouth and covered his ears, motioning for Cato to do the same.

The real shock came a split second later, as the sound of the explosion—twenty eight-inch cylinders of black powder, releasing 10 megajoules of energy—burst from the tower's crown, a wave of overpressure and sound so powerful it took on a physical presence, shooting outward across the park, the traffic circle, and the surrounding walls of buildings to the east and north. Though he'd pressed his hands to his ears, the blast was nevertheless painful. As he looked around, feeling the ground tremble under his feet, he could see that—almost as if with the flip of a switch—the relative calm of a quiet winter sunset had been transformed into chaos. Pedestrians staggered or fell to the ground. Horses reared and whinnied, some breaking free from stunned coachmen and rushing this way and that, colliding with other carriages or overturning them. Dandies in evening dress threw themselves into manure-clogged gutters. Lower windows along Central Park South imploded in sequence, as if at a cadet review. A surprising number of people drew pistols from places of concealment. Under the stroke of his calming caress, Diogenes felt Bad Influence tense. He was concerned the horse might bolt, not out of fear but out of excitement, thinking—after being long conditioned to loud reports at the track—that a race had begun. But Cato held him steady, and as a reward he reached into his pocket and fed the horse a watermelon-flavored sugar drop.

After the passage of the wave of overpressure, Diogenes closed his mouth and looked up again. A black cloud was thrusting like a fist into the sky, along with bits of debris that tumbled even higher, lit from below.

And then the second explosion went off, tearing away the top part of the structure, adding more fuel to the growing conflagration. Diogenes, ears uncovered now, could hear the full power of this report ring off the buildings around him, a thunderclap that echoed and reechoed over Central Park, ricocheting from one line of buildings back to the other. He felt immensely gratified. A third explosion blasted out the middle part of the remaining tower, rocking the ground and prompting still more screaming, firing of shots, and crashing of glass.

And then the fourth and final detonation tore out the lower sides of the structure, sending another series of echoes booming down the stone canyons and shattering whatever nearby windows remained intact. At this, the unflappable Cato glanced over at Diogenes, raising one eyebrow as if to ask out of mild curiosity: *How long is this to continue?* Diogenes smiled and shook his head. *Study to be quiet*, he signed in return, quoting Paul but thinking with equal irony of Izaak Walton, and the admonition with which he'd closed *The Compleat Angler*.

The rumbling died away, while the ruins of the observation tower were rapidly engulfed in fire. Another sound rose up: a loud patter as a rain of grit and debris began to come down around him.

The first three sets of charges had destroyed the framing in the upper section of the tower. The final, fourth charge had been detonated where the brick cladding ended. But the brickwork encircling the lower half, along with the structural steel supporting it, now performed Diogenes's second purpose: that of a chimney. A huge column of sparks and embers from the burning wooden beams within mounted up several hundred feet, the bottom of the tower turned into an eight-story kiln. The only comparison that came to his mind was that of a monstrous afterburner. Glancing upward at the tower of fire and sparks, Diogenes saw to his satisfaction that the engine he'd created was coloring the bellies of the gathering clouds with an angry orange glow.

This was a signal that no one within a hundred miles could miss.

There was nothing more to do. Like the watchman in *Agamemnon*, he'd lit the beacon, heralding the news: his assignment complete, it was up to its intended witnesses to act. Time to return to Smee's Alley. He saw the chaos in the street was only growing worse—they'd better hoof it before the route became impassable.

Back to the alleyway, please, he said in ASL to Cato as he gave Bad Influence a final pat and made for the carriage door. Cato nodded and stepped up into the driver's seat.

Another thing, Diogenes signed, leaning out from the step, one hand on the window frame. *Once all this calms down, we'll celebrate with a drink.*

And with that, he slid into his seat and closed the door as the cab lurched forward. Cato had yet to fully appreciate the virtues of absinthe, but—like Livia—he had the makings of a model pupil.

✻ ✻ ✻

D'Agosta, sitting moodily in the iron cell, heard the turn of a lock. Then the door opened—but to his surprise, the party that had come to take Pendergast downstairs was now reduced to two: a single guard and Pendergast himself, a revolver held to the guard's head.

Thirty seconds later, D'Agosta had stepped outside and the guard had replaced him as resident. Pendergast slammed and locked the door behind him, then pocketed the key.

"How in the *hell*—?" D'Agosta began in a loud whisper.

"I made a loop with your shoestring, slipped it into the handcuff lock, lassoed the lock screw, and then drew the pin back. An old Houdini trick. Well, not *old*, yet, but... Listen, we must hurry—we have very little time."

"Time for what?"

But Pendergast was already moving along the hallway, and the question remained unanswered.

63

"Excellent!" Leng said as he entered the room and saw Constance pinned to the floor. "Hold her tight, fellows; she's a catamount." He strode up as Decla remained hunched over Constance, the knife's point planted in her scalp, blood running out of a half-inch cut. Decla paused.

Leng looked down into those strange violet eyes. "I've never met a demon quite like you."

"Your cowardly assistant was about to scalp me."

"Barbaric. But fully deserved."

"She's too scared to fight me properly," Constance said. "She needs a platoon to help her."

"Shut your bone box," snapped Decla.

Leng stared at Constance. It was quite astonishing what this vixen had been able to do, how many she'd killed in his very own house, under his very nose.

He started to speak again, but at that moment a distant rumble passed through the house—something had happened far to the south. The others in the room noticed it, as well. But Leng paused for only a few seconds. His own mansion had been echoing with sporadic gunfire for the last half hour—and his interests lay here.

"Before you continue your work," he said to Decla, "and she's no good for conversation anymore, I have a few questions I'd like to ask."

"Go ahead."

He looked back down at the pale, beautiful, defiant face. "Where are Mary and the two children?"

"Far away by now."

"No matter—I'll find them later. Were you living in my house?"

"She was," said Decla. "We found her lair down below. And a tunnel, like, straight out to the Hudson. Figure she came and went that way."

"How intriguing. One final question: I've tried to accept it as a given, under the circumstances, but at the same time I still find it hard to believe. Are you and the waif you call Binky truly one and the same person?"

Constance laughed. "Since you ask: yes. How strange are the byways of time. And now, I'll answer a question you are unable to ask, being ignorant of its circumstances—but that will nevertheless be of great interest to you."

"By all means, enlighten me."

"You've been poisoned."

A silence, and then Leng said, "Really. And how might that be?"

"Remember the excellent meal you had several nights ago? *Filet de bœuf*, consumed with a bottle of Clos Saint-Denis."

Leng paused. "Decla, please rise, just for a moment; you others, let the girl free, but keep your weapons trained on her." Leng waited for them to clear a way so he could move in still closer.

"You spied on my dining?"

"More than spied. I poisoned the Bordelaise."

"What nonsense. That was..." He thought for a moment. "Five days ago. I'm fine."

At this, the woman smiled. "Since you're a connoisseur of poisons, perhaps this detail will help convince you: alpha-amanitin, extracted from the death cap mushroom—taken from your own basement storeroom."

"You couldn't possibly perform the biochemical extraction."

"Ah, but I can. Here's something else you don't know: in the future—or what, for me, is now the past—I become your assistant. You see, *I* was the guinea pig whose survival finally convinced you the Arcanum was a success. The half dozen before me had *appeared* successful—but you forced some to live imprisoned for observation, while you dissected the rest in search of internal damage. One way or another, you killed them all. *I* happened to be the guinea pig at the time you finally convinced yourself the Arcanum worked. And one thing else: you didn't just let me live. As it turns out, I not only lived in this house during Pendergast's time—I lived here for over a hundred years before, as well—*with you*."

Leng felt a most unpleasant sensation of cognitive dissonance wash over him: one of utter disbelief combined...with certainty the woman must be telling the truth.

"That's how I was able to create the poison," she said, her voice rising. "And that's how I know there's no antidote, none whatsoever—*not in this century!*" And she broke into a peal of laughter that rose toward a scream.

Leng stared at her—and believed. She would not tell such an obvious untruth. And the fact was, he'd already noticed since first rising that morning he wasn't feeling quite himself.

His thoughts turned wildly to his predicament. Five days had passed already...He knew, given the properties of the death cap mushroom, that gave him another week to live, at the most. *Another week to find an antidote.* There must be one, somewhere, in his vast chemical arsenal. Hadn't she just said there was no antidote? Was she lying—toying with him?

He glanced at Decla. "Don't kill her—not yet. Make her suffer infinite agonies until she provides me with an antidote. You'll find me in my lab!"

"With pleasure, Doctor." Decla prepared to reinsert the stiletto into the cut she had begun.

As Leng turned to go, he abruptly stopped. In his panic at Constance's sudden revelation, he'd forgotten: Ferenc. Pendergast. And Constance herself—the time machine could save him.

There's no antidote—not in this century…

As this thought burst into his mind, the house itself suddenly shuddered with a deep bass roar: the walls split and snapped; the chandelier and half the ceiling dropped with a shower of plaster; and a huge gout of flame and smoke burst through the lathing.

64

Choking and coughing, Decla clawed away the dust and pieces of plaster, her immediate instinct to locate, by feel, the stiletto she'd dropped in the explosion and collapse. The room was so filled with dust she couldn't see, but—as she struggled to her feet and took stock of herself—the air began to clear. She was not hurt, beyond cuts and bruises. But the rest of the gang, which had been standing back, lay crushed and buried under heavy timbers.

What the hell had happened? And where was the doctor? She could see no sign of him—no doubt he was buried under one of the numerous piles of debris. Some of these piles were moving, a few forcibly, others more spasmodically. But there, right in front of her, was the duchess, rising unsteadily to her feet.

Constance wiped away a rivulet of blood on her forehead—and then their stares locked.

"Looks like we're the last ones at the party," said Constance, flicking away bits of lath clinging to her clothing.

"You're one lucky bitch," said Decla. She advanced, wielding the stiletto.

"So you've decided on a fair fight—now that your Neanderthals are incapacitated?"

Decla knew she was being goaded, knew the bitch was supremely dangerous. But she also knew there was nobody who could best her with a knife. That's why she'd risen to lead the Milk Drinkers, why members of other gangs leapt for cover when they saw her coming. There was no way this young woman—with her milky skin and fancy clothes—knew how to handle a knife. The bitch had cut her hand, but that was only because she'd been taken by surprise. This time, there would be no such surprises. Keeping her eyes on Constance, she flexed first her arms, then legs, before crouching into her favorite fighting stance.

"I'd like my stiletto."

"I bet you would. It's mine now."

At this, Constance merely smirked. She took one step back, then another. With a quick movement she plucked a four-foot piece of wooden molding out of the debris. She held it by one end with both hands, like a golf club, twisting it first one way, then another, as if testing its tensile strength and elasticity.

"What do you plan to do with that?" Decla asked, laughing despite herself. "The javelin competition isn't until tomorrow."

Suddenly, Constance planted the staff-like piece of molding hard against the ground, lifted herself into the air, and—legs horizontal—swung toward Decla. Taken by surprise, Decla staggered back, but Constance kept pivoting around the staff like an acrobat, feet toward Decla's face, and then suddenly emitted such a bloodcurdling cry that Decla stumbled backward, dropping the knife and scurrying out of the way.

Constance immediately threw aside the molding and grabbed her stiletto.

But Decla, looking around at the motionless bodies, first spotted, then snatched up, a twenty-inch sawback machete—once Fishbait's pride and joy, now hers.

Constance glanced from Decla to the evil-looking knife, then took a step back.

"Nowhere to run, bitch," Decla said. "Your carnival tricks aren't going to save you. You're the one who's about to be slit like a Christmas goose... and I think I'll start with the giblets."

Even before she finished speaking, she leapt forward, blade whistling. Constance leaned backward as the machete carved air her breast had occupied a moment before. Then, using her loss of balance to best advantage, she pivoted ninety degrees, one hand planted on the floor, then leapt to her feet again as Decla got a fresh grip on her blade and tightened its lanyard around her wrist.

Decla took a moment to size up her opponent, who looked back at her expressionlessly, violet eyes narrowed to slits, doing the same. They'd keep this game up awhile longer, see how well her stamina lasted.

Decla lunged. Constance swerved—but in the direction Decla anticipated. She J-hooked the arc of the blade, cutting through the sleeve of Constance's dress.

Her opponent spun away, but the damage was done. With satisfaction, Decla saw blood darken the sleeve. It was not serious, any more than the wound in the shoulder had been. She could keep this game up for quite a while, carving here and there.

Constance held her stiletto out, its tip bobbing up and down slightly, and, her head lowered, in a half crouch—circled Decla. She suddenly whirled, sweeping the knife in an arc at belly level, but Decla once again anticipated the move and hopped back, rotating to one side like a matador. As Constance's arm flashed by, she gave her another cut with the machete—just for fun—parallel to the slice she'd already made on Constance's arm.

The bitch recovered her balance and once again went into a crouch. But the blood was now spreading across the tears in her sleeve.

"Those are gonna scar up good," said Decla. "Or they would, doll—if you survived."

She circled Constance, who rotated in turn.

Constance swept again with the knife toward Decla, but it was a feint and she finessed the move with sudden, startling speed, the blade of her knife just catching the fabric of Decla's sleeve.

"Not good enough," said Decla.

And it hadn't been—but the feint itself, along with the alarming speed with which it had been executed, was a reminder to Decla not to get too confident: this opponent was as lithe and fast as a weasel.

Suddenly, Constance kicked up a piece of plaster; Decla dodged, only to realize this had been yet another feint—the plaster had not been directed at her at all, but Constance used her rival's countermovement to artfully slash at her again. Decla responded quickly, but not quite quickly enough, and Constance's knife—which had been aimed for her throat—swiped instead across her chin.

"There's a scar for you," Constance said, falling back into position.

"*Bitch!*" Decla was breathing hard now—and she was angry. Nobody had touched her face before.

As she stood back, gathering her wits and taking fresh stock of her opponent, she saw one of the numerous heaps of debris—one directly behind Constance—begin to shift.

Suddenly, Constance—who had been standing utterly still—exploded into movement. Airborne for a moment, she then came back down into a low crouch, lunging forward, thrusting the stiletto into Decla's thigh and giving the blade a sharp twist before pulling it out.

With a curse, Decla staggered back, partly in pain, but mostly in astonishment at the sudden display of skill and the cleverness by which she'd been duped. She backed away farther as a figure rose up behind Constance, the noise obscured by the cracking and moaning of the dying mansion.

She raised her machete to distract Constance just as the figure, whom she recognized as Trotter, used a broken board to slam Constance across the back of her head. The young woman was knocked to one side, yet somehow managed to slash Trotter across the neck as she recovered her balance. But it was just the opening Decla needed and she lunged forward, thrusting the blade deep into the bitch's vitals.

Constance's eyes went wide and she fell onto the debris-strewn floor, clutching her abdomen and trying to stem the flow of blood from the wound. Decla stepped back and gave a whoop of triumph, raising her arms. Her opponent was a goner, gut cut like that—but there would be time and pain before the end came.

Giving a second victory cry, she glanced over to where Constance had stood a moment earlier and saw Trotter. The hand that had held the board was now pressed against his neck where the knife had cut him.

Suddenly, as she stared, Trotter's head vanished into a pinkish mass of blood, brains, and fluid. It was as if someone had taken a baseball bat to a balloon filled with butcher's offal—while a deafening report boomed through the room.

She whirled around and saw a pale highwayman emerge from the dust like a ghost, gun pointed; a great explosion of white light was followed immediately by a devastating blow to her head—and then, sudden darkness.

65

D'AGOSTA HEARD THE TWO shots and, waving away the clouds of dust, saw Pendergast kneeling over someone on the floor—Constance, gasping, lying in a pool of blood. Nearby were two figures, their heads mostly gone. Muffled cries, moans, and calls for help came from scattered spots under the collapsed ceiling, primarily from the far end of the room.

"The children," Constance said in a whisper. "The children got out."

"We're going to get you out, too," Pendergast told her.

He eased Constance onto her back. Pulling off his coat, he tore it into strips, balled up one of them, and pressed it hard against her abdomen; Constance cried out once, then fainted. He then tied the remaining strips around her midriff in an improvised tourniquet.

"Go first and clear the way!" he called to D'Agosta, heaving Constance up and draping her over his shoulders. "Keep an eye out for any resistance!"

D'Agosta stumbled forward, Pendergast calling out directions through the wrecked house. They had to negotiate fallen beams and push aside sections of plaster and lath. The fire above was now working its way down with frightening speed, filling the corridors with smoke. They ran into a couple of Milk Drinkers, but they were disoriented and terrified, trying to find their own way out; the two groups ignored each other.

Finally they reached the central staircase and descended to the main floor. A tremendous amount of destruction in the reception area blocked the front door. Turning, Pendergast directed them through the salon instead.

"Take that battle-axe," he said as they passed a suit of armor.

D'Agosta wrenched it from the knight's hand with a rattle of steel. He'd always wondered if these suits of armor on display were real or not—he wondered no more; the axe weighed at least twenty pounds. They continued around to the side of the house to an oaken door. D'Agosta tried it, found it locked.

"Use the axe!" Pendergast said.

With a mighty swing, D'Agosta split the door down the middle; two more strikes opened it wide.

Pendergast carried Constance outside. They paused, coughing from the smoke and sucking in the fresh air. D'Agosta peered into the fading light; they had exited on the northern side of the mansion.

"Vincent," Pendergast said, "go around to the mews and get the carriage."

But just as D'Agosta was turning to run, wondering how the hell he was going to drive a carriage—assuming its horses were even hitched—there came a clatter of hooves... and then Leng's barouche came flying out from behind the house and onto the drive. Murphy, sitting in the coachman's seat, pulled on the reins and halted the stamping animals.

"Oh, my dear Lord!" Murphy cried, seeing Pendergast holding Constance, the two of them covered in blood.

"Who's driving the clarence?" D'Agosta asked.

"Gosnold, sir. He insisted on coming along. Shall we follow them back to the mansion, guv?"

"No!" Pendergast said as he eased Constance's body into the coach. He leapt in behind as D'Agosta climbed up next to Murphy.

"Longacre Square!" cried Pendergast. Then he murmured, to himself rather than the unconscious Constance: "That signal from Diogenes is our only chance."

"*Hyaa!*" Murphy shook the reins and the horses took off at a gallop.

66

Twenty minutes after leaving the chaos at the Grand Circle, Diogenes pulled up at the fortified entrance to the alleyway. Bloom must have been waiting just inside, because now he pushed his way past a couple of burly roustabouts and stepped onto the pavement.

"Milord!" he said, looking Diogenes up and down. "What's happened? Have you been accosted?"

Diogenes realized the man was referring to his once-resplendent outfit, now bereft of its ruffles and lace. He was also covered with soot and ash. Above the tops of the buildings on the north side of the avenue, the conflagration was still visible: the tower of fire had subsided, but black smoke was belching upward as thickly as ever.

"We almost got caught in an explosion in the park," he told Bloom. "Anarchists, maybe—but *I* think it's the Theosophical Society, creating a diversion. If I'm right, that means an attack might be imminent. They must have learned about the nexus and are preparing an assault on our barricades."

As he listened, Bloom's expression wavered between

incredulity and alarm. The latter won out—thanks, in part, to the inferno. "Those blasts got the men riled up," he said. "They're ready for anything."

"'Anything' is the perfect word," Diogenes said, a not entirely theatrical quaver in his voice. "A mob might descend upon us. My brother will certainly be here momentarily. God only knows what will happen—" He paused to look at Bloom. "You haven't let anyone near—"

"Lord, no, sir!"

"Good. Now, tell your men: we might have to open the alley barricade for my brother at a moment's notice... while preparing to repel anyone else. Lively, now!"

As Bloom took off, yelling for his men inside the tenements to rally round, Diogenes made his way through the barricade that blocked the alley entrance. Here, between the unlit buildings that rose on both sides, night had fallen—save for the barrier of thick tarps in the very center of the alley, where an unearthly glow shone from behind the canvas shroud.

Diogenes dashed forward and ducked inside. There it was, strong and stable as before: the gateway, not only to his home, but to countless distant worlds beyond. With its brilliance and fearsome power, it had an ineffable attraction, awe inspiring in its promise of the unknown...

...Forcing himself to look away, Diogenes ducked back out of the enclosure and glanced down Smee's Alley toward Seventh Avenue. Half a dozen men, at least, were now manning the barricade.

He paused a moment, thinking. When the three of them—Pendergast, Constance, and himself—had held their meeting at the bordello, they had agreed on one crucial element: a deadline. Since Constance knew the Riverside Drive residence intimately, she was key to the plan; Pendergast was to find Binky, get captured, and ensure she was brought back with him to the mansion, where Constance would find a way to free her and, if necessary, Joe. It was a desperate and unlikely stratagem, but then so were their circumstances. Constance had set the deadline at January 9—she refused to say why exactly but insisted that if the day should arrive without at least Binky being back at Leng's mansion, all would be lost.

There was, of course, a codicil to this plan: in addition to impeding Leng's access to new victims, Diogenes was to keep an eye on Smee's Alley and—in the unlikely event the portal should reappear—contrive to send out a signal that would reach the length and breadth of Manhattan, and that could not be missed by Pendergast, wherever he might be.

And late this afternoon, that event had—remarkably—transpired, and the signal had been duly sent: the destruction of the tower.

Diogenes now went deeper into the alley and through the door leading to the rambling ground floor of the northern tenement. The building was by now a virtual armory, and he grabbed a brace of pistols as he followed the twists and turns leading at last onto Forty-Second Street. There he stopped, tucking one pistol into the waistband of his silk trousers and the other into his vest. If everything had gone according to plan; *if* Pendergast had found Binky and returned with her to Leng's mansion; *if* Constance had managed to slip past Leng and his gang and freed Binky; *if* Pendergast had been able to extricate himself from the mansion... if, if, if.

Diogenes was certain of one thing: they could not fail to notice his signal—and if all was well, they would now be coming to Smee's Alley at a gallop.

Thanks to the explosions, the thoroughfares surrounding Central Park were full of panicked people, carriages, and horses...no doubt impassable. If they'd still been in Leng's mansion, Pendergast's group would come down the Post Road, then remain near the Hudson as the road became Tenth Avenue, not turning until Forty-Second—which meant they would probably be approaching from the west, if they were coming at all.

He surveyed the broad street. Here, ironically, there was less traffic than usual; the confusion and frantic bottleneck seemed to have created something of a ghost town on these cross streets to the south. A few carriages and pedestrians jogged up Seventh Avenue and Broadway, apparently spurred on by curiosity. A greater number were making their way south. He could hear the frantic ring of distant fire bells and the occasional gunshot from the direction of the Grand Circle.

Diogenes squinted westward through the intersecting pools of light the gas lamps cast along the boulevard. As he stared at the scene, a strange sensation of past, present, and future images overlapped in his head, along with a succession of conflicting emotions. And then he saw a large black shape—a four-in-hand barouche coach—emerge from Tenth Avenue and swerve east onto Forty-Second Street. It was Leng's: Diogenes recognized it from that first day, when he'd seen it pull up at Bellevue. As Diogenes stared, his heart accelerated when he saw Murphy, Constance's coachman, at the reins.

The coach was moving like the devil. Having navigated the turn, it accelerated toward him at breakneck speed, the horses thundering along the cobblestones at more of a stampede than a run.

No sane person would drive as recklessly as that... unless it was a matter of life and death.

Turning abruptly and breaking into a run, he cried to the bodyguards maintaining watch. "Open the gate!" he yelled. "Open the gate!"

He reached the corner and turned onto Seventh Avenue. His shouted commands had preceded him: the massive construction of lumber, prepped for such an occasion, crept open like the gates of Troy. Now a dozen or more men were rushing over the scaffolding like ants, pushing boards and metal columns out of the way, while others fanned out across the alley and beyond, firearms at the ready, keeping watch. Diogenes glanced into the alley in time to see Bloom appear out of the darkness. The black of night was diluted by gas lamps, but the alley itself had an illumination all its own: an unearthly glow that, for all their efforts, still permeated the heavy tarps. Bloom had trained his men well; although they had to be curious, and perhaps fearful, of whatever was within that enclosure, his sharp orders—and the promise of a thousand dollars each—kept them at their posts.

The rattle of iron horseshoes ringing off the cobblestones approached, and a second later the big coach turned into the alley at full speed, wheels screeching, forcing men to jump out of the way. There was a commanding shout from Murphy and the horses reared, skidding on the bricks, half falling in the effort to stop. Flecks of foam from their bits spattered Diogenes as he ran past them toward the carriage door, which burst open even as his fingers grasped its handle.

Diogenes was stunned by the scene within. The dark interior of the carriage was in a state of confusion, the coppery smell of blood overpowering.

"Hurry!" Pendergast cried from the darkness. "Get her to the portal!"

He emerged, carrying a bloody body slung in a blanket. With a profound shock, Diogenes realized that all was, in fact, not well—Constance had been terribly, if not mortally, wounded.

"Good God, what happened?" Diogenes cried.

"Clear the way!" Pendergast shouted. D'Agosta jumped off the coachman's seat, and the two of them carried Constance toward the shrouded enclosure.

Diogenes turned and ran before them. "Bloom! Open the canvas!"

The workmen fell back in a scramble, Bloom untying and pulling aside the heavy tarps. In an instant they were bathed in a kaleidoscope of light. As if from far away, Diogenes could hear shouts of surprise and dismay rise from the workmen as they shrank away in fear. As the unnatural light spilled across the alleyway, thousands of cockroaches stirred in alarm and scuttled, in disgusting chitinous waves, every which way.

The portal was exposed, coruscating.

"Is she alive?" Diogenes shouted at Pendergast.

"I don't know. We've got to get her back." He turned to D'Agosta. "We can't all go through simultaneously. You go first; tell them we're coming. I'll follow with Constance in a few seconds once the portal recharges."

He turned to Diogenes. "You guard the portal, keep everyone back, and follow last. As soon as you come through, we'll shut it down on our end."

"What about Leng?"

"Dead—or as good as dead. Constance poisoned him with an extraction from the death cap mushroom."

Diogenes looked into his brother's face, smeared with blood. "I'm not coming, *Frater*."

Pendergast stared back. "What?"

"Go on, get her through—save her life, if you can!"

"We'll never open the portal again. This is your only chance."

"I made a hash of my life in your time."

Pendergast looked carefully at him. "If there was ever a time for jokes—this is not it."

"I'm not joking. For me, this world is a fresh

start—and I have things to do here. Enough said. *Ave atque vale!*"

Pendergast stared at him, the expression on his face unreadable. "Goodbye then, Brother," he said, and turned away. "Vincent," he cried: "*Go!*"

67

D'Agosta didn't hesitate—not even for a second. On the other side of that shimmering door was Laura.

He stepped up to the portal—feeling again that sense of unearthly energy, hot and cold simultaneously, that made the hairs on his neck stand at attention—and jumped.

At the same moment, the gateway flickered—a piece of gossamer, sliced diagonally from top to bottom by an invisible knife—wobbled, weakened, then disappeared.

Caught unawares, D'Agosta fell onto the cobbles of the alley. He rolled, instinctively using his shoulder to break the fall. It still hurt like a son of a bitch.

"*What the hell?*" he cried as he lay on the ground. The look on Pendergast's face was one of pure horror and despair. He felt the same sudden madness and fury: what kind of sick, twisted joke was fate doing to—

With a snap that was not a sound, but some phenomenon having nothing to do with his five senses, the portal abruptly came back to life, its brilliance once again filling the alley. D'Agosta didn't need a second invitation. He leapt...

...And found himself half staggering, half falling onto the floor of Pendergast's basement laboratory. He glanced around on his knees. Proctor was there, staring at him, along with some guy in a wheelchair.

"Get ready!" he cried. "We've got Pendergast and Constance coming through. She's stabbed in the abdomen, bleeding out!"

The portal rippled briefly, brightened, and a moment later—with a glittering, blinding flash—Pendergast staggered through, Constance in his arms. He was caught by Proctor's steadying hand.

"Call an ambulance," Pendergast cried. "We need AB negative blood—lots of it." He turned to D'Agosta. "Please assist me."

As he helped Pendergast carry Constance out into the hallway, the last thing D'Agosta saw was Proctor, raising a phone to his ear at the same moment the stranger in the wheelchair shut off power to the machine.

68

It was five days before D'Agosta took Pendergast up on a standing invitation and returned to the Riverside Drive mansion for afternoon tea. Everything looked the same; everyone acted the same: Mrs. Trask opened the front door with the usual blandishments, and as D'Agosta approached the library entrance, he saw Pendergast seated in his usual chair by the fire. The harpsichord bench held a neat stack of densely notated music, Constance's newly polished stiletto lying atop like a paperweight, both music and weapon awaiting the recovery of their mistress. Yet for D'Agosta, everything had changed. His venture into the nineteenth century had given him a new and much darker worldview that no ordinary far-off vacation could have. Ever since returning, after a joyful, awkward reunion with Laura, he felt unsteady—like a sailor just back in port, still encumbered with sea legs. He found himself waking in the middle of the night, sitting up and drawing in a lungful of breath, just to make sure the air was reassuringly clean, without the constant background odors of coal smoke, tallow, and manure.

As he stepped in, Pendergast looked up at him, then gestured languidly toward a chair. "Vincent, my friend, so good of you to come—at last."

"Sorry," D'Agosta said as he came over and sat down. "I had a lot of fancy footwork to do, after going missing for two weeks."

"Everything all right downtown?"

"It is now."

"And how is Laura?"

"Fine, thanks." This, in fact, had been the other, marvelous, side effect of his strange journey: one that had brought his life back into balance. The longer he was away, the longer he was missing—with everyone thinking the worst, with an ever-widening search turning up nothing—the more anxious she became. Her imagination (she'd told him) had run wild; crazy scenarios had gone through her mind: he'd decided to just chuck it all and go back to Moose Jaw, Canada, to write another book. He'd run off to Ibiza with some sidepiece he'd been hiding from her. After a week with no news, her scenarios had grown morbid: suicide; a Turkish prison; murdered by the mob, his body joining Jimmy Hoffa's.

When he'd told her the bizarre reality, she had listened quietly. When he asked if she believed him, she'd responded, "Nothing that happens when you partner with Pendergast would ever surprise me." And she added, "It doesn't matter now, Vinnie. I have you back. I learned the hard way that's all I care about."

When D'Agosta had first arrived at the library, Proctor had been standing by the door, a study in taciturnity, and that odd guy in the wheelchair he'd seen briefly on their return was parked on the far side of Pendergast, in half darkness, sipping hot cocoa. His name was Mime, some sort of computer maven Pendergast occasionally consulted with, and who'd helped Proctor fix the machine. D'Agosta had never met him before, but Pendergast had spoken of him several times, and on one occasion explained that thalidomide embryopathy had left him with malformed legs and one nearly useless hand. But nature had bestowed the gift of transcendental intelligence to that otherwise compromised body. From an early age, he'd shunned the company of others and devoted himself to mathematics, cryptography, engineering, and computer programming. Apparently, once Proctor finally convinced Mime to leave his sanctuary in River Pointe, Ohio, via private medical jet, the hardest part of repairing the machine was already done. Mime had succeeded brilliantly.

But now, as D'Agosta sipped his tea, he could see that Mime, for all his alleged reclusiveness, loved to talk and relished an audience. In front of the fire, he proudly recounted the steps he'd taken to render the device not only workable, but improved. As he talked, Proctor eased himself into a wing chair near the library entrance to listen.

"... The most difficult part was the downtime," Mime was telling them. "It took me two days—well, closer to three—to understand the basic functionality. That was some righteous, righteous shit! After that, I spent ages waiting on *him*." Here, an eye was cast toward Proctor. "The dude took, like, *forever* to get the parts."

"Try acquiring a palladium bolometer and a unimetric thermopile... at three o'clock in the morning," Proctor replied. He did not seem to hold Mime's genius in high regard. D'Agosta could only imagine the long hours they must have spent together—Mime giving the orders, Proctor doing the work.

"Pendergast, my man, don't get me wrong: Wild Bill Hickok here is an ace when it comes to cleaning guns and sharpening knives... But ask him to do some delicate soldering?" He shook his head, pale and bald save for a few blond hairs laid flat across the dome. "Sweet sister Sadie."

"You have to admit," Pendergast observed gently, "that Proctor turned your instructions into reality. And he provided you with invaluable information on how the machine initially worked."

Mime appeared ready to object, then changed his mind and took a swig of cocoa.

"Thanks to the two of you," Pendergast continued, "one using his mind, the other his hands—we are safely back home. And for that, we'll be eternally grateful."

At this, Mime beamed. Proctor, meanwhile, remained expressionless—but, though he couldn't be sure, D'Agosta thought the man's chest swelled slightly with pride.

"How's Constance doing?" D'Agosta said, taking the opportunity to change the subject.

"Steady improvement, thanks. She has a remarkably strong constitution. Another fifteen minutes' delay in 1881, and..." He shook his head. "A massive transfusion was required—six units of packed red blood cells in under an hour. Not to mention surgery and an infusion of antibiotics to address a severe laceration in the peritoneal cavity."

"Six units?" D'Agosta echoed.

"In under an hour."

"Jesus." Six units for someone as petite as Constance... He could only shake his head. "What about the kids—Binky and Joe?"

"No doubt she would have liked more time to say goodbye to her family. But it's done now, and for the best. During those last weeks, she prepared matters carefully, set everything up for them to be well taken care of. The mansion is in their name, as is a considerable fortune. Féline and Mary will be able to make sure their education

back and forth for a minute in silent annoyance. "I guess I'll take what I can get."

"You may, in the meantime, continue to examine it—as long as you promise not to use it."

"Oh, I'll just use it once or twice. You know, make a few trips back to 1983, so I can take care of Johnny Williford—the bully who kept putting baking soda in my Cream of Wheat at lunch break."

This was met by a frosty silence.

"That's a joke! Didn't I agree I'd just study it? Of *course* I won't turn it on. Jesus, has everybody lost their sense of humor here?"

And then he laughed—but he laughed alone.

He bent forward suddenly, coughing, a spasm racking his guts. As he recovered, his hungry gaze probed the lab, taking everything in by the reflected light. His eyes stopped their circuit at a far corner, still in shadow despite the portal's violent intensity.

"You!" he cried, staggering.

"Me," a dulcet voice replied.

Constance Greene sat in a wheelchair, wearing a silk dressing gown, her face pale, dark circles under her eyes. Her legs were covered by a heavy blanket. Beside her was a small wheeled lab trolley, made of steel that winked and shone in the light of the portal. On it sat three items: a book, lying open; a small bottle of medicine; and a large surgical scalpel.

Their eyes met. Then, while still looking at Leng, Constance reached for the scalpel.

Leng raised the gun, while at the same time shaking his head with a *tut-tutting* sound. "Hands back in your lap, my dear."

She complied. Leng stood before the glowing portal, grasping the railing.

A beat passed, and Constance spoke again. "I knew that, sooner rather than later—assuming you hadn't been crushed in your own mansion—you'd appear in that rathole of an alley, waiting. I could have kept the machine off and left you to die, but I didn't. Instead, I turned it on—knowing you'd come through."

"I see *you've* managed to cheat death," Leng said after a moment, his voice thick and raspy. "Thanks, no doubt, to the miracles of twenty-first-century medicine."

She did not reply. Leng remained where he was, listing slightly back and forth.

"I'm glad you survived," he continued. "I, too, seek the miracles of twenty-first-century medicine—and you're going to help me with that." He gestured with the muzzle of the gun, keeping it aimed even as he turned partially away, coughing and retching, seized by another bout of cramping. But he recovered quickly, spitting a mouthful of phlegm toward the nearest wall. "When you disappeared, I knew you'd all gone through that magic-lantern show. Well, now, so have I. Expected that, did you? Never mind: I'm here now—and you're going to undo the pain and suffering you've caused me." He again waggled the gun. "So: where are we?"

"In a basement."

"Don't be daft. Where *are* we?"

"New York City. In our home."

"'Our'?"

"Aloysius and mine."

"Aloysius... Pendergast. How domestic." Leng tried to smile, but his face was contorted by another spasm of pain.

"In your former house."

He took a deep, shuddering breath. "Enough persiflage. I need you to get me the antidote—the one you told me didn't exist in *my* century. And for your sake, I suggest you hurry—I may be losing my grip on reality, which makes me unpredictable."

"A side effect of the poison?" Constance asked. Then: "What happened to your face?"

"When I was waiting in the alley, that pernicious cleric paid me a visit."

"You don't mean Reverend Considine?"

"He had something glowing in his hand, and before I could gather my wits, he branded me—across the face! The brand exiles bore when bound for the penal colonies of Australia. As I fell back, I heard him say: 'Here's a farewell gift from Constance.' I see now, you little vixen, that he was one of yours."

"Thoughtful of him," Constance murmured.

"No more wasting time. I want medical attention, and right away—as I implied, the last thing you'd want is my growing delusional. I know what a telephone is: use it. Get me a doctor. Now."

"No need for threats," she said. "And in fact, there's no reason to leave this room. I have the antidote right here." And she nodded toward the metal table at her side.

As Leng followed her glance, she picked up a medicine bottle, sealed, with a tiny label covered in writing.

"That is certainly most convenient. And how do I know it's not just another poison?"

"Because that would be too cheap a trick." She twisted the top of the bottle, cracking open the seal. "Your timing is good; indocyanine green only became available as an alpha-amanitin inhibitor quite recently. Before that, there was no true cure for the death cap mushroom."

As he watched, she took a sip.

"Ugh," she said, recapping the bottle and returning it to the medical trolley. "Bitter."

"Let me have it." With his branded face, his crazy eyes, and the infernal halo of the portal ablaze behind him, he could almost have been one of Lucifer's fallen angels.

"I will. Do you think I've been waiting here, in the dark and the damp, for my health?"

Leng scoffed, then looked at her narrowly, as if she might still be feverish. "I tire of this. *Let me have it!*"

"Very well." As he kept the gun aimed, she reached over, grasped the trolley, and rolled it across the uneven floor. It collided with the vertical post of the emitter railing, then rolled backward a few inches, the scalpel and medicine bottle wobbling slightly under the impact. Leng watched as Constance sank back in the wheelchair. Despite her bravado, it was obvious that simply pushing the tray was still not only painful, but exhausting.

Grabbing the scalpel off the tray and throwing it into a dark corner, he put the revolver down, picked up the bottle, read the label with streaming eyes—there it was: INDOCYANINE GREEN, neatly and officially printed. Steadying himself against another wave of spasmic pain, he twisted off the top, threw it aside, and drank half of the bottle down. It *was* bitter. He couldn't feel any worse off than he did already, and it wasn't a large bottle—he lifted it a second time and drained it to the dregs.

Then he tossed it away. As he heard it shiver into pieces against the floor, he raised his eyes to Constance.

She was seated in the wheelchair as before. Now, however, the blanket covering her legs had dropped away, revealing a pump shotgun leveled at him, her finger on the trigger.

"You must have wondered why that portal suddenly appeared, after five days of nothing but agonized waiting," she said. "It was bait—and you swallowed it. You see, it wasn't enough for me to kill you in *your* century. I wanted to see you die in *mine*, as well."

"You *hell-bitch!*" And, as Leng snatched his revolver from the tray, she unloaded the 12-gauge into his chest.

The load of double-aught buck knocked him off his feet, throwing him back toward the portal and ripping a hole in his midsection, even as his own gun went off uselessly, the round going wild. Constance's wheelchair lurched under the recoil, impacting the wall behind it. She watched as Leng somersaulted backward into the glowing tunnel, blood and viscera erupting in a fountain of gore. The portal dimmed briefly, as if absorbing a meal, then flared back once again to its full, awful power.

Constance sat for a moment, breathing hard. The lab hummed with the low song of the device; there were no other sounds. It was as if Leng had never been there.

Wheeling herself a few yards along the closest wall,

she reached up and painfully opened the dual industrial breaker boxes that fed the machine its 100,000 watts. As she snapped off each SF6 breaker in turn, the portal winked out; then the humming whined to a stop. She took a final glance at the panels, then twisted the three-phase main lug into the off position.

Now she moved the wheelchair to the center of the room, dark save for the glow of Mime's rack of monitoring equipment. She stopped once to check the dressing beneath her robe and to regain her breath. Then, turning the wheelchair with one hand, she faced the machine, racked the shotgun, and raised it.

The first blast tore apart the main control console, ripping it wide open, exposing a fantastically intricate web of circuits and wiring, flinging fragments of logic boards and chunks of microcircuitry outward. Pumping another round into the chamber, she noticed that the impact of her blast had torn away a reinforcing internal panel, exposing a section of much older technology. She lifted the shotgun, aimed with great effort, then sent a load of buckshot directly into the heart of the machine, smashing it into a chaos of pulverized transistors, vacuum tubes, and copper.

This blast sent her wheelchair lurching backward once again, this time tipping it over. Strength gone, in pain, Constance let the weapon slide from her hand as she rested her head on the cold floor...even as rising voices sounded in the corridor outside.

70

D'AGOSTA WAS HARD ON the heels of Pendergast and Proctor as they raced down into the basement, following the sound of a shotgun blast. As they reached the landing and ran down a corridor, he heard a second blast, followed by a third. The echoes died away as they approached the laboratory door. It was closed, but Pendergast shouldered it open and they stormed inside.

The room was dim. Acrid smoke filled the air. The glow of red emergency lamps flickered and danced, coming in and out of view as the haze drifted by. It stank of burnt electronics and nitrocellulose.

As D'Agosta stood, uncomprehending, Pendergast and Proctor fanned out ahead of him, their figures growing ghostly in the pall. He heard the sounds of switches being turned on and off fruitlessly. There was a loud spark, followed by a curse from Proctor. And then lights in the ceiling sprang to life—one, two—and the roar of an exhaust fan came from somewhere overhead. The light revealed Constance Greene on the floor, propped up on her knees, in a dressing gown. An overturned wheelchair and shotgun lay nearby.

"Constance!" Pendergast cried. "What happened?"

"Help me up, please," she said with a gasp.

Gently, Pendergast helped her rise as D'Agosta righted the wheelchair and eased her into it.

"Are you all right?" Pendergast asked.

"Rarely better," Constance managed to say, even as she winced in pain.

Proctor watched them silently for a moment, then approached the smoking wreckage, surveying the damage. "Mr. Pendergast?" he said, turning.

The agent looked over. Proctor silently pointed to a section of the device that had received the brunt of the blast. The central brain of the machine was a violent tangle of copper wire, bits of plastic, ruined circuit boards, and other detritus stamped with various colors and labels. The damage was so great D'Agosta could see right through the ruined guts of the machine to the wall behind, peppered with shot.

"It's finished," Proctor murmured, almost to himself.

There was a brief silence as Pendergast came over and the two men surveyed the damage. Then Pendergast turned back to Constance, looking at her silently.

"Why did you destroy the machine?" he asked after a moment.

"Because none of you would," came the reply.

"Before that first shotgun blast, I thought I heard the faint sound of a raised voice. Who...?" Pendergast stopped, looking most uncharacteristically baffled.

"Leng," she said.

"What?"

"He—" She paused, closed her eyes, and took a moment to regain her breath. "He came through. He wanted something."

"And?"

"I let him have it."

This was followed by another silence, during which Proctor knelt to pick up the shotgun. He turned it over in his hands, then racked the slide a couple of times. Two shells sprang out, which he picked up and put in his pocket. Then he leaned the weapon against the wall and turned toward Pendergast. An odd look passed between them. Pendergast's glance shifted to the shotgun, then the portal, and finally to Constance, his eyes glittering with growing understanding.

Then he returned to the wheelchair and gently gathered her into his arms. "I'm taking you back to bed," he said in a low voice that sounded not quite paternal, and not quite fraternal. "Vincent, if you wouldn't mind getting the door and assisting with the elevator, please?"

"You got it." D'Agosta moved to the exit, holding the door open. "What—" He hesitated. "What are we going to tell Mime?"

Pendergast made a pained face. "Later, my friend." Cradling Constance, he walked toward the door.

As he did so, D'Agosta saw Constance bring one hand up to caress Pendergast's cheek. At the same time, she raised her head to murmur something in his ear. D'Agosta, embarrassed, looked away, but heard her words nevertheless: *Thank you for bringing me home.*

"Proctor," Pendergast said over his shoulder, "if you wouldn't mind making sure this mess is stabilized and not about to burst into flame, before following us back upstairs?"

"Of course."

"Much obliged." And Pendergast vanished around the corner and into the hallway, D'Agosta following.

* * *

Proctor spent ten minutes checking the main electrical leads and a few of the more unstable components, satisfying himself that the thing was inert—and would stay that way. Task accomplished, he made a circuit of the room, his flashlight illuminating every corner. He picked up the empty buckshot shells and pocketed them with the others. Then, as he rose in preparation to leave, he noticed three small droplets of blood. They were at the base of the platform where the portal normally appeared. Dipping a hand into his jacket pocket, he pulled out a handkerchief, knelt, and carefully wiped them away.

"Neatly done, Constance," he murmured in a low, admiring voice, as he returned the handkerchief to his pocket. "Very neatly done indeed."

Then he rose, turned off the emergency lighting, stepped over to the door, exited, locked it behind him—and vanished into the gloom of the basement hallway.

EPILOGUE

Five Months Later
(One Hundred and Forty-Five Years Earlier)

THE AFTERNOON SUN SHONE benevolently over the Austrian town of Baden bei Wien, nestled deep in the heart of the Vienna Woods. In the late nineteenth century, a time when people were obsessed with European spas, Baden was distinguished for its long history. The town dated back to the Romans, when it was known as Aquae Cetiæ. For centuries the area's fourteen hot springs, rich in healing minerals, had drawn people from all over the world. These were pilgrims eager to "take the cure" and bask in the town's lush gardens and brilliant promenades, seeking a restorative retreat from the bustle of the Gilded Age.

Among the finest of Baden's establishments was the Grand Hotel Flußblick. It had been built two centuries earlier, sited next to a dramatic waterfall. Over the years, the force of the water had widened and deepened the flume, and the hotel had responded—not by retreating to safer ground, but by reinforcing its granite footings and adding top-floor suites with magnificent views. In some future day the entire construct, foundation and all, might tumble into the spume like the Rhodian Colossus—but at present it was quite safe, if vertiginous, and the presence of the mighty waterfall only added a delicious thrill to the wealthy and privileged who stayed there.

A second-floor balcony, perched alongside the great falls, presented guests with a dramatic view of the rushing water. In the calm of a bright and sunny morning, this L-shaped balcony afforded a direct view over the thundering cataract for breakfast or lunch. But as the sun made its way across the sky, afternoon zephyrs began moving through the gorge—frequently carrying a fine mist toward that section of the balcony—and the staff moved the furniture around the corner, facing the hotel's front. Everything, naturally, would return to its original place overlooking the waterfall in time for the next morning's breakfast.

On this particular afternoon, Cedric, Lord Jayeaux, reclined on a chaise lounge placed on this forward-facing balcony, next to his traveling companion, Livia. He was occupied by a languorous admiration of his clothing and its accoutrements: a linen suit the color of faded apricot; bicolored cap-toe oxfords; and his favorite snakewood walking stick, freshly waxed and gleaming. A few minutes earlier he had given it a lazy roll into the sunlight, the better to admire its subtle taper, the rich cloisonné enamel inlaid with Chinese cinnabar that adorned the handle. At last, he glanced at his pocket watch, then raised his eyes to look beyond the topiary, toward the Schwechat River, the Casino dì Baden, and the verdant green bowl of the Vienna Basin beyond.

In such idle moments, Diogenes Pendergast would occasionally reflect on his decision to remain in this nineteenth-century world. As the weeks had passed, he'd come to realize more and more that it had been an excellent, if not brilliant, choice. It was a simpler world than the one he had fled. A compromised world, of course—as dispassionately cruel as it was dispassionately just—but the cruelties were of a more straightforward nature, done with less hypocrisy and self-justification. In places like Dodge City and the Black Hills, men of ugly aspirations were busily killing off the buffalo and forcing Native Americans from their ancestral lands. Black people, although technically freed by the Civil War, remained disenfranchised in the South. Nobel had recently invented dynamite, naively believing that the horror of its destructive power would make war obsolete. Cruel: yes, without a shred of doubt. At the same time, in Menlo Park, New Jersey, Thomas Edison had just created his first high-resistance incandescent bulb—and in Berlin, Robert Koch was doing work leading to the discovery of the tuberculosis bacterium.

A waiter in tails and a starched white shirt approached their balcony table and spoke to Diogenes's companion. "*Möchten Sie noch etwas trinken?*" he asked in an unctuous tone.

"*Noch ein Campari und Limonade, danke,*" said Livia. Diogenes glanced at her; she looked resplendent in her pale-lime gown, with its plunge neck and half a dozen ruffled tiers.

"*Das gleiche,*" Diogenes told the man, who bowed and disappeared. His musings interrupted, he kept his face toward Livia. "My dear, I believe you're picking up German even faster than Italian."

"When the subject turns to such things as ordering dresses, dinner, or diamonds—at least—I do appear something of a savant."

Livia, to his good fortune, was turning out to be the perfect traveling companion for a grand world tour. A literary upbringing had endowed her with a curious mind and charming turn of phrase. A nasty change in the family's fortunes as a child had acquainted her with self-reliance and self-preservation. And she displayed an in-the-moment philosophy that could best be described as cultured hedonism. Diogenes, who previously had been forced to play tutor to his *affaires de coeur*, was astonished to find Livia teaching him things—not only in the elegant halls of art museums, but in the boudoir as well.

"I'm glad to see you enjoying your Campari," he told her. "It's rather an acquired taste."

"One of many highlights of Italy, thanks to you. Along with the *Pietà*, the chiffon peignoir you gave me... and the bout of amoebiasis from those mussels you insisted I dine on in Napoli."

"Shigellosis. My apologies."

Livia shrugged it off with a laugh. "It's always a gamble, isn't it? Eating in the most expensive restaurant isn't necessarily safer than a Sullivan Street watering hole."

This was a perfect example of what secretly pleased him most: her insouciance at his offering the medical term for her discomfort... despite the fact shigella would not be discovered for another decade or two. He knew that Livia, nothing if not observant, understood there was something absolutely unusual about him, but she was also clever enough not to question or become too curious.

"As to the Campari," he went on, "do you suppose the crushed cochineals add flavor to the liqueur or simply give the drink its carmine hue?" He was referring to the soft-bodied insects that endowed the drink with its distinctive color.

"I assume that observation was intended to disgust me?" She smiled, then took a sip, pretending to consider. "Since you ask, I suspect the bugs' only contribution is to the hue. But I must admit each time I take a sip, I expect to find a tiny, hairy leg on my tongue: like a burdock on some cowboy's chaps."

Diogenes allowed himself a laugh. "Touché!" The fresh drinks arrived and they raised glasses; then Diogenes sat back again, sipping his drink and enjoying the warm air.

Earlier, he'd toyed with the idea of using his knowledge to gain power and prestige, but he quickly realized this would be a terrible mistake. Hubris like that always led to a downfall, usually a fatal one. He now saw himself as someone more like Charles Swann—though Proust would not create this literary character for another thirty years—a man of taste, erudition, and wealth, who could move easily in circles beneath or above his own without bringing attention to himself.

After he'd satisfied himself that the portal was well and permanently closed—thus severing all connection with his former world—he had Bloom and his men quickly deconstruct and clear the alley. He paid them off handsomely and sent them on their way. In their absence, Enoch Leng, poisoned by Constance, had taken up residence in the alley almost immediately, waiting for the portal to reopen, and Diogenes had taken advantage of this opportunity to brand the dying man's face... a suitable parting gift, all things considered.

He quickly got rid of the Right Reverend Considine—called back to England by an urgent summons—although to quell any inquiries, Diogenes made sure Considine donated a most handsome sum to the local Methodist elders, ensuring the House of Industry and the Mission would be well provided for... and serve the purpose their founders had intended.

That left him with one more duty to perform before he and Livia could begin the grand tour he envisioned. He went up to the wreckage of the Riverside Drive mansion and explored the debris for incriminating details.

He was satisfied to see that the basement and its collections and labs were thoroughly destroyed, and the pirate lair now hidden under rubble. When the Aloysius of this timeline ultimately made his way north from New Orleans to New York, Diogenes mused, his brother would simply have to make do with the Dakota. And, of course, there would be no Leng for him to deal with in that timeline. But having settled these matters, such thoughts were no longer Diogenes's concern—he'd brought along enough medicine, and other useful items, in his valise when he'd leapt through that portal to keep himself and Livia relatively insulated from the problems of the day—and he was now embarking on a new life.

His musings were again interrupted, this time by movement: a man, approaching in the distance. "Livia," he said, "princess of my violet-scented dreams—would you mind raising your lorgnette and directing it toward the main stairway for just a moment?"

His companion did as requested.

"Now: do you see that officious-looking man, whiskers quivering with self-righteousness?"

Holding the spectacles up by their gold handle, Livia peered through them. "No... Yes!" A pause. "What an odious little creature. He reminds me of that official who stopped our train at the Austrian border, then insisted on opening my trunk and putting his grubby hands all over my scanties."

"How precisely you hit the mark! That man is, in fact, a customs official—and not unlike the homunculus you describe, he is full of the self-importance common to minor bureaucrats. As it happens, he's here to see me."

"Whatever business would you have with a man like that?"

"Very important business, my dear. He's the illegitimate child of a woman named Maria Schicklgruber. His father's name is unknown: the stories of his birth are as legion as the number of illegitimate children he's sired—and will sire."

"I see." She lowered the lorgnette. "But why is he here to meet with you?"

"Before I answer, allow me to acquaint you with one more fact about the man: when he came of age, he changed his name from 'Schicklgruber' to something equally ludicrous: in demotic old German, it means 'someone who lives in a hut.'"

"I have little doubt he does—but that still doesn't explain your interest in him."

"We'll discuss that shortly; he'll be here any minute. You see, I let it be known that were he to stamp some counterfeit export papers for me, he would receive a very handsome bribe, making his journey here most worthwhile. Ah—here he comes now."

Grasping his cane, Diogenes stood up to greet the approaching guest. "*Guten Abend, mein Herr.*"

"I speak the English well enough," the man said with a heavy accent.

"All the better. This is my companion, the Lady Livia. Would you care to join us?"

"Thank you, I would not." The official eyed Livia up and down, not bothering to conceal his assumption she was a courtesan. Then he flicked some stray dust from his forearm. "Let us please transact this business of yours—the two of us, privately. I had a long and uncomfortable journey here."

"Very well." Diogenes gestured toward the turn of the balcony. "Shall we talk there, with a view of the waterfall?"

The man followed Diogenes as they turned the corner to face another long stretch of balcony—invisible from the frontage, and uninhabited at this hour of the afternoon. As they stopped short of the railing, a stray breeze—coated with fine mist from the waterfall—drifted over them.

"*Verflucht!*" the man said, annoyed.

"The wind drives in a bit of *Nebel* from the waterfall now and then during the afternoon. That's why this balcony is so desolate at the moment. Refreshing, don't you think?"

The man waved this away impatiently. "*Lasst uns unsere Geschäfte schnell erledigen.* You have some papers you wish stamped, *nein?*"

"No."

The official gazed at him uncomprehendingly. "No? What do you mean?"

"That was a deception on my part. I called you here on account of our maidservant at this hotel—one Fräulein Rostig. When she was crossing from Slovenia with her fiancé last week, you gave her a difficult time at the border. In fact, you made the two of them wait for over an hour. I summoned you to compensate her for your rudeness."

As the affront to his person began to sink in, an especially large spray—driven by the wind—doused the man from head to foot.

"Taking the waters, I see," Diogenes went on, swinging his cane. "An excellent idea."

"How *dare* you—!" The man turned to leave. Diogenes blocked his path.

"I'm not finished. Not only did you hinder our maidservant but, in pawing through her luggage, you managed to tear her most expensive frock. So: I shall collect twenty gulden from you as restitution for your rudeness—*and* your clumsiness."

"Get out of my way!" the man said in red-eyed fury.

"Not until you do the gentlemanly thing: pay up."

With an oath, the man raised a fist and charged like

an enraged bull. Diogenes, however, merely swung his walking stick up to meet the rush—and in so doing triggered the eight-inch sword cane that sprang out the end, fast and silent as an adder's tongue, so that the man impaled himself up to the hilt by his own furious inertia. The angry look on his face turned to surprise. Diogenes walked the man two steps back to the railing and hoisted him up, letting him dangle a moment. He tipped him over, watching as he slipped off the blade, and then—drumstick legs churning—tumbled down into the thunderous waterfall. Diogenes pushed the dagger back into its sheath by pressing the cane against the floor with a resounding flourish. He glanced around again: no witnesses. He leaned over the balcony for a final look into the waterfall. The body had vanished.

He strolled back around the corner and sat down. "Well now, where were we? I believe we were about to discuss our next destination."

"My darling, you're a little damp. What happened to that unpleasant little man?"

"He left the balcony by another way." He paused. "Actually—just *entre nous*, you understand—I assisted him over the railing and into the *Katarakt*."

Livia looked at him for a long time and then said, "Why?"

Why indeed? Though he had no desire to make this parallel universe his domain, Diogenes nevertheless had begun, unexpectedly, to feel a proprietary interest in its well-being. And he'd realized that a few small adjustments—tweaks, one might call them—could save his adopted world great agony...and loss of innocence.

He took a sip of his drink. Then, with sudden decision, he put it down and sat up again, swinging his legs onto the ground and leaning forward. "May I confide something in you, my nereid of the azure Danube?"

"Only if it's incriminating."

"It is indeed. You recall my telling you that execrable customs official had changed his name? It used to be Schicklgruber." He paused. "It is now Hitler."

Livia looked on, her expression unchanged. "Never heard of him."

"Of course you haven't. But the twentieth century *will* come to know that name in the person of his son, born eight years from now, named Adolf. Or rather, the world would have known. But thanks to this little accident today, the name Hitler will remain obscure forever—and, if fate is kind, many millions of lives will be saved."

Livia's gaze remained very steady, and her face had paled somewhat.

"There are two other places I'm anxious to visit on our grand tour," Diogenes continued, "for the very same reason."

"And those are...?"

"Have you any desire to see the Hermitage—in St. Petersburg, Russia?"

"Not particularly. I hear Russia is cold."

"In the summer, parts of it are quite lovely. I would propose we visit the incomparable Amber Room in the Catherine Palace—the most beautiful chamber in the world—while it still stands. Our next stop will be Beijing—I mean Pekin—in China."

She gazed at him steadily. "Whom will you be seeking in St. Petersburg and Pekin?"

"Two other fathers."

"For the same purpose?"

"Yes. And after that," he went on with sudden cheer, "we book passage back to San Francisco—on our way to, dare I hope, nuptials in New York?" And he tapped something hidden in his jacket that may or may not have been an engagement ring.

She remained silent so long he began to fear he'd revealed too much. At last, she spoke. "Before I answer, I have a question of my own."

"What is it, my dove? Do you wish me to go down on one knee?"

But she'd fallen silent once again. Then, abruptly, her color returned. "Will I become Lady Jayeaux? Or shall I be taking your *real* name—whatever it is?"

And as she burst out laughing, Diogenes realized he'd just—for lack of a better term—gotten some of his own back. "You...!" he began, then stopped, momentarily at a loss for words.

"That, darling, was in return for the Campari-colored bugs. But you never needed to ask, you know: dearest Cedric—you lead, and I shall follow."

He looked at her, returning the smile. Then he took a sip of his aperitif and reclined once again in his chair, closing his eyes to reflect on the vagaries of fate and time, as the setting sun poured cinnamon light over the lowering clouds of the Vienna Woods.

Turn the page for a preview of the next thrilling tale in the Nora Kelly series, in which archaeologist Nora Kelly and FBI Agent Corrie Swanson, while investigating bizarre deaths in the desert, awaken an ancient evil more terrifying than anything they've faced before.

Available Now!

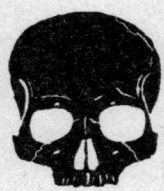

1

August 2020; precise date uncertain

THE WOMAN PAUSED and raised her head, looking over the wavering landscape toward the horizon. She blinked, then blinked again, dazzled by the light. As far as she could see lay a land dotted with hoodoo rock formations: spires and domes of rock, giant boulders balancing on slender stems, trembling and ghostly in the heat. This madness of rock and sand rose into a burning sky dominated by the implacable sun. She could see no traces of life: no trees, no grass, nothing beyond a few stunted prickly pear cacti hugging the sand, shriveled up, dead, more spines than flesh.

The woman lowered her head and continued walking, concentrating on placing one foot in front of the other, always northward, where she knew her destination lay. If only she could get there soon, she would be safe.

She finally understood the expression *raging thirst*. She thought she had been thirsty before, sometimes very thirsty; but that had been nothing. Nothing. She thought of the Coleridge poem she'd taught so often in English lit it had become a drone in her head. This was what that Ancient Mariner must have felt watching the very boards of his ship shrink under the sun. The thirst that was upon her now was one that seized her mind, refused to let her think of anything else. She could feel her pulse thundering in her temples; the muscles of her legs were shaky and trembling. Her mouth had dried up many miles back, and now her tongue was cracking and swelling. She could taste the iron of blood.

But to stop now would be the worst possible mistake. She had to keep walking.

To get her mind off the thirst, she tried recalling the last few days, but the memories would come back only in pieces: long, dusty bus rides; furtive traveling by night; the air-conditioned Walmart with its racks of cheap clothes; the shabby gas-station restrooms and McDonald's dumpsters. She recalled burning her money, watching with fascination as the twenty-dollar bills wrinkled in curlicues of flame. The phone had been harder to destroy; in the end, its innards had nevertheless crackled and popped under a burning glaze of lighter fluid.

One foot in front of the other.

A sudden surge of dizziness forced her to brace one hand against a rock. She took a deep breath, let it out slowly. The sun stopped wheeling overhead, returning to a fixed position, a hole of omnipotent heat punched through the fabric of the sky. She spat out the blood weeping from her tongue and continued on.

All she had to do was endure. She tried to say it out loud, *endure*, but no sound emerged beyond a breathy hiss. It was hot, brutally hot, but nowhere was it so hot as at ground level. She could feel it through the soles of her running shoes. It was a miracle they weren't actually melting. And, in fact, maybe they were melting: she had once read that in the desert, in full sun, the ground temperature could exceed a hundred and fifty degrees.

Time passed. She walked on. And then came to a tottering stop, feeling a rush of... what?

Of what? She couldn't articulate what she felt. Everything was so different now. Here in this inferno, it was as if she'd already begun her transformation. The way she felt now was different from just a quarter of an hour before—and light-years from the beginning, when she first realized she'd lost sight of a road.

Deliverance. That was the one word that echoed louder than anything else in her mind: louder than the baking heat, louder than even the dreadful thirst. Even now it rose before her. *Deliverance.*

She could feel the anvil of the sun directly on her head. She counted ten steps forward.

She took off her shirt, peeling it off over her head, and dropped it.

Ten more steps.

She unhooked her bra and shrugged it off. The radiation of the sun now penetrated into her skin.

As she reached for the button of her shorts, she saw movement out of the corner of her eye. She swiftly moved and crouched behind a rock: she'd already seen many things that were merely tricks of her sun-blind vision, but she had to be sure.

This time, it was no phantom or mirage. There was the dot of a person in the distance.

How strange: out in the middle of nowhere, a woman was herding a small flock of sheep. She was maybe a mile away and headed in the opposite direction, and she'd become visible only because she was climbing a low rise with her sheep, taking them over the brow of a ridge.

Had the woman seen her?

She waited, hiding. Nothing. After a while, once she was sure the woman was gone, she eased back up.

She unbuttoned her shorts and took them off, dropping them, following with her panties.

The running shoes came off next, and finally the socks. When she placed her bare feet on the hot sand, she felt a sudden, searing pain so excruciating she almost fell to her knees—but she pushed this away as best she could, focusing instead on clenching her last possessions: the objects that, unlike things of this world—money, clothes—she could not, *must* not, give up.

It was like walking on fire. Her body, not her brain, warned her that this could not last long. But there was no reason to be afraid, no reason at all.

One step. Another.

And then, with unexpected abruptness, her legs gave way and she fell to her knees. Her bare skin hit the ground like meat dropping on a searing griddle. She screamed involuntarily, then fell back, writhing in a useless attempt to escape the heat, every fresh contact with the sand scorching anew, as she felt her skin crack and pop. Fluid sprang out from her skin, but it was like no sweat she'd ever experienced. It made a hissing sound. Through a screen of agony she realized she was cooking. *Her body was cooking...*

The screams stopped. There was a brief flurry of echoes before silence fell over the landscape once again. Her body went slack against the sand in a dreadful mockery of ease as the first stage of postmortem change—primary relaxation of the musculature—began.

Only her fists remained clenched.

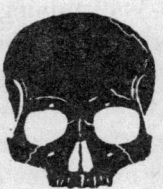

2

Present day

ALONG THE REMOTE eastern border of the Navajo Nation, dawn broke over the Ah-shi-sle-pah badlands, the sky lightening from midnight blue to pale yellow.

"We're gonna lose the best light," the director told Alex Bondi, who was crouched over a small landing pad, preparing a drone camera for a flight. "*We're gonna lose the light!*"

Bondi ignored him and continued calibrating the drone's compass and IMU. He did not point out that the reason they were late was due to the director's carousing the night before. In order to arrive by the 6 AM sunrise in these remote badlands, they'd had to get up at 2 AM and make a bone-jarring drive over terrible roads. When the director was assisted into his vehicle, he was still drunk. The horrendous drive had shaken the booze out of him—leaving him hung over and pissed off.

Bondi was already beginning to regret accepting the job as cinematographer for the film, an indie Western called *Steele* being financed by a bunch of Houston oilmen. It had sounded like fun—five weeks in Santa Fe, shooting at the Lazy C Movie Ranch, staying in a downtown B and B near the plaza. He'd heard that the director, Luke Desjardin, was "a bit of" a maniac, but he'd worked with maniac directors before and felt he could handle it. But Desjardin had turned out to be not just a lightweight maniac, but a fanatically committed one: a Clase Azul–chugging, Montecristo-smoking, coke-snorting tornado who never seemed to sleep and resented others for doing so.

Two dozen crew were on site—grips, PAs, camera operators, a breakfast caterer, the works. They'd hauled out an RV with AC and a flush toilet. There was no lack of money being spent. A large shade had been erected to keep people out of the July sun, with big coolers of ice water set up on tables. At least the backers weren't parsimonious—or maybe they'd already figured out that filming without basic comforts in a place so brutally remote might cost them a lot more in the end.

Calibration complete, Bondi stepped back. "Ready to fly," he said.

Desjardin's voice was almost as high pitched as a girl's, and so loud that it cut the desert air like a knife. "About time! The sun's going to be up in less than five minutes." He took a deep breath. "Here's the shot I'm looking for—a long, establishing sweep over these badlands just at the crack of dawn, getting in all that golden light and the long shadows."

"No problem."

Bondi's PA stood next to him, ready with a pair of binoculars. He was the spotter, whose job was to keep track of the drone—as much as was possible—in this landscape. But Bondi had plenty of experience flying drones out of sight, using as guidance the video feed on his handheld console.

"I want you to fly past that peak over there," said the director. "You see it?"

Bondi did indeed see it—a creepy fifty-foot spire of black rock that looked like a crooked finger pointing into the sky, cut off flat on top. It was about a mile away, across a maze-like terrain of hoodoos and balancing rocks, riddled with dry washes and miniature ravines. Bondi had to admit it was a perfect location. It was also a hellscape like nothing he'd ever seen before.

"I want you to fly over to it, camera looking straight down, then come around in a circle, raise the camera to center on the spire, and speed past it, panning back as you go by. Can you do that?"

"Of course." This was the shit he got paid for. His only real fear was some mechanical failure that might put the drone down somewhere in that crazy landscape.

"Okay. Roll."

Bondi fired up the drone and raised it to an altitude of ten feet, paused to make sure its GPS made satellite contact and knew where it was, and then bumped it up to sixty feet, high enough to clear the rock formations. He started it off northward at a medium pace, while Desjardin peered closely over his shoulder at the screen, cigar breath washing over Bondi.

"Go lower."

Bondi lowered the drone to fifty feet.

"Lower."

Bondi took it down to forty. This was risky, because many of the hoodoo formations were higher than that. But Bondi had confidence in his ability to navigate through them, and besides, the drone had a radar avoidance system that would stop it from flying into a rock even if he tried it. He normally turned this safety feature off when getting closeups, but in this landscape he decided not to risk it.

"Good…good…that's it…steady on…," Desjardin murmured, peering at the screen, watching the footage from the drone's perspective.

"Lost it," said the spotter with the binocs.

"No worries," said Bondi. "I got it under control."

Christ, what a landscape! It was hard to believe it wasn't some surrealist painting, all the little balancing rocks and spires and arches and twisty little dry washes casting long shadows. As crazy as Desjardin was, he knew how to get incredible footage: this should be fabulous, totally worth the effort.

The cut-off spire was coming up now. It was so prominent, he figured it had to have a name. He flew past it, then brought the drone around in a long, sweeping turn while smoothly raising the camera as he did so. The lens caught a brief moment of the fiery gleam of the rising sun before centering again on the spire. Bondi knew immediately that he'd nailed it, feeling the sudden adrenaline rush of a shot perfectly executed.

"Okay...," said Desjardin. "Good...now lower the camera back down to the ground."

He manipulated the controls and the ground loomed up, a pool of fire in the early morning light.

"Lower," said Desjardin.

Bondi brought it lower, keeping the camera focused on the ground.

"Wait," said Desjardin. "What's that?"

Bondi had seen it, too: something on the ground. But the drone had passed by and it was no longer in view.

"Turn back around," Desjardin said.

Bondi brought it around and retraced.

"There!" Desjardin said.

Bondi brought the drone to a halt, hovering over a whitish object partially obscured by sand.

"What the fuck? It's a skull!"

"Yeah," said Bondi.

"And look, there are some bones, too...See them?"

"I do."

"It's a skeleton!" Desjardin said. "Oh my God: someone died out here!"

As Bondi panned back over the scattered remains, he saw nearby a rotten old shirt and a shriveled-up running shoe.

"Take the drone a hundred yards north," said Desjardin, "and then fly it back over, slow, another hundred yards south. Track the skull with the camera."

"Yes, but..."

"Just do it!"

Bondi did as he was told, flying the drone past the remains.

"Again! This time, raise the camera slightly to pick up the horizon, then pan across the skeleton as you go past."

"Um, that's not a prop," said Bondi.

"Who the hell cares? It's perfect!"

Cobb, the AD, spoke up. "Luke, there's nothing in the script about a skeleton."

"There will be! I can promise you that!"

Bondi flew past again, panning over the bones.

"Those are human remains out there," said Cobb. "I mean, are we even going to be able to use this footage?"

"You're damn right we will. They show shit like this on the news every day! Okay, Bondi: do that pan again. That first take was a little rough."

The drone's monitor began beeping and flashing, indicating a low battery. "I should bring it back," Bondi said.

"I can read a meter, too. It's still at fifteen percent. We've got time for another pass."

"It's almost a mile out. We need enough juice to bring it back."

"Do the pass!"

Bondi didn't argue; it wasn't his drone. He did the pass again, but his hand on the camera wheel was trembling slightly and it wasn't a smooth take.

"One more pass!"

The alarm grew more insistent.

"I need to bring it back," Bondi said. "Now."

"One more!"

He sent it back out a hundred yards, then turned it around. Abruptly, the screen went pixelated; the alarm beeped—then blackness. Fifteen seconds later, a stark warning message appeared on the screen. EMERGENCY LANDING EFFECTED.

Bondi lowered the monitor. "We lost it."

"Get the backup drone."

"It crashed—remember? We've got another one in shipment."

"What the hell?" Desjardin roared with frustration. "*Fuck me!*" He stomped around, cursing and yelling, as everyone else stood around looking on in silence. This was not the first time he'd lost it on set.

Finally, he rounded on Bondi. "Well, do you know where it is?"

"I've got the GPS coordinates."

"You saw the message. It didn't crash; it did an emergency landing. It's still good. Let's go get it."

This was met with silence, until finally Cobb said: "You can't be serious."

"What do you mean?" screeched Desjardin, whirling toward the AD.

"In July, hiking a mile into those badlands, with the sun up? It's already close to a hundred degrees. It'll be death out there."

"Who made you the expert?"

But Cobb stood firm. "Don't take my word for it, Luke—that skeleton says it even better. I, for one, have no wish to join it." And then, as the director fumed, the AD added: "I think we'd better call the cops."

About the Authors

The thrillers of **Douglas Preston** and **Lincoln Child** "stand head and shoulders above their rivals" (*Publishers Weekly*). Preston and Child's *Relic* and *The Cabinet of Curiosities* were chosen by readers in a National Public Radio poll as being among the one hundred greatest thrillers ever written, and *Relic* was made into a number-one box office hit movie. They are coauthors of the famed Pendergast series and the newer, popular Nora Kelly series, and their recent novels include *Badlands*, *Angel of Vengeance*, *Dead Mountain*, *The Cabinet of Dr. Leng*, *Diablo Mesa*, *Bloodless*, *The Scorpion's Tail*, and *Crooked River*. In addition to his novels, Preston is the author of the award-winning nonfiction book *The Lost City of the Monkey God*. Child is a Florida resident and former book editor who has published eight novels of his own, including such bestsellers as *Chrysalis* and *Deep Storm*.

For more information you can visit:
PrestonChild.com